Salavandra: A Coffee Tale

A novel by Theodore Erski

David,
I had a great time cupping with you. Thanks for the opportunity.

ISBN-13: 978-1-4303-1363-2

Copyright © 2007 by Theodore Erski

With sincerest thanks:

Tracy
Jessica
Anne
Deb
Janet

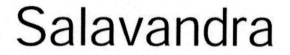

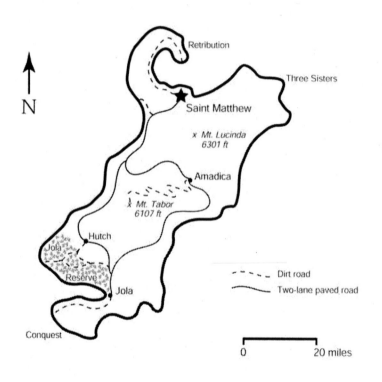

One

Antonio Richards awoke to a familiar, earthy aroma, vaguely reminiscent of ripe fruit, as it drifted through his small home. A spoon tapped three times on a battered and charred pot his father Victor used to make the morning coffee. The sound of a chair scraping against the kitchen's well-worn floorboards interrupted his parent's hushed murmurs. These comforting routines drew the sleepy nine year old out from beneath his thick blankets and into the chilly morning air. His stomach rumbled. Coffee, tortillas, fresh fruit and fried plantains. More coffee.

Victor always offered Antonio just enough sugar to sweeten the young boy's cup. The mornings when Antonio wanted to show his father how much he had grown, he refused the sugar and gritted his teeth against the thick black brew. His mother Rene rolled her eyes at this gesture while exchanging a knowing grin with her husband.

This morning Antonio accepted the sugar with a small nod when Victor quietly held up a spoonful and raised an eyebrow to his son. Each sip chased away the morning chill with comfortable familiarity. At over three thousand feet, the coffee growing region of Salavandra was ideally suited for cultivating high quality Arabica. The mornings, however, seemed downright chilly, even for well-bundled Antonio. This morning he savored the coffee's warmth on his small but calloused fingers and snuggled deeper into his thick sweater. He looked forward to peeling off the woolen layer as the sun rose and work warmed his body.

Half a sack of coffee cherries by the afternoon. Half a sack would prove to his father that he could work hard. Last year's harvest found Antonio staying at home helping Rene while hired hands worked the fields with Victor. All January, February and March Antonio anxiously arose each day, hoping to be invited out into the fields. When he finally worked up the courage and asked to go, Victor promised him the next year. Antonio expected the hired hands back again this year, but since January was still young, about two weeks would pass before they arrived. By then the trees would be heavy with ripe coffee cherries and additional hands would be needed all over the region.

Harvest was busy and exciting, filled with strangers coming from Saint Matthew, Hutch and Jola. Small bands of men also arrived from other Caribbean islands, hitching rides on fishing vessels in search of work. This pattern of labor, with extra workers arriving during the dry harvest months, sustained Salavandra's coffee yields for generations.

Breakfast was usually quiet at the Richards' home, a pleasant and sleepy hush broken only by the creaking of late-morning insects and later by Henry, the obnoxious rooster. After lunch was wrapped in a bit of cloth Victor finally spoke, softly telling Rene that he loved her. Then they were off, father and son, each carrying several large burlap sacks. The canteen of water hung heavily at Victor's side as the two stepped onto the road leading away from home. Rene stood watching from the porch, smiling at Antonio and cautiously waving when he turned back for one last look.

"There's Mary, son," said Victor softly, gesturing towards a small home a few doors away.

Antonio's heart skipped and he wished away the hot blush suddenly covering his face. He stared at the ground and kept walking, acknowledging his father with a small grunt.

Victor chuckled, "You need to look them in the eyes, Antonio. Be a man. People respect that. Women respect that. Even young Mary."

Heartened by his father's encouragement, Antonio forced his chin up. He already knew where to look for her. It was the same place she always stood, right next to the steps leading off her front porch. With a deep breath he bravely turned his head and caught Mary staring at him. She smiled and waved.

In a sudden act of bravado, Antonio greeted her loudly. "Morning, Mary," he called out to her, his thin voice cracking horribly. Victor coughed wildly as he fought to suppress a laugh.

"Good picking today," she called, and quickly stepped inside. Antonio could not be sure, but Mary seemed to show a little more color in her cheeks too.

"One year behind you, right?" asked Victor as Mary's home disappeared behind thick trees a few moments later. Antonio nodded.

"She's very pretty, son. Watch to make sure the other boys don't distract her when school starts again."

Antonio, already awash in emotion, felt excited and anxious all at once. He crinkled his eyebrows at his father as they walked.

"School? But I thought I was helping you now, Papa. There aren't any other boys to distract her. They're all helping in the fields and don't come to school anymore."

Victor looked down at his son. The eyes of his nine-year-old son gleamed up hopefully, trusting him to make the right choice, hoping it was for work and not school. It pained Victor, knowing his son wanted nothing more than to work the coffee fields. He stopped walking and bent to look at Antonio. He took his son firmly by the shoulders, wishing Antonio could understand the importance of what he was about to say.

"Listen, Antonio," he paused, searching for the right words. "I know picking the coffee is fun for you, and I certainly do need your help. But after harvest the work is very unpleasant and requires a lot of spraying. Your mother and I don't want you around all those chemicals. Besides," said Victor softly, "boys that work the fields during the wet season do so because their parents can't afford to send them to school."

"But they're really working Papa, even in the rain. Ignacio's father even lets him tote the sprayer when it's half-full. Otherwise it's too heavy."

Victor nodded, "I know, I know. I see Ignacio out there with his father. But we're different, Antonio. We have a little more money because we have a few more trees. Also, Ignacio's parents are sick a lot, and they desperately need his help. As badly as the Munoz's need Ignacio to work the green coffee cherries, your mom and I need you in school."

"Need me in school?" Antonio asked, confused and a little hurt. "Why would you need me in school?"

Victor looked around at the forest, still holding his son by the shoulders. He considered the mountain, the island, his hard life and the harder lives of his neighbors. Antonio had never left Salavandra. He barely understood what lay beyond the Caribbean. Europe, Canada, even the United States; anywhere but Salavandra, thought Victor.

"So you can leave Salavandra, Antonio. So you can forget coffee, get off this island, and live free."

Picking only ripe coffee pained Antonio's little fingers. Each red cherry had to be gently twisted off its branch without disturbing the unripe beans. Dew-soaked twigs poked him mercilessly, and the occasional spider kept him on edge throughout each day of exhausting work. Fortunately, the red, ripe beans stood out in clear contrast to the green, unripe coffee. In a few weeks, however, most of the coffee would turn red, and then it would be suddenly difficult to keep pace with the ripening.

Antonio worked the bottom half of trees deliberately left unpicked by Victor. The burlap sacks grew heavier as the hours passed, and by late morning Victor had picked almost an entire sack.

"They're coming fast, Antonio. Finally that Rocanophyl seems to be kicking in." He lifted a branch and peered beneath the leaves. "Look, no leaf-rust anywhere!" He handed Antonio the canteen and motioned to take a break.

They sat and rested on the hillside overlooking a valley that fell away to the northeast. Several other coffee fields clung to the steep slope, and in the next orchard down Antonio could just see their neighbor Juan Munoz walking from tree to tree checking his coffee. Looking closer, he saw Ignacio following behind his father, mimicking his movements.

"What did you mean about leaving Salavandra, Papa?" Antonio asked. He handed Victor the canteen and laid back against the hillside. Clouds gathered in the distant sky and marred an otherwise perfect blue.

Victor paused before answering. Antonio heard water bubble in the canteen as his father swallowed.

"Salavandra's more than what you see, Antonio. Right now the island's nice for you because you're young, and it's probably very exciting. When this is yours," Victor swept his hand across the orchard, one of several plots he owned, "you'll see things differently."

Antonio felt a swelling pride as his father gestured across the hundreds of trees clinging to the steep mountain soil. He imagined pruning, spraying and harvesting the orchard, just like Victor. He neither wanted nor could imagine anything else in the world.

"But we stay on Salavandra, Papa. Does that mean we don't live free?"

Victor looked down at Antonio and experienced a profoundly aching heart blended with immense pride. He realized that right before him his only son was growing, thinking and trying to figure out the world. Too young right now, Victor thought, too young and too innocent.

"In a way, I…"

Antonio waited patiently for his father to continue while gazing into the immense sky. He imagined what Salavandra must look like from above, just a small speck in a glittering sea, hardly anything at all.

When Victor's pause grew long Antonio sat up and turned to him, suddenly concerned. Victor's glazed eyes drifted unfocused across the valley while his hands desperately clutched the canteen.

"It's ok, Papa. I'm right here."

Victor did not answer or even acknowledge Antonio's presence. It was like this often now, with spells occurring more frequently and lasting longer than before. Antonio patted Victor's big shoulder, trying to bring his father a modicum of comfort deep inside his seizure. This always made Antonio feel horribly awkward, but he forced himself to continue, to be responsible as he told himself a man ought to be responsible.

"Come on back, Papa. Everything's fine."

Rene would be worried all over again. Neither he nor Victor would tell her when they returned home, but she would know just the same. Upset and perhaps tearful, she would insist that Victor go to Saint Matthew's clinic for an examination. Antonio could already see his father gruffly refusing, insisting that he would not get any real care anyway. A thin stream of drool leaked from Victor's half-opened mouth and Antonio quickly wiped it away.

"Come on, Papa. Wake up. Please."

Nothing. Antonio knew he could only wait; perhaps a few more seconds, perhaps five more minutes. With each passing moment Antonio choked down the urge to start running for help, reminding himself that nobody would come in time and that he would only embarrass his father. Finally Victor uttered a small grunt and blinked.

"You ok? You had another attack."

Victor turned slowly, and looking bewildered addressed his son in the blank manner Antonio learned to expect following a seizure.

"Hmm."

He patted his father's hands, now loosely holding the canteen on his lap. With each passing minute Victor became a little more lucid, and after about twenty minutes said he was fine. Then, standing slowly, he insisted on getting back to work.

Victor's attacks had become more frequent and severe in the past several months, and with each one he became more short-tempered about his worsening condition. Three years of fighting seizures took its toll, and though he would never admit it, Antonio could see weariness gripping his father. With a sad irony the attacks coincided with steadily increasing coffee yields and more food on their table. This year, Antonio thought while gazing at the heavily laden trees, was surely a bumper crop.

Later that afternoon, clouds thickened and the sky threatened rain. Antonio scowled from beneath the coffee branches and muttered about the dry season never being dry enough. He listened to his father's steady and comforting rustling from a nearby tree. As expected, Victor spoke no more than necessary. Antonio expected him to remain quiet for the rest of the day.

A light mist dropped, cooling the air and making Antonio brace himself against the chilly showers that he came to expect so early in the harvest. Victor's rustling never slowed, so Antonio continued working and hoped his father would notice his effort and throw him an encouraging word. When the sky darkened a few moments later and a hard rain began to fall, Antonio ignored his chills and continued picking, just like Victor.

From within the steady rain he listened for his father's faint rustling, barely audible over the heavy raindrops. High above, thunder suddenly cracked, and then the sky really opened.

The heavy downpour made the work slippery and frustrating. When dry, coffee picking took considerable effort but was not immediately exhausting. Soaking rain made finding beans difficult and picking quite challenging. Each little orb slipped out from between Antonio's fingers as tried to grab hold. The trick, he learned after several frustrating minutes, was to grip harder than normal before twisting the coffee cherry. Locking a bean between his fingers, he forced it to come loose despite the rain.

The burlap sack, weighed down with product and made heavier from the downpour, dragged behind Antonio as he struck out for the next tree. Sheeting rain roared down the hillside, obscuring the entire orchard. Swaying branches twisted away from his grip and provided little cover as he crouched beneath the next tree's leaves. Overwhelmed by the torrent, he shamefully tucked his head to his knees and waited for the deluge to slacken. He thought only of his father noticing that he had stopped picking.

Gradually the rain slowed and then disappeared altogether as sunlight streamed to the ground. Thousands of dripping leaves still made considerable racket, but the rain's deafening roar was blissfully absent. Antonio took little notice, however. He immediately began picking and hoped to make up for lost time by doubling his efforts.

After several minutes of furious work he felt a creeping sense of distress. An unfamiliar quiet disturbed him in its obvious contrast to the harvest's normally energetic and rustling noises. This quiet shouted want and signaled that something stood amiss in the orchard. The leaves still dripped, but an opaque silence flowed beneath the trickling water. He paused, suddenly fearful to turn around, as if some creature sneaked up the mountain and crouched behind him, slavering, waiting, hungry.

"Papa?"

The thick, moist air swallowed Antonio's voice. He waited for a response and turned from the tree to carefully survey the orchard. Nothing seemed out of place.

"Hey, Papa?"

No sound responded to his call. No rustling disturbed the peace.

Concern tripped into panic when Antonio suddenly spotted his father lying face-up on the muddy ground. Victor had clearly slid several feet down the hill before coming to a stop against a large clump of weeds. Dropping his sack, Antonio ran towards his father but immediately slipped on the wet ground and began sliding down the steep slope. Coated in thick mud, he clawed at the ground and tried stopping himself from sliding. He finally caught a tuft of grass, and as he lay panting, wracked with fear, he looked up the slope to see if his father was breathing.

"Hey Papa," he screamed out in desperation, "Hey Papa, get up. Roll over, please!"

The harsh absurdity of a quiet evening several months ago crashed into Antonio's mind.

"If you ever find him lying on his back, roll him to one side quickly, or else his tongue will choke him," Rene told him privately. She found Victor face up earlier that day in the midst of a seizure and suffocating from a swollen tongue.

Antonio clawed up the hill, gathering massive clumps of sodden earth in his little hands. It was like a bad dream. The faster he tried to go, the slower he actually went. Victor did not move. Sharp rocks and scrubby twigs tore mercilessly at Antonio's hands and knees, but he felt nothing even as mud pushed deeply into his cuts. All that mattered was reaching Papa.

A minute passed, then another as he made his way slowly back up the hill. Finally his father lay beneath him. A blue hue touched Victor's lips. It contrasted sickeningly with his waxy face. Eyes stared blankly, dryly, deeply up into the peaceful blue as if lost in thought. With fearful tears Antonio pushed hard against Victor's side, trying to roll him. He succeeded only in pushing himself down the hill again, slipping away from Victor's much heavier frame.

Crying with fear and unable to stand on the slick mud, Antonio screamed out and swore loudly at his father. If anything would move him, a curse would. Victor always forbade expletives and punished Antonio whenever one slipped out. Victor, laying a few feet up the slope, did not move even after Antonio screamed out several harsh comments. Antonio reached him again after another mad scramble across the sticky mud. He unsuccessfully tried once more to roll his father to one side.

Blinded by frantic tears he pried opened Victor's mouth and tried to clear his throat. Thick saliva made Victor's tongue slip maddeningly through Antonio's muddy fingers. Each time Victor's throat cleared, his tongue quickly slid back and blocked it again. Antonio's dread grew as the minutes passed and no breath escaped his father's lips. He slowly realized that his panicked fight for Victor's life was lost.

"Come on, Papa. Help me out, Papa!" Antonio screamed into Victor's face with a shattered voice. Victor's muddied mouth remained bizarrely open to the sky as Antonio sank weakly onto his father's motionless chest. Beaten and exhausted, he wept.

"We're on our way down. Phillip wanted to watch the storm break over the mountain. It was quite a sight, very dramatic. I got a few pictures that might be good for Marketing. I'm sending them now."

Tom Penkava, President and CEO of Penkava Incorporated, lightly touched a button on his Link communicator. In two seconds all twenty snapshots passed to a satellite orbiting high above the Caribbean and landed on a partner's desktop computer in Lower Manhattan.

"We should be in Saint Matthew in three hours. I'll Link again when I'm on the jet."

The partner's image, clearly displayed on the three-inch square screen, nodded quickly and faded out. Tom tossed the communicator toward the Hummer's open trunk, aiming for the large pile of camping gear. He missed, and the Link clattered loudly across the rocky ground.

"Phillip," Tom called out loudly. "Let's get moving."

A young boy's voice called out from somewhere below. After a few minutes his son's head appeared as he climbed back up towards Mt. Tabor's peak.

"There're caves down there, Dad! They go way back into the mountain. I left my mark in one of them." He ran over to the Link and carefully picked it up.

"Is it broken?"

Tom shook his head and tossed more camping gear into the truck. "It's virtually impossible to break that thing. You could throw it on the ground and it would still be fine. It's specially made for the outdoors."

Phillip, Tom's son and heir to the Penkava fortune, promptly hurled the Link back onto the ground. The unit hit a sharp stone but failed to break. His father chuckled as he threw the Hummer's back gate shut with a loud thump.

"Bullet proof, Phillip. I don't think either of us could break it. Come on," he said, motioning to the passenger side of the vehicle, "it'll be tricky driving after all that rain."

Over three thousand feet above the Richards' orchard the Hummer's engine cranked to life and the Penkava's waved goodbye to their campsite. The two nights spent camping atop Mt. Tabor made a pleasant end to an otherwise bland business trip. Tom was grateful for the brief vacation, rough though it was, and for the time spent with his son.

Numerous switchbacks made the drive from Mt. Tabor's peak to Amadica challenging on dry days. Now the slick mud threw the Hummer around on the steep road and threatened to toss it off the mountain. Tom gripped the wheel hard as he made his way down, grateful for the four-wheel-drive and the Hummer's heavy ride.

Phillip, oblivious to his father's driving challenges, connected to the orbiting Link satellites and began team-playing a search-and-destroy game. The game's objective was to find an enemy commando's hideout and release a melee of destruction with seven compatriots simultaneously playing around the globe. The rough ride interrupted his game several times as the Hummer slid across the road.

"What the...?"

Tom slammed on the breaks and sent the vehicle sliding across the mud towards the road's precipitous drop. Phillip's concentration broke as the Hummer slammed against a boulder and shuddered to a stop. He carefully peered out his window at a steeply sloped coffee patch tipping away to the northeast while opening one of Salavandra's grand panoramic views.

"What happened?" he asked with a heavy breath as he stared down the steep hillside. The truck seemed to barely cling to the road's edge.

Sighing with relief, Tom looked at his son while pointing through the windshield. Sunlight sprayed crazily across the mud spatters and partially obscured the view, but as Phillip turned to look he saw the strangest sight. A boy stood directly in front of them, caked in mud and staring quietly. He did not move. It was as if Salavandra's mud encapsulated and transformed him into a bizarre statue, a mockery of a boy.

"Is he real?" Phillip whispered, unable to tear his eyes from the living sculpture now blocking the road.

Tom nodded slowly. He released his seatbelt and opened the door.

"Stay here Phillip. I'll see what's going on."

Tom cautiously approached Antonio asking if there was trouble and watching carefully for some response. He crouched down and looked into the eyes of the little muddy figure. There was definitely life in there, panicked life by the way the pupils danced. He took the boy's shoulders in his hands and gave Antonio a little shake.

Rene would step from the porch and immediately begin crying. Antonio quivered at the thought. His mind raced with ways to avoid going home, to avoid bringing his mother the news. Alone with her, but somehow Victor always stood there too, as he imagined awkwardly telling her that Papa had died. Victor, Papa, he always stood strong and unmovable like the mountain. Now he lay in a damp heap far down the orchard's slope, cold, dead and very heavy. Antonio never imagined his father being so heavy.

Antonio snapped out of his daze and found a stranger peering into his face. He smelled clean and looked important, and shaking Antonio gently asked if there was something wrong.

"My father," he whispered in a voice just audible over the Hummer's engine. He pointed down the slope.

"Your father?" Tom Penkava asked, eyebrows wrinkling. "Is he ok?"

Antonio shook his head. He could not bring himself to say anything more. He felt heat coming into his eyes and suddenly large tears formed and ran into the muddy furrows on his cheeks.

"He's too heavy," he croaked and slid through Tom's arms, dropping heavily to the road.

Tom stepped to the edge and peered down into the orchard. Tree after squat little coffee tree, arranged in a crazy patchwork that somehow proved productive, made it impossible to see many details. This meager patch, perhaps a bit larger than others but just barely, was so very similar to the hundreds of others peppering Salavandra's coffee region. Combined, they made Tom a wealthy man and Penkava Incorporated stockholders very happy. Coffee, in addition to the island's numerous other operations that Phillip would control in due time, made his family's business one of the most stable investments on Wall Street.

Antonio's wrenching sob distracted Tom and he turned quickly.

"Sorry kid, but I can't see anybody. Can you point?"

Antonio gathered his strength and did better. He guided Tom down the hill and stood several paces off to the side while Tom drew in for a closer look at Victor. The mud around Victor's mouth was beginning to dry and crack, and recognizing death, Tom did not try any resuscitation.

"Damn, kid. Is there anyone around that can help you?"

Antonio's eyes quickly welled with tears again.

"Now you knock that off," Tom said sharply while pointing a stern finger at Antonio. The last thing he needed was a weeping kid mucking up his plans to get back to New York. Surely there were other people around that could get this corpse off the mountain, he thought. Besides, the muddy road had already put him well-over his scheduled departure time.

Antonio forced back his tears. This adult, with his big truck that could move him and his father, was the only blessing of the day. He stared at Tom, looking especially miserable. Surely, he thought hopefully, this man would not abandon him to dragging his father up the hill.

Tom stared at him, judging, considering. "Shit, kid. You gotta help. Now get back up to the truck."

The bumper winch whined mechanically as Antonio played out the cable just as Tom instructed. "Keep it taut, kid, otherwise the whole thing gets tangled. You got it?" Antonio nodded and slowly let the cable out as Tom descended with a large blue tarp tucked under his arm. He caught sight of Tom's son in the Hummer's front seat, curiously watching the entire operation from behind the huge dashboard.

"Don't let it get tangled," Phillip yelled from his open window, "or you'll get smacked for sure." Antonio nodded and turned his attention to the winch.

A long silence ensued after Tom yelled up to Antonio and told him to stop playing out the winch. The late afternoon air, clean from the rain and beginning to cool, seemed to mock Antonio's misery. He hated the day, the coffee, even the orchard that just hours ago seemed the most important thing in the world. He despised his own life. That it seemed so promising and exciting earlier was now just a bad joke. All was mud, and misery. He ground his heels deeply into the road's pebbly muck while waiting for Tom's signal.

"Not so fast," Tom screamed up the hill a few minutes later after telling Antonio to begin winching. "You're ripping my fucking tarp!"

His booming voice echoed across the hills. Antonio suddenly wanted to run far away from the shiny black truck, from Tom and his unfriendly son. He wanted to escape, but Salavandra's sticky mud seemed to root him firmly to the ground.

He pulled back on the winch's lever, stopping the cable and pausing operations. Tom swore again from somewhere down the hillside. Antonio gently eased power back into the winch and carefully wound the cable into the spool. With each turn he dragged his father up and out of the orchard. Tom's head finally appeared after half an hour of barked profanities. The blue tarp followed. Antonio's father lay wrapped in that thing, with a booted foot poking out of one end. The winch jerked to a sudden stop.

"A little more, kid. I can't get him over the road's edge without the winch."

Antonio checked his urge to run. He stared coldly at the large blue wrapper and gave the winch one last gentle nudge. With an unnerving jerk Victor's body popped up onto the road and slid a few inches before coming to a rest at Antonio's feet. Sweating, red in the face, Tom followed and looked little worse from his efforts.

"Phillip, toss out two drinks."

Tom eased himself onto the bumper and considered the tarp at his feet. It was a tricky job wrapping up Victor without rolling him further down the hillside. This would definitely be a story the Board would appreciate. Tom could already see their faces staring in amazement at his incredible adventure. He quietly chuckled at the thought until he noticed Antonio staring at him in horror.

After resting, Tom hoisted Victor's body up onto the Hummer's hood and drew several lines across the muddy tarp.

"To secure him, kid," he said after seeing Antonio watching him suspiciously. "We can't have him sliding off, now can we?"

The afternoon sun hung low in the sky when Tom turned his attention to Antonio. "Now, about you," he started, standing tall and imposing. First, you can't get in my truck covered in all that mud. The seats are leather, kid, and you'll ruin them. Since I can't waste another second unpacking any of Phillip's stuff, you're going to have to strip down to your underwear. We'll pile your muddies out here on the hood with Dad. Ok?"

Antonio stared at him, not immediately comprehending Tom's words.

"Second, you have to tell me where to go. Right after I Link, we're going to get the hell off this mountain and take you two home. You must live somewhere around here, right?"

Antonio nodded and fearfully imagined riding naked in the truck. Phillip would surely snicker. A hot flush bloomed across his cheeks.

"Ok then, get out of those clothes while I call New York. Phillip, toss out that Link, would you?"

Antonio's heart pounded. His head swam with the impossibility that he was being told to strip. His father would never allow this humiliation. He would crush this man for suggesting such a thing. His father, he remembered with a wave of nausea, lay dead inside the muddy blue tarp stretched across the Hummer's hood.

"Come on, kid," Tom scowled between sentences to New York. "I have to get off this island tonight."

Slowly, staring at the ground, Antonio peeled off his shirt, boots and pants and left them in a heap at his feet. He drew his hands protectively over himself and refused to look at Tom.

"Damn, kid, like I don't have one of those. Why the hell aren't you wearing any underwear?"

Antonio could only shrug and stare at his clothing. He wished he could pull on the filthy garments.

"We'll, it's better than wearing your clothes."

Tom pointed to the Hummer's door. "Phillip," he yelled, "unlock the passenger door and let naked boy squeeze into the back."

The Hummer's rear passenger door opened but Antonio stood frozen to the ground. He worried that Phillip would see him as he climbed into the truck.

"Get moving before I smack your butt," Tom ordered gruffly. "Damn, kid! Do you think I have all the time in the world?"

Phillip mercifully ignored him as Antonio scrambled into the truck. He sat next to a large green blanket. It looked dry and clean. He desperately wanted to cover himself with it but refused to allow his filthy body closer than a few inches. With a quick roar the Hummer jerked into motion and began making its way down the mountain. Antonio quietly gave directions as they drew closer to the hollow in which his home nestled against Mt. Tabor's slopes.

"Don't you have any underwear?" Phillip asked, after cautiously peering around his seat.

Antonio's face flushed and he barely shook his head. He stared down at the Hummer's black carpet, embarrassed about his lack of clothing. Large flakes of drying, reddish soil lay at his feet. He could see bare patches on his skin where the mud had peeled away. The truck would be dirty, he realized. Expecting to get yelled at, he braced himself against the Hummer's frame and lifted his feet from the floor.

"Here?" Tom asked suddenly, slowing and pointing down a narrow side-road leading away to the east.

Antonio let out an affirmative grunt, but with a jolt of horror realized that his neighbors would want to see who was in the truck. Normally the rusting and battered coffee truck drew out several people wanting news or gossip. Surely this huge black vehicle would draw everyone from their homes. Mary's face suddenly appeared at his tinted window. He looked longingly at his clothing tucked under a line strapping his father down. Another wave of nausea rolled through his stomach when the Hummer jerked to a stop in front of his home. A small crowd quickly gathered.

Through the dirty windshield Antonio watched as a familiar figure appeared in his doorway. His mother's shape, framed against his home's dark interior, paused before stepping out into the late afternoon. She stood motionless for endless moments, and Antonio suddenly realized he would escape having to explain that Victor had died. Rene knew, of course. She knew the instant she saw the blue tarp.

More people gathered in front of his home, in front of the Hummer, all whispering and pointing. Mary ran behind the adults as she searched for a better view.

"Shit. This is going to suck," said Tom, and released a tremendous sigh. He unbuckled his seatbelt and quickly threw open his door.

The cool outside air immediately settled into the cab and displaced the comfortably warm interior. At any other time Antonio would have breathed deeply, enjoying the refreshing and energizing air. Now he grew increasingly anxious. The cool air seemed to mock his feelings of dread.

"Let him out, Phillip," Tom called from the front of the truck as he unfastened the lines securing Victor to the hood.

Always obedient, Phillip reached around and opened Antonio's door. To Antonio's horror all his neighbors peered inside and stared directly at his nakedness. Forgetting about being dirty, Antonio shrank from their stares and huddled against the clean green blanket. He vaguely heard Tom addressing the crowd and saw his neighbors parting as Rene stepped towards the truck.

Mary's out there, Antonio thought. His desperate mind raced for a solution to his awkward nakedness but no answer came. His heart hurt from its heavy pounding. He felt suddenly lightheaded.

"Well…" Phillip looked at Antonio with an expectant gaze. "You can't stay in our truck forever."

Antonio stared at him, astounded at Phillip's failure to notice his dilemma.

"You need to look them in the eyes, Antonio. Be a man." His father's comment somehow rang out, distant yet clear. In his haze of indecision Antonio grasped these words and held them, drawing strength from their simple message. Wishing to please Victor even in death, he took a deep breath and boldly stepped out of the Hummer. Behind him Phillip closed the truck's door with a sharp click. Antonio stood naked before his neighbors, before Mary, before the entire island.

Silently defiant and with a challenge in his eyes, he dared anyone to comment. Mary's face appeared and blushed quickly. He held her gaze as he held all the others, strong and unyielding. Victor's words grew more powerful with each second and strengthened Antonio's courage. His stubborn confidence reflected in his neighbors' stunned faces, and they looked at him first with concern, and then with suddenly expectant expressions. Serious faces, Antonio thought, that somehow showed respect despite his nakedness, as well as a nervous kind of aggression as their eyes flickered from him, to the Hummer and back again.

A neighbor stripped off his own shirt and quickly covered the young boy.

Two

"Honestly, Tom, just between you and me, I think it was a late twentieth century mistake. But trying to undo a nature reserve is like trying to sell Internet stock, it's impossible."

Tom Penkava nodded somberly at Senator Bill Wilson from across the ornate rug. A fire crackled comfortably in the cozy office and warded off February's damp misery. He took another sip of scotch and set the heavy crystal tumbler aside. As an afterthought, he placed the glass carefully on a marble coaster after recalling the scowls and short comments of his housekeeper.

"Well," he sighed, looking carefully at the Senator, "I expected as much. I was just hoping you might have some advice from when Alaska's North Slope was finally opened."

Senator Wilson shrugged and leaned back into the leather sofa. He was enjoying this visit to his old friend's home and was always ready to help Tom whenever possible. Penkava's contributions had kept his campaigns running smoothly for over twenty years.

"Oil's a lot harder to live without than wood. Besides, from what I hear, Jola's reserve status isn't much of a deterrent."

"That's true," Tom quickly agreed, noting Bill's scotch tumbler with mild amusement. Whenever they got together they both seemed to drink too much. "But it's the damn Board, Bill. Chambers and Hill are clamoring about some crappy NGOs, and Franklin has Princeton University pressuring him." He threw up his arms in frustration. At seventy-three, his arms did not move as well as he intended, but he could see Bill got the point. "Princeton! Can you believe it? I built two fucking buildings on that campus and now some snot-nosed Dean is pressuring my Board about the legality of our logging operations."

"Thankless wretches," the Senator muttered while shaking his head. He tossed back his last bit of scotch. The smoky fluid rolled heavily down his throat. It was always a pleasure visiting Tom. "I'll see what my staff can dig up," he offered. "There must be something in those files that could ease the pressure on you."

"I'd appreciate it, Bill."

"Always ready to help."

A young man, smiling broadly, leaned into the room knocked politely. Tom turned his head to the door. At thirty-two Phillip had matured into more than Tom had ever expected. He smiled and quickly waved his son into the room.

"Heck, Phillip here would appreciate it more than me. He's basically running things now."

"Bill," Phillip said loudly as he approached the Senator. "Nice of you to stop by. My old man isn't boring you, is he?" He held out his hand and the Senator shook it firmly.

"Good news, Dad," said Phillip without waiting for the Senator's reply. "The market went up today. We gained three percent."

Tom grinned and remembered a time in his life when he watched the company's stock as closely as Phillip. He knew the rise and fall on any particular day mattered little. It was a fever for Phillip, however, and one that Tom remembered well.

"You'll have to do more than watch the stock, my boy," he replied. "Real growth means stability. That's what it's all about. Rock solid stability."

"Yeah, yeah," Phillip said, half-joking while dismissing his father's concerns. He heard the same lecture dozens of times. "Ten year window, thirty year window, all that's great but man, it's boring." Phillip turned suddenly to face the Senator.

"What about you, Bill? Your shares must have looked nice today."

"Nice enough, Phillip. As usual." Uncomfortable with such open talk of money, Bill set his tumbler on the table and changed the subject. "Tom tells me you're heading to Salavandra tomorrow."

"Anything to escape New York in February."

Phillip threw himself on the couch. "Besides," he continued, pouring himself a glass of scotch. "The Board's anxious about operations and wants my assessment. I'm sure it'll be business as usual, but who knows? Maybe I'll find some excitement."

"You be sure to do some actual work down there, Phillip," said Tom. I'll be looking for your reports. You've got the new Link, right?"

Phillip nodded and jerked a thumb towards the door. "Just picked it up. It's basically the same, just tougher and faster, like every other model. Don't worry, you'll be getting those reports."

"While you're down there, why don't you talk to some of the locals in Hutch. See how the logging extractions are coming along, despite our little…problem."

Phillip nodded vigorously and read into his father's comment. "Already arranged, Dad. I have a few people lined up. I expect we'll be fine if half of what I've heard is true."

Tom nodded, pleased at his son's foresight.

"Will you be a guest of President Vasquez?" the Senator asked hopefully. Jorge Vasquez was on Bill's cooperative list, and that pleased a lot of people on the Hill. To Bill's surprise Phillip shook his head.

"El Presidente?" said Phillip. "Nope. Oh, I'll stop in and make nice, but we've got the new cabin out on Retribution Point. The Company's decked it out with all the amenities." He gestured widely with his hands. "And get this, we've actually tapped into Salavandra's aquifer. I've got running water out there!"

"Sounds nice, Phillip," said the Senator soberly, "but I'm sure Jorge would appreciate your visit. Be sure to say hello from us, ok?"

Phillip smiled and nodded, understanding Bill's persuasive tone. "Can do, Bill. I like Jorge too and I know how you guys in Washington feel about him. Heck, without him, Penkava would be adrift in the primaries markets. I make it a point to see him every time I visit Salavandra."

"See, Bill," barked Tom. "He may seem a bit rambunctious but Phillip here knows exactly what's important. What's good for Penkava is good for Washington. Everybody wins."

A sudden gust of wind rattled the antique leaded glass windows of Tom's study and howled mournfully through the vacant streets of the Upper East Side. Snow drifted heavily against the building. The fire flickered as a rogue gust burrowed down the chimney and threatened to snuff the flames. All three men paused, and gazing out the window shook their heads at the unusually harsh winter weather. Tom broke the silence, concerned about his friend.

"Looks pretty bad on the outside, Bill. I'll have the Hummer warmed up for you."

During the afternoon siesta on the second day of February a small jet circled once over Saint Matthew before landing at the airstrip to the west of town. The few people strolling along the seafront took notice; it wasn't everyday that Salavandra played host to people important enough to fly in private airplanes. The temporary excitement passed quickly, however, and the town soon returned to its quiet afternoon slumber.

Christopher Knox was not one of those asleep. He was hungry, and the pain in his stomach kept him awake while others slept. Slouched against a corner building on Nelson Street, Knox watched Philip Penkava's plane and wondered what new Yankee had just arrived. He spat in disdain. An unemployed logger from Hutch, Knox hitched a ride to Saint Matthew two weeks ago to find work. So far the experience in Salavandra's capital proved quite unsatisfactory.

Dockside work was hard to come by, especially with the influx of other workers from nearby islands. The jobs he did find paid poorly and were always temporary. Life in Saint Matthew was hardly easier than in Hutch, and Knox was now considering returning to his home town. At least there he had friends that would help him in a pinch.

A short time later he heard Phillip's vehicle. The smooth engine echoed through the mostly empty streets and bounced off the concrete buildings. Knox stared when the shiny black Lexus SUV rolled around a corner and began moving toward him. The truck's sheer size and high polish made it stand out in stark contrast to the more humble cars and trucks common in Saint Matthew.

He checked a second urge to spit as the Lexus drew near. His anger suddenly bloomed as the driver came into view. Coveting such wealth and despising his own misery, Knox began unconsciously following the shiny vehicle as it moved slowly down the street.

The old British colonial port looked much the same as Phillip remembered from his trip two years earlier. A few squat buildings, none taller than four stories, lined the streets in various states of disrepair with pathetic and nearly colorless facades. Dilapidated trading houses that once controlled vast shipments of sugar and coffee to England now housed bars and brothels catering to Saint Matthew's fishermen and migrant workers. Some time ago Saint Matthew's buildings were bright and lively, with owners maintaining their homes and shops with meticulous care. That was well before Phillip's time, however, and now Saint Matthew looked poor and rundown. The brightest spot in town was on the eastern slope of Mt. Lucinda. Here, in a bright white estate towering over the tiny capital rested Jorge Vasquez, Salavandra's president for life if Penkava Inc. had any say in the matter.

Phillip parked in front of the only open restaurant. After his flight he wanted a cold beer and a big meal. Remembering his promise to Senator Wilson, Phillip reminded himself to visit Jorge right after he ate. Before clambering out of the cab he reached over to the passenger seat and grabbed an automatic pistol from beneath a heap of supplies.

"Never know," he muttered, and tucked the heavy piece deep into his pocket.

Sipping beer while two fans blew aromatic, warm air around the empty restaurant, he turned his attention to the sole waitress and guessed her age at about fourteen. Too young for the Manhattan crowd, Phillip thought, but on Salavandra she might be just the ticket for a little excitement.

As she set a plate of steaming rice and beans in front of him he suddenly leaned forward and grabbed her wrist. Her eyes widened and she pulled back instinctively, but Phillip tightened his grip, thrilled by his own aggressiveness. She stared down at him silently, with large, cautious eyes.

"No siesta for you, huh?" Phillip asked, grinning slightly. Her obvious anxiety and steady pulling made his heart pound. He quickly looked her up and down, pausing obviously at her gently sloping breasts. This island, this girl, awoke in him something caged and restrained in New York. Anything seemed possible on this vast Caribbean playground.

"No siesta, Sir," she said quietly and nervously looked toward the kitchen. Phillip was certain that one of her parents stood back there working the stove. He almost let her go, but then suddenly clamped down even tighter, electrified by the added danger.

"What's your name, sweet?" He fought back a blush from his own ridiculous machismo. He suddenly pictured his friends rolling with laughter at this story. They would probably ask to join him on his next trip down.

"Miranda. Let me go," she whispered furiously and gave her arm a firm tug.

"Nervous?"

Miranda suddenly calmed and looked directly into his eyes. "For you, Sir. My mother will take her biggest spoon to your skull when she sees this." She looked down at her wrist, slightly red under Phillip's tight grip. "Last week a man was taken to the hospital. He has not returned."

Phillip's enthusiasm abruptly chilled. He recalled seeing a large woman wielding a massive spoon when he first entered the restaurant. Now that he thought of it, she seemed to grip the thing like a club and could undoubtedly swing it like one too. He felt Miranda's hand jerk away as she took a few steps back from his table.

"Anything else, Sir?" she asked coolly, as if nothing had transpired between them.

In his mind's eye Phillip's friends were laughing again, but this time their amusement was directed at him. Humiliated and unable to look her in the eyes, he shook his head and waved Miranda away.

"Rice and beans. Rice and beans. It's always the same on this fucking island," he muttered bitterly and took a few bites. The food was good but his injured ego blunted an otherwise sharp appetite. He ate in a sour mood and finished everything without looking at Mirada.

Unknown to Phillip, Knox lounged outside and cast furtive glances through the restaurant's small window into the dark interior. A cold sweat broke out on his forehead and chilled him despite the warm afternoon sun. He was not a criminal, he kept reassuring himself as his mouth watered with the smells of cooking. He was simply hungry, and the man inside seemed to have money to spare.

He saw a movement a few blocks away. A woman, fresh from her nap, strolled across a distant street carrying a large bag. She made Knox nervous if nothing more than because she was the first of many people now waking from their siesta and going about their business. More people meant more chances to get caught. He desperately wished the Yankee would finish eating before the entire town awoke. Already a truck's engine roared to life a few blocks away. Even its muted rumble made Knox's heart race. The dockside whistle blew loudly from across town. Saint Matthew was waking up.

Unable to contain himself, Knox looked again through the restaurant's small window and nearly choked. The Yankee's table was vacant and being cleared of dishes and beer bottles. The man seemed to have disappeared. A vertical slash of blazing sunlight abruptly illuminated the far side of the restaurant's gloomy interior and Knox instantly understood. After all those beers the man probably had to relieve himself. A mugging in the relative privacy behind the restaurant, Knox thought excitedly, would be much easier than on the street. He spun on a worn heel and raced around the small building.

Beer and Salavandra's high temperature, combined with Miranda's acidity made Phillip's head swim as he stepped through the rickety door into the bright sunshine. Squinting furiously he groped the wall to catch his balance before making his way across the back yard to the ramshackle stall. Various kinds of junk lay strewn across the yard. He picked a path through broken crates, several planks of rotting wood and numerous pieces of rusted and ancient looking machinery. Weathered barrels full of rainwater stood solemnly in the sun with oily rainbows glittering across their surfaces. Sunlight pounded onto Phillip's skull while the acrid smell of dried urine permeated the air.

"Thank God for my own bathroom out on Retribution," he muttered.

Breathing through his mouth to avoid the smell, he opened the stall's door and peered inside. A cracked, shit-spattered porcelain fixture lay embedded in a board a few inches from the ground. Phillip groaned, unable to stop visualizing various people squatting unceremoniously over this primitive fixture. Several sheets of old newspaper lay piled in a corner covered with flies. The oppressive heat inside the stall cooked everything into an atrocious stew.

Hesitating, debating about peeing outside, Phillip suddenly found himself stumbling uncontrollably towards the fly-covered newspapers. His knees buckled and he just barely caught himself on the commode. He turned to look at his right hand weakly gripping the toilet and pulled away in horror as hard black flakes broke away. With his suddenly aching head near the ground, the smell of drying sewage bloomed in his face and pulled up his lunch. In this convulsing daze, a pair of rough hands patted him down.

"Not so nice in here, eh Yankee?"

A calloused hand, solid like steel, gripped the back of his neck and roughly pinned his head to the ground. More vomit rolled out of him and Phillip began dry heaving uncontrollably. Another searching hand found his wallet and Phillip felt it disappear from his pocket. Suddenly the violent searching paused. Through his sickness Phillip actually managed a weak groan.

"Hey!" exclaimed his assailant in an excited whisper. "It must be my lucky day." With a little struggling, the heavy pistol disappeared from his pocket.

"I will take this too, I think," the man above him whispered roughly.

Phillip grunted and tried to lift his head out of the pool of vomit and bile. Hair stuck to his forehead in a wet and smelly patch. Knox pressed Phillip's head more firmly into the ground when he noticed him struggling.

"You want up? Not so quick. I can't have you seeing me."

Phillip gave up and lay meekly on the ground, too weak to try moving again while pinned so securely. He wished his assailant away, wished he could get off the disgusting ground and wash off. A moment passed and still the strong man held him down, seemingly undecided.

"I won't look," Phillip mumbled. "Just let me go."

A soft chuckle sounded above him.

"I know you won't look. Because of this."

Knox brought the butt of the gun down on Phillip's head with a sharp crack.

Antonio's machete bit into an old stump with a sudden squeak. He gave the blade a hearty tug but the rotting wood refused to give up his broad blade. Sighing, he sat down heavily and took a long drink from his canteen. Some of the coffee trees looked sick and he worried that their illness might spread to the rest of the orchard. Wilting leaves and fading green foliage during the height of harvest was a very bad sign. Luckily there was no sign of the dreaded leaf-rust, the fungus that arrived without warning and coated the underside of coffee leaves with its fine brown powder. This new problem was sneakier, but just as devastating to the coffee. Some trees yielded half or even one third of their expected output.

"Looks like you've got a root problem, Antonio, especially over on the southeast side." Marco Iglendza, one of Antonio's more seasoned hired hands, reached into his burlap sack and pulled out a handful of sick-looking coffee cherries.

Antonio shook his head. The year's harvest already looked thin, and this new problem spelled serious financial hardship down the road.

"Mix them with the better ones," he said to Marco, grimacing. Antonio prided himself on producing high quality coffee; mixing sick beans with healthy ones was difficult. "Maybe we can sneak them by."

"Already done, Boss," Marco said with a small grin. Antonio nodded, expecting as much given Marco's twenty years experience picking coffee. At somewhere around fifty, even Marco didn't know his own age, the wiry older man still out-picked his two younger companions. Antonio reminded himself to tip Marco well as the man strolled away dragging his coffee sack behind him.

Very soon, Antonio thought, the disease specialist from Saint Matthew's Coffee Institute would have to visit his orchards. That meant more expenses, but without a soil and root analysis there would be no way to attack this new problem. Antonio's jaw clenched at the thought of ripping up trees to take samples. Each coffee plant was precious and represented untold hours of care and worry. He gazed over the orchard and wondered what new treatment could bring all the trees back to health. More spraying, perhaps, or possibly a heavy mixture of some new pesticide dumped directly over the trees' roots. Whatever the solution, Antonio knew he had little choice but to invest his meager savings into the recommended care.

"...forget coffee, get off this island..."

His father's words, spoken the day he died over twenty years ago, echoed clearly in his head. Antonio now knew how a man with hundreds of trees and the respect of his neighbors could still live a trapped life. Salavandra's beaches could well be the edge of the world, Antonio thought. He had no prospect of leaving coffee, much less Salavandra, especially with an aging mother and barely enough money to make it to the next growing season.

Then there was Mary, gorgeous and lovely Mary. The thought of her lightened his heart and made him momentarily forget his sick trees and poor harvest. Mostly he thought of her flowing black hair and large brown eyes that sparkled whenever she looked at him. Mary was all encouragement, always positive and energetic even when facing her own tiresome work schedule at the greenhouses.

Antonio brushed his pants pocket and felt the well-worn bills folded neatly against his leg. Forty dollars, all the money he dared save for a ring, lay stashed in his pocket at all times. It wasn't much, and he constantly wished he could spend more on her, but too many years had already passed and it was high time that he proposed.

"Now I remember," said Marco later that afternoon, huffing a bit as they all walked back up the hill. The four men, having picked over a large portion of the orchard, left six sacks of coffee by the roadside for tomorrow's pick-up and were making their way back to Antonio's home.

"It was on Jamaica, about three years ago," Marco continued. "Not quite in the Blue Mountains, but close enough. It was an orchard like yours with many trees looking as sick as those we picked today."

"What happened?" asked Antonio anxiously, fearing the worst. He had heard of entire orchards being ripped up and burned in a futile attempt to rid an area of a particularly difficult pest. Marco saw Antonio's worry and shook his head.

"Some new pesticide was used. I forget the name, but in two or three seasons all the trees were fine. That's what I heard, at least."

"Was that Rocanophyl?" asked one of Marco's companions. Antonio's attention spiked. The most effective leaf-rust abatement ever used, one season it simply disappeared from Amadica's coffee mill. Nobody could say why the shipments stopped. The Celeste, the huge ship docked in Saint Matthew, simply stopped carrying the spray.

Marco shook his head. "That was for leaf-rust, not this problem. I didn't see any rust out there, did you?"

Marco's coworker quickly shook his head and looked at the ground. Clearly Marco was in charge of his two companions.

"Besides," Marco continued, satisfied with his friend's humility, "the World Health Organization banned that stuff years ago."

Antonio was so surprised that he stopped walking. If the WHO banned Rocanophyl it must have posed a serious threat to people's health. He vaguely remembered his father praising the fungicide before dying.

"Banned for what," he asked suddenly, with a hard edge to his voice. The other men gathered around him with their faces shadowed in the late afternoon light. They were a rag-tag bunch with worn clothing and tired bodies.

"You didn't hear?" Marco asked, looking both smug and amazed. "It was a big story, especially with the law suits dragging out in the courts for so many years."

"Lawsuits? What are you talking about?"

"Man, you've got to get off this island, Boss," Marco exclaimed.

"Yes, yes," replied Antonio impatiently. "Get off Salavandra. I've been hearing that for years. What about Rocanophyl?"

Marco quickly saw Antonio's agitation and immediately changed his tone. "Three or four groups sued the maker. They claimed some kind of heath problem. I don't remember the details except that the company fought them in court."

"What happened?" Antonio asked impatiently.

Marco shrugged, clearly uncomfortable with his sudden lack of knowledge. "Don't know, Boss." He kicked a clod of dirt down the road. It tumbled to a stop several yards ahead. "The story just faded away and then suddenly nobody could buy Rocanophyl. No explanation. It just wasn't available anymore. Then one day I heard the WHO banned the stuff. End of story."

Antonio turned suddenly and with a disgusted sound continued walking home. Marco and his two silent companions followed, wondering at Antonio's sudden interest in the old story. Images of the day his father died flashed through Antonio's mind. The blue tarp, his father's face covered in mud, his own nakedness; all the images that lay buried for so many years now rose and festered.

After several minutes Antonio finally noticed Marco and his companions' uncomfortable silence. He realized the need to lighten the mood and keep his hired hands in good spirits. With such a poor harvest he could ill-afford his workers thinking he was a grumpy employer.

"I guess a newspaper or two might be good up here sometimes," he said heartily, and lightly smacked Marco across his back.

Marco nodded, "That or a Link, Boss."

Antonio nodded, "Yeah, a Link. That would be better."

He remembered using a Link several years ago while studying Arabica hybrids at the Coffee Institute. The handheld communication device was similar to the one in the big black truck that carried him and his father home on that fateful day so many years ago. The quiet and strange kid in the front seat was playing with it, Antonio recalled. Mill managers too, Antonio remembered, used them a lot when they punch in weights and values for international bean buyers. Mostly, however, Links were rare pieces of technology available to only a select few of Salavandra's residents. Poor coffee farmers were not included.

"Yes," Antonio murmured, "a Link would be much better."

As the road forked toward home he saw her climbing the hill with a few other women. The greenhouse bus was unable to navigate up Mt. Tabor's steep slopes, so it always dropped them off a quarter of a mile down the road.

"You guys go ahead. Tell Rene I'll be home soon. She'll have a meal ready for you." Antonio waved his workers home and waited for Mary. She and the other ladies walked slowly, clearly tired from standing all day tending flowers. Mary's good cheer, however, shined through the group's fatigue. She smiled as she talked and Antonio could see that she lifted their spirits with her animated conversation. He loved her, and his heart swelled waiting for her to notice him.

As if sensing him she looked up and with a broad smile waved and quickened her steps, leaving her friends behind. Breathless from the climb, a deep red bloomed on her cheeks as she neared.

Antonio gathered her tightly in his arms. She folded herself into his hug and turned her face up for a kiss. It was not a passionate kiss, not in front of her friends, but certainly more than a casual peck. The passion would come later, Antonio sensed, as Mary provocatively crushed her body into his.

"I missed you today," she said quietly, aware of her approaching friends.

Antonio gathered her flowing black hair into his hands and gently held her head. He stood completely absorbed, breathing in her scent, oblivious to everything else. As the shadows lengthened and cool evening air enveloped them, he felt that they alone occupied Salavandra.

"Every moment we're apart hurts," he whispered. Her friends passed, smiling and acknowledging Antonio with quick nods.

"Tomorrow I want to meet you here, just like this," Antonio said quickly. He waited for Mary to nod, and when she did she had a questioning look in her eyes. Beautiful eyes, Antonio thought, even as he noticed the swollen and red irritation common with all the greenhouse workers.

"I'm going to Saint Matthew tomorrow. I'll be back in time to meet you here."

Her breath drew in sharply and tears suddenly threatened to flow. Only one reason could draw Antonio from the harvest. He held her shoulders tightly but pulled away a fraction to see her face more clearly. He looked into her eyes with a pent-up intensity.

"I love you, Mary," he began. "We've waited long enough. My mother's finally well and strong enough to handle a celebration, and I know your family's ready too."

A small tear rolled down Mary's cheek and left behind a damp line. She sniffed lightly and nodded, overcome with emotion.

"Thank you very much, Mr. Richards, for making it impossible for me to sleep tonight," she said sarcastically with a big smile. She punched him lightly on his chest and laughed.

Antonio laughed and drew her close again.

"Oh, I wasn't planning on letting you get much sleep tonight anyway," he said in a shallow whisper and lowered his eyes. He confidently slid his hands to her narrow waist and pressed firmly.

"Mr. Richards," she replied coyly, feigning a struggle to break away from his grasp, "I'm sure I don't know what you're talking about." She turned her head and looked down the road while pretending to ignore him. Her pressing body and caressing hands belied her interest, however, and Antonio suddenly gripped her more firmly.

"Just meet me later."

Antonio set out from his home the next day before Marco and his men finished eating breakfast. Fog still clung thickly to the dense forest and a damp chill hung stubbornly over the early morning. Before leaving, he instructed them to return to yesterday's unfinished field and continue picking. Despite the sick trees, Antonio remembered that many branches sagged heavily from their coffee cherry loads and knew that many more burlap sacks could be filled.

Last night's bliss with Mary kept his spirits high on the way back up the mountain to the bean stash. As he climbed through the thinning mist, his mind drifted back to yesterday's conversation with Marco. It worried him that Rocanophyl was linked to health concerns significant enough to warrant WHO involvement. He now held suspicions about his father's death and how it might be linked to the banned fungicide. Without newspapers or a Link, however, hunting for more information would be nearly impossible. A gritty diesel rumble interrupted his thinking as he neared his six coffee sacks waiting by the roadside.

It was a small flatbed truck, well suited to navigate the often muddy and narrow roads common to Mt. Tabor's coffee zone. It already carried four sacks of coffee, most likely from Antonio's nearest neighbor. Seeing Antonio wave, the driver pulled to a stop and hopped out of the cab.

"Six today, Antonio?" he asked, seeing the sacks waiting by the road.

Antonio nodded and wished John Doddard a good morning. He was an old acquaintance, having driven the same coffee pick-up route for the past fifteen years. He helped Antonio lift the heavy sacks and position them securely on the truck.

"Six bags, six tickets, as usual," John said in his regular business-like manner. He reached into the cab and withdrew a large pad of official mill certificates. Antonio and hundreds of other coffee farmers regularly exchanged these for cash or credit at the mill in Amadica. It was the enduring economic pattern that sustained Salavandra's coffee farmers for generations.

"Actually, John," Antonio said with a small gesture, "I think I'll hop in and take care of these personally. I'm going all the way to Saint Matthew today."

"Hey, good. I could use the company," replied John with a smile. "Let me clear a spot for you."

Antonio pitched in on the way to Amadica, steadily loading the flatbed with more sacks and watching each farmer receive his respective certificates. Some received as many as seven, but more often only two or three. It was not a good sign at the peak of harvest.

"Slim pickings all over the place, it looks," he commented as they pulled away from the last coffee field before reaching town. He jerked a thumb over his shoulder at the pile of bulging sacks, recalling that in previous years the truck carried nearly double the number.

John nodded somberly. "It's like this on the other routes, too" he replied and spat out the window in disgust. "We're all going to have trouble paying our bills this year. Plus," he added as an afterthought, "a lot of the beans look wrong." He cast a quick look at Antonio but was too polite to ask if his beans were also sub-par. Antonio only nodded and watched the small town of Amadica come closer.

Amongst the single-level ramshackle homes, many with fenced yards holding chickens or goats, loomed the giant coffee mill. It stood three stories, larger than the church on the eastern side of Amadica's main square. Made of corrugated steel and baked for years in the tropical sun, the mill's gray surface cast an ashy and somber hue about its extensive yard. The entire town seemed eclipsed by this towering, foreign processor looming on Amadica's western edge. Across the mill's front side, splashed in narrow white letters as tall as a man, the name Penkava Incorporated NYC, left no doubt about who owned the operation.

John turned a practiced hand on the truck's cracked steering wheel and navigated expertly through Amadica's narrow lanes. A roar of machinery echoing through the streets greeted them as they entered the expansive yard in front of the mill.

Several large trucks, able to carry much more coffee than John's flatbed, waited in line at the mill's gaping door. Inside, smaller trucks transferred their loads to those bound for Saint Matthew, or offloaded their sacks into massive holding areas for immediate processing.

The dockside coffee mill in Saint Matthew normally received those coffee cherries picked within twenty-four hours. Amadica's mill, smaller by many times over, usually processed only those beans picked over twenty-four hours ago and therefore threatening in-sack fermentation. Whichever mill eventually received a farmer's coffee, all of it was normally processed within three days of picking.

Many people moved about the mill as John finally pulled up to the main entrance. Some men ripped open burlap sacks and dumped coffee cherries into massive sluice gates, some weighed the bulging sacks on huge scales while others secured loads on larger trucks in preparation for the trip to the coast.

Antonio pointed to one of the large trucks preparing to leave and John eased his flatbed up to the rumbling giant. The driver of the larger truck understood immediately and quickly helped Antonio transfer his six sacks. When everything was in place and Antonio positioned comfortably on the load, the massive vehicle rolled out of the mill and onto the paved highway. The entire process took fewer than twenty minutes.

Thin, cool air quickly gave way to heat and humidity. Antonio savored the steep drop from Amadica, enjoying the scenery and the relaxation as the truck carried him down to sea level. He shed his heavy sweater shortly after the ride began and was soon riding comfortably with the warm wind whipping through his loose T-shirt. The forty dollars in his pocket felt heavy, and he nervously wanted to count it again but feared the wind might rip the precious bills from his fingers.

By the time the truck slowed just outside Saint Matthew the sun was high in the sky and Antonio's shirt hung damply in the clammy air. He did not recall Saint Matthew ever being so hot, and was suddenly thankful for the cooler and drier air around Amadica.

Barely pausing at the narrow intersections, the coffee truck made straight for the docks where another giant gray coffee mill stood next to a row of seven large and somber looking warehouses. By the thousands, sacks of processed beans waited for export in those buildings. Some sacks held beans as long as three years until Penkava Incorporated decided to release them into the marketplace.

The beans' sole means off Salavandra, the hulking and rusted Celeste, lay tied to the dock next to the mill. Two cranes dropped heavily loaded pallets deep into the ship's hold. The name Penkava Incorporated adorned nearly every structure, from the mill itself to the warehouse roofs and even the Celeste's stern, just below the ship's name.

Inside the mill's cavernous interior four trucks, each as large as the one on which Antonio rode, waited for offloading. Steel catwalks and well-illuminated air-conditioned offices lined the loading bay's ceiling perimeter and allowed plant managers unobstructed views of the floor.

Antonio's truck pulled up next to a large sluice gate and grumbled once before coming to a stop. With a signal to a nearby office that six sacks needed special attention, a net suspended by four massive steel hooks lowered from the ceiling. Antonio and the driver rolled his six sacks into the large net for weighing.

"How's the coffee up there, Mr. Richards?" asked the weigh clerk as he checked the digital readout on his desk.

Antonio shrugged, worried about the handfuls of ugly beans strategically buried amongst the healthy ones. "Same old beans, same old harvest," he lied, hoping the clerk had not heard about his particular area of the coffee zone yet. Usually if one farmer had a problem, everyone soon struggled with the same problem. The clerk nodded once, ripped six certificates off his pad and handed them to Antonio.

"You probably won't like the payout on these six," he said quietly, knowing Antonio's future lay heavily in their value. "A lot of the coffee coming in is a little light, and some looks kind of sick." He gestured at the bright red digital readout displaying the coffee's weight. "The company's not paying too much for those certificates this season."

Antonio's hand tightened around the thin sheets. Their fanciful lettering mocked him, and he found himself once again hating his absolute dependency upon the certificates. Victor's words of escape surfaced in his mind, and again he saw his father dying on Mt. Tabor's slopes.

"Mr. Richards," the clerk asked cautiously, "are you ok?"

Antonio shook himself out of his daze.

"Fine. I understand. Where's the cashier?"

The paltry sum netted only two thirds of last year's value for six sacks. Antonio stalked from the mill fuming, worrying about curing his trees and convinced that he would need yet another loan from Amadica's mill. It occurred to him that no matter how hard he worked or cared for his trees, one or two bad years always seemed to knock his finances back to zero. In productive years, he remembered with frustration, loans and interest payments took what little extra money appeared. He gritted his teeth thinking about this cycle and nearly bumped into a dockside worker rushing to the Celeste.

A crane gently lowered a pallet to the dock where a small crowd gathered. Instead of coffee, a man lay sprawled across the splintered wood with a broken leg and blood dripping from a large cut on his face. A plant manager pushed his way into the crowd and knelt at the man's side while telling everyone that an ambulance was coming and to clear away from the pallet. Antonio crept in as close as he dared but stayed well behind the crowd in an effort to avoid the confusion. He caught bits of conversation across the dock as an ambulance siren grew louder.

"A sack just fell off, nobody saw it in time," said one voice from the crowd.

"A hundred twenty pounds from fifty feet," said another. Astonished murmurs followed this comment.

As the siren grew closer Antonio felt a light tap on his shoulder. He turned and found himself looking at an agitated manager.

"Need a job, mister?" he asked Antonio in a low voice. "Quiet like, get up there and into the hold. Come see me in Office B when the last load's in and I'll pay you cash."

He pointed at a rickety gangway leading up to the Celeste's deck high above the docks. Antonio hesitated, thinking about Mary's ring and hitching a ride back to Amadica.

"You or someone else," the manager said quickly. "She's got to sail today." He looked around the dock for someone more interested. Antonio gestured quickly.

"How long?" he asked.

"No more than two hours, I expect."

Antonio estimated the time. Two hours loading, an hour to find a ring, and another couple to hitch a ride back to Amadica. If everything worked out, he might be able to afford a slightly better ring for Mary.

"Office B," he confirmed, and ran up the gangway as the ambulance pulled to a stop on the dock.

Within a few minutes Antonio stood inside the Celeste's yawning steel hold looking up at a perfectly square patch of blue sky. He stood surrounded by massive, dimly lit steel holding bins filled with coffee and freshly cut lumber. A large pile of loose green beans lay swept to one side of the hold as men sifted through the contents of the accident trying to salvage the remaining coffee. Smells of wood sap, dust, oil and diesel fuel filled the hold and made Antonio wish for the refreshing ocean breeze outside.

Two men motioned him away from the floor's center as a shadow suddenly blocked out the sunlight. A pallet, nearly bursting with coffee sacks, lowered slowly to the floor. The heavy chains suspending the load twisted lazily as it dropped.

"You have to stay away from the floor's center, mister," shouted one of the men above the Celeste's diesel rumble. Antonio nodded and mimicked the others as they backed cautiously away from the dropping pallet. The heavy load twisted and creaked twenty-five feet above, and each corner threatened to burst loose from the heavy metal hooks securing it to the crane's immense chains. Antonio imagined one of the sacks dropping to the floor and the shattering mess it could make of a man's body. He wondered if the man outside would be all right.

"Got to stay safe, or you're going to end up like Ricardo," another man shouted.

Antonio turned when a terrifying, ripping crack erupted above his head. Under the excessive weight, one of the pallet's four corners suddenly gave way. The other old planks, never designed to support such a massive load, quickly buckled with ear-wrenching shrieks as nails tore violently from the dry wood. Antonio saw the other men covering their heads with their arms while diving away from the collapsing load. Splintered chunks of wood embedded with rusted nails flew through the air and showered men with debris. Antonio reacted too slowly to escape the onslaught. A large corner of the pallet, misshapen beyond recognition, slammed into the right side of his face. He dropped unconsciously to the floor amongst a cascade of polished green beans.

Three

On a broad volcanic plain southwest of Amadica, where the rocky earth stubbornly refused any attempts at cultivation, twenty-six massive greenhouses did what the thin soil could not accomplish. Roses, carnations, lilies and even orchids grew in abundance under the careful pruning and spraying administered by dozens of women. Salavandra's greenhouse project was started as an experimental investment by Penkava Incorporated thirty years earlier. Over time it gradually expanded into a substantial revenue source. The greenhouses now kept Saint Matthew's little airport humming year-round with aromatic and colorful cargo flights.

"Well where do you think he could be?" Mercedes asked Mary for what seemed the hundredth time. She paused at a rose and pinched off a deformed leaf. She kept her voice low and watched the supervisor across several rows of neatly laid flowers.

Mary just shrugged, too upset to even comment. Her drawn face revealed deep worry and she furiously blinked back another urge to cry. Shivering half the night at the fork in the road while waiting for Antonio took its toll. Only after midnight, when Mercedes came and pulled her away, did Mary finally return home.

"I'm sure he's ok, Mary. He probably just couldn't get a ride back in time. He's probably waiting for you right now." Mercedes tried her best to sound optimistic as she unsuccessfully comforted her longtime friend. She wished they could sit, rest, and decide what to do next.

The supervisor snapped his fingers at them from across the flowers. Both women immediately looked down at their work. Early February was no time for casual greenhouse labor. Valentine's Day loomed, and every woman looked ahead to fourteen-hour workdays over the next week and a half.

"I'm just convinced that something terrible happened," whispered Mary while tending her rose bush. She pulled a spray bottle off her belt and gave the plant a thorough dousing. Green fluid dripped heavily from the red petals. The spray sickened and killed any pests landing on the rose over the next few days. Its lingering effects, mostly an irritating itch, gathered in Mary's eyes and nose. She sniffed heavily and clipped an errant shoot.

"You can't keep thinking that," Mercedes replied firmly. She sharpened her voice to strengthen Mary's resolve in dealing with Antonio's absence. Her own rose looked fine but she angrily doused it with spray anyway. As with every Valentine's season, all the greenhouse flowers would be pest-free and perfect during the frantic cutting sprint a few days before the holiday.

"I know," Mary replied with a desperate sigh. This time a few tears escaped. She wiped them away and immediately stamped her foot in frustration as pesticide residue burned her eyes.

"Hey," the supervisor called from across several rows, "I've been watching you two. Separate now or you'll be assigned to different houses."

Both women began protesting, but they immediately quieted after seeing the impatience carved into their boss's face.

"I don't have time today, ladies," his voice softened a bit as he sensed their somber mood and serious tones. "I just got word that Mr. Penkava is visiting. In fact, he should be here any minute. So everybody get busy." With this last comment he raised his voice to the entire greenhouse and several pairs of women briefly looked up from their work.

A large black shadow suddenly rolled by outside the transparent walls. Every eye turned to look at the massive truck as it pulled to a stop directly in front of the main office door where a No Parking sign kept other vehicles at bay. The driver gunned the engine once and then cut the motor. For several moments nothing moved, and the truck's heavily tinted glass obscured even the most intense stares. The supervisor recovered first, and immediately ordered the stunned women back to work. Inside the truck, Phillip was Linked to New York.

"And you're ok to stay down there?" asked Tom Penkava. His miniaturized face wrinkled with concern on the Link's small screen.

Phillip nodded vigorously and wondered how many times he already answered that question.

"Like I said before, Dad, the clinic fixed me up just fine. It was just a little bump, nothing more."

"How many men did Jorge send?"

Phillip shrugged and remembered Salavandra's president showing up at his bedside.

"I think he mentioned a dozen or so, but I forget. I was really tired when he stopped by."

"I'm sure he'll get the guy," Tom confidently replied. He scrawled himself a note to give Jorge a call. He knew that a concerned voice from the north would spur on the investigation.

Phillip glanced out the windows at the colony of glass buildings. He picked out numerous movements inside the greenhouses and reminded himself to get to work.

"I've got to get moving, Dad. I'm at Amadica's greenhouses now."

Tom nodded and waved his son off. "Wait," he called suddenly, and returned to the screen. Phillip paused just before switching off his Link. "The cabin out on Retribution. Is it ok? Did we build it right?"

Phillip smiled while remembering yesterday's pleasant afternoon spent quietly nursing himself back to health. The cabin's air conditioning, clean running water and satellite communications helped ease his recovery.

"All of civilization's amenities, Dad. As usual, the company knows how to travel."

Tom smiled, relieved with the knowledge that his son at least had comfortable lodging on Salavandra.

"Well you be careful, my boy," he half-joked in a stern voice and pointed a steady finger at Phillip over thousands of miles. "I've got enough worry up here without wondering what you're doing too."

Phillip nodded at his father and gave him a winning smile. "Always careful, Dad. Just slipped up once. I learned my lesson." He pressed the Link's power button and watched his father's image fade from the screen.

Phillip sighed as he considered the hours of work waiting for him outside the SUV. Seed, fertilizer and pesticide stocks needed verification with his records. The labor needed a quick look-over to make sure everyone was working well and had no explosive grudges. All physical logistics of the expected Valentine's Day shipment needed confirmation. Normally these on-site tasks warranted a manager with field experience. In their infinite wisdom, however, the Board requested Phillip's special attention to specific operations once every several years. Normally he didn't mind such trips, but after his violent encounter in Saint Matthew, Phillip began wondering if his talents might be more appropriately, and permanently, applied in Manhattan.

He reached under his seat for a small revolver, an apologetic gift from President Vasquez, but then thought better of taking it with him into the greenhouses. This was Penkava Incorporated property, after all, and worrying about muggings here seemed a little ridiculous. Still, upon exiting the SUV, Phillip carefully locked the doors.

"Is there anything you two can think of that might make your job better?"

Phillip looked carefully at Mary and Mercedes as they sat across the desk. Seed catalogues and samples from all over the world littered the office and gave the small room a stuffy sense of disarray. He longed to leave and return to the cabin.

He chose the two women at random after an afternoon of searing boredom brought on by all the mundane tasks required by the Board. The questions he asked them were standard procedure, demanded by the public and eventually reported to stockholders in the form of employee satisfaction reports. He watched as both ladies squirmed under his watchful gaze and silently swore this would be his last visit to Salavandra.

"The same question was asked by another about three years ago, Sir," answered Mercedes. "We told him as we're telling you," she looked at Mary for support. "The spray hurts our eyes and noses. It burns."

Phillip nodded once, well-apprised of the burning pesticide issue. He privately recalled the reams of studies back in Manhattan supporting the contention that no long term effects stemmed from prolonged exposure to the greenhouse sprays.

"A little itch in the eyes and nose?" he asked, hiding a sigh and pretending to make a notation on his Link. The screen glowed brilliantly green and the unit responded beautifully to his gentle tapping with a series of important sounding beeps. Both ladies nodded and looked pacified. Mercedes actually smiled.

"What about you, Mary? Is there anything you'd like to add?"

Phillip imagined the dozens of contrived employee interviews transmitted to Manhattan, all slightly different but ultimately satisfying the Board, the stockholders and especially the prickly labor-rights activists. Mary looked up from her lap, clearly surprised he addressed her alone. Phillip suddenly noticed her striking but unassuming beauty.

"I'm sorry, Sir. What were you saying?"

Mary envisioned her supervisor scolding her for not paying close enough attention to Mr. Penkava. She could hardly help herself though, because even though she savored the time to sit and rest, she constantly worried about Antonio.

"You look tired," Phillip replied honestly. "Rough night?"

Mary nodded once and tears suddenly glistened in her eyes.

"Thank you for asking, Sir," Mercedes replied quickly. She reached out for Mary's hand and squeezed firmly. "My friend is missing her significant other. He didn't return last night and there's no news yet."

Mary squeezed her eyes shut, painfully aware of her inability to speak. She held her friend's hand and breathed deeply while trying to restore her composure. Surely Antonio would return today, she told herself.

Phillip found himself squirming under the expectant gaze of the two women, as if he could suddenly solve their problem. It was an absurd thought. The man, whoever he was, probably got drunk and stumbled into a ditch. Maybe he had his way with a lady and was too ashamed to return home. Whatever the case, Phillip did not care and certainly did not want to get involved.

"I keep saying that her Antonio will return, today I'm sure, but of course she worries all the time." Mercedes shook her head. "I can't blame her. I would be a wreck too."

Caught between being a tactless jerk and a concerned boss, Phillip chose the path of least conflict and looked forward to leaving the greenhouses in under a minute. He moved to lift himself from his chair. "I'm sure he's..." Phillip paused, his mind stuck on Mercedes's comment.

"What did you say his name was?" he asked, and sat back down.

"Antonio."

"Antonio what?" Phillip asked, remembering a memo flashing across his Link earlier that morning. He dismissed it as one of the innumerable, annoying memos passed back and forth amongst Penkava employees everyday. He suddenly realized that both ladies were staring at him, expecting some kind of magic trick that would produce this missing man.

"Richards," Mary whispered with unmistakable hope in her voice. Mercedes seemed to hold her breath as Mary pronounced the name.

The memo suddenly snapped into Phillip's mind. Antonio Richards, coffee farmer, hurt on the Celeste while loading coffee. He was now hospitalized on the company's dime in Saint Matthew's clinic. Phillip nodded, impressed at his own ability to retain a message glanced at for the briefest of seconds.

"I think I might know something about this Antonio," he said, but instantly regretted opening his mouth. Mary and Mercedes leaned across the desk with expectant looks. He held up his hands in protest at their sudden pressure.

"Hold on now. Hold on. I have to check some documents."

With the Link, Phillip accessed recent memos and quickly scrolled to the one mentioning Antonio Richards. He gently tapped a contact line and in a few seconds was speaking to a mill manager in Saint Matthew. Between sentences it soon became clear that the Antonio Richards hurt on the Celeste was the same missing man.

"What's his status?" Phillip asked the manager as he held up a hand to shush the ladies.

"Still out, last I checked. Lost his right eye."

Gasps from across the desk obscured the manager's next sentence, but Phillip did not care. He suddenly wished himself far away, back in the big city where anonymity was a footstep away from his company's front door. Responsibility weighed heavily upon him and he thoroughly disliked the feeling. He felt trapped in this little office, pressured by the two women across the desk, and longed to leave them immediately. With a click of the Link's power button the manager thankfully disappeared.

"It sounds like Mr. Richard's is in good hands at Saint Matthew's clinic," he said with a false sense of optimism.

The manager's comment about Antonio losing an eye tickled the back of his mind, but he pushed away the thought and moved to escape into the cool outside air. A strangled sob from across the desk shoved him back into his chair. Despising his own weakness and privately rolling his eyes, he turned to face Mary.

"Look, Mary," he began, horribly uncomfortable with the whole consoling routine. "He was hurt, but the company's looking after him now, and everything is going to be fine. You can go see him at the clinic and..."

Phillip suddenly realized the remote likelihood of Mary being able to visit anybody outside Amadica. All the greenhouse labor arrived and departed on company buses. He felt a chill coming over him and stood quickly, intending to get out of the office.

"I'm sure you are correct, Mr. Penkava," Mary began, somehow finding strength with news of Antonio's location. "But you see, I have no way..."

He gritted his teeth against Mary's words, realizing the entire scenario began with his own foolish pride about recalling a two-sentence memo. He reminded himself to keep his mouth shut in the future. A long and uncomfortable silence followed Mary's comment as both ladies stared at him intently. Mercedes even went so far as to cast a quick glance out the window towards the SUV. She finally broke the silence when he made no move to say anything, and was instead standing foolishly in the cramped office.

"Of course, Sir, you're undoubtedly returning to Saint Matthew in your truck. Will you be passing near the clinic?"

Phillip almost laughed out loud. He swallowed his bitter smirk as he considered Saint Matthew's diminutive size. One could hardly help passing near everything when traveling through town. At least Mercedes allowed him the opportunity to save face.

"Of course, of course," he replied, feigning surprise and growing more irritated thinking about the next few hours chauffeuring Mary down to Saint Matthew. "In fact, I'd be happy to drive you there, Mary. I'm leaving now, though, so go tell the supervisor we're leaving."

"What about my hours, Mr. Penkava?" Mary asked hopefully.

"Forget about them," he said, now completely committed. "I'll see that you get paid for the full twelve. Now go get your stuff. I guess I'll talk to the supervisor personally."

"It so nice in here, Mr. Penkava," Mary said later while riding in the passenger seat. With unmasked awe she gazed wide-eyed around the SUV's plush interior. Phillip shrugged and wondered what about it impressed her so much.

"It's nothing. It's just a dumb truck."

Mary shook her head. Her thick, shining black hair glistened and flowed heavily off her shoulders. "You're a lucky man to have this. I can't imagine having such a thing."

"It's not mine, really," Phillip demurred. "It's the Company's."

He noticed Mary's innocence and suddenly appreciated how it heightened her natural beauty. The past hour spent privately fuming over his unfortunate luck blinded him to the fact that an attractive young woman sat across from him. He looked at her, this time as a woman instead of an annoying employment liability. His gaze lingered too long, however, and Mary suddenly blushed.

"I hope he's ok," she said quickly, staring out the broad windshield at the winding black ribbon of road stretching towards Saint Matthew.

Phillip nodded but sensed a familiar predatory urge and tried to concentrate on driving. With a sudden thought he knew he could force himself on her, but thought there might be other, more gently persuasive means, to get what he suddenly wanted.

"This is just a crappy company truck, you know. I've got much nicer ones back home in New York."

"New York City?" Mary asked, temporarily forgetting her concern for Antonio.

Phillip nodded. "Manhattan, actually. It's full of huge buildings and nice shops. It's really gorgeous. Lots of nice restaurants for couples to sit in and talk."

Mary's eyes widened. "What else is there?" she asked, enamored with his description of the big city. She looked at Phillip expectantly and he suddenly felt an urge to possess her.

"You're curious about New York?"

Mary nodded enthusiastically. "Very much so. I've always wanted to go there, or meet someone who's been there so they could tell me about it."

"Oh, you know how it is," Phillip began, strategically making her feel small and isolated, forever tucked away on Salavandra. "Any night you want there's something going on, like a show or a movie or some kind of concert. There's really never a dull moment."

Mary nodded but remained quiet. Phillip's world seemed a million miles away. She looked at her clean but threadbare skirt, her strong hands roughened by the greenhouse work and her clunky work shoes. She felt suddenly provincial, even ignorant sitting next to Mr. Penkava in his nice truck that he thought was not very nice at all.

"I can hardly imagine," she said softly, and once again turned her gaze to the road.

"Some day you'll get there," Phillip said quickly. "I always say that if you want something badly enough, all you have to do is work hard and it will be yours. Do you want to see Manhattan some day?"

Mary's face lit up at the question, and he smiled at her.

"Most certainly, Mr. Penkava. I dream of seeing America, the people and the cities. I would love to see Man-hat-tan." The borough's unfamiliar name felt strange and exotic as she mouthed it again. "But I've never even left Salavandra," she continued, her enthusiasm fading. "Getting there from here, even with working hard, seems impossible."

"Life can be hard," Phillip said. He switched on the truck's headlights to illuminate the road in the late afternoon sunlight. He began planning the trip back to Amadica later that evening.

"Are you hungry, Mary?" he asked. "We could get a bite to eat after we visit the clinic. I can't be taking you home hungry."

"Thank you," Mary said and smiled briefly, "that would be nice."

Saint Matthew materialized a few minutes after darkness fell. The stars above shined clearly as they drove through the quiet streets towards the tiny clinic. It stood isolated from other buildings and was little more than a two-story cinder-block square, painted white with light blue trim. Phillip remembered his own experiences inside the clinic just a few days ago and thought that anything more serious than a sore throat or broken arm would require a flight off the island. He pulled to a gentle stop in front of the building.

"Now Mary," he said, turning to her with his most concerned look, "I want you to know something." He placed his hand firmly upon her knee and gave it a light but reassuring squeeze while looking directly into her eyes. Her leg felt warm beneath her skirt, but he resisted running his hand up her thigh. That would come later, he assured himself. "No matter what, the company's going to make sure Antonio has the best possible care, ok?"

"Thank you, Mr. Penkava."

"Call me Phillip. I feel like we've known each other forever." He gave her knee a firm pat. "Now let's go help Antonio get better."

"He looks so pale," Mary said softly after a few silent moments at Antonio's side. She ran a hand through his hair and tucked a few loose strands behind his left ear. The right side of his face lay buried in thick gauze that clearly hid a terrible wound. "I can't believe his eye is gone. It's so terrible."

From across the room Phillip agreed. He approached her side and put an arm around her shoulders.

"Tragic," he agreed. "Apparently he was lucky though. It could have been much, much worse."

Exhausted, Mary leaned into Phillip and let him support her. She felt absolutely tired and wished that she had gotten more sleep the previous evening.

"I hope he wakes up soon. Isn't there anything they can do to pull him out of the coma?"

"Not safely," Phillip sighed and shook his head. "They say the best thing right now is rest. That way his body can really begin healing itself. Why don't you sit, Mary? You look exhausted."

He dragged a chair over to Antonio's bedside and eased her into the seat.

"You rest here awhile. I've got to make a few calls so I'll be outside. Do you need anything before I go?"

Mary shook her head and thanked Phillip for his kindness.

Outside the hospital Phillip grabbed the Link and dialed one of the Company's lawyers.

"He looks pretty hurt, Dan," Phillip said over the Link. "What the heck is Company policy with this kind of thing?"

From his home in New Jersey Dan responded. "Standard procedure is medical care and a ride back home. That's it." He glanced away briefly then returned to the Link. "I see that's all being taken care of, Phillip. You need not worry too much about this case. As soon as Mr. Richards is awake, everything will get back to normal."

"Is there any chance of this coming back to haunt us?"

Dan laughed confidently. "Sure, and that same team of lawyers are now gearing up to prosecute us for the ninety-two other cases we've taken care of over the past ten years. You're pretty funny for a Penkava. And I thought you inherited Tom's sense of humor."

"You lawyers are all the same," Phillip replied with a laugh. "Sorry to bother you at home, Dan. Give my best to your family."

"Hey Phillip," Dan called out quickly before breaking the connection. "Just for my own peace of mind, why don't you visit him tomorrow morning? Call me then so I can see him over the Link."

As Dan's image faded from the screen Phillip surfed to the Company's page and checked the stock. "Up again," he murmured and roughly calculated his net worth. "Not bad for a hard day's work." He glanced at the hospital and thought of Mary sitting inside and needing some comforting. "And things are going to get a whole lot harder pretty soon," he whispered, tossing the Link into the SUV.

"This will make you feel better, Mary," Phillip said at dinner as he passed her a glass of merlot. He played with the idea of taking her out to the cabin, but thought better of it when he realized it would mean driving her home tomorrow. "A good solid dinner will do you good."

"Thank you so much, Mr.," Mary paused as Phillip quickly held up his hand. "Phillip, I mean," she said, smiling and swallowed the wine.

"Like I said, I'm sure everything will be fine." Phillip avoided using Antonio's name whenever possible. "Now let's talk about you. What would you do if you were in New York?"

Over the course of dinner Phillip filled and refilled Mary's glass. Between bites of food and tales of life in the big city he gradually warmed her over until she actually grasped his hand several times in excitement over stories about Manhattan, Paris and Tokyo. He marveled at her innocence and wondered why he failed to take advantage of similar opportunities on previous trips to Salavandra.

"I've never eaten so much, or so richly, Phillip," Mary said after a bite of chocolate cake. Phillip insisted on sharing the dessert, alleging he was too full for his own while carefully watching Mary for any hesitation. She seemed to have cast aside any worries about him, and Antonio's name had not been mentioned for over an hour.

"It's good stuff, isn't it?" he asked, pointing at the cake while thinking about his favorite restaurants back home. The best Salavandra has to offer, he thought, and still nowhere near acceptable. He sighed, growing a bit weary of Mary's endless enthusiasm.

"We've got to get you back, I think," he said shortly after she finished the last bite of cake.

As he expected, Mary tried to mask her disappointment. She failed miserably, having virtually no practice at this kind of socializing. He jumped in quickly to lift her spirits.

"Well we don't have to go *right* back," he said with feigned hesitation. "I know a nice place we can go first. It's really beautiful."

Mary immediately took the bait while Phillip privately congratulated himself. He could already feel her firm thighs pressed against him and her hot breath in his ear. He quickly ordered another bottle of wine, bought two glasses and a corkscrew, and paid the entire bill in cash with a healthy tip for the waiter. Mary eyed the money on the table as they prepared to leave.

"Not enough?" Phillip asked, knowing Mary had little clue about an appropriate tip. He quickly pulled out a few more bills and tossed them onto the table. "That ought to do it," he said, humorously considering the ridiculously large tip. He wrapped his arm comfortably around her shoulder and hustled her to the door.

"It's just down the road a bit," he said later as the SUV's headlights pierced Salavandra's darkness. The island's lack of light always impressed Phillip. Nighttime here was really dark, unlike in New York where the sky rarely turned anything less than a deep purple. He looked at Mary sitting comfortably in the passenger's seat with an expectant look in her glazed eyes. Antonio might as well be on Mars, he thought happily.

"It's really nice. Sometimes I come down here just to get away from everything."

Mary nodded and smiled. The bottle of wine felt heavy in her lap and she carefully held the glasses so they did not knock around.

A dirt lane veered off gently from the main road several miles from town. Phillip slowed the SUV to a crawl as he navigated through overgrown ruts and gradually made his way down the easy slope to a narrow band of white sand. As they approached the beach, Mary stuck her head out into the pleasant air and breathed deeply.

"It smells so clean and fresh," she called back into the truck. "And it's so warm. It's chilly at night around Amadica. You can't go anywhere without a sweater."

"No need for those down here," Phillip said and stopped the truck in front of a small dune. Well-packed, pristine white sand reflected brightly under the SUV's headlights.

"I think there's a blanket and a lantern in back."

He killed the engine and while Mary explored the beach he rummaged around the truck looking for supplies. In a few moments he emerged from the back with his arms full. He could just see Mary's silhouette down by the water's edge, lifting her skirt and testing the Caribbean with her bare feet. Illuminated only by dense starlight, her delicate figure cut a striking shadow against the nighttime sky as she moved carefully through the stars fixed to the horizon. Gently lapping water accentuated her movements and seemed to beckon him to the ocean's edge.

"Is it warm?" he asked a moment later after setting up the blanket and lantern further up the beach. He held out a full glass of wine for her to take.

"It's like magic, Phillip. The water, the stars, everything seems so unlike anything I've known, yet I've been here my whole life."

"Some evenings are like that. They're always the best ones."

Mary smiled at him. "Come feel the water," she said and kicked a little spray towards him while laughing.

He stepped confidently out into the quiet surf. More self-assured than with any woman he immediately took her into his arms and kissed her passionately. She let out a surprised murmur first, but he held her firmly and moved his body closer. Firm breasts and hips pressed against him provocatively and after a second of hesitation she kissed him back, carefully, experimentally. She tested these new lips that were so unlike the ones she had kissed for so many years. Her head swam with wine, with visions of their rich dinner and the cash left on the table, with images of New York City. She swayed under his grasp and let him hold her firmly.

"Let's go back to the blanket," Phillip whispered and drew her from the water with a steady hand. She followed willingly, stunned at what was happening. Mr. Penkava, sweeping her off her feet. She could hardly believe it was real. Mercedes would never believe her.

The thought of Mercedes banged home the realization of what she was doing outside Amadica in the first place. Antonio, with his battered face and lost eye, lay unconscious and suffering from a trip that began around her. He planned to propose, she remembered suddenly as she took a few steps up the beach. I should be formally engaged tonight, she thought again, and would be were it not for the accident. She pulled away from Phillip's grasp.

"It's just up here," Phillip gestured to the blanket and tugged her arm. The lantern stuck out from the sand at a crazy tilt and partially illuminated their nearby shoes.

"Wait," she said softly. "Maybe this isn't good idea."

Phillip paused, stunned but not completely surprised. She seemed quite cooperative the entire evening. Completely forcing her might still be unnecessary, he thought bitterly.

"Live for right now, Mary," he whispered into her ear. "I know what you want, and it's alright."

Mary hesitated and tried to focus on Phillip's eyes. She looked down at the wine glass in her hand and was surprised to see it nearly empty. Somehow in the past few minutes she drank some, but could not remember doing so. Phillip tugged at her arm again. She tipped towards him and stumbled into his grasp. The wine glass flew from her hand and they both landed in a heap on the blanket with Phillip kissing her before she recovered. In a swooning daze she tried to resist, but the wine and fatigue blended her emotions until she helplessly succumbed to Phillip's insistent attentions.

Somewhere in the minutes that followed she tried pushing him off as he pressed down upon her bare chest and exposed legs. She pleaded no, weakly, several times but the words somehow smothered into increasingly sloppy kisses that were more Phillip's than her own. Mostly she fought against a curtain of blackness that shrouded reality and threatened to blot her consciousness. Vaguely, distantly, she felt Phillip thrust deep up inside her. She gasped once before blacking out.

"It looks like you've been up half the night, Phillip. Is Salavandra keeping you entertained?"

Phillip gazed bleary-eyed into the Link's little screen at Dan. Over the thousands of miles separating them Phillip could easily make out the lawyer's crisp clothing and well-groomed hair. Having not slept more than a few hours after dropping Mary off, and not bothering with a shower or a shave, Phillip felt especially gritty as he spoke to the attorney.

"You might say that, Dan," Phillip croaked. He fingered a bit of sleep muck from the corner of an eye as images of the previous evening swept through his mind. Mary had regained consciousness, but only after he had his way with her for nearly an hour. He felt almost evil about that but shrugged it off as a wild night out. The drive back to Amadica was a little uncomfortable, he remembered, with Mary drifting in and out of sleep and refusing to speak.

"Too much wine. And too much local talent, Dan. You ought to visit sometime."

Dan chuckled and waved a hand in front of the Link. "You forget, Phillip, I'm a family man now. None of that for me. Now what about this Antonio Richards character? How is he doing?"

Phillip glanced over at Antonio resting comfortably in his bed. A little color flushed his cheeks and his breathing seemed stronger than yesterday.

"He's honestly looking better. The doctor seemed optimistic this morning." He briefly held the Link's screen up towards Antonio so Dan could see him.

"That's good, really good, Phillip. We've got a little pressure up here from Labor Watch and need to keep this sort of thing quiet."

"Anything to be concerned about?"

Dan shrugged. "I seriously doubt it, but why tempt fate? As soon as Mr. Richards is conscious, have the mill pay his bill and get him home quickly and quietly. Then we'll put all this behind us."

"Consider it done, Dan," Phillip said.

"You should get yourself cleaned up Phillip! Isn't there any running water on that island? You really look like hell."

Phillip nodded. "At the cabin, Dan. As soon as I'm done here, I'm heading back out to the cabin to freshen up."

"Tom told me about that place. Pretty nice?"

"It's the only civilized place on this entire rock."

Phillip abruptly severed his connection with the lawyer. He poked around on the Link for the next few moments and surfed to various sites checking the international news and commodity markets. He did not notice Antonio's bed sheets rustle.

"Who are you?" Antonio asked, suddenly breaking the room's silence and startling Phillip. The Link slipped from his grasp and clattered loudly to the floor.

"Sorry, mister," Antonio said more softly. "I didn't mean to scare you."

Phillip grabbed the Link off the floor and turned to face Antonio. "You didn't scare me...Mr. Richards." Phillip recovered, "glad to see you're finally awake. I'm Phillip Penkava, from the Company."

Antonio nodded. "I'm in the clinic," he observed after looking around for a moment. "I remember the pallet breaking," he said slowly and lifted a hand to his bandaged head.

"Oh, God," he whispered while gently running his fingers over the thick gauze. Phillip watched with macabre wonder as Antonio realized the seriousness of his injury.

"I'll get the doctor," Phillip said quickly and darted from the room.

From the tiny waiting area Phillip heard Antonio's anguished cry a few moments after the doctor entered. A new eye might be necessary, he thought for a moment, depending on how vocal Mr. Richards became. The expenses of a flight off Salavandra, as well as the surgery, would be steep. He could see the Board frowning at the precedent.

"Time for some damage control," he mumbled after listening for several minutes to the muffled voices flowing from Antonio's room.

"Mr. Richards," Phillip said confidently as he stepped back into the room and nudged the doctor aside. "I want to assure you that the Company's taking care of all this," he waved the Link around the sparse room and included the doctor in his sweeping gesture. "As you can probably tell from my clothing and hair, I've been up half the night talking with the mill and the pallet construction company about what happened. Heck, I even called the crane manufacturer. We've jumped on the case and are investigating it with everything we've got. In the mean-time, don't worry for one second about any medical bills."

Antonio looked at him quietly while the doctor shuffled out of the room. He noticed the Link in Phillip's hand and eyed it carefully. "You're from the Company?" he asked quietly, still grasping the news about his right eye. Phillip nodded and held his breath while waiting for a storm to erupt.

"And that's a Link in your hand?"

Phillip glanced down at the Link and then quickly held it up and nodded again. He could not quite read Mr. Richards yet, and did not exactly know how to treat him.

"Do you want to see it?" he asked carefully, doubting that Mr. Richards even knew how to read. He held out the Link and wondered if the lowly device might somehow keep Mr. Richards quiet. To his relief Antonio took the machine and looked it over from top to bottom, carefully considering every button, the strong casing and the little screen.

"Do you know how to use it?" Phillip asked.

"One of the instructors at the Coffee Institute showed me several years ago."

Phillip looked surprised for a moment. "So you've been to our little institute. Did you learn anything useful?"

"The Institute is yours?"

"The Company built it to help people like you grow better coffee."

Antonio nodded, appreciating the explanation. He never considered how such a school might get started. "I learned a lot about new Arabica hybrids, as well as some things about financing and the interest on my debts. My instructor sometimes let me surf around to various Link sites."

"Well on this model the red button turns it on and off," Phillip said helpfully and turned on the communicator. The Link's diminutive screen flickered once and then snapped to life with a warm green luminescence. Antonio looked completely absorbed.

"You've been through a lot, Mr. Richards," Phillip said gently and began backing away from the bedside. "I've got some business to attend to, but why don't you take my Link for the afternoon? Get some rest, surf around, and I'll come by later to see how you're doing."

Antonio breathed deeply after Phillip left the room. He could do little more than quietly reflect, and was grateful for the lack of any additional visitors. Phillip's conversation with Dan still echoed in his ears, and though lacking some details, Antonio understood the intent of their discussion: keep him quiet to avoid problems.

Antonio sadly thought about Mary as a humid breeze slipped in through the open window. He was sure she had waited for him, and for the first time in his life, he had failed to show up for her. His heart ached wanting to see her and to explain what happened, but an unfamiliar weakness clung heavily to every limb and there was nothing he could do but rest.

With his hand resting on the Link Antonio drifted off into a light sleep. Fitful dreams plagued his nap as pallets fell from perfectly square holes in the sky and Mary repeatedly cried out for him. He awoke sweating, but only after the attendant firmly shook him and offered up a pain killer and damp washcloth.

"What time is it?" he asked as the young man checked his bandages and applied fresh tape.

"It's around noon. You've been sleeping for about an hour. Are you hungry?"

"I'll eat whatever you've got," said Antonio, abruptly feeling the depth of his hunger.

The food was pleasant enough and Antonio ate everything while feeling his strength slowly returning. Near the meal's end he began fidgeting with the Link, figuring out how the buttons worked and poking the screen with the stylus. He comfortably cruised through the Link's introductory pages as the attendant whisked away the empty tray.

Antonio reviewed information about the satellite network orbiting far above him and how it transmitted information from anywhere on the planet. He discovered that using these satellites was free, provided one acquired a hand-held communicator, the user portal for hundreds of millions of people. News, entertainment and personal communications flowed around the Earth at incredible speeds while users stood anywhere on the planet.

Remembering his conversation with Marco, he punched *Rocanophyl* into a search engine. The word led him to a series of data connections listing archived materials from the World Health Organization and major newspapers. First looking up to quickly check his privacy, he carefully selected a connection and immediately found a lengthy document displayed on the screen. After trying for several minutes to make sense of the report's weighty legal jargon he gave up and surfed to another site. His second attempt yielded more fruitful results and displayed a brief history of the fungicide controversy.

"It seems Marco is correct," Antonio mumbled as he read the first few paragraphs. The clinic's attendant suddenly popped his head into the open door and looked inside.

"Need something?" he asked, and made to enter the room.

Antonio waved him away with a slightly guilty feeling. All this attention made him uncomfortable, and no matter how many times he reminded himself that it was the man's job to look after him, Antonio still found himself wishing for more privacy.

> *Rocanophyl was banned by the World Health Organization after numerous organizations levied joint suits alleging neurological pathology resulting from prolonged, unprotected exposure. Claims ranged from mild dementia to full blown, chronic seizures striking individuals exposed to the banner fungicide for no more than three consecutive years. Labor Watch led the charge in global health claims, representing over ten thousand coffee workers, the vast majority of them living in South America and Africa.*

Antonio set aside the Link's stylus and considered the information displayed on the small screen. He remembered two uncles caring for him and his mother after Victor died. All three adults stubbornly ignored his demands that he be allowed to work the coffee trees like his father. After Victor's death Antonio saw very little coffee work until returning from the Coffee Institute. Doing some quick calculations, he determined that the WHO probably banned Rocanophyl about seven years before he returned to the coffee fields.

As he considered these issues and reminisced about his uncles helping for so many years, Antonio caught sight of the Link's cursor blinking wildly. He poked at it with the stylus and the text immediately flipped to another page revealing more information about the Rocanophyl story.

> *Penkava Incorporated, the fungicide maker and defendant in all said cases, commissioned numerous studies to counter claims by Labor Watch. Nearly all tests yielded mixed results, leading to additional testing and legal delays lasting many years. Although a multitude of circumstantial evidence pointed toward Penkava Incorporated's culpability, no study by either*

side produced a smoking gun. Ultimately most cases fell into dismissal and as the plaintiff's funding dried up, all remaining cases were eventually dropped. Finding the product steeped in potential problems, the World Health Organization banned the fungicide when new farming inputs eliminated the need for Rocanophyl.

The cursor no longer blinked at the page bottom, but Antonio stared at it while considering the impact of this dated news. Surely, he thought, the Penkava Incorporated mentioned with Rocanophyl was different than the one buying his coffee and employing Mary and her friends in the greenhouses. He found it difficult to imagine any company producing fungicide while also buying coffee and flowers. Anxiously considering this possibility, Antonio turned the stylus to the data connection for Penkava Incorporated.

"Everything ok in here, Mr. Richards?" asked the attendant helpfully. Antonio's head shot up from the Link. His left eye, already strained from watching the Link's screen, took a moment to focus. He felt a slight headache pushing through the pain medication.

"Fine, thank you. Shut the door, please. I need some rest."

The attendant looked at the Link lying on Antonio's lap and shook his head. "The doctor said to go easy on your good eye until it's strong enough to work by itself. Cruising around on a Link isn't going to help."

Antonio guiltily looked down at the communicator. His eye took a moment to refocus, which was just enough time to remind himself of his injury.

"Everything looks flat," he said quietly, not looking at the attendant.

The man walked into the room and stood next to him. Antonio strategically moved the Link to the opposite side of the bed and listened as a sigh escaped the attendant's lips.

"It'll take some getting used to, Mr. Richards," he began, trying to look at Antonio's good eye which was still turned to the bed-sheets. "I've seen this injury a couple of times and though it's hard at first, you'll adjust and have a pretty normal life."

Antonio nodded and considered farming coffee with only one eye. Picking might be challenging, he thought, but not so much that the harvest would suffer. He always had hired hands too, so if he was a little slower, they could always pick up the slack.

"There's no fix to this?" he asked hopefully, looking up at the attendant while pointing at the bandages covering his face.

"You know there isn't, Mr. Richards. I'm sure the doctor told you."

"Right," Antonio nodded, shaking his head. "Can I at least have a patch?"

"I'll see what we can do. In the mean-time," he said, pointing at the Link, "try to give that a rest. It'll just make your head hurt." He turned and left, pulling the door shut behind him.

"Just a few more minutes, I promise," Antonio called after him.

> *Welcome to Penkava Incorporated, home of one of the most successful public agribusinesses ever listed on the New York Stock Exchange. Our mission is simple: to provide a wide range of high quality agricultural goods to the world's consumers. Choose from the following data connections and explore our core business themes: stock value, stable growth, quality products, and competitive exchange.*

Antonio selected stock value and found himself whisked away to the New York Stock Exchange. A detailed stock listing popped up on the Link's screen, complete with comparative statistics and a miniature time-elapsed graph that could be expanded on demand. Antonio selected the graph and watched as the stock's trend-line illustrated a steady climb over the past twenty years. He returned to the company's main page and selected the stable growth data connection.

> *Penkava Incorporated rewards long-term investors with superior average returns that regularly eclipse all major indexes. Careful planning, judicious attention to environmental and human inputs, and a keen sense of opportunity continually push our superior growth. We work closely with the governments of our Caribbean, South American, African and Southeast Asian partners to promote stable working conditions that ensure long-term expansion. Together, a relationship built on mutual*

> *trust and financial reciprocity stimulates additional business-building enterprises.*

"Sounds like a solid company," Antonio murmured as he flipped back to the main page. He was anxious to see what products, other than those produced on Salavandra, Penkava Incorporated supplied to the world. He thought of his own experiences with the coffee mills and wondered if his certificates were part of the mentioned reciprocal relationship. Then he remembered their value, and his endless debt, and doubted that the Company intended that such credit slips be included in their commentary.

He gave the next data connection a poke with the stylus and considered the displayed text.

> *Penkava Incorporated is engaged in two main product lines. Our earliest line, and upon which the company was founded, is in the primary commodities markets. Products here include coffee, lumber, soybeans, corn, numerous ores, and flowers. Our second line, developed in the late twentieth century, is designed to secure and stimulate our investments in the primary markets. These products include a wide range of agricultural inputs designed to minimize the threat of pests and invasive plant species, as well as boosting yields.*

Antonio poked curiously at an icon illustrating corn. The image expanded and a brief text description emerged beneath the picture. Other commodity icons behaved similarly when tapped. No icons illustrated the company's second product line, but Antonio hardly needed any pictures. Familiar with controlling insects and weeds on his own land, he immediately realized that such inputs included the pesticides, herbicides and chemical fertilizers he so desperately needed to keep his farm operating.

"I guess a single company can buy my coffee and help me grow it too," he said aloud, wondering how many Penkava Incorporated inputs went into his coffee. The Rocanophyl story grew clearer by the minute, and Antonio began wondering when Phillip would return so he could ask him some questions.

Under the competitive exchange data link Antonio found a series of pictures displaying farmers from all over the world. Many worked in fields similar to those on Salavandra, while others used massive tractors to reap huge yields from farms stretching thousands of acres. All the workers smiled happily for the photographer.

The page also displayed data connections to Penkava Incorporated's four geographic operating arenas. Antonio carefully selected the Caribbean link and waited for the page to load. A small regional map popped up along with instructions to narrow one's inquiry. Remembering his geography lessons, he poked at a group of highlighted islands. A moment later Antonio found himself mired in documents about competitive worker compensation and long-term financial security.

> *Our Caribbean operations consist of the governments and people of numerous islands, including but not limited to Cuba, Haiti, Dominican Republic, Salavandra and Jamaica. To ensure financial success we recognize and respect the varied histories and governments of these countries and thus practice targeted, one-on-one face time with all our working partners. Although this raises initial costs, our returns continue to out-pace other companies operating within this arena. Extensive worker interviews and community-building efforts, in addition to competitive compensation for labor's often heroic efforts, make Penkava Incorporated the most conscientious employer in the Caribbean. Our coffee certificate exchange system, for example, provides long-term financial security for thousands while offering our buyers some of the world's most competitive prices.*

His father's words seemed to suddenly echo off the room's cinder-block walls.

"It seems the dead talk more loudly as I age," Antonio said. He heard voices outside his door and clamped his mouth shut. A gentle knock sounded at the door.

"Mr. Richards?" Phillip called softly from the other side of the door. "May I come in?"

Antonio paused while looking at the door and waited patiently for his eye to focus properly. He felt overwhelmed with fatigue and knew he needed some rest and time to think. Mary was surely sick with worry, and Marco and his crew undoubtedly wondered if he fell off the island somewhere. Coffee needed picking. He looked at the Link guiltily and felt that he had just frittered away the afternoon with a play-thing.

"Are you awake, Mr. Richards?" Phillip called, a little louder this time. An undeniable edge tinged his voice and Antonio thought it unlikely that Mr. Penkava waited for anyone. Steeling himself against exhaustion, Antonio called out in a firm voice. Phillip swept in followed closely by the attendant, who immediately began examining Antonio's bandages.

"I hear you've eaten all your lunch, Mr. Richards," Phillip announced heartily. "That's great. And I hear you're quite adept at navigating the Link. I had no idea you had such skill."

"It takes little skill," Antonio replied dryly, too tired to participate in Phillip's jocularity.

"Still, Mr. Richards...may I call you Antonio? I hate these formalities. I'm a lot more comfortable with Phillip, myself. What do you say?"

Antonio nodded and winced as the attendant removed a piece of soiled bandage.

"Antonio is fine. Thank you for stopping in to see me again. Is there any way to get news to my mother and Mary Gonzalez?"

"Your mother and Mary already know," Phillip said quickly. "In fact, I personally brought Mary down here yesterday to see you. She was worried sick of course, but the doctor assured her you would pull through. I'm heading up to Amadica again later today and I'll personally tell your mother that you'll be returning soon."

"Tonight. I'll return tonight. I'm sorry to bother you for a ride."

The attendant shook his head and chuckled briefly. Antonio turned to face him, and the young man swallowed his laughter after seeing Antonio's scowl.

"You can't leave, Mr. Richards," he said, taking a step away from the bed. "The doctor says you need observation for at least two more days. Then you can go."

Antonio paused as a stone-like weariness weighed him down. He respected the doctor's opinion and knew that more rest was essential. Sleep beckoned, his head ached and he longed to close his left eye and give it a rest.

"Fine. Two days," he said with a heavy sigh. Suddenly determined to shorten Phillip's visit, he quickly looked up and gathered his little remaining strength.

"Phillip, tell Dan that I accept your offer."

Instant confusion registered with Phillip and a pale sheen crept across his face.

"I'm sorry, Antonio. What offer?" Phillip's voice almost trembled. Were it not for his hushed tone, Antonio was certain it would crack. He grasped the Link at his side and held it up toward Phillip.

"Tell Dan he won't get any trouble over this," Antonio pointed at his wrecked face with his free hand, "if I can keep this Link." He gave the Link one firm shake and let it fall to the bed.

Both the attendant and Phillip seemed frozen.

"But I still need a ride home in two days, by you or someone from the mill. Ok?"

Phillip recovered and gave Antonio a big smile. He agreed with a firm nod, pleased that Antonio's gloating sense of cleverness ultimately let the company off so cheaply. Images of Mary's nakedness, of her succumbing beneath him, flashed through Phillip's mind and he grinned more deeply thinking about who in fact was the cleverer.

"A man with your insight is uncommon," he said, and shook Antonio's free hand. "The Link is yours. I'll tell Dan immediately. After two more days I'll see that you get a ride back home."

"Thank you, Phillip." Antonio cracked a smile for both men.

Phillip turned to leave, followed by the attendant. Antonio called after them as they passed through the doorway.

"Phillip, one last thing," Antonio said loudly. The effort sent a bolt of pain though his head. Phillip stopped and turned to face him.

"When did your company stop making Rocanophyl?"

"Oh God, Antonio, that was years ago. I'd have to check."

"Never mind. I was just thinking about my trees. There's something wrong with them."

"Tell you what," Phillip said after a brief pause. "Just to put the finishing touch on our deal with the Link, I'll have the Institute's specialist drive you back home. While he's there, he'll do some investigating. The company will absorb the cost, ok?"

Antonio nodded and managed a small smile. It was much more than he expected.

Four

Later that night in the depths of dreams where endless rows of ancient coffee trees stood in fading twilight, Victor pleaded with Antonio to again leave Salavandra. Mary stood quietly by Victor's side, saying nothing and looking forlorn and remote. She avoided Antonio's eyes and gazed instead to the slope across the orchard where a sheer cliff dropped into a pounding sea. Tremendous black clouds obscured the horizon and kicked up a noxious northeastern wind. Suddenly alone, Antonio cried out at trees that were somehow stripped clean of coffee cherries. Mill certificates scattered at his feet and he scrambled to catch them, but they all blew through his fingers.

While Antonio wrestled with his nightmares, Christopher Knox peered down the inside of a heavy shot glass and licked away the lingering rum. Cigarette and cigar smoke hung about in thick clouds and softened the loggers' boisterous voices echoing through the bar. In one quick motion Knox flipped the glass upside-down and slammed it onto the rough table. A smile cracked the corners of his mouth as he watched his three friends slam down their glasses too. It felt good to be home.

"Another," he yelled above the din while he and his friends cheered.

They had no place to go tomorrow, no trees to cut or boards to saw. They could drink all night. Unemployed loggers make the best drinking companions, Knox thought sourly as four fresh glasses appeared on the table.

"All on my tab, Jenny," he said to the waitress, "and here's a tip for you." He poked a crumpled bill deep into her plunging neckline. She smiled and expertly backed away before he could squeeze a breast.

"Hooray for Knox," yelled Stephen Sorrell as he lifted his glass. "Somehow he gets us drunk when nobody else has any liquor money."

Four glasses drained again as Knox lost count of all the rounds he bought. With Phillip's stolen cash creating a large lump inside his boot, Knox knew he could buy rounds for the entire bar and still have money left for food, a room and a lady. The thought made him chuckle, but then immediately wince as a few bruised ribs strained painfully under his breath. Salavandra's Federal Police inflicted the injury after escorting him outside Saint Matthew where three heavy-set privates convinced him that staying in town was a bad idea. They were looking for a mugger and thief, they said, and did not want to question him again. Taking a careful breath, Knox thought he paid a fair price for Phillip's money and gun.

Stephen slammed down his glass and smacked his lips with a smile. "This is the best damn night I've had in months," he said happily, and patted Knox heartily on the shoulder. "There's been absolutely no work since you left for Saint Matthew. I was planning to go there myself until you showed up tonight."

Heads nodded in unison around the table. Will Finkle, laid-off from Sawmill Number One on Hutch's northern edge, grunted his discontent and took a long drag on a cigarette. He had a family to support and virtually no savings.

"I don't know what I'm going to do," muttered Will while exhaling a cloud of smoke and shaking his head. "Another week of this and I'm sunk. The bank won't lend me another cent, my kids are hungry and one's coughing up a lung. All I can do is wait until Mill Number Two has a slot open."

"If one opens up over there, I'll split the time with you," said Stephen bitterly. "Hell, I'll go for just thirty percent of your hours. Anything. So many fucking trees that you can't see through them, and some asshole from up north says we can't cut." Stephen's voice rose above the bar's rumbling murmur.

Diego Garcia eased back into his chair and puffed out a long smoke stream. A lifetime logger like Knox, Diego managed unemployment better than either Stephen or Will. With no family and no loans, he managed to save a little money over the years and slowly lived off the pile while waiting for work. Diego rarely spoke, but his comments always charged his friends and seemed to turn the course of any conversation. Knox noticed this trait a long time ago and always pegged Diego as more cunning than the average man, including himself.

"Jola's crews are taking all our wood."

Diego's comment floated out above the table and clung to the heavy smoke tendrils drifting in the dense air. The men fell silent as it settled, and Knox was again struck by his friend's capacity to say so few words that carried so much weight. The stolen gun, tucked securely in his pocket, suddenly felt heavy against his leg. He shifted in his chair and winced again as his tender ribs forced him to recall the unpleasant encounter with Salavandra's Federals.

"Nothing to do about that," said Will, casually breaking the table's silence. "Hutch or Jola, we all take the same trees. Jola's Number Three and Four mills operate when Hutch's One and Two stop, and we're up when they go down."

"Shut the fuck up, Will," said Stephen roughly. Knox saw the liquor affecting him and briefly considered slowing down the rounds. He watched slightly amused as Stephen continued. "You're fucking cousin in Jola isn't even a logger so quit defending those fucks. Diego's right. In fact, you might even say Jola's crews are taking food right off my table."

Will held up his hands in protest and shook his head, quickly giving way to his aggressive friend. "I'm just saying," he said carefully, leaning away from Stephen, "it's not us who decide when and what to cut. As far as we know, the whole Reserve is off limits."

Everyone laughed out loud at this comment, including Stephen. Trees regularly disappeared from the Jola Reserve whenever the mill's saws spun. Several large, barren patches already broke the forest's continuity where crews from Jola or Hutch clear-cut twenty or more acres.

"You're a funny guy, Will. Very funny," said Knox between chuckles. "So I guess it's a good thing we're not out there everyday. Got to save those trees for something. For what I don't know, but it must be goddamn important if Stephen can't keep food on his table."

"What do you care anyway, rich guy?" Will asked, smirking at Knox's comments. "You can sit pretty with your mystery cash. Something good must have happened in Saint Matthew. What was the job, Knox?"

With the liquor settling in Knox felt like talking about his exploits in Saint Matthew. It was a good story, especially the part about stashing the money and gun just seconds before the police cornered him for questioning. He looked around the table at his friends. They were all good men, he thought, and he knew he could trust them to keep their mouths shut even under pressure. He leaned above the table and motioned them to come closer.

"Let's just a say a certain fancy Yankee suddenly ran out of spending money for a few days."

He looked around the table waiting for his comment to register. Diego's face immediately lit up and a small smile crept onto his lips. Stephen and Will both smirked, and then all three men leaned closer for more of the story.

"You can't just stop there," protested Stephen after Knox deliberately made no move to continue telling the story. "Come on, you can't just leave us hanging. Out with it."

"If I say anything you could all be in danger." Knox lowered his voice even more and cast a quick glance around the bar. "The Federals questioned me."

That comment sobered the men for an instant. Unofficially known across the island as President Vasquez's personal thugs, Salavandra's Federal Police enforced the president's authoritarian presence in each of this island's five districts. People often simply disappeared whenever these soldiering police got involved in a case.

"Holy crap, Knox," said Stephen, looking quickly around the dimly lit bar. Knox felt Stephen's hot, rum-laced breath on his cheek and turned his eyes to his friend. "Three Federals came to Hutch this afternoon," Stephen continued. "They were looking around, asking questions."

Knox's heart skipped as his thrashing outside Saint Matthew flashed through his mind. He steadied himself and felt the automatic pistol in his pocket while staring back at his three electrified friends.

"I'm not worried about those idiots," he said in a voice just barely audible over the bar's noise. He tucked himself even closer to the table and carefully pulled the gun from his pocket. "Besides," he continued, lifting the weapon to the table's edge and letting his friend's have a peek at its polished nickel surface, "I've got a sure way to fix any problems."

"Holy crap, Knox," Stephen exclaimed again while the others quickly looked around the bar. Knox immediately tucked the gun away and waved Jenny back to the table.

"Double shots for everyone, Jenny," he cried out loudly.

Knox's story flowed as quickly as Jenny served the rum. Stephen and Will interrupted frequently and pressed for more details, especially about the actual mugging. As Knox expected, Diego sat quietly and chuckled appreciatively when hearing how Knox eluded the Federals for a few days. Over a dozen men scoured Saint Matthew, interrogating hundreds of people and demanding to know their whereabouts on the day of the mugging. When they finally caught up with Knox he claimed to be working the docks that day and provided a convincing alibi from all the rumors about the two accidents on the Celeste.

"Of course," Knox said with a sigh as the story came to a close, "they took my picture and then gave me this going away present."

He lifted his shirt on one side revealing a patchwork of blackened ribs and the distinct tread of a boot imprint. "This hurt the most," he said, pointing at the waffle-like pattern where one Federal gave him a departing stomp before leaving him by the roadside. "I think a rib's actually cracked there."

"Those fucks do whatever they want," growled Stephen, gripping his shot glass and firmly rapping the table. "I'll bet you wish you had that gun when they were kicking you. Hell, I'd like to shoot them myself, the way they strut around as if they own everything."

Knox vividly recalled his plan to retrieve the gun and immediately hunt down his three assailants. He eventually thought better of it, however, and left Saint Matthew for Hutch where he could escape their notice and enjoy the fruits of his crime. Unknown to Knox, the Federals managed to narrow their search over the past several days. They tried unsuccessfully to corroborate his story with Saint Matthew's coffee mill and were now actively searching for him all over Salavandra.

"Three Federals at the door," observed Diego softly, staring at the bar's entrance with no expression on his face.

Knox and the others froze and made a point not to look up while a hushed silence rippled through the patrons. Most loggers had nothing to fear, but the Federals' hard stares made even the most innocent man wonder what crime he committed.

Knox's hand moved to the gun. He did not intend to be questioned again.

Stephen's youngest son Carlos slammed the front door and sprinted through the darkness towards the bar his father liked to frequent. His mother's anguished cries pushed him to run faster, and though only thirteen years old, he covered the five ramshackle blocks in good time. A cold panic and nervous energy surged through him. He longed for the firm assurances of his father to quiet the fluttering in his stomach. Carlos was certain his father would take care of things. It was only a matter of pulling him from his table and showing him Vicente's broken body.

Breathing heavily outside the bar he hesitated while catching his breath and listening to the loud voices and harsh laughter seeping through the thin walls. The darkness around the building seemed threatening, and though grown men stood just a few feet away, he drew little comfort from their drunken presence. Why his father frequented such a place he could not imagine. Carlos suddenly found himself unsure that he could actually open the door and step inside.

Images of Vicente's broken arm and bloody face, with his mother weeping over him, finally cracked his hesitation. Taking a deep breath Carlos grasped the worn handle and threw open the bar's door. He dashed inside and crashed headlong into the khaki legs of the three Federals standing in the doorway.

"Watch it, Kid," growled one and roughly shoved him away. Carlos slammed into a wall and hit his head with a heavy crack. His knees started buckling but he managed to remain standing while scowling fiercely at the Federal who pushed him.

"Serves you right, you little shit. Now stay out of our way."

The soldier's voice echoed as Carlos tried clearing his head. He looked around at doubling images of laughing men, bar stools and rolling cigarette smoke. A few men turned to look, but their faces twisted oddly under the poor lighting. They turned away smiling, assuming Carlos drank too much liquor.

"Don't hurt him, you idiot," snarled the tallest Federal. "He's probably some logger's kid, and we don't have any backup for another thirty minutes. Now spread out and look around. I'll watch the door."

He waved his two companions into the bar and withdrew a wrinkled photo from his pocket.

His head finally clearing, Carlos pulled himself away from the wall and tested his legs. They seemed stable so he bravely ignored his blooming headache and carefully made his way towards his father's regular table at the back of the bar. The three Federals ignored him as they squinted into the smoke-filled darkness and compared loggers' faces to the photograph.

Carlos saw his father crouched over his table with three familiar men. Probably playing cards, he thought, remembering the numerous nights when Stephen arrived home with pockets full of winnings. Lately his father carried empty pockets, and with no work Carlos was certain his mother would have a strong word to say about any poker games. To his surprise, when he stepped up to the table no cards littered the surface.

"Carlos," Stephen said softly, keeping his face low and looking at the ground. He gathered his son protectively under his arm. "Those Federals at the door, what are they doing?"

Feeling the bump on his head Carlos began telling his father about being pushed into the wall but stopped mid-sentence. He suddenly remembered Vicente, lying at home and muttering weakly about getting back at the Jola crew.

"Vicente's beaten up," Carlos sputtered, overwhelmed with responsibility. Stephen suddenly looked him in the eyes and forgot the Federals making their way through the room to his table.

"Beaten up? How badly? Who did it?"

"We were in the Reserve coming home when we came across a Jola camp…"

With his back to the front door Knox quickly interrupted. "Later, Stephen. We'll go to your home right away. What about the Federals, Carlos. What are they doing?"

Carlos sensed Knox's tension and turned his head to the Federals. One stood two tables away and was looking down at the seated men comparing each of them to a photograph.

"They're looking at a picture, Mr. Knox," Carlos said politely. Stephen always taught him to be polite to adults. He was sure his father meant the Federals too, but after tonight Carlos swore to avoid them at all costs. He noticed Knox shifting something beneath the table and turned to look at his father. Stephen suddenly gripped him tightly and cast a quick glance at the closest Federal.

"Not that, Knox," Stephen said firmly. Carlos heard an unfamiliar shake in his father's voice and was suddenly scared.

"What's going on?" Carlos asked, clutching his father while peering beneath the table. A silver flash sparkled briefly in Knox's hands.

"You got a better idea?" Knox asked gruffly. "I'm not going with them, no matter what."

Carlos suddenly understood and pressed himself firmly into his father's embrace. Vicente forgotten, he wanted only to get out of the bar and away from the Federals.

"Aw, fuck it," said Will and suddenly stood. "We all leave now, by the back door. Knox, put that fucking thing away before you get one of us killed."

"Time to go," Diego said and also stood while motioning to Stephen and Knox to follow him to the back door. Will pushed two people out of the way, clearing a path to the bar's shabby back door where a ripped calendar hung. The Federal moved to the neighboring table and peered down at the patrons' faces.

"Carlos, follow Will," Stephen said quickly. Carlos picked up on his father's urgency and ran towards Will while Stephen stood up from the table. Only Knox remained seated with his back to the Federal standing just feet away. Stephen caught a quick glimpse of Knox's face on the crumpled photo and turned to look down at his friend. He nodded, showed Knox a tight fist and nudged his head a fraction of an inch towards the Federal. Knox understood and pocketed the gun. In such close quarters, he realized, fists might do even better than a weapon. Taking a deep breath Knox finally stood. He could feel the Federal standing behind him.

"Hey, you at the back, stop right there," the Federal suddenly shouted across several people towards the back door. Carlos pushed heedlessly towards the door, ignoring the Federal and wanting only to escape the terrible bar. He suddenly remembered Vicente and quickly turned to his father when the entire bar seemed to erupt in an angry mob of fists and screaming curses.

Stephen threw the first punch, landing it squarely on the Federal's nose and sending the man crashing into three other people. Already tense from the soldiers violating their space, three men turned and cuffed the bleeding officer several times before throwing him back across the room. He flew into Knox as a helpless and groaning heap of agony, while the two other Federals tried pushing towards the back of the bar. Drunk loggers tripped and kicked them, and several beer bottles crashed open on their skulls as they tried unsuccessfully to reach their comrade.

"It's you!" cried the Federal as he dangled limply in Knox's arms. Knox gave him a firm blow with his forehead and sent the man crashing unconsciously to the floor. A hard kick curled the Federal's limp body around his boot. He drew back for another, this time aiming for the officer's skull. He felt nothing but pounding bloodlust. A crushed skull, Knox thought, would square the pain and humiliation the Federals inflicted on him outside Saint Matthew.

"Knox," screamed Stephen above the roaring bar. He pulled roughly at his friend's arm. "We're leaving. Now!" He pulled more firmly and managed to yank Knox away from the Federal before the fatal kick landed. Both men stumbled through the chaos towards the back door and spilled out into the quiet night where Will, Diego and Carlos waited nervously in the shadows.

"Home," shouted Stephen fiercely and grabbed Carlos's hand as he broke into a quick trot. The men followed suit and quickly made their way down into Hutch's dark streets.

"Vicente, how bad is he?" asked Stephen as he pulled his youngest son along the street. He suddenly remembered holding Carlos as an infant and how he pledged at the time to spare him from a logger's difficult life. Tonight's mayhem brought a crashing end to thirteen years of futile effort.

"He's all bloody. His nose is broken and his arm too. Mom got Mr. Broderick to help."

Stephen felt a deep rage building. Now seventeen, Vicente carried himself like a man and contributed to the family's income like an adult. He looked out for his little brother and never complained when work became long and tiresome. Cutting trees together for the past two years, Stephen grew more fond and proud of his eldest son with each passing month.

"What was that about a Jola camp?" he asked as they neared the last block on the street. Stephen saw a light on inside his home and a shadow move through the room.

"There were fifteen loggers from Jola, Dad. They cornered us in the Reserve and caught Vicente. I ran away but watched it all from behind a tree. They really beat him badly."

"Can you lead us to that camp?" Stephen asked, stopping just before the door to his home. The other men gathered around in a tight knot while looking out for trouble. Dark streets stretched into the night with the sounds of insects interrupting the humid silence.

Carlos looked up into his father's eyes and Stephen suddenly witnessed his son's innocence drain away. He nodded once and looked at the face of each adult surrounding him, clearly understanding everything.

"Good boy Carlos. Now let's go see your brother."

Stephen's wife Marla, with the help of neighbor Logan Broderick, finished setting Vicente's arm just minutes before they arrived. Both stood resting from their efforts with Logan holding a half-empty bottle of Salavandra's infamous rum. A blood-soaked basin of water rested on the battered wood floor with filthy rags floating in the red mess. Vicente's bruised and swollen face turned to see his father and a weak mumble escaped his lips.

Ignoring his wife and Logan, Stephen ran to the bedside and gripped his son's right hand. Vicente squeezed back and Stephen nearly broke down and sobbed in front of everyone.

"I'm alright, Dad," Vicente whispered through rum-soaked lips. "Just have to rest now."

Stephen only nodded, afraid his voice might crack if he opened his mouth. He looked to Logan and whispered a quiet thanks, then stood and held his wife tightly as they both looked down upon their broken son.

"Same as the Warwick boys last month, Hank Campbell two months before that and Franklin earlier last year," said Logan. "And now Vicente. Meantime we're all getting poorer."

"He's been mumbling all night about the Jola crew camped in the Reserve," Marla said with fresh tears springing into her eyes as she looked around the room. "Where's my Carlos?" she asked fearfully.

She quickly grabbed her youngest son and held him tightly against her leg.

"I'd say this is the last straw," said Logan, watching Vicente carefully and wondering what kind of brutes could pummel a kid so badly. He recalled many shouting matches in the Reserve when men from different crews accidentally stumbled across each other. Over the past year as the mills in either Hutch or Jola stopped operating for weeks on end, the loggers' shouting and posturing had elevated into violent confrontations. Loggers now carried machetes for more than cutting underbrush.

"Little payback's in order," Diego said from the back of the room.

Stephen turned and for the first time really noticed the crowded room. His lifelong friends looked back at him, ready to do whatever he asked without question. Knox pulled the gun from his pocket and held it carefully in his clasped hands while waiting for Stephen to say the word.

"Carlos," Stephen said, staring at each of his friends. "Go get the machetes."

A minute later three machetes lay on the floor in neat formation and reflected the light from the room's single bare bulb. Stephen's, the longest and newest of the three, still held a blue patina and a sharply machined edge. The other two, each at least a foot long, showed various states of rust and small cavities from years of field work. Everyone gazed silently at the neat row while listening to Vicente's labored breathing.

"I'll get mine," Logan said quietly and disappeared through the back door.

"I prefer bullets anyway," said Knox, and cocked the automatic pistol. The gun clicked loudly as he drew back the barrel and set a bullet in the chamber. "Too many years of this crap," he continued while shaking his head, "I'm sick of it."

Stephen nodded and somberly handed Will and Diego the two extra machetes. Hefting his own, which seemed more like a sword than a tool, Stephen realized that the decision to enter the Reserve tonight would forever change his life. A weak groan from Vicente cast aside any lingering doubts, and Stephen suddenly gripped the machete tightly.

"Enough of this shit," he said softly. "Tonight Vicente gets revenge and tomorrow we get our fucking trees back."

Diego and Will nodded firmly as Logan returned through the back door carrying his own machete and a grim face. Setting Vicente's arm put him on edge and he could not shake the queasy feeling in his stomach.

"All set then," said Stephen. "Carlos, stay close to me. When I tell you to stay put, you stay put, got it?"

Carlos nodded silently but stood close to his mother and tightly gripped her hand. Stephen's heart ached for his youngest son. More violence loomed in his future and though he wanted to protect him from it, he also needed his youngest son to lead them to the Jola camp.

"I'll keep him safe," he said to Marla. "I'll tuck him out of the way as soon as he shows us the camp."

Marla shook her head and wiped a fresh tear from her face. "You send him home instead," she insisted. "I can't stay here waiting and not knowing if he's coming back. I need you here with me, Carlos." She shook her son's shoulder and looked at him sternly. "You run home as fast as you can when your father says so, ok?"

Carlos nodded with relief while looking up at both his parents. The last thing he wanted to do was return to the Reserve. At least now he would return home even if it meant running alone through the darkness.

"The Warwicks and Hank will want to come, no doubt," said Logan.

"What about Franklin?" Knox asked. "Is he still limping?"

Logan and Stephen both nodded but quickly dismissed Franklin. "He's too old and tired," said Will quickly as the group shuffled out the front door. "He doesn't go out much since he got hurt so bad."

"We'll even things out for him too," Diego mumbled quietly.

The five men and little Carlos struck out into the humid night air and steadily made their way to the home of Jonathan and Daniel Warwick. Hutch's streets were very dark, and whatever terrible things transpired in the bar after they left remained hidden under a blanket of quiet now covering the town. Knox worried that the Federals might be looking for him, but reminded himself that more pressing concerns now weighed on his shoulders. Besides, he thought, each Federal could help himself to a bullet if they cornered him.

The Warwick brothers both lived at home and cared for their aged and sickly parents. In their late twenties, the men worked the trees around Hutch, and like all the residents found these times financially challenging. Several months ago the two of them traveled to Jola's Mill Number Three seeking work and accidentally ran into six men drowning their own unemployment sorrows in a series of rum shots. A brief altercation evolved into a fight, and then into a severe beating, as the alcohol-sodden men passed the brothers around in a melee of fists and kicks. Both spent the night curled in a ditch, regaining their strength before hitching a ride back to Hutch the next morning.

As they neared the Warwick home Knox recalled seeing Jonathan and Daniel a few minutes after they arrived back in Hutch that day. Though Vicente's beating looked worse, the two brothers clearly bore the marks of a sound thrashing. Both of Jonathan's eyes remained a sickly purple for nearly three weeks, and Daniel lost a good number of teeth on the right side of his jaw.

"I'll go get them," said Knox, unknowingly taking charge of the small group as they neared the house. "I don't want us waking up their parents."

Knox left his friends and quietly approached the home's front door. It opened suddenly, revealing a man's thin physique cast entirely in shadow against the dark interior.

"Knox?" the shadow's voice whispered cautiously. "I thought that was you. What's going on?"

Knox recognized Daniel's voice and remembered that he rarely slept. He did not waste time explaining the menacing cluster of men standing behind him with machetes.

"A Jola crew camped in the Reserve got Stephen's son Vicente. Beat him up pretty bad. We're going in to settle things. Permanently."

Daniel waited a few moments before responding. Knox imagined him poking his tongue around his mouth and feeling the gaps that once held strong teeth.

"Wait here," Daniel said in a full voice, forgetting about his sleeping parents.

Daniel left the door wide open and disappeared inside. Seconds later low, mumbling voices emanated from the tiny house, followed by silence. Knox turned to his friends and nodded, certain that the Warwick's were coming. He did not have to wait long.

"Been waiting for this, Knox," said a deeper voice from the shadows.

Knox squinted into the darkness but saw nothing until Jonathan Warwick stepped to the door. He stood taller and more muscular than his brother, and fiercely gripping his own machete stepped outside and joined the men. Daniel followed after a moment, also carrying a machete and a determined look on his face.

"Now for Hank," Knox said confidently, and briefly looked over his friends. He suddenly felt an odd sense of pride. All of them clearly knew what was coming and each looked as determined as the other to go forward, regardless of the looming danger. Logan's bottle of rum suddenly appeared and they all passed it around.

"Save the last for Hank," said Knox after each man took a swallow.

He led them all down the alley past the Warwick's home to the next street where Hank Campbell rented a room in a dilapidated row house. The low building housed six other renters, all single men that frequently slept off their alcohol binges in jail rather than home. Knox slowed as they approached the building, not wanting to startle anyone lingering outside and risk waking the neighbors.

"He's probably up boozing," Will said, pointing at Hank's illuminated window. Hank was known around town as a heavy drinker and he usually stayed up late into the night. "You sure we should save Hank that last drop of rum, Knox? I'm sure he's got plenty."

Despite the obvious tension in the air Knox managed to chuckle at Will's lame attempt at a joke. Will was right though, Hank would probably offer them a drink in a few minutes. Before Knox could answer, a voice called out of the darkness near the building.

"Will Finkle, I thought better of you."

The men stopped dead, startled by Hank's powerful voice ripping through the darkness. Apparently Hank did not care if he woke the neighborhood.

"Taking a man's rum is grounds for a beating," Hank's voice continued from the shadows. Knox smiled, recognizing Hank's familiar tinge of off-humor. He pictured his old friend quite amused with himself for startling everyone.

A creaking chair announced Hank's location as he stood up and stepped away from the building.

"What the heck, boys?" he asked, seeing their machetes and grim faces. "I sure hope you didn't come looking for me with those things." He pointed at them with an empty beer bottle and looked at Knox expectantly.

"We thought you might want to lend a hand, Hank," Knox said quickly. "Can we talk inside?"

"Better inside than out here," Hank replied somberly. "I don't expect you all know anything about a truckload of Federals driving around?"

"Truckload?" Knox asked quickly. "We saw only three tonight. There was a little, uh, altercation at Jenny's earlier."

"Well…there's a lot more than three now," Hank replied. "Drove by about five minutes before you all showed up, going real slow and scoping out my building, as if I'm suddenly guilty of something."

Hank led the cluster of men into his home and predictably passed around his own rum while Knox and Stephen explained the evening's situation. Hank listened carefully and asked about the extent of Vicente's beating. He also asked Carlos what he saw in the woods, and how certain he was of the number of men in the Jola camp. As drunk as he often became, Hank knew when to be deliberate and calculating.

While gathering in all this information Hank repeatedly made a fist with his right hand, closing stiff and deformed fingers into a tight ball. The index finger looked particularly wrong; it twisted at an odd angle against all the other fingers. Knox noticed the misshapen fingernail growing back in a painful-looking curl and remembered how black and swollen Hank's entire hand looked after his encounter with a Jola crew.

"Well," said Hank after a pause, "it's not pretty but it's a better plan than I had for tonight."

"You had a plan?" asked Will, surprised.

Hank nodded sadly, opening and closing his right hand repeatedly in front of everyone. "Yep, I had a plan. It was to get drunk, keep sitting on my ass and stay out of trouble."

He looked around at the men crowded in the small room and suddenly smiled.

"I'm in boys," he announced heartily as if deciding to go to the bar for a drink after a hard day's work. "Somebody ought to pay for my hand, and so far nobody's paid nothing. Damn thing still hurts. We owe it to Vicente, too."

Knox clapped him on the back. "I knew you'd want to help Hank. You still have that old shotgun?"

Hank nodded grimly and accepted a swallow of rum as the bottle appeared. He took a long drink before retrieving the gun from beneath a floorboard. Well wrapped in oiled rags to protect it from Hutch's moisture-laden air, the gun really belonged in a museum rather than in a logger's hands. Two earlier Campbell generations used it to hunt, but Hank rarely even looked at the thing and shot it even less.

"Twenty-seven cartridges," he said seriously while wiping away excess oil from the stock and checking the fittings. "That's all I got, and I have to go to Saint Matthew to get more, which is a big pain in my ass."

"Carlos said fifteen men," Knox replied. "I don't expect you'll need to use any more than three or four. Not with six machetes and of course, this..."

Knox showed Hank the automatic, tipping it against the room's harsh light so he could see it better. Hank whistled his approval, but knew better than to ask how Knox acquired the thing.

"We'll surprise them too," said Stephen, anxious to get moving. "It'll be over before they know it."

"Besides," Jonathan said, flourishing his long machete, "all of us want a little piece of the action, so don't bring all those damn bullets."

With a sudden motion Hank cocked his shotgun and slid a bright yellow cartridge into the gun's chamber. The resounding click hung in the air as the lights suddenly went out and cast the eight men into darkness. Carlos let out a yelp before Stephen barked at everyone to be quiet.

"Need darkness. Federals outside," Diego said in a low voice.

All eyes turned to the street where a large flatbed rolled by carrying six Federals. Four men stood on the back and carried automatic rifles strapped to their shoulders. One swept the length of the building with a spotlight.

"Everybody down," Hank whispered fiercely. A second later the dense shaft penetrated the window and jabbed the room's far wall with a blinding white circle. Everyone threw themselves to the floor. The bright spot hung on the far wall as the Federals peered into Hank's room.

"Did it get anyone?" Hank whispered loudly, confident his voice would not carry over the truck's heavy rumble.

"It might have got me," said Will, strangling a curse. "I couldn't tell."

"Knox, I don't know what you did in Saint Matthew," Hank growled, annoyed that the Federals were targeting his home. His friendship with Knox was well-known, and he expected that somebody had talked following the bar incident. "But you must have pissed off somebody really important."

Knox grunted and mumbled something about telling him the details later.

The spotlight suddenly slid off the wall and moved out of Hank's room. Heavy voices barked orders and the truck's motor suddenly roared. It grew quieter as the Federals moved on to the next block. Hank stood first, telling everyone to stay put while he peered out the window.

"Ok, they turned up the next street. We leave now and go straight for the Reserve."

Everyone filed out of Hank's room and began trotting towards the Reserve. Stephen watched Carlos, concerned he might be too tired for the trek so late at night, but his son kept pace with everyone and needed no encouragement. A grim look clouded his face though, and Stephen thought sadly that his youngest son suddenly looked much older than his age.

The land on either side of the dirt road leading from Hutch lay mostly barren. Stripped of trees but not put under the plow, the once forested land seemed oddly empty in the faint light of the quarter moon. All around them insects screamed and strange rustlings disturbed tall grasses as they passed. No one spoke as each man considered what lay ahead. Revenge filled the hearts of Stephen, the Warwick brothers and Hank. Logan felt a sense of responsibility towards Vicente and his neighbors. Will and Diego just wanted to work, and ran towards their destiny hoping it might somehow ease their financial pain.

Knox stomped steadily down the heavily rutted road feeling nothing. Revenge was a fine excuse he thought, but he did not feel the driving need like Stephen. Work might be a fine reason too, but deep down Knox loathed logging and wanted to escape the difficult life of sweat and falling trees and aching muscles. Knox ran down the road towards something else. What little he could see led him to believe that whatever happened in the next few hours, there was little chance he would ever again wield a chainsaw. That part of his life lay behind him forever.

The edge of the Reserve emerged after nearly an hour of steady hustling. From their perspective it looked like a tall dark wall that occasionally wavered in the humid wind. Towering mahogany and teak grew in a tangled mess with dense walnut and other less valuable trees. When the mills asked for them, these trees eventually provided food, clothing and a little school for Hutch's strapped citizens.

Knox just made out the huge white billboard down the road and spat in disgust at the restrictive language painted on its surface in tall black letters. The sign marked the edge of the Reserve, established years ago by a global environmental group hoping to protect Salavandra's unique island habitat. To Knox and other loggers, the big white sign marked the beginning of Yankees telling them how to live their lives.

Carlos suddenly called out to his father and Stephen quickly ordered everyone to stop. They all clustered around the little boy and looked as he pointed far off to the left of the sign. Just barely visible in the dense blackness at the forest's edge a single weak yellow light pushed back the night. Someone's fire, thought Knox, left unattended while the camp fell into sleep after a long day of work.

"So damn close to us!" cried Logan.

"You'd think they'd stick closer to home," Will agreed. "It can't be good moving those trees to Jola when Hutch's One and Two are so close."

"Teak's always been the thickest here," said Diego, pointing beyond the fire where several giant vehicles stood silently in the darkness. Each was nearly loaded with long, trimmed timber.

"Don't know and don't care why Jola gets our trees. All I know is who's taking them, and who hurt Vicente." Stephen's voice grew hard as he gazed toward the fire. "Carlos," he said to his boy sternly, "you did good and I'm proud of you. You run home now. If I hear you took too long getting there, you'll get it, ok?"

Carlos nodded and immediately turned and ran back down the road. In seconds the darkness swallowed him, leaving the men looking ahead to their grisly work.

"He's a good boy, Stephen," Hank said. "It's too bad we had to drag him into this."

Stephen nodded and gritted his teeth. "Nothing to do about that," he mumbled. "The time was coming anyway." He took a step off the road towards the distant fire.

"Do we have a plan?" whispered Will to Knox a few minutes later as the fire grew more distinct. His heart pounded in anticipation and he feared the machete might slip from his sweaty palms. Knox shook his head and kept walking.

"No plan yet, Will. Just think about Vicente. That, and how your wife and kids will look at you in another two months when all these fucking trees are standing right here and they haven't eaten a full meal in weeks."

Will nodded and shut up. He did not want to think about his wife and kids. As far as they knew he was getting drunk in Hutch, not hunting men in the countryside. He focused on the camp ahead where he could just make out four big tents ringing the fire. When the camp's layout became more visible, Knox motioned everyone to stop.

"Four tents," Knox began, crouched in the grass and speaking softly to his friends. "That's at least three, probably four in each tent." He paused and looked around at the somber faces before continuing. Clearly in charge, he did not remember accepting the responsibility.

"We split up," he ordered. "Hank and I get our own tents because we've got guns and can easily take out four. I'll get the furthest one. Hank, you take the one to the right of mine." Knox pointed through the darkness at the tents and looked back to make certain Hank knew which was his tent. "Will, Diego and Jonathan," he continued, thinking fast and trying to tap each man's unique quality to ensure success, "you three get the one next to Hank's, and Stephen, Logan and Daniel, the last one. Everyone got that?"

Knox paused, half expecting someone to object, but nobody said a word.

"All of us go in at the same time," Knox continued. "Nobody comes out until it's finished. Remember Vicente."

Seven heads nodded quickly and with a racing heart Knox stood, pulled out his gun and sprinted toward the furthest tent without looking back. He worried that any pause might jeopardize the entire evening.

Feet immediately pounded behind him and at that moment he knew everyone was committed beyond the point of turning back.

The fire burned brighter and larger than he expected and cast rippling, dancing shadows across the heavy white canvass tents. Floating into the ring of light Knox lost all sense of peripheral noise and motion while concentrating on his target. He no longer heard the others but knew they ran just steps behind him. In seconds he bent to grab a heavy flap and vaguely heard scuffling somewhere behind him. No shouts, no other noise, just a quick scurry of feet. He knew that the others had reached their tents, and then he threw back the canvass and burst inside.

Fire erupted from his fist and illuminated the tent's interior with a mean orange glow. The vague shape on the cot nearest the door jerked once and laid still. Three other shapes immediately bolted up from their cots and screamed out while a shotgun blast echoed loudly through the camp. Another bolt of fire leapt from Knox's fist and threw back a man just beginning to stand. Screams erupted from somewhere far behind him and the ring of steel bit through the darkness as Knox imagined a machete slipping through flesh and hitting a cot's steel frame. Another blast from Hank's shotgun, then another as yells and shouts erupted all through the camp.

The two remaining shapes cowered against their cots. The darkness made them more shapeless blobs than men. He took a deep breath and aimed at the head of the closest man. He thought a sound escaped the man's lips, but whatever he said died when Knox pulled the trigger a third time. Hank's gun blasted once more, simultaneously. Somewhere in the back of his mind Knox counted four shotgun blasts and realized Hank was probably finished. Again steel on steel rang from the other tents. Sobs and cries of fear echoed through the camp. Never taking his eyes off the last man, Knox swept the gun around and took aim.

"Please no," the voice from the shadow cracked in fear. "I have a son and daughter. What will they do?"

Hank's voice suddenly yelled clearly and Knox heard his footsteps pounding away towards the other tents where the machetes still worked through the Jola crew. In seconds another shotgun blast burst through the humid night air. A smoky and burned smell drifted into the tent where Knox stood towering over the last man. Again the man pleaded for Knox to spare his life.

"Get up," he ordered, his mind racing with possibilities. He suddenly wanted to give his men one final act of machismo. Knox wanted their collective vengeance to really sink in and give Stephen, the Warwicks, and Hank some real satisfaction. This last man, Knox thought, blubbering in fear, would serve nicely. He pulled the man up by his hair and roughly shoved him outside.

A weak scream that cut off sharply came from the furthest tent. Stephen, Logan and Daniel already stood by the fire wiping bloodied machetes on their victim's clothing and refusing to look at each other. Hank stood outside the last tent and held the flap open for Will, Diego and Jonathan. The three emerged covered in blood. While everyone gathered near the fire, Knox pistol whipped the last man and watched as he crumpled to the ground.

"Nice work, boys," yelled Knox, breaking the sudden and heavy silence. A few eyes turned to him and questioned the man at his feet. "Tonight Hutch got some payback, and tomorrow we'll finally get back to work. Now about this last guy…"

Knox grabbed a handful of hair and twisted the Jola man's face towards his friends. "Stephen, Daniel, Jonathan, Hank," Knox called, deliberately singling out those who suffered the most and looking carefully at each man as he called their names. "This is our problem." Knox pushed the man closer to the fire for everyone to see.

Bleeding from his head where Knox cuffed him, the Jola logger gazed back fearfully at all the men. Jonathan, who shed his own soiled shirt, looked especially menacing as he swung his machete like a pendulum and stared at the man. Death lay behind those eyes. The Jola logger realized the futility of pleading for mercy.

"Just do it fast," he croaked.

The logger swallowed once and stared into the flames seeing his wife and children. He barely listened as Knox declared sentence over him. He sadly recalled the various beatings, including Vicente's, that he administered with his friends. Lost in a year's worth of poaching, in which both sides dipped into the Reserve, lay hidden the reasons why arguments with Hutch's loggers evolved into tonight's slaughter. He acknowledged some guilt towards the crimes Knox proclaimed, but also knew he would commit them again under similar circumstances. Too much mahogany and teak stood waiting for the chainsaws. Seeing the neat stack of tree trunks towering in the darkness just beyond the fire, he suddenly wondered at the futility of it all.

"All for that fucking wood over there," he mumbled, suddenly hating the Reserve.

Knox finally quieted and silence filled the camp. Will threw his bloodied shirt on the fire and flames shot up into the dark sky. Jonathan stepped away from the light and approached the kneeling man. The Jola logger, suddenly awash in a grinding anger, stubbornly refused to cry out and steeled himself against the machete as it bit deeply into his neck.

Carlos heard the distant gunfire and kept running towards home. His feet ached and his mind tricked him with fatigue and stress. Several times he hallucinated and saw a bright wavering light ahead. He stumbled on the heavily rutted road. With knees blackened and muscles aching he willed himself to keep moving away from the violence and towards home. He nearly ran straight into the flatbed truck carrying the six Federals. The light he saw was not imaginary. It was the same spotlight he managed to avoid at Hank's place.

"Hey, stop right there, kid," shouted a uniformed Federal. The heavy spotlight pinned Carlos in his tracks. He was too tired and disoriented to try running and actually sat down on the ground in relief, breathing heavily and suddenly, oddly, smelling the earth beneath him. His head swam and he fought back waves of nausea as rough hands gathered him up and passed him onto the truck's expansive back. Someone shoved a flask into his mouth and poured a vile, burning liquid down inside him. He choked and sputtered, but his head momentarily cleared.

"What the hell are you doing out here in the middle of the night, kid?" asked the man with the flask. Carlos tried to focus on him but failed. He shut his eyes and saw his father's disappointment when hearing how the Federals caught him. A rough hand slapped his face, but Carlos could not bring himself to respond.

"It's no good," said another voice above him. "Handcuff him to the back. We'll sort it out in the daylight when we find his parents. I want to get closer to those gunshots."

The truck lurched heavily in the deep ruts then rolled forward, taking Carlos back towards the Jola camp and the carnage he desperately wanted to avoid. In moments he passed out.

Five

Antonio stared down at ripped black vinyl as the truck finally lurched through the roadblock. His seat looked oddly flat and the inside of the truck, with its cracked windshield and missing rear-view mirror, appeared strangely monotonous. When he dared to look at the sparkling Caribbean, it pulsed with an uninspired and somehow lifeless radiance that sent waves of vertigo surging through his head. Fighting back nausea, he shut his eye and took a few deep breaths.

"Hey, if you need to vomit let me know, ok?"

Through his self-imposed darkness Antonio nodded and waved a hand weakly towards the road. Two full days of rest deadened the horror of losing an eye but were insufficient to accustom him to the world's new, weird bluntness. The doctor said he needed a few weeks of practice before he could enjoy an end to the dizziness and headaches.

The coffee specialist grunted and accelerated past the two jeeps packed with Federals. Displeasure registered on his face. Phillip Penkava had personally asked him to do this unpleasant favor, so he picked up Antonio early in the morning and headed up the road towards Amadica.

"Any idea who that guy in the picture was?" Antonio asked after a few minutes. He remembered the Link shoved into the cab showing a man's grizzled face with dark, angry eyes. "Why are the Federals looking for him?"

"You didn't hear?" asked his companion.

Antonio shook his head and pointed at the black patch covering his right eye. "Been occupied lately, remember?"

"Right, sorry," the specialist said. "I'm still surprised you didn't hear anything. Mr. Penkava was mugged and beaten up a while back.

Vasquez put his men on the case and they have a suspect but can't find him."

Antonio remembered seeing Phillip a few days ago and thought he looked no worse than having spent a late night out. He guessed his mugging was not too bad.

"All those soldiers can't find one guy?" he asked. "But Vasquez has hundreds of men."

The specialist nodded energetically. "It gets better," he continued, suddenly forgetting that he did not want to be driving to Amadica. "They almost caught him in Hutch a few days ago, but he and a bunch of friends slipped through their fingers after beating up three Federals in some dive bar."

"Sounds like the Federals need some practice," Antonio mumbled, remembering the assault rifles strapped to their shoulders at the roadblock. "I sure wouldn't want to be that guy," he continued, "he'll be sorry when they catch him, I'm sure."

The specialist nodded vigorously, savoring the fact that Antonio did not yet know the best part of the story. "I don't think we'll hear much about it when they finally do get him." He smiled and waited for Antonio to acknowledge the pause. Antonio turned, appropriately expectant after a few moments.

"They connected him and his friends to the Jola Reserve massacre."

Antonio scowled in confusion. He suddenly felt as if years had passed while he recovered in Saint Matthew's clinic.

"Massacre?"

"Fifteen loggers from Jola were hacked up and shot dead near Hutch the night of the fifth. The Federals are all over it. They even arrested family members and friends. Anyone remotely connected has been brought in for questioning."

Antonio stared in disbelief.

"Fifteen? Dead? Are you certain?"

The specialist nodded. "Hell, you're the one with the Link. You ought to know this stuff."

Antonio looked down at the bit of clothing scrounged from the clinic. The Link lay tucked between two shirts, turned off and looking quite innocuous. The information it revealed about Penkava Incorporated raced through Antonio's mind. He still was unsure who to tell, or even if it all mattered. He planned to tell Mary, and possibly Marco if the seasonal worker showed any interest.

"I'm still learning how to use it," he said truthfully. Over two days he learned a lot about Penkava Incorporated's culpability in the Rocanophyl case. He also realized that he was tapping into just a minute portion of the Link's vast information network.

"It takes time," the specialist nodded in agreement. "Just do a search for current Caribbean news and you'll get reams of information."

"Thanks for the tip," Antonio responded, "but what about these fifteen men. Why would someone want to kill them?"

The specialist shrugged. "Maybe the guy who attacked Mr. Penkava is just psycho and likes killing people. That doesn't explain his friends though. They were all involved. The Federals say there are eight men total, and this Christopher Knox guy is the leader."

"Christopher Knox," Antonio mumbled, letting the name sink into his memory. "Maybe the Federals can't find him or his men because they all left the island."

The specialist gunned the engine and shifted the truck into low gear as the road curved left and they started climbing towards Amadica. He shook his head after a moment. "The Federals are searching all the boats in Jola and Saint Matthew. Unless they had something planned from a beach, they're still here."

Antonio felt a sweaty dampness beneath him and squirmed uncomfortably on the vinyl seat. He looked gratefully up the hill where the cool and dry air around his coffee plots never made him sweat so profusely. His mother and Mary both waited for him up there, and he looked forward to returning to the fields and finishing the harvest with Marco and his two helpers. He expected a quick return to normalcy, especially after the specialist recommended a cure for his sick trees.

"Well," he said after watching the road in silence for several minutes, "I hope they get caught soon. Salavandra's got enough going on without a bunch of maniacs running around murdering people."

"They both left early yesterday, Boss," replied Marco when Antonio asked him why his two companions were missing. "They were worried that you couldn't pay, being in the clinic, so they went up to one of your neighbors to help with his harvest."

Seated at the table Marco looked tired as he gratefully accepted a cup of coffee from Antonio's shuffling mother. He spent the past day alone in Antonio's fields, racing against time to pick the ripe coffee cherries before they rotted on the branches. His lone, monumental efforts were nowhere near sufficient.

"I couldn't convince them to stay," he continued after a healthy sip of the black brew. Antonio blew across his own cup and savored the rich smell curling into the air. Even in the most difficult times, a solid cup of freshly brewed black coffee made him feel better. The sugar, loved long ago as a child, sat forgotten in a small bag inside a heavily lidded pot to keep out hungry insects. "I told them you were good for their work, but you know how youngsters are, always needing money right now and spending it as fast as they get it. Those idiots waste most of it every night in Amadica, anyway."

Antonio remembered the sour smelling, alcohol and smoke sodden men emerging from sleep to come inside for breakfast. It was nothing unusual for the pickers, he reminded himself. Ever since he could remember, seasonal workers disappeared into Amadica after a day's picking and stumbled back to his front porch to crash for a few hours before returning to the field the next day. It was a timeless pattern, like the ripening of the coffee.

"I'm sure glad you stuck around, Marco. My mother kept you well fed, I expect?"

Marco nodded and patted his stomach. "I think I took your place for a few days, my friend," he said smiling and looked over at Rene now resting in an old rocking chair. "She insisted I eat all the time, and yesterday packed a huge lunch for me. I think I actually gained a few pounds."

Antonio chuckled and leaned back in his chair. The cool evening air felt great, especially compared to Saint Matthew's oppressive heat. Twilight's shadows lengthened as Marco explained the state of Antonio's various coffee plots and laid out a strategy for picking over the next few days.

"We can still get a good number of sacks picked," Marco assured him after Antonio expressed his doubts about the quantity of the harvest. "Luckily the two northwest fields are a little higher up than the others. Those cherries look a lot healthier than the others."

"How are the certificates?" Antonio asked, remembering his dismal returns in Saint Matthew.

Marco shook his head and pointed at a burlap sack on the counter. "Not too good, Boss," he replied, shaking his head. "I keep asking John for a few extra certificates when he picks up the coffee in the morning, but he won't budge an inch. That guy's straight as an arrow."

Antonio smiled. "He's been at this too long, Marco. He's a good guy though, and he'd give us more if he could. What's the news from the other farms?"

Marco shook his head and swallowed a little more coffee. His wrinkled eyes and gray hair belied an otherwise tough and optimistic attitude. Antonio noticed how tired he looked, as if too many years had passed and there was still no end to his working life. "They've all got sick trees like you," he said while shaking his head. "It's spreading, too. I'm sure they'll want to know what that specialist finds."

Antonio nodded and remembered the specialist heading down into one of his coffee plots with a chainsaw and a shovel. He promised to take only a few root samples, but Antonio knew that meant cutting at least two and probably three sick trees.

"As soon as I know, I'll spread the news around," he said to Marco. If his neighbors' trees looked as sickly as his own, Antonio expected them to jump at the cure. With next year's crop already threatened, anything less amounted to financial suicide.

"Did I see a Link in your stuff, Boss?" asked Marco, remembering their discussion about Rocanophyl before Antonio left for Saint Matthew.

Antonio looked over at the small pile thrown on a chair. The Link's blank screen reminded him of his missing eye, and that suddenly made his good eye ache. He shook off the slight pain and nodded.

"I got it after the accident," he began with a sigh. "I found out a lot about the Rocanophyl story and Penkava Incorporated. They made the stuff, you know."

Antonio watched Marco pause. "The same Penka..."

Antonio nodded and held up a hand. "The same Penkava that buys all Salavandra's coffee," he said. "It's the same company that has bought our coffee for generations, too."

Marco looked a little stunned. He prided himself on knowing more than the average person, and this new information surprised him. "So all those lawsuits that failed in court, they were against *our* Penkava Incorporated?"

Antonio nodded and finished his coffee in one long swallow. He set the plastic cup on the table and leaned towards Marco. "That's not all I found out," he said softly. Marco looked at him, wide-eyed in the failing light.

"What else, Boss?"

Antonio got up and switched on the light. The bulb glowed weakly above the table and cast dark shadows in the corners of the room. Rene snored softly in her chair and Antonio reminded himself to tuck her into bed.

"All these years I guess I knew on some level that I actually worked for Penkava," Antonio began while staring outside into the darkness. "We've always lived off their certificates, after all. I guess I just never put together the extent of control the company has over Salavandra."

"What do you mean?" asked Marco. "What kind of control?"

Antonio returned to his chair and sat down heavily. Gleaning all this information off the Link over the past two days was tedious work. "Those greenhouses on the road to Jola, they're Penkava's too. That means Mary, Mercedes, and all those other ladies work for the same company I do." Mentioning Mary made Antonio note the time. In a little while he planned to meet her at the fork in the road.

Marco nodded. "But everyone knows those are Penkava's greenhouses. Why is it such big news?"

Antonio nodded and remembered feeling the same thing the day before. Then he stumbled across several pages listing economic statistics for countries around the world. Salvandra's data revealed compelling information.

"Salavandra exports only one other major thing, Marco. It's wood, almost all of it high value teak, mahogany and walnut." Antonio remembered the environmentally dedicated Link site showing this information. It listed the Jola Reserve as one of the world's most threatened protected lands. Antonio suddenly remembered the specialist telling him about the Jola massacre. He paused and tried to piece together the disparate bits of information.

"I know that, Boss. I worked the Number Three mill in Jola a few years back after the coffee harvest. It was a good year, if I remember right."

"On your checks, what was the company's name?"

Marco shook his head and smiled. "No checks, Boss. Cash only. Number Three didn't even give us a choice. It was cash or nothing. I didn't mind, of course. President Vasquez shouldn't get any more money from me."

Antonio nodded and recalled how the coffee certificates stated that all appropriate taxes were automatically deducted and paid to the state before any cash changed hands with the farmers. Antonio never heard of anyone objecting to the system.

"Guess who owns Mills One and Two in Hutch, along with Three and Four in Jola."

"Not Penkava again?" Marco said, nearly holding his breath.

Antonio nodded, relieved to finally be telling someone about his findings.

"So coffee, flowers and wood leave Salavandra," Antonio said, looking at Marco to make certain he understood. "The coffee and wood leave on the Celeste, the same big boat I was hurt on." He pointed to his eye patch. "The flowers are regularly flown out of Saint Matthew's airport. Together these three products make up a huge percentage of Salavandra's yearly earnings."

"Gross domestic product?" asked Marco. Antonio nodded in surprise and then reminded himself that Marco was older and better informed than the average seasonal worker.

"Yes, right, the GDP." Antonio tried to keep his voice down in spite of his excitement.

"Well that means if Penkava controls the coffee and saw mills and the green…"

"Right, right," exclaimed Antonio, quite animated. "That means Penkava Incorporated basically owns Salavandra."

Marco sat back in his chair and looked up at the ceiling, absorbing the new information. He knew that large commercial forces controlled many Caribbean products. He worked the islands' fields and forests too long to overlook that fact. Never once, however, did he consider that one company might have such a lock on an entire island.

"You're certain of all this, Antonio?" he asked skeptically.

Antonio anticipated Marco's response and reached for the Link. In a few moments the two men surfed to Antonio's bookmarked sites.

Half an hour later Marco sat back shaking his head, quite convinced of Penkava Incorporated's monopolistic control over Salavandra.

"Wow," he said softly. "I never imagined."

"One more thing," said Antonio, maneuvering the stylus over the Link's diminutive screen and selecting the final bookmark. "This is the most important thing, at least for us coffee growers." He pointed at the bookmark and after a quick flash a new Link site popped up on the screen.

"The New York Board of Trade? What's that?" asked Marco, tired of looking at the little screen and rubbing his eyes from the effort. He wondered how Antonio managed with just one eye. Antonio looked more than a little possessed as he gazed into the Link.

"This," Antonio said in a low voice, "I found late last night. It's where I figured out how much we're all getting screwed."

The sound of a smoothly humming motor suddenly interrupted the early evening's quite peace. Both men looked up from the Link, first at each other and then out the window. A perfect square of darkness stared back at them, broken only by the occasional bit of starlight leaking thought the leafy canopy cloaking Antonio's home. Antonio stood and peered outside into the darkness.

"Strange to have a truck up here at this time of night," he said to Marco.

He watched as a pair of headlights sliced through the darkness. The piercing beams jerked violently as the truck hit a deep rut. It looked to Antonio as if the vehicle stopped in front of Mary's home.

"Same as yesterday, actually," said Marco. "About the same time of night, too."

"It's not the Federals, is it? I heard about the Jola thing. They're looking all over the island, I guess." The sound of the truck's door closing echoed over to Antonio. It began turning around on the bumpy road.

"No Federals that I can tell," replied Marco, standing next to Antonio to get a better view. Already its red taillights moved down the road and in a few seconds disappeared around a bend. As the motor's hum grew distant, the evening's normal tranquility returned. "It's a fancy truck," Marco continued. "Nothing Vasquez would have his soldiers riding around in."

"Fancy truck? What kind of fancy truck?"

Marco looked at Antonio with a slightly confused expression. "It's black," he said, trying to be helpful when he saw Antonio was more than just curious. "It's black and shiny. I saw it last night close up. That's all I know."

Antonio stood thinking for a moment while gazing out the window into the darkness. His was one of many small homes, some closer to shacks really, clustered within a picturesque hollow on Mt. Tabor. Everyone living in the hollow farmed coffee on the nearby slopes and Antonio knew all his neighbors. Nobody owned a vehicle or was even friendly with an owner of a fancy truck.

"Wait here, Marco. I'm going to go see what that truck was doing up here. I don't want to be surprised by that Christopher Knox guy showing up."

Marco chuckled, "Knox and his friends won't be showing up here, Boss. We're too far out of the way. Besides, they don't have any vehicles. I've heard they're a dirt-poor lot from Hutch. There's no way it was them in that truck."

"Still, I want to go check. Besides, Mary should be coming home soon and I want to meet her and explain everything that I told you."

Marco returned to his seat and stretched out his long legs. "Fine with me, Boss. I'll be hitting the hay soon anyway. Give me a kick tomorrow morning?"

"You got it," replied Antonio. "I want to tackle one of the northwest plots you were talking about."

"Good choice. On the way, you can tell me about the New York Board of Trade and how we're all supposedly getting screwed."

Antonio gently woke Rene and helped her into bed. His elderly mother still moved around well, but lately her sleep was deeper than Antonio remembered. Just another sign of her age, he thought, and pulled the bedspread up to her chin to ward off the night's chill. He wished her goodnight and by the time he left she was already sleeping again.

He buttoned his coat against the cool nighttime air, feeling slightly dizzy as his left eye lamely sought out recognizable shapes amongst the confusing array of shadows and suddenly unfamiliar silhouettes. This difficulty would pass too, the doctor assured him, and he would soon see during the nighttime almost as well as before the accident.

Ignoring the growing tension in his forehead, Antonio made his way down the road more by memory than sight. Occasionally stumbling in the many ruts, he eventually made it to Mary's home where a light burned inside. He paused outside her home and considered the mysterious truck stopping and letting someone out. The ladies should be returning from the greenhouses soon, he realized, and listened for their quiet chatter on the road but heard nothing. Suddenly Mary's familiar figure passed quickly in front of the lighted window. Antonio smiled and walked briskly to the door. It opened before he knocked.

"Antonio!" cried Mary, startled to find him at her door. She rushed into his arms and hugged him tightly. "I was just coming to see if you got back yet." He hugged her tightly, and looking over her head, nodded once to her father. He came to the door with a concerned look on his face.

"I heard about the wrecked eye," he said in his familiar, gruff manner. Mary pulled away and looked up into his face. She reached a hand up to touch the black patch covering his eye.

"Does it hurt?" she asked.

"Not anymore. But I get headaches from the stress on my left eye. They'll pass."

"Tough break, Antonio," Mary's father said curtly and grasped the doorknob. "You two probably want to catch up, and it's cold out there so either go for a walk or come in, but decide quickly because I'm shutting this door."

Antonio chuckled comfortably and held Mary tightly around her shoulders. "I'd like to walk a little, ok?"

The door clicked behind them as they stepped away from Mary's home and onto their familiar walking route. It led along the road past the other homes and further up the mountain. During the daytime the two moved along small footpaths, but in the darkness the road was the only comfortable place to walk and chat.

"Are you warm enough?" he asked.

Mary nodded and stopped walking. She looked up at him with her eyes glistening in the weak light. "I was so worried for you, Antonio," she said with her voice cracking. "I waited where you told me. So long and…"

"Shhh, Mary," he gathered her up in his arms and held her tightly, rocking slightly back and forth to comfort her. "I'm ok now. I'm so sorry I missed you. That was the worst part of the whole thing. Wondering about how you managed."

A muffled sob escaped from his coat where she buried her head. Her body shook and he felt her take a deep breath. "Mercedes helped me a lot," she said, finding her breath and resting her head heavily against his chest. "I don't know how I could have managed without her."

"She's a good friend," Antonio replied. "I'll have to thank her when I see her."

They continued strolling up the road holding hands and squeezing their fingers together as they talked. Mary told him about the endless work hours spent preparing for Valentine's Day. She mentioned how frazzled her boss was and how he snapped at anyone not paying close enough attention to the flowers. A deep red, almost purple rose was all the rage in the United States this season, Mary told him, so her boss was especially nervous whenever anyone worked around these precious flowers.

"Your eyes," Antonio asked. "How are they?" He saw the familiar swelling and irritation outlining her brown eyes. After her normal ten-hour workday she often complained about itching and burning eyes. The fourteen-hour days before Valentine's Day were especially difficult.

"Not good," she replied quickly. "I want to rub them so badly, but it only makes them hurt more. The boss hands out eye drops halfway through the day now. It makes some difference."

"Eye drops?" Antonio said, surprised. "That's an improvement. Why the change?"

After some hesitation, she replied. "Phillip Penkava is coming around nearly every day to check on our progress and see how we're doing. He asked a few of us about the pesticides, and then ordered some eye drops."

"Phillip Penkava is being a nice guy? Really?"

Mary shrugged and looked up ahead into the darkness. "He gave me a ride to see you and kept me updated on your progress."

"He might seem ok at first, Mary, but he's a criminal. On a scale you can't even imagine."

Vague images of her dinner and ride around Saint Matthew flashed through Mary's mind. She remembered the money he left on the table, the wine on the beach and her futile attempts to resist him. She remembered him insisting on seeing her again the very next day. The rape was already becoming something else in Mary's mind. Recalling yesterday's willing encounter with Phillip was clearer. Darkness thankfully hid her face as guilt washed over her.

"Criminal?" She pulled her suddenly sweaty palm from Antonio's hand and put it into her pocket.

"It's a long story and I don't feel like talking about him right now."

Mary breathed a sigh of relief. She did not want to talk about Phillip either. Mercedes was already scandalized, and Mary was too tired to handle any more drama this evening.

Antonio wrapped his arm around her shoulder and drew her close. She felt so familiar to him, and he realized again how much he missed her.

"Mary," he began after a moment, "I still want to go to Saint Matthew for your ring. I was thinking…"

"Not tonight, Antonio." Mary stopped and turned to look into his eyes. She dreaded this topic and had already calculated an excuse. Trimming flowers all day gave her plenty of time to strategize. "You just got back after a horrible experience, and I can't have you worrying about me right now. I can wait until after the harvest."

Antonio smiled at her but it was a sad smile and he wished that they had married years ago. Between work and sickly parents, there was never an appropriate time. "That would help me get the coffee in," he said somberly, suddenly hating the beans and despising his responsibility to pick the stuff. "I'm behind, as you probably know. Luckily I have Marco."

"Several more weeks won't kill me after all these years," she said quickly, turning towards home without seeing the hurt expression on Antonio's face. Last night Phillip promised to take her to New York following the Valentine's Day flower shipment. She willingly gave herself to him then, succumbing to his violent lovemaking while thinking about escaping Salavandra and seeing the streets of the United States. The end of the coffee harvest seemed years away.

"Hey," Antonio said firmly and stopped her as she took a step back down the road. She turned to look at him and saw a tried, broken man.

The eye patch, she suddenly thought with a tinge of guilt, made her longtime friend and lover look sad and a little hopeless. Phillip's glossed perfection certainly outshined Antonio's gritty, earthen look. Mary astounded herself that she could even think such a thing.

"I love you. You know I wanted to marry long ago. That's all I ever truly wanted."

She smiled up at him but was unable to say anything. Years had passed waiting for these words, but they now sounded irritatingly flat. Instead of speaking, she hugged Antonio tightly and wondered desperately how she could avoid hurting him.

They returned to Mary's home in a brooding sort of silence as Antonio worried about her feelings and Mary's stomach did flip flops thinking about her promised encounter with Phillip tomorrow.

"Hey, before I forget," said Antonio as Mary put a hand to her doorknob after a quick goodnight kiss. She turned to look as the door cracked open. A vertical ray of light escaped into the night and temporarily blinded Antonio. "Do you know anything about a truck coming up here just before I came over? I thought it stopped nearby."

Mary froze and then steadied herself against the sudden pounding of her heart. She took a deep breath to calm her voice before speaking, and did not turn to look at Antonio.

"Mr. Penkava came by just before closing. He dropped me off again."

"Dropped you off? Again?"

At that moment the gentle sound of women's voices drifted up the road. The other greenhouse women finally arrived after walking up the hill from the bus stop. He turned to look into the darkness and saw nothing, but from his blinded right side he vaguely noticed the light from Mary's door suddenly widen. She stepped inside and quickly closed it behind her.

"Wait," he said, just as the door banged shut. He stood suddenly alone outside her home as a cluster of women approached in the darkness. Blinking hard to clear his eyesight and wondering at Mary's odd behavior, he greeted the ladies tersely and quickly returned home.

"I'm really not in the mood to talk right now, Marco," said Antonio the next morning after they set out for the northwest plot and Marco asked about the New York Board of Trade. Even a double helping of coffee failed to jolt him awake this morning. He tossed uncomfortably throughout most of the night, worrying first about Mary then about the information gathered from the Link. Jola massacre nightmares interrupted what little sleep washed over him in the small hours, and he awoke groggy and in a sour mood after Rene shook him lightly.

Luckily Marco understood perfectly and did not pry or even open his mouth again until they reached the orchard. They stepped quietly through the misty, wooded slopes listening to the piercing bird calls and feeling the early sun slowly warm the mountain through breaks in the forest canopy. Marco prided himself on reading people and knowing what to say at the right moment. Mornings, of course, were touchy for many people. He also suspected that Antonio's meeting with Mary did not go very well, and therefore planned to steer well clear of that subject.

"Over there, Boss. That's where I looked the other day."

Beneath a tree lay a large pile of empty, dew-soaked burlap sacks. The one acre, steeply-sloped plot, lay covered in ripening trees with their branches hanging low under heavy coffee cherry loads. Antonio gathered a few branches in his hands and looked closely at the ripe fruit.

"Nice, red and perfect," he said to Marco, a little heartened at the good sign. Perhaps, he thought hopefully, the root problem missed this plot. He remembered his father talking about the importance of having many different plots on various mountain sites. That way, explained Victor one afternoon many years ago, a single plot might succumb to disease while others survive to produce healthy beans.

"Tackle this field now, Boss?" asked Marco, wondering about Antonio's other trees and when they might be harvested.

After careful consideration, Antonio decided to harvest. The other plots could wait, he thought, and in the meantime these trees would yield a nice crop. Besides, Antonio argued to himself with a touch of bitterness, harvesting perfect coffee cherries was always more pleasant than picking deformed and often blackened beans. He picked up a sack and tossed it to Marco, and the two men began rustling through the dew-soaked trees dropping handfuls of ripe, red coffee into the burlap.

The sacks filled quickly. They made their way from tree to tree, keeping an even but non-rushed pace with each other. Entire branches held only red cherries instead of the more common jumble of red ones mixed with green, unripe coffee. The two men could therefore often strip entire branches in one sweeping motion, rather than carefully going through each branch and selectively picking.

Antonio's mood began to lighten after two hours. He always liked the harvest, despite it being the busiest time of year. After almost year of careful preparation, the several harvesting months finally revealed the sum of all his efforts. He paused before moving to his next tree and proudly looked at the neat rows as they marched down the slope. His father may have wanted him to leave Salavandra, but Antonio was certain Victor would also be pleased with the morning's progress. Marco picked up on Antonio's mood and rested for a moment while sipping water from his canteen.

"Very nice so far, Boss," he said, also pleased with their progress. Though owning no land, Marco still appreciated a bountiful harvest. When his employer paid well, which Antonio always did, he felt connected to the land and somehow personally responsible for the crop's quality.

Antonio agreed and accepted the canteen from Marco. He thought about where his crop would soon travel.

"You know where all this coffee eventually goes?" asked Antonio after a moment.

Marco nodded, seeing that Antonio was ready to talk. "The U.S., Boss. Always the United States takes Salavandra's coffee. The U.S. takes all the coffee from all the islands I've ever worked."

Antonio nodded. This was common knowledge to coffee workers, whether land owners or landless pickers. The Caribbean people rarely consumed more than two percent of their crop.

"Yes, the U.S., but before the American's drink it, almost all of it goes through the New York Board of Trade. That's where the big buyers line up and purchase thousands of tons of beans. Maybe even Salavandra's entire crop."

Marco nodded and listened intently. This was something new, and he always liked hearing fresh information. Seeing Marco listening, Antonio continued.

"Yesterday, when I said we're getting screwed, I meant because of the prices on the New York Board of Trade."

"What about the prices?"

"They're much higher than what the mill gives us in certificates."

"Much higher?" Marco asked. "How much higher?"

Antonio steadied himself on the steep slope and looked carefully at Marco. His employee was really more a friend, and seeing him poor and landless year after year made this information especially painful. "Sometimes over one hundred fifty times as much," he said quietly.

Marco's jaw dropped and he looked at Antonio in disbelief. "That can't be possible, Boss. Surely the certificates match better."

Antonio shook his head slowly. At first he too did not believe the numbers until many hours of searching the Link confirmed the pricing pattern over dozens of years. In his searching Antonio also found various coffee retailers occasionally lobbying the governments of countries for more equitable pricing schemes, but these efforts usually failed to produce any significant results. The real culprits, Antonio was convinced, were giant food and agricultural corporations culling favor with pliant, corrupt governments. Penkava Incorporated and Salavandra stood out as good examples.

"I'll show you on the Link when we get back home," he said sadly. "I checked and double checked to make sure."

"One hundred fifty times," Marco said aloud, still looking stunned. "Over my life that would mean…"

Antonio took another sip from the canteen while watching Marco make rough calculations. His facial expression revealed a progression of thoughts that quickly turned to anger. Antonio harbored the same feelings of being cheated, still fresh from making his own, similar calculations.

"It means you would not be picking with me today, my friend," Antonio said, deliberately interrupting Marco so he failed to tally a grand total.

Marco slowly nodded while casting a hard look at Antonio. "I could have my own land, a farm even, maybe like you."

"Better than that, Marco," replied Antonio, gesturing to the sky. "You can think even bigger. How about not farming at all? That would also be possible. No more calloused hands, no more back-breaking lifting and no more living year after year on loans and certificates."

Seeing Antonio's point, Marco nodded and smiled briefly. The smile faded quickly, however, and he immediately shook his burlap sack and asked, "How do we get one hundred fifty times more for this, right now?" He held Antonio's eyes with an intense look as his well-muscled forearm flexed and held the heavy coffee sack off the ground.

"I don't have an answer, Marco," replied Antonio, shaking his head and picking up his own sack. A lot of trees still needed picking. "I think President Vasquez is part of the problem, though. I don't think he does us any favors."

Marco snorted in disgust at the president's name. "Vasquez? Doing us favors? All he cares about are his precious Federals and his huge estate overlooking Saint Matthew. He lives off my sweat. He lives off your sweat and all your neighbors' sweat too. I think he's a crook."

"Wait until you see the Link," Antonio agreed. "Vasquez is mentioned a lot, but not by any source on Salavandra. Those Federals of his, they're mentioned a lot too, mostly by groups watching human rights. A lot of people outside Salavandra think they're nothing better than well-armed tyrants."

A sudden rustling sounded to his right and Antonio turned to look. His patched eye blinded him, so he heard a voice before seeing anyone.

"Not just outside Salavandra," growled a man.

Christopher Knox stepped out from behind several coffee trees. More men suddenly materialized from other areas of the orchard until a total of eight haggard men surrounded Antonio and Marco. They all stood quietly on the slope, unshaven, nervous, and clearly exhausted. Knox, the closest of the eight, had dark and heavy rings under his eyes. Most of the men carried a machete tucked into their belts, and three held the same automatic rifles the Federals carried.

Antonio and Marco both dropped their coffee and gazed at the ring of silent men. At a clear disadvantage, neither considered running.

"Mr. Christopher Knox," Antonio broke the quiet with false confidence ringing in his voice. "I'm surprised you made it here. Getting to Amadica through the roadblocks couldn't have been easy."

Knox grunted once and furiously chewed a little stick poking out from his mouth. He looked at the two coffee men suspiciously.

"I have friends. How do you know me?" he asked.

"How? The entire island knows you and…" Antonio looked around to verify the number of men and nodded, "and your seven companions. The Federals are searching everywhere."

Mentioning the Federals clearly upset Knox's men and they shifted uncomfortably on the steep slope while casting nervous looks through the coffee trees.

"We don't fear the Federals," Knox replied. "They die like other men."

Antonio thought he felt Marco suddenly tense-up. He did not remember hearing about Federals getting killed from his brief conversation at the roadblock near Saint Matthew. If Vasquez's men were killed, Antonio thought quickly, it would explain the intense manhunt all over the island. It also explained the three assault rifles which Antonio knew were far too expensive for any of the men to have purchased.

"You killed Federals at the Jola Reserve too, didn't you?" Marco asked. "It wasn't just loggers. Vasquez doesn't care that much about loggers."

Knox smiled bitterly and looked up and down the slope at his ring of weary men. Marco saw pride flash in Knox's eyes. "How right you are, coffee man. Vasquez doesn't care a lick about us. If I heard you two correctly a few moments ago, he doesn't care much about coffee farmers either."

"Why did you kill those guys from Jola?" Marco asked.

Knox sighed while looking at the ground for a moment and kicking a clod of earth. He privately marveled at the extent of their revenge, especially the morning after when the alcohol finally wore off. He never revealed these thoughts to his men, however. They were all in too deep to turn back now, and Knox felt a certain sense of leadership and responsibility towards his friends. Antonio and Marco saw his hesitation, though, and they realized that on some level Knox carried a heavy burden.

"It's too long a story to tell why," Knox began. "We're hungry. Do you have anything to eat?"

Antonio considered the food that Rene had prepared earlier that morning. He looked to the nearby cloth bundle and thought how ridiculous it would be if eight men consumed a lunch packed for two. Besides, he thought uncomfortably, the Federals might consider him an accomplice if he fed Knox and his men.

"We have very little. Why should we feed you?"

Knox shrugged, clearly understanding Antonio's dilemma. He harbored no ill will towards these coffee men, but he was short on patience after spending the past several days on the run. For a second he considered threatening Antonio with his pistol. He was in no mood for that sort of fix, however, and looked at Antonio and Marco, simply hoping they would agree.

"I'm asking you as a man in need, please," he said softly. "If not me, at least feed my men."

Antonio and Marco looked at each other in surprise. Here stood what the Federals called the most dangerous man on Salavandra, who admitted to killing many people, and he just politely asked for something to eat.

"If we refuse?" asked Marco, daringly.

Knox only shrugged again and held up his palms. Neither Antonio nor Marco could interpret this gesture, and Knox himself had little idea what he would do if the meager lunch was not forthcoming.

Profoundly suspicious of Knox, Antonio looked at the gaunt men standing amongst his trees and took pity on them.

"I will give you our food," he said suddenly and watched as relief flooded across Knox's face. "But I need a favor in return."

Knox hesitated a moment and gave Antonio a hard look. An affirmative murmur from one of the nearby men convinced him to listen. He nodded once, quickly.

"I will listen," Knox said.

Antonio waved his arm across the remaining unpicked coffee patch. The acre plot held well over one hundred trees and innumerable coffee cherries still clung thickly to many branches. The few hours spent picking before Knox appeared barely dented the work ahead.

"I need this picked," he said, loudly enough so his voice carried to all Knox's men. "I'll give you our small lunch now and feed you well, later tonight, if you stay and pick until evening." He paused and looked around at Knox's men, wondering how they might react to such a bargain. Some shuffled their feet while others shifted the heavy automatic rifles on their shoulders. Other men just stared at Knox waiting for him to make the decision. For Antonio and Marco, the moment of silence stretched endlessly.

"Accepted, coffee man," said Knox finally. He smiled and offered his hand first to Antonio and then to Marco. "Come on over, boys," he called out to his seven hungry men. "Have a nibble now, and there'll be lots more when we've earned our keep."

"Lots more," affirmed Antonio, smiling nervously while thinking about how much food his cupboards held. Feeding these men, plus Marco, Rene and himself would certainly strain his supplies. The certificates earned from today's picking, however, could easily replenish the food. He reminded himself to make a trip into Amadica tomorrow.

Knox introduced each man as they came closer. Each politely shook hands with Antonio and Marco, and then stood waiting for everyone else to gather around. Marco retrieved the lunch and began dividing the food under Knox's watchful eyes.

"We're not thieves, Mr. Richards," said Hank Campbell, leaning his old shotgun against a coffee shrub. "We might be on the wrong side of the law, as far as Vasquez and the Federals are concerned, but we're all hard workers."

"The Jola families might think less of you," Marco said under his breath as he finished parceling the lunch. Hank and several others stared at him. Jonathan Warwick stepped threateningly towards Marco until Hank held out his arm.

"What we did, Marco, we're not proud of," said Stephen Sorrell, thinking of his sons. He learned the other day, through a friend, of the painful interrogation Carlos suffered. He now lay recovering at home with Vicente. Weeks would pass before either boy felt normal again. "But you know nothing of our lives over the past year," he continued. "And I'll not have you judge me."

"Enough of this," interjected Antonio. "I want no tension here, Marco." He did not like reprimanding his friend, but seeing Knox's men near desperation, he was keen to avoid even minor confrontations.

"Good, good," said Knox, handing each man a handful of food. "No fighting, any of you. We eat, we work, and then we eat again. That's all I want you to think about."

Stephen and Jonathan nodded obediently to Knox, and Antonio breathed a sigh of relief. Marco acquiesced with a nod while Knox and his men quickly devoured their food. They inhaled it like starving men, and Antonio wondered how long ago they last ate.

"Ok, Mr. Richards," said Knox when he finished swallowing his morsel. "I don't think any of us have ever picked coffee." He looked around at his men as they shook their heads. "Tell us how to do it correctly."

Over the next few minutes Antonio and Marco demonstrated the efficient stripping method, for those limbs covered in ripe coffee, as well as the more time-consuming pinch, twist and pluck method of more selective picking. They both stressed picking only the red ones as the mills refused bags holding too many green coffee cherries.

"If you have too many unripe beans," Marco said, "they can make you toss out the green ones and re-sack on the spot. Or they'll just keep dropping the certificate cash-out value for everyone." His comment received many nods and the men began test-picking. Will Finkle popped a bright red coffee cherry into his mouth and chewed thoughtfully.

"It's really sweet, but somehow mixed with something bitter," he commented. "Sticky too," he said, and spit out the yellowish pulp along with the rock-hard bean. "No wonder coffee tastes so bad," he joked. "The beans are surrounded by all that crap."

Everyone chuckled at Will's comment and Knox quickly distributed the burlap sacks. Antonio directed where each man should start, and in a short time everyone began rustling through the coffee trees steadily picking through the peaking crop. Standing next to Knox, Antonio watched them for a moment and smiled as he considered this twisted stroke of luck.

"Not too bad for you, eh Mr. Richards?" asked Knox as he stripped an entire branch. Dozens of red coffee cherries tumbled into his burlap.

"Call me Antonio, and yes, this is fortunate. I was afraid of losing this coffee. Now I can pay my bills."

"You get a lot from this business?" asked Knox, grasping another branch.

Antonio smiled sadly and shook his head. "If you only knew how little, you'd be amazed." He stepped to Knox's tree and began picking his own branch. "Just before you came I was telling Marco about how we never receive anywhere near what Penkava gets for my beans in the United States."

"Penkava!" growled Knox, "I spit on that company." He moved to another branch and aggressively tackled the ripe coffee. Antonio noticed how he paused before picking and decided that the stripping method was not appropriate. "I hate logging," Knox continued, and threw a few carefully selected coffee cherries into his sack. "I've always hated it. It's too hot, too dangerous and too sporadic. Penkava doesn't spread out the work, either, so the mills run off and on. A man can't live right or support a family when he doesn't know if he'll be working tomorrow. Then the loans come due. They're always coming due, and it's always hard to pay."

Antonio nodded and recognized a common hardship with Knox and his men. Many coffee farmers experiencing a bad year or two fell into the familiar pattern of circular debt that their sons later inherited. He recalled many times sharing food with neighbors who would otherwise go hungry while trying to square their balance sheets with the mill.

"Plus," Knox grumbled, "that Reserve has so many trees, but some rich fuck living in America decided we're not supposed to cut."

Antonio nodded again and pictured the Jola Reserve with its densely forested growth. His single trip there long ago impressed upon him what Salavandra must have looked like many years ago. He vaguely remembered his school lessons about the Reserve and saving the environment, but recalled no mention of loggers.

"While drinking my beans," Antonio said softly, "and paying me nearly nothing for the pleasure." He shook his head and sighed at their unfortunate circumstances.

Knox stopped picking and looked sharply at Antonio. His fingers, unfamiliar with harvesting, already held a touch of discomfort. The hours of work ahead suddenly loomed large and he wondered if he could continue working until evening.

"And while Vasquez and his bullies cozy up with Penkava Incorporated," he said to Antonio.

"It seems we have some things in common, Christopher. You need to see my Link. There's a lot of information about him and Penkava we can dig up."

"Knox, I prefer Knox. Yes, most definitely. I'd very much like access to a Link. I'll take a look after we eat tonight."

The two men continued picking in silence and made good progress as everyone moved steadily through the orchard. As late morning turned into noon, Antonio noticed Marco and Will working together and occasionally racing through the trees to see who could finish faster. Marco usually won, of course, but Will remained determined even after being soundly beaten several times. Many sacks bulged with coffee by the day's end and though pleased with the progress, Antonio could not stop thinking about his brief conversation with Knox. So many seemingly related forces somehow controlled his life, Marco's life, and the lives of these desperate loggers-turned-outlaws.

Six

"We've got some gear so we'll camp a little ways from your home," said Logan, helping himself to another tortilla and scooping more rice and beans onto his plate. He sat on the floor with Knox's other men, devouring massive quantities of food while enjoying the comfort of being indoors. The other men nodded as they chewed, understanding that sleeping on the front porch, a common practice amongst temporary workers, might imperil Antonio and his neighbors.

Antonio thanked the men for picking throughout the day. The loggers proved hardy workers and helped pick over eleven sacks of coffee cherries. The certificates earned from those sacks would more than pay for the food and Antonio actually looked forward to meeting John Doddard in the morning. He harbored deeper plans than simply exchanging the sacks for certificates, however, and anxiously awaited seeing his neighbors and telling them about the prices they ought to receive for their coffee.

"And your decision to stay and pick tomorrow, is everyone still agreed?"

Antonio directed his question to Knox but made it clear that anyone could answer. Shortly after completing the day's work the men unanimously offered to help pick the next day, provided they were fed and paid the going rate. Having no stable source of food and with their money running low, all of them realized they needed to work. Knox replied with a hard nod and kept eating.

"A little spending money would be good tomorrow evening, too, Mr. Richards," said Hank Campbell. "I've got a mighty thirst for a drink, and I'm just about out of my stash."

Daniel and Diego nodded and smiled. After several days on the run both men looked forward to several shots of rum. While at first generously sharing his flask, Hank grew considerably less charitable as the drink ran low.

Rene shuffled over to the men and set down another big plate of steaming food. She smiled at everyone and quickly returned to the stove, unaware that she served eight men hunted by the state. Antonio struggled to tell her about Knox when inviting the men inside, but finally decided to keep his mother in the dark. He convinced himself that there was no point in worrying her about Salavandra's problems. As he expected, Rene insisted on cooking for everyone and stubbornly refused to leave her pots even when Antonio scolded her for working too hard.

"Nobody goes to town, not for anything," said Knox harshly. He cast a quick glance towards Rene and lowered his voice. "You'll have to go without for a while, Hank."

Hank looked hard at Knox but finally agreed. Over the years he managed to control his itch to drink and could usually handle the occasional dry spell. Too long without, however, inevitably found him at a bar staring down the inside of a bottle. Daniel and Diego both looked at each other and shrugged.

Antonio suddenly wondered if Knox's order also applied to him and Marco. He looked at his friend, but Marco seemed absorbed in understanding another of Will's tired jokes. With their guns, Antonio thought with a chill, Knox and his men could order just about anything.

"I still need to show you that Link, Knox," said Antonio.

"When we're finished eating I want to take a look at it. How is it that a coffee farmer ends up with a Link?"

Antonio pointed at his patch. "I guess you could say it was payment for losing an eye. Besides," he continued, "I wanted it to research a fungicide for coffee."

Knox nodded but seemed surprised at Antonio's quick answer. "An eye is an expensive thing to exchange, even for a Link."

"I'd trade it back in a second," agreed Antonio.

Rene produced a final large bowl of rice and the men grew more comfortable as the evening lengthened and they polished off every last morsel. Each man ate to his content, and Antonio was pleased that he could deliver on his promise to feed everyone. A few battered cigarettes appeared after the meal and everyone settled back and talked about the challenges of growing coffee and cutting trees. Much to Antonio's surprise, the Warwick brothers immediately tackled the dishes after thanking Rene for the meal and actually forcing her to sit down in her chair. She beamed at the men sitting around her home and remembered the times when Victor also filled the house with workers.

Knox walked over to Antonio later in the evening as his men filed out the door. "Tomorrow, since we'll be camped near the other field, we'll just wait there for you and Marco." He waved quickly to Stephen and Hank as they followed the others out into the darkness. Marco eased into his blankets spread out on the porch. Antonio's little home suddenly fell into quiet.

"That's fine," Antonio agreed. "But I've got to get certificates from the mill's driver first, and then buy more food in Amadica. Marco will be along early enough, though. Let me get my mother to bed and then we can have a look at that Link, ok?"

Knox paused briefly, weighing Antonio's intentions the next day.

"Just for food supplies, right? You won't be making any other stops in Amadica?"

Antonio looked at Knox and saw a tired and suspicious man but one that wanted to trust. "You and your seven men are saving my harvest this season, Knox," Antonio said seriously. "I'd be a fool to visit anyone else in Amadica."

After tucking in a still-smiling Rene, Antonio joined Knox at the kitchen table and tapped the Link's power button. As it warmed up, Antonio still sensed Knox's suspicions, but knew the hardened logger had little choice if he wanted his men paid and something to eat.

The Link carried the men from site to site where they learned about the extent of logging activities in the Caribbean and the kinds of forest reserves scattered across the region. Some sites displayed logging anecdotes collected from workers like Knox, while others reported on the manufacturing of various hardwoods. Knox studied one site in particular that displayed price lists for various exotic woods and included listings for Salavandra's mahogany and teak.

"I did the same with sites listing international coffee prices," said Antonio. He understood Knox's feelings of somehow being cheated and saw a remarkable similarity to Marco's revelations earlier that day.

"Of course, there are costs of getting my wood and your coffee off Salavandra," said Knox after careful consideration.

Antonio nodded. "But so much?" he asked, unconvinced that mere transportation explained such a tremendous price gap.

"I agree," said Knox, looking away from the screen for the first time in half an hour. "It's not as bad as the coffee discrepancy you mentioned, but the prices are definitely lopsided."

A heavy rumble of a large truck suddenly interrupted the nighttime calm. Both men sprang from their chairs and peered out the window towards the road.

"Marco," whispered Antonio fiercely, "Can you make out what's coming?"

A tense voice drifted up from the porch amidst a shuffling of blankets.

"It's not that fancy truck, Boss. This one's way too loud, and sounds too big."

A massive truck quickly rounded the bend in the road and made Antonio's heart leap. By the light of the nearly full moon he spotted several soldiers riding on the back and two inside the dimly illuminated cab. Every one of them carried an automatic rifle. Before either Knox or Antonio could react, the truck jerked to a stop nearly in front of his home and all the Federals jumped off the back. One quickly approached Antonio's home while the others began knocking on his neighbors' doors.

"Into the bedroom, quick," Antonio ordered Knox. "My mother won't wake up unless I shake her. Stay quiet." He pushed Knox into Rene's room and pointed at the dark gap beneath her bed. Knox took three fast steps and slid beneath the bed as a heavy knock sounded at the door. As he quickly stashed the Link, Antonio heard Marco asking the Federal something, clearly stalling the man and giving Knox time to hide.

Antonio considered revealing Knox. His legality with the Federals would be assured after a few questions, he thought, and Antonio was confident in his ability to spin a convincing story of coercion by the hardened murderer. That thought abruptly reminded him that Knox and his seven men were in fact murderers, something that now seemed unlikely after they spent the day working in the field and eating in his home. Convinced that harboring wanted men invited harsh punishment from the Federals, Antonio almost decided to wash his hands of Knox and his friends.

He paused, however, with only two steps to the door. Marco still talked loudly and now carried a slightly panicked tone. The Federal harshly told Marco to shut up and again pounded the door as Antonio stood paralyzed. His mind flashed to the trees heavily laden with ripe coffee ready to pick. He thought of the certificates earned from the harvest and the food and clothing the cash would purchase over the next year. Rene could see Amadica's doctor, he realized, and possibly relieve some of her arthritis pain. Mary would finally get a ring; one he could be proud of buying. He reached for the door and quickly swung it open.

"You'll wake my mother with your pounding," he said sternly to the Federal. "What do you want?"

The Federal actually took a step back as Antonio stood tall and moved into the doorway. The eye patch, Antonio realized, must seem threatening because he had no recollection of anyone ever reacting to him in such a manner. The soldier quickly recovered, however, and looked once towards Marco who awkwardly stood a few feet away.

"We're searching for a man and his friends," the Federal began. Barely in his twenties, the soldier felt out of place addressing Antonio and Marco with an authoritative voice. In a swift but fumbling motion he produced a Link from his belt pouch and shoved it towards Antonio. "Have you seen this man?"

Knox's gruff and sour image showed clearly on the Link's illuminated screen. It was the same grizzled face shown to him at the roadblock when he left Saint Matthew. Antonio studied the picture carefully. On his blinded side, Marco exhaled heavily.

"That's the same picture you guys showed me in Saint Matthew," Antonio said with an accusatory tone. He swallowed hard to keep his voice from cracking. "How is it that you haven't found him yet? Is it true he's wanted for murder?"

The young Federal nodded and looked apologetically at Antonio and shrugged. "We're doing our best, Sir, but Salavandra's bigger than it seems."

"Well you're not going to find him here, young man," said Antonio gruffly. "Why aren't you guys in Hutch? The Federal in Saint Matthew said that's where he lives."

"We're looking there too, Sir," said the young soldier as he showed the Link to Marco. Marco shook his head and shrugged.

"I'm sorry to bother you gentlemen but we have orders to search everyone's home. I'll be in and out in a second."

Marco picked up on the soldier's discomfort. He immediately saw that Antonio still held some power with the Federal.

"I'd be real quiet if I were you," Marco said under his breath, nearly whispering. The Federal turned to him, clearly wondering what he meant. "His mother's a tough old root," Marco continued. "Wake her up and you'll probably need to call for reinforcements." He grinned at the Federal and quickly returned to his blankets, dismissing the entire incident as a minor inconvenience. What the Federal could not see was Marco's pounding heart and sweating palms as the older man sank back into his bedroll and turned away from the front door.

Antonio realized that Marco knew the most likely place Knox could hide and was trying to steer the Federal away from the bedroom. He sighed loudly and backed into the house, opening the door wide and flooding the porch with his home's weak light. The two Federals in the truck's cab turned to look and watched carefully for any signs of trouble.

"Search away, Sir," Antonio said casually, but held his breath as the Federal stepped into his home.

Like most homes in the hollow, Antonio's had only two rooms. Rene now solely occupied the tiny bedroom she once shared with Victor. Antonio slept in the same corner of the main room that he occupied as a child, which was near the small kitchen. The Federal swept through the main room in a few seconds and seeing nothing out of the ordinary immediately pointed to Rene's bedroom door with his rifle. Antonio held his finger to his lips as he grasped the doorknob and carefully cracked open the door.

"Just my old mother, thankfully sleeping now," he whispered.

The Federal strained to look inside the dark room.

"Stand away from the door, please, Sir. I have to get a better look."

Antonio shushed the Federal, "she's a light sleeper, mister," he whispered again. "My employee on the porch wasn't kidding. If you wake her up, you're on your own."

The Federal nodded and took a careful step to the bedroom door and peered inside. Rene's relaxed and wrinkled face shone clearly in the light from the adjacent room and her chest rose and fell smoothly as she slept. The soldier leaned into the bedroom and quickly looked around. He backed up suddenly and began to lean down near the floor to have a look beneath Rene's bed. Antonio futilely tried controlling his pounding heart and hoped that Knox buried himself into the furthest and darkest corner next to the wall.

Rene shifted and let out a small noise. The Federal abruptly jumped up and fearfully looked towards Antonio and then back to the bed. His mother's long gray hair now spilled over the pillow and her breathing looked faster and less regular. A small scowl furrowed her brow.

"It's the light," Antonio managed to choke out quickly. "It disturbs her sleep."

The young man nodded and motioned Antonio to quickly shut the door. As it closed, Antonio heard him breathe deeply.

"That was close," Antonio said, noticing the Federal's tight grip on his rifle. "Another couple seconds…" Antonio shook his head and shrugged.

"No need to disturb an old woman's sleep," the Federal said amicably. His grip relaxed and he moved away from the door lest his voice carry into the room. A few muffled shouts from outside signaled the return of several Federals to the truck. Antonio looked outside and saw three soldiers lounging next to the cab, sharing a cigarette.

"One last thing, Sir," said the young man in front of him. "I need a quick snapshot. For our records, you know."

"You want my picture?" Antonio asked suspiciously. "What kind of record needs my picture?"

"Don't know, Sir. Sorry about this but that's the order. It'll only take a second."

Antonio sighed and shrugged. He wanted to object again but knew the more important issue was to have this soldier leave as quickly as possible. "Where should I stand?" he asked, clearly annoyed.

"Thank you, Sir," the young man said, relieved that Antonio submitted to being photographed without being forced. "Anywhere is fine." He pulled the Link from his belt and tapped lightly on the screen several times with the stylus.

"Ok, ready?" he asked, and held up the Link so the screen faced Antonio.

"You take pictures with that thing?" Antonio asked.

The soldier looked confused for a moment but then realized Antonio meant the Link in his hands. "How else?"

"No camera?"

The soldier shook his head and smiled as he remembered the old-style cameras. "This little thing does everything," he said, smiling. He lowered the Link and showed Antonio a tiny circle of dark glass near the top of the unit. Antonio recognized it immediately. "That's how it takes pictures," the soldier explained. "You just tap the screen like this," he showed Antonio the simple command layers in the Link's software, "face the screen toward the person, and then push this green button."

Antonio shook his head in wonder. "Amazing," he replied honestly. "And the picture just pops up on the screen?"

The Federal smiled again and nodded. He reset the picture command and again held up the Link. A quick flash later and Antonio's image suddenly appeared on the Link's screen. The Federal recorded Antonio's name just beneath his picture by tapping out the letters with the stylus.

"And on it goes to the central database," he said, tapping the screen one last time. The picture disappeared and was replaced with a database confirmation code. Antonio leaned in for a closer look. The Federal nonchalantly accommodated his curiosity and showed him the long row of letters and numbers.

"So my picture is not inside your Link anymore?" he asked.

The Federal shook his head. "Just its locator number. I can retrieve the picture from a database if I need to, but this way the unit doesn't get overloaded with information. Also, your picture is now accessible to anyone with a Link and permission to access the database."

Antonio's wide eyes did little to hide his amazement. He actually forgot about Knox for a moment while considering this newly discovered dimension of the Link. "And I thought those Links were just for looking at information. I had no idea they also took pictures."

A loud horn suddenly blared twice and an officer outside gruffly ordered all the soldiers back to the truck. Sliding the Link into his belt, the Federal shrugged once and nodded while adjusting his rifle strap. "Sorry to bother you tonight, Sir. Like I said, it just took a second."

Antonio waved him through the door with a casual smile and wished him a good evening. He stood and watched as all the soldiers piled back onto the truck. The driver maneuvered a tight three-point turn, and in under a minute all that remained of the dangerous encounter was an occasional hint of cigarette smoke dissipating in the cool air. Marco stood up and shook his head as he watched the truck's bright red taillights disappear into the darkness.

"Too close, Boss," he said in a low voice. Antonio nodded as he waved to a neighbor now closing her door.

"My heart was pounding," Antonio replied honestly. "That was fast thinking about my mother, Marco. I had no idea you could spin a lie so quickly."

Marco chuckled a little but it was a tense laugh of relief. "I can hold my own under pressure," he said with a sigh and stretched his aching arms. "But I impressed even myself tonight."

"You both impressed me, gentlemen," said Knox's voice from the kitchen window. The hardened logger kept out of sight, but his voice carried out onto the porch. Antonio and Marco went inside and shut the door as Knox approached them and shook each man's hand.

"I owe you both. Thank you."

"Hell, Knox," replied Antonio heartily, "you and your men can't pick my coffee if you're in jail."

The three of them laughed quietly over their luck as they recounted the Federal's movements and questions. Knox heard everything through the thin walls and even described the young soldier's face from the glimpse he caught just before Rene shifted in her sleep. Antonio found a bottle of rum and they all took a celebratory swig.

"I'll tell my men what happened," said Knox, grimacing at the rum's harsh aftertaste. "They need to thank you. You protected them tonight, too." He then wished them goodnight and disappeared into the forest.

Early the next morning as fog tendrils drifted through the trees and pooled deeply in the hollow amongst the homes, Antonio set out along the road to his stash of eleven coffee sacks. John Doddard's pick-up route reached Mt. Tabor's northwestern area first, and Antonio had to arrive before the flatbed. He paused momentarily in front of Mary's home, remembering her as a child wishing him a good day's picking. He sadly realized that they failed to see each other last night. Worried and mulling over her strange behavior the previous evening, he gathered up his coat against the chilly morning air and stomped his way steadily down the road. Some time later he stood next to the bulging coffee sacks listening to the familiar sound of John's truck straining up the mountain.

"I heard about your accident, Antonio," said John as he stepped out of the cab after Antonio waved him down. He walked over to the side of the road and his eyes widened. "What's that? Ten, no eleven! Looks like you've made up for lost time." He turned to Antonio, forgetting about the coffee for the moment. "How's the eye?"

"Useless," replied Antonio, adjusting the string holding the patch in place. He realized it was getting easier to live with only one eye. The headaches plaguing him over the past several days had weakened and this morning his head was blissfully pain-free. "It's completely blind, but I'm getting used to it."

"I also heard about the other accident on the Celeste. You couldn't get me to work on that boat for anything." He bent down and helped Antonio heft a sack of coffee up onto the flatbed.

Antonio's mind's eye flashed to Saint Matthew's mill. He remembered the poor cash payout from the certificates and the Celeste's rusted hulk towering over the docks. Forty dollars would have bought Mary a fine ring, he considered sadly.

"I needed the money," he grunted, lifting another sack and nudging it into place.

"Don't we all," agreed John. "This year's light harvest means I don't get any raise. Everybody suffers."

They piled another sack onto the truck. "Everybody but Penkava and Vasquez," said Antonio.

"What do you mean?" asked John curiously. He heard Antonio's tone shift and become more aggressive than the every-day grumbling about prices that he heard so frequently.

"Let's just load. When we get to José's stop, I'll tell you both at the same time."

"You're riding today again? Good. Not going to Saint Matthew though, are you?"

"Just Amadica's mill today. Hopefully with a few others."

With the eleventh sack tucked securely onto the truck, John and Antonio made their way slowly up the mountain. The switchbacks and rutted road made the drive challenging, but John's practiced hands found the most stable ground as the truck gradually climbed up into Mt Tabor's coffee region. Thousands upon thousands of coffee trees, many already picked clean, stood interspersed within the natural forest vegetation. Songbirds roosted in the higher trees and took to flight as the truck rounded the sharp corners and roared up the steeper road sections. Ahead, a thin man wearing a red bandana around his neck waved them to a stop.

José Vazzana's fields were as old and profitable as Antonio's. Both his and Antonio's family had farmed coffee since the British left the island over one hundred years ago. Like all the other farmers, his fields lay scattered amongst other properties and it was only through common knowledge that everyone knew who owned what parcels. José also lived a few doors up from Antonio in the hollow, and the two often talked about growing conditions and the state of the harvest.

John drew the truck up close and parked it next to José's three sacks. "That's quite a pile, Antonio," said José, acknowledging John with a friendly nod. Antonio smiled and got out of the truck to help load. José also heard about the accidents on the Celeste and pressed Antonio for a few of the more dramatic details. Antonio obliged, but did not look forward to repeating himself at each stop along John's route. When John ripped off three certificates, José roughly folded them into his shirt pocket with a sour grunt.

"Slim payouts this year, José," said Antonio, nodding at the certificates now making a mangled stack inside his breast pocket. José shook his head and spat on the ground.

"Cashed out a pile about a week ago," he replied, "and got about sixty percent of last year's pay out."

"Same here," Antonio grumbled. "Are you having any problems with your trees?"

José nodded and pointed up a nearby slope to an orchard with a lot of sun exposure. "A patch up there looks like it's dying off. No mold, just pathetic little coffee cherries and hardly any yield."

Antonio told him about his own tree problems and José appeared hopeful when Antonio explained that a specialist was currently diagnosing the problem.

"What about coming with me to Amadica this morning?" Antonio asked when John made it clear that he had to continue on his route. "I found out a few days ago that the mill can pay us a lot more for our coffee, and if we go together, they just might listen to us."

Both John and José paused and looked confused for a moment. Antonio quickly told them about the information he found on the Link, and how much price difference existed between the cash they received for certificates and the amount that their coffee sold for in New York City.

"The price difference is way too big, even when roughly figuring Penkava's expenses, such as John's salary, coffee processing, and transportation to America. We're scratching by on almost nothing while Penkava's stock keeps climbing. It's not fair."

"Are you supposed to know this?" asked José. He remembered the Federals coming by last night and wanted no trouble. "This kind of information seems like it belongs under wraps."

Antonio shrugged. "I didn't break any laws finding out," he replied. "It's all public information accessible by my Link."

"Since when do you have a Link?" John asked, amazed that Antonio could afford such a thing. José nodded and looked suspicious.

"Just ride with me and I'll explain everything before we get to Amadica. I'm going to try to convince a few others to come along, too."

José looked up and down his nearby fields and roughly estimated the harvesting time lost while in Amadica. Most of his fields were already picked over at least once. The few remaining trees could wait a half day, he argued to himself. He also knew that if he received more cash for his certificates as a result of the trip, the time would be well spent.

Having quickly convinced himself, he clambered into the cab between Antonio and John as Antonio began explaining the details of his discoveries on the Link. By the time Leonard Sherman waved them down, both John and José were fully convinced and excited to get to Amadica.

Leonard Sherman's grumpy attitude was infamous. Ironically, of all the nearby farmers, Leonard had the least to be sour about. He held the most land and always harvested the largest number of sacks in any year. He rarely conversed with his neighbors, however, and led a solitary life in a modest home at the edge of the hollow where Antonio and José also lived. Antonio remembered going to school with him many years ago, and wondered how such a happy and popular kid grew into such an irritable recluse.

"I don't know about Leonard," said José as the truck pulled to a stop. "I don't think he likes me much."

"You, me or anyone," said John, remembering the many brusque mornings exchanging certificates for Leonard's coffee. The man walked under a perpetual cloud, John thought, and he wondered how anyone could live such an ill-tempered life.

"He's not so bad," replied Antonio. "Felix likes him and he usually listens to me."

Leonard acknowledged the three men with a nod and hefted one of his ten sacks up onto the truck. Besides being Salavandra's most irritable farmer, Leonard also carried the reputation of being the strongest. Most men could heft a full sack and even carry it some distance. They usually shared the work, however, because each sack weighed well over one hundred pounds. Leonard never really acknowledged this tradition. He always tackled full sacks by himself, and his sheer stature and great swinging arms kept others at a distance while he worked. He tossed another sack up onto the flatbed while Antonio and José struggled with one of their own.

"You handle those burlaps like puppies," said José after helping Antonio position a bulging bag.

"Got to load 'em," replied Leonard with a little grunt.

John switched with Antonio and helped José load another sack. Antonio rested by the truck's side and considered the best way to approach Leonard. He had to talk fast because the coffee cherries were half loaded already.

"Hey Leonard," began Antonio, "I think the mill can pay us more for our certificates. We're all going into Amadica to find out."

Leonard paused in mid stride with a nearly bursting sack gripped tightly in his massive, gnarled hands. José and John continued loading.

"How much more?"

"At least fifty percent and maybe even one hundred percent or more, if the numbers I've seen from America are correct."

Leonard threw the sack up onto the truck and looked steadily at the three men with his hands on his hips. He towered over everyone and his chest rose and fell from the effort of loading. Antonio had the impression of standing next to a powerful beast.

"How do you know the American numbers?"

Antonio explained how he came to acquire a Link and what he found while surfing from site to site. He pointed to his eye patch for effect, but did not embellish the story the way he did with José and John while riding in the truck. The truck's load continued growing as he explained. Antonio finished recounting the details as Leonard situated the last burlap.

"We thought that several of us should show up at the mill," said José as John ripped ten certificates from his pack. "That way the mill might be more likely to listen."

Leonard nodded as he accepted the certificates. "I'll ride on the back," he said immediately. Without pausing he stepped up onto the flatbed and reclined across the load.

"Well that was easier than I imagined," said John as the truck pulled forward. He looked back at Leonard sprawled out across the coffee and shook his head. "I always forget how huge that guy is. Seeing him toss those bags around really drives it home."

Antonio and José agreed with a little chuckle. Antonio thought how fortunate they were to have Leonard accompanying them to the mill. Though prepared to argue with the cashier, he realized that having a man of Leonard's stature standing next to him would heavily favor him receiving the attention that he wanted.

"How many stops, John?" asked Antonio, wondering how many more people they might pick up along the route.

"Could be as many as seventeen," replied John with a shrug. "But lots of people are nearly done picking the first round, especially on the little farms. I expect we'll see around ten more."

As John's route continued winding across Mt. Tabor, eight additional farmers waved down the truck and loaded their coffee cherries. Most loaded only two sacks, with the help of José or Leonard. John prepared certificates while Antonio explained the presence of so many people. While expressing a desire to join them at the mill, most farmers shook their heads and pointed to nearby fields where red coffee cherries showed clearly through the waxy green foliage. Antonio expected as much and assured everyone that he would spread the news and let them all know about the mill's responsiveness. By the time the sun burned off the morning's fog, John was headed downhill with only one stop remaining on the route.

Craig Palmer and Felix Ramirez stood next to each other as the truck slowed to a stop. Their farms occupied opposite sides of the road and they often found themselves waiting together for the coffee pick-up. They were old friends, had small and about equal amounts of land, and were destined to become relatives when Craig's son Eric married Felix's daughter Rosemary. Both men were in their usual good-spirits as everyone poured out from the cab and Leonard jumped off the truck's large load.

"What's this," asked Craig smiling, "some kind of party? Why weren't we invited?"

Leonard suddenly and awkwardly stooped near Craig and grasped a sack from the ground. Craig backed up a few steps, but stopped when he saw Felix smiling at him.

"He won't bite you, Craig," Felix joked as Leonard grunted and gently tossed the sack to the top of the truck's load. "You already ate breakfast, right Leonard?"

Leonard acknowledged Felix, about half his stature, with a nod and a small but genuine grin. Felix was one of the few people actually comfortable poking fun at Leonard for being such a cantankerous giant, and Leonard never seemed to mind.

"Seriously though," said Felix, bending down to help José load a sack. "Why so crowded this morning?"

"We're all going to the mill to get a fair exchange for these certificates," replied Antonio. "Can you two come along?"

A few minutes later Antonio sat next to Craig and Felix on the back of the truck as it coasted down the dirt road towards Amadica. Having picked over most of their trees, the two friends readily agreed to go to the mill and chattered excitedly as John's truck lurched through the potholes and ruts peppering the road. Antonio found himself filling in details about his research on the Link and answering questions about his eye. When they finally passed Amadica's first few dingy homes, Craig and Felix knew all about the coffee prices listed on the New York Board of Trade and how Penkava Incorporated artificially deflated prices on Salavandra by being the sole coffee bean buyer.

"There's a personal reason I'm mad at Penkava, too," said Antonio as the hulking steel mill appeared in front of them. Craig and Felix looked at him, waiting for an explanation.

"I believe the Company is responsible for my father's death."

John suddenly braked hard. Felix nearly rolled off the truck as he lost his balance. Another flatbed, this one loaded with Federals and painted dark green suddenly roared by just inches from John's bumper. The truck's horn blared loudly and the driver shouted an obscenity about stinking farmers as the soldiers passed in a choking dust cloud. Craig started to flip them off, but Antonio quickly grabbed his arm.

"We don't want any extra trouble this morning, Craig," said Antonio, knowing the Federals could easily stop and harass them for even minor infractions.

"I hate those guys," said Craig loudly, and sneezed as the dust settled. John yelled out of the cab to make sure everyone was still on board, and then carefully eased into the intersection.

"Who doesn't?" asked Antonio, "but we've got certificates to deal with right now."

"You can tackle them later, Craig," said Felix sarcastically as he repositioned himself securely on the sacks. "They'll never know what hit 'em, you coming on all tough and threatening with your fists flying. They'd drop their guns in a second and run back down the mountain to Vasquez, I'll bet."

"Funny, very funny. And I'm sure you'd be right there to help me out."

Felix nodded seriously. "I'd be right behind you, buddy."

John finally pulled into the mill behind two similarly loaded trucks. Drivers from other routes, thought Antonio, and anxiously looked for additional farmers amongst the myriad of people bustling about the mill's floor and along the catwalks suspended high above. The few farmers he saw either sat on their loads or lounged next to the truck that brought them down the mountain. All of them waited for the coffee to be off-loaded and exchanged for certificates. Looking at his own cluster of friends, Antonio's heart started pounding as he realized that his plan amounted to little more than making a raucous demand for more money. Suddenly he wondered if the morning might have been better spent picking coffee cherries instead of disrupting the status quo.

"I'll tell you what," said José, watching an old farmer carry his certificates to the cashier's office. The aged man walked slowly with a slight limp. "If what you say is true, Antonio, there's going to be some problems around here soon."

Craig and Felix agreed while Leonard calmly watched the floor.

"It's true," replied Antonio. "Unless the entire Link network is designed to deceive me, what I discovered is true."

As their turn for off-loading arrived, Antonio suggested they all approach the cashier's office at once and present a unified voice. Everyone agreed while John excused himself from their plan. "It's not that I don't want you guys getting more money," he explained. "But I'm just a driver. Hell, I don't even know one coffee grade from another."

The weigh clerk looked mildly surprised that five farmers rode in on a single pick-up route, but he made no noise about it and politely handed each man his respective certificates. Antonio tried calculating how much food and supplies eleven certificates earned at the going rate and realized that he might be able to put away another dollar or two for Mary's ring. Stashing away little crumbs of money made him feel pathetic, but it was the only way he could afford anything as luxurious as an engagement ring. He felt a gentle nudge on his left arm and turned to see José looking at him expectantly.

"You brought us down here, Antonio. You lead us to the cashier's office."

Antonio shook off his daze and swallowed hard. He looked to each of his neighbors and saw trust on their faces. They looked to him with hope and a willingness to follow. Even mighty Leonard, who normally followed his own lead, waited patiently for him to take the first step. Antonio suddenly recalled many years ago standing naked in front of his neighbors while caked in Salvandra's mud. People looked expectant then, too. He took his first step towards the cashier's office.

"That's not enough for my work," Antonio said politely as the cashier slipped a small pile of bills across the counter and filed his eleven certificates. The man looked up in surprise and Antonio felt his friends step in close behind him. He heard their anxious breathing and a thick tension immediately charged the small office. The cashier looked nervously from man to man with a confused look on his face.

"I would like to request a more equitable payment," Antonio explained, strategically seizing the silence enveloping the office. "Something more in line with the prices paid in New York City."

"We all request the same thing," said Leonard in his lowest and most heavy voice. Antonio imagined the glass panes in the office rattling as Leonard spoke, and silently cheered his huge friend. The others chimed in behind him and affirmed Leonard's comment. The cashier's eyes widened and a worried look spread across his face.

"I don't know what to tell you," shrugged the clerk uneasily. "I only do the exchanging. The people upstairs set the price." He pointed through the windows to the catwalks and well-lit managerial offices lining three sides of the mill.

"Well tell them it's time to begin paying us properly," said Antonio firmly. He surprised himself with his steady voice and tapped firmly on the counter with a finger. Inside him a newly discovered sense of power suddenly bloomed. With the support of his four friends, Antonio suddenly felt that anything was possible.

The cashier's office door opened and two more coffee farmers strolled in with certificates ready to exchange. Antonio looked at them quickly and turned back to the man behind the counter. "I'm sure these men would also like to be fairly paid for their work, too."

The strangers, older men with tanned faces and wiry bodies, stopped in mid-stride and looked intently towards the counter. One let the door swing shut with a bang. The other nodded thoughtfully as he sensed the delicately balanced conflict within the tiny room.

"Let me call upstairs," said the clerk, quickly tapping a computer screen containing a list of names. A man's face appeared on the screen and looked expectantly at the cashier.

"These men want more money, Sir," said the cashier nervously. "They're saying something about prices in New York City."

"New York?" asked the well-dressed manager. "What are you talking about?" The cashier shrugged and turned the screen to face the farmers. Antonio repeated his request and this time quoted the huge price imbalance between the certificate payouts and coffee figures listed in New York.

"How in the world do you know that?" asked the manager, making no attempt to conceal his surprise. He momentarily looked away and shrugged at someone not visible on the screen.

"It doesn't matter how I know," replied Antonio, "just that I do know. Now what are you prepared to offer us for our work?"

A muffled voice interrupted the manager and he again looked away from Antonio. A few brusque words exchanged, and the screen's view abruptly slid to another part of the manager's office. Antonio suddenly found himself staring at Phillip Penkava.

"Mr. Richards," said Phillip smoothly and smiled an oily grin. If Phillip was surprised by Antonio's presence it did not show. "It's so nice to see you again. How's the eye?"

Antonio straightened and forced his breath to calm as he tried to slow the sudden leap in his heartbeat. "No problems," he replied, trying to sound composed but imagining that Phillip sensed his tense nerves. The men crowded even closer behind him and strengthened Antonio's resolve. He pushed forward with his demand. "We're requesting a more equitable payment for our coffee, Phillip. Something more appropriate, compared to the prices paid in America."

Phillip raised his eyebrows in surprise and then leaned back in his chair. His image on the screen, now considerably smaller, seemed less threatening. After a lengthy pause and a loud sigh he clasped his hands behind his head and looked at the ceiling.

"Look, Antonio," Phillip began in his most placating tone while continuing to stare at the ceiling. He suddenly leaned forward so his entire head occupied the screen. Antonio heard someone behind him take a step back. "It's nice to know you're able to figure out how to navigate on my old Link, but there is no way you can just walk in here and demand more money. Larger market forces are at play."

"I know all about your larger market forces," replied Antonio, slightly louder this time as he sensed Phillip's condescending tone. "I know about your company's stock and its quarterly earnings. It's not just coffee, Phillip. I also know about the lumber. It's time Penkava Incorporated began paying us better."

Phillip rolled his eyes and thought about his father sitting comfortably in New York. The Board too, Phillip deliberated, would find this Antonio character quite amusing. Control the potential damage, they would advise him. He peered behind Antonio at the cluster of coarse farmers gathered in the cashier's office. Patience might serve well here, he thought quickly, but then cast aside the notion as he considered its substantial effort.

"Hold on a minute, Antonio," he said quickly. The screen suddenly went blank. Not a sound broke the silence in the small room. Even the cashier stood frozen as he gazed from man to man wondering how Mr. Penkava might resolve this issue. Antonio listened but could not even hear his men breathing. The oppressive office, Amadica and even Salavandra seemed locked in time. A minute crawled by, then another and soon Antonio wondered if Phillip intended to respond at all. After ten minutes the loud grumble of a truck suddenly echoed in the mill and brakes squealed in protest as a flatbed slowed to a stop. Heavy footsteps pounded across the cement floor and suddenly the cashier's office door flew open.

"I think it might be best if everyone accepted the going rate, gentlemen," said Phillip, his face suddenly flashing back onto the screen.

Heads turned quickly back and forth between Phillip's image and the soldiers. Federals now crowded the doorway gripping their rifles. Leonard and Felix moved slightly, suddenly, and Antonio immediately yelled for everyone to clam down.

"Just wait," he continued loudly, taking a deep breath. He looked at the closest soldier, keeping his distance so that his rifle had clear range of the room. "None of us want any trouble, Sir."

The Federal looked at him but did not reply. With a free hand he pressed a headset closer to his ear and listened intently while never taking his eyes off Antonio. Two other Federals behind him stood like statues and grimly stared down the scruffy farmers.

"Cashier," the soldier with the headset suddenly yelled. The clerk jumped to attention. "Cash everyone out, now."

"Goodbye Antonio," said Phillip. He dismissed the entire scene with a quick wave of his hand and the screen went blank.

With a shaking hand the cashier motioned for José to hand over his certificates. José looked to Antonio, who gritted his teeth and nodded. Several crumpled certificates appeared on the counter and the clerk immediately gathered them up and pushed back a small stack of bills. Other men quickly followed suit. Antonio felt a sense of frustration settling over the room. Craig strained especially hard to keep his anger bottled. The Federals backed out of the doorway and watched as each man silently exited the office.

Cloistered behind thick blinds in an office high above the mill floor Phillip gazed out at the dissipating men and smiled. He remembered Antonio lying in Saint Matthew's stinking clinic with a bandaged head. Perhaps, he thought, giving him the Link was not the best solution to the Celeste incident. Who would guess that a mere coffee farmer could grasp the Company's quarterly earning statements? Phillip sourly admitted that Antonio surprised him.

A side door opened to another office deeper inside the mill and interrupted his musings. He turned to see Mary glide into the room holding two steaming mugs filled with black coffee.

"What are you looking at down there?" she asked curiously and set the mugs on the table. She strolled over to Phillip and leaned into his embrace.

"Nothing interesting," he replied and nonchalantly moved away from the window. Antonio had just looked up at the offices, searching the windows for Phillip's location. "It was just some annoying little business thing."

"The coffee is freshly roasted," Mary said cheerfully, "just how you like it." She looked up into Phillip's eyes and saw his promise to carry her away from Salavandra's gritty reality of farmers and greenhouses. He promised again this morning when he insisted that she leave the greenhouses and spend the day with him. He walked to the table and picked up a mug.

"Cheers," he said lightly, and smiled as he thought about having a delicious quick morning romp.

Seven

From his narrow porch Antonio looked out across the hollow at dozens of farmers. They waited in the flickering orange light of several hastily made torches, silently staring at him hoping for some expressions of guidance. Short and tall, wearing the various trappings of a working man's life, torn and patched clothing, an occasional machete, every one of them thin, hardened and seeking leadership. Neighbors and friends appeared in the gathering crowd while children chased one another through the darkness. A festive atmosphere for them, thought Antonio, planted absurdly within a looming crisis for the older generation.

Marco stood on his right side while Mary helped Rene out of the house and to her chair on the porch where she could see the people. After the morning's failure at the mill, Antonio had returned to the fields to recount his tale and continue picking. He picked with despair though, and was filled with an emptiness that even Will's lame jokes failed to penetrate. The ten sacks now waiting for John's pickup felt like leaden weights, dragging his spirit down into Salavandra's hungry soil. Victor's words of escape echoed in Antonio's mind.

"What was that?" asked Mary, now standing on his left side. Rene sat behind them but with a good view out across the crowd. She looked at the people with quiet understanding.

"You said something about leaving?" continued Mary.

Antonio shook free any thoughts of his father and looked into Mary's eyes. Dark hair played against the dancing torch light and made her appear mysterious and seductive. A lustful thought bloomed in his mind but he stamped it down and forced himself to consider her question.

"It was nothing," he replied, embarrassed that he murmured anything at all and wondering how much she actually heard. "Something my father said to me a long time ago."

"I can't believe word spread so quickly," said Marco from his side as he gestured out across the hopeful faces. Antonio spotted Craig and Felix standing near a cluster of men from Mt. Tabor's southern coffee area. Leonard stood by himself at the edge of the torch's illumination and quietly observed the crowd.

Antonio nodded and remembered the anger he and others felt as they left the mill. Craig in particular seemed more worked up than the others and spent a considerable time ranting against the Federals and proclaiming new rules for Salavandra if he were in charge. José chimed in and actually suggested tonight's meeting so that the certificate problem could be discussed with as many farmers as possible. Both looked to Antonio as their natural leader, and after some consideration he agreed. Now, as he gazed over the crowd, Antonio soberly realized the large number of farmers whose lives he might influence.

"What are you going to say?" whispered Mary. She barely seemed to breathe next to him.

"The truth," replied Antonio. "How Vasquez and Penkava get rich off our sweat." Antonio remembered Knox, now camped far from the hollow with all his men, saying the same thing as he helped pick the second northwest field. "That, and how the Federals are nothing but a bunch of well-armed thugs."

"But you'll get them all riled up," Mary protested. "Don't you think we'll all get in trouble?"

Antonio turned to see her eyes. The shadows flickering across her face created a strange vagueness and he momentarily saw her as a stranger. He shifted against the feeble light and the illusion disappeared. "Perhaps that's the point," he replied. "Perhaps a little trouble is the only way things are going to change."

A few more farmers strolled into the ring of light and were greeted by their neighbors. If this crowd showed up at the mill, Antonio thought, an entire truckload of Federals would have a difficult time forcing a cash-out at gun point.

"Think about it, Mary," continued Antonio. "My father's lifetime of work, his death, your discomfort from the greenhouses and my missing eye are all are related. That we work so long and earn so little, too.

These kids running around," he pointed at two children as they scampered past the porch, "they've got this to look forward to." He held out his calloused hands, "and of course, endless debt."

Mary already looked beyond these things however, and pinned her hopes on Phillip's promise to take her away from Salavandra to a place where men never had calloused hands and never smelled of sweat and dirt. She remembered his baby-soft fingers running across her abdomen, his peppermint breath and fragrant hair as he rocked into her that morning. She nervously felt the wad of cash pressed against her thigh that he gave to her this afternoon.

"Just be careful what you say," she pleaded. "The Federals are all over the place."

"We don't have to worry about them surprising us tonight," said José as he materialized out of the crowd and stepped up onto the porch. "I set lookouts and quick runners. We'll know at the first sound of an engine or the sight of headlights coming up from Amadica."

"Nice work," said Antonio, pleased that José so readily followed his suggestion for lookouts. It felt like an order when he asked that some kind of watch be placed along the road. However José understood the charge, he did not hesitate. Antonio momentarily felt that he was slipping into something larger than he was prepared to handle.

"You better say something to them, Antonio," said José, and stood next to Marco looking over the crowd. Antonio nodded and took a single step forward. These people needed leadership, Antonio reminded himself. They lived a hard life, and right now had hope that some form of relief might be coming. He cleared his throat and spread his arms as if embracing all his neighbors.

"Good evening, everyone," he said firmly. He heard his own voice sounding confident and strong and listened appreciatively as the crowd greeted him warmly. "I assume most of you know why we've gathered here tonight, but in case you don't, I'll give you a quick account of our experience at the mill today."

Dozens of men and women listened intently to the story and several interrupted to shout profanities about Federals and certificates. Marco and José appealed for calm whenever too many voices sounded together and drowned Antonio's words.

"The question is," said Antonio finally, "what are we going to do about this?"

The crowd grew silent and several men shrugged hopelessly.

Finally one man shouted out so everyone could hear him. "Can't do a damn thing," he began sourly. "They've got all the guns."

Several men agreed loudly while more nodded their heads. Antonio remembered Knox and his handgun, Hank holding his old pump-action shotgun, as well as the other Hutch loggers carrying the Federal's assault rifles. None of those were available, he reminded himself, having deliberately kept Knox and the others out of sight for fear of stirring up even more confusion. The Federals did not have *all* the guns, but certainly more than this crowd.

"I do not accept that we are completely helpless, even if they do have all the guns," replied Antonio as the crowd's noise died down. He noticed Leonard leave his place at the edge of the light and move deeper into the crowd.

"If enough of us put pressure on the mill, Penkava will have to pay us more," continued Antonio. "Besides, with my Link I can upload information to the satellites and let everyone know what's happening here." He recalled learning the steps just an hour ago when he finally discovered how to place a few lines of text on a message bulletin board and communicate with people anywhere on the planet. Ironically, the bulletin board on which he posted his first message was Penkava Incorporated's own stock page.

"They haven't cared before," replied another voice from the crowd. "What makes you think they'll care now?"

Antonio was surprised that nobody questioned the fact that he had a Link. Perhaps that story spread too, he thought quickly, and considered the man's question.

"Nobody's ever told the world about Salavandra," he replied hopefully. "If we pressure the mill and let the Yankees know what we're doing down here, Penkava might be embarrassed into responding."

"How do we pressure the mill?"

"What about the Federals?"

"What if the mill doesn't pay us anything for the certificates?"

Antonio volleyed question after question, but more came with each response until he felt overwhelmed and struggled to maintain his own optimism. Responsibility weighed upon him heavily. Finally he noticed Leonard, who had gradually moved through the crowd until he stood in front of Antonio's steps. Suddenly the giant man turned and raised his hands high above his head and let out a huge bellow. Silence rippled through the crowd and children clung tightly to their parents' legs.

"Enough," shouted Leonard impatiently. He looked over the crowd and somehow managed to make each person feel personally responsible for angering him. "I know many of you find me a bit cranky. I've even heard that some of you think that I don't like people, especially my neighbors."

Antonio watched the crowd's silent astonishment and wondered what finally drew Leonard out of his shell. His massive neighbor seemed charged tonight, and Antonio tried to recall a similar time when Leonard spoke so many words to anyone.

"I worry," continued Leonard, more quietly and with a hint of sadness. "I worry, perhaps too much, about the coffee, the land, and especially making sure everyone I hire to pick coffee gets paid well."

The crowd murmured appreciatively. Leonard's picking-wages remained high even when certificate cash-outs grew light. Many smaller farmers picked Leonard's crops after harvesting their own, in order to make a few extra dollars. What they all failed to calculate was the loss Leonard took on much of his crop in order to maintain the high payments.

"I am behind Antonio all the way," shouted Leonard, nearly as loud as when he commanded the crowd to be silent. Antonio felt the blood rush to his face. He bit back an urge to cry out, and stood tall while proudly looking over the multitude of anxious faces.

"We cannot keep living like this," continued Leonard. He pointed at a man and asked how long his mother had been ill. At another he asked how long his child managed to stay in school before being called to work the fields. He asked a last man, his closest neighbor and now showing signs of age, how many months had passed since he visited Amadica's doctor for his stomach pain.

"All this crap," Leonard yelled with growing fury, "can be alleviated. Doctors, school, food and medicine all cost money. We all produce something that Penkava and the Yankees want. I say, let them pay for it."

Felix shouted out to Leonard and began clapping. Craig joined him and soon the entire crowd was shouting loudly and calling for Antonio to say something. Mary lit another torch and its light played with the firelight flickering across people's faces. Antonio suddenly felt tired, but he looked over the crowd appreciatively as José gently nudged him.

"Tell them about our plan for tomorrow," he suggested. "I think they're ready now."

Antonio loudly thanked Leonard who remained standing next to the porch. "Tomorrow," he began, "we'll return to Amadica's mill and demand more for our coffee. Today we were turned away by a truckload of Federals. Tomorrow, when all of us show up, we won't be so easily turned away. We'll refuse to exchange our beans until we're assured the cash-out is raised. So we're not alone, tonight I'll upload our efforts onto the Link's network. Let February eleventh be remembered as they day that Salavandra's coffee farmers finally demanded fair prices."

Antonio initially hesitated to include the last embellished sentence but could hardly help himself as he looked over the mass of hardened farmers. Each now seemed as charged as Leonard, and through the clapping and cheering now echoing in his head, Antonio felt confident that he was moving in the right direction. He raised a fist above his head and people cheered and chanted his name. He turned to his mother, who smiled at him and nodded. He turned to José, who concentrated on the crowd and cheered them on to ever more enthusiasm. He finally looked to Mary, but she was missing.

Mary slid off the porch as Antonio finished telling people about tomorrow's plan. She had to warn Phillip, she thought desperately, or else tomorrow would catch him unprepared and ultimately she would feel the brunt of his anger. Her mixed emotions pained her stomach and she sadly realized that she was about to betray Antonio once again. With a growing sense of anxiety she quickly walked down the road towards Amadica while thinking up excuses for the lookouts. She stopped several times, standing alone in the darkness and struggling with her emotions. Phillip angry or Antonio deceived, she thought, neither choice was appealing. Eventually, Mary's own dreams of escaping Salavandra convinced her, and from that moment she never hesitated until reaching Amadica where Phillip rested in the executive guest room deep inside the mill. The night attendant escorted her into the building and towards the catwalks.

"It's the last door on the left," he said, pointing at a rickety steel walkway. "Go through there and down the hall to the last door. That's where Mr. Penkava's staying." He left her standing at the foot of the catwalk steps and disappeared thought a side door.

Mary stood alone in the mill's yawning chasm. A few dim lights illuminated portions of the giant interior, but most areas lay cloaked in darkness. A multitude of odors hung thickly in the stale air. Dust, rotting coffee husks, oil and burlap, sweeter aromas combined with heavy industrial odors all woven together in a nauseating mixture that spoke of work and endless, repetitive toil. She suddenly feared the mill's great empty space. Her footsteps echoed hollowly on the steel walkway.

"I don't think they'll take anything less, Dad." Mary heard Phillip's voice through the door and paused before knocking. "A few came by today actually wanting more. A team of Federals had to convince them to cash out."

Mary listened intently but could not understand the muffled second voice coming from the room.

"Yes, Vasquez was incredibly helpful. I already personally thanked him. God I hate this island. There are just too many things to look after. Has the Board mentioned to you when they might want me back?"

Mary leaned in closer to the door and strained to listen as her heart pounded. The sooner the Board asked Phillip to return, the sooner she too could leave the island. She straightened suddenly as Phillip said goodbye, and then she gave the door a few confident knocks. Phillip answered in his underwear while holding a Link. He was obviously getting ready for bed and making some final calls before turning in for the night.

"I thought you said people would get suspicious if you stayed away at night," he said upon opening the door.

Mary looked at him sadly and wished he would greet her with just a little warmth. She remembered how he approached her the day after their first encounter. At the time she felt as if Phillip was conducting a business transaction rather than pursuing her as a man might seek out a woman. Then she considered New York, and her misgivings vanished.

"They all saw me. I can't stay but I have to tell you what happened tonight."

Phillip invited her in and shut the door firmly behind him. One final go at Mary, he thought lustfully, before sending her on her way back up the mountain. He sat her on the side of the bed and pushed himself into her.

"Tell me when you're done," he ordered, and dropped his underwear to the floor.

The next morning, Leonard looked out over the crowd congregating at the mill's entrance and considered that such a gathering was long overdue. Several generations had passed since the British left the island, and since that time the coffee farmers never created a unified voice or emerged from their cycle of debt. February eleventh began as any other day, waiting for John Doddard's truck and loading sacks of coffee. The similarities ended there, however, and now, as he stood next to his coffee outside the mill, he privately considered the momentum gathering behind Antonio and wondered how much resolve his fellow farmers truly carried.

He estimated about seventy-five to one hundred farmers stood outside the mill in the cool morning air. Each waited next to one or several stuffed burlap sacks, and everyone seemed to be talking at once but in low voices, as if anticipating something momentous. Antonio moved amongst them, thanking them for coming and encouraging everyone to stand firm against the mill's managers that now weaved through the crowd trying to convince people to exchange their coffee at the going rate. Not one farmer took their offer, and those who at first seemed reluctant to follow Antonio's lead soon had their neighbors encouraging them to hold out.

For his part Leonard needed no encouragement. Several farmers quietly gathered around him and occasionally asked his advice on what was going to happen. He answered everyone the same. He truly did not know, but pointed to Antonio and assured them that the mill's management would listen when he spoke. He watched as one manager approached Craig and Felix. The two stood predictably together, joking around even as the tension in the air seemed to rise with the sun.

"Care to exchange those sacks, mister," asked a heavy-set manager with pasty skin.

Craig nudged Felix and both men grinned. "Can't just yet, Sir, but thanks a lot for asking," replied Felix.

"You know, gentlemen, there's no guarantee that we'll take those sacks later. Might be that we're just about filled up with beans right now and can only take a few more loads. What do you say?"

Craig suddenly lost his grin and stared down the manager. He took a step forward but Felix lightly grabbed his arm and held back his friend. "You're trying to tell us that after years of taking our coffee, today, the very day we're asking for a fair exchange, you might just have enough beans?"

Craig's voice rose above the general din and nearby men stopped talking and turned to look. Felix's knuckles whitened as he gripped Craig's arm more tightly. Despite his tendency to joke, his friend harbored an explosive temper and Felix did not want to see it getting loose this morning. The manager backed up a step and nervously looked around at the sun-browned and lined faces of the hardened farmers. Nobody stepped in to mediate, and the nearest mill employee stood halfway across the crowd working a group of three men.

"Take it easy, mister," said the manager quickly. "It's just what we've been told to say."

"Told to say? By who, you jerk? We know you want our coffee. It just depends on how badly you want it." Craig was relaxing now but Felix still held his arm tightly. Craig often only acted pacified when actually planning to throw himself at someone.

The manager backed away waving his palms. He finally turned around and pushed through the crowd. Mr. Penkava would want to know about this hostility, especially from this last one who seemed ready to explode. He looked around expectantly, hoping to see Phillip working the crowd, but only saw two managers shaking certificates at farmers while making futile attempts to exchange their beans. He looked at his watch and remembered the instructions delivered late last night.

"Work them until quarter to nine," said Phillip over his Link. He woke all five managers with a conference call near midnight. Somehow he knew what was going to happen this morning. "If nobody exchanges by then, return to your offices and sit tight."

The instructions seemed cryptic at the time, but as he considered the crowd and Craig's threatening stance, he was thankful that Phillip seemed prepared to deal with the obstinate farmers. Someone roughly bumped into him, but nobody acknowledged this when he turned to look. Five more minutes, he told himself, and approached a man standing by himself next to a single sack.

"You can still exchange that, Sir," he said to José.

José shook his head and inhaled deeply from a broken cigarette. He pointed to Antonio, now at the other side of the crowd and still encouraging people to stand firm against any exchange offer. "Not until you guys speak with Mr. Richards," said José, and blew a cloud of smoke into the air.

The manager turned and grew more aggravated at the one-eyed man working the crowd. "Whatever he says," the manager responded heatedly, "he can't change the certificate cash-out value with just a few words. It's a lot more complicated than that."

José flicked ash from the cigarette and watched as the tiny pieces fluttered through the air and landed on the manager's polished shoes. "It doesn't matter how complicated," he replied. "We deserve more."

The manager shrugged and gave up trying to convince anyone else to exchange his coffee. Obviously Mr. Richards carried a significant presence with the crowd and nobody seemed ready to sell without his direction. He thought it odd that Mr. Penkava instructed them to try convincing the farmers to sell rather than approaching Antonio.

"I'll talk with their leader if they refuse to sell," said Phillip, just before he ended the conference call last night. "Just me," he continued quickly. "I'll be the only one talking to Mr. Richards."

Antonio turned from the two farmers he just met. They were unable to attend last night's meeting, but heard about it and joined him on the ride down to Amadica this morning. They came from the eastern part of Mt. Tabor's coffee region and assured him that word had spread quickly about his attempts to improve the certificate exchange.

Many familiar faces appeared in the crowd. He easily spotted Leonard standing tall and observant amongst a small cluster of farmers. Antonio took him aside last night after the meeting and thanked him for stepping in when he did. He picked out Craig, Felix and José too, all the men that first ventured with him to the mill seeking an equitable exchange. His neighbors, especially those unable to leave their fields on that first day, now supported him by being present and refusing to sell until he said it was time. Feelings of compassion, of responsibility, which might otherwise weigh him down, now lifted Antonio's spirit as he walked amongst the men and saw their hopes lift when he passed.

Rene gave him an especially tight hug as he left this morning. She looked at him proudly and told him how pleased she was even in the face of such controversy.

"Victor would be proud of you," she said.

"It's something I have to do, Mother," he replied. "For the first time in my life I feel like I'm doing something significant. Something that Papa would be proud of. I can't explain it any better."

Before leaving home Antonio quickly checked his Link to see if the message he posted the previous evening received any attention. It already recorded hundreds of hits, mostly from traders who quickly moved in and out of stocks. Most did not leave any response, but the few that did confused Antonio more than anything. They asked questions about tonnage, negotiations and union activity. Some compared his message to a similar one that kicked off a general strike over a decade ago in Vietnam. Most, however, only wanted to know how much more money he thought was appropriate. They did not ask why or even suggest how one might calculate the figure. It was less heartening than Antonio anticipated, and as he stashed the Link high in the rafters of his home, he made a mental note to post another message on a different board.

"You ready, Boss?" asked Marco, standing at his side. His friend and employee stuck with him all morning and insisted on coming to Amadica even though more coffee needed harvesting. Antonio agreed, but only after Marco assured him that Knox and his men were anxious to continue working and could easily handle an entire plot.

Antonio clapped Marco on the back and was glad to have him along for support. He nodded towards all the farmers.

"Who would have thought they'd all show up?" he asked quietly.

Marco helped Antonio up onto a large pile of coffee sacks where he commanded a sweeping view of the entire crowd. The turnout was much greater than he anticipated. A cheer arose as he positioned himself securely on the sacks and several men began chanting his name. Antonio wanted to smile, to greet his neighbors and join them in their excitement, but he soberly reminded himself that they needed guidance right now, and that a leader had to place himself somewhat apart from his men. The mill's management, he also reminded himself, was undoubtedly looking for him to speak for the crowd and would not respect a cheering man lounging about with his fellow farmers. He straightened, held his arms aloft in a large embrace of the crowd and cleared his throat. Quiet pockets materialized throughout the crowd, and soon complete silence lay over the entire yard.

"Friends and neighbors," Antonio began, quickly reminding himself what he intended to say. "Today we ask, demand, that Penkava Incorporated recognize our work and pay us accordingly." A cheer rose up and Antonio felt flushed with excitement.

"As you know, I too work the coffee fields and like you find myself wracked with debt and humbled with each pathetic cash-out. For over one hundred years we've withstood this pattern of abuse at the hands of one company, Penkava. Today it ends. Today we finally demand a fair price for our product."

Another cheer, this one greater than the previous, roared through the farmers. More chanted his name and several groups of men raised their fists into the air. Antonio waited for the roar to die down and then turned from the crowd and looked to the mill. Raising his voice, he shouted at the hulking building where he knew the Company's management listened intently.

"Penkava," Antonio bellowed, "A fifty percent increase in certificate cash-outs is well within your means. We ask that you agree to this in addition to negotiating a long-term plan that ensures our quality of life and your marketable product."

Silence reigned for a moment and then a lone figure stepped out from the mill's gaping black door and walked confidently into the sunlight. Phillip Penkava, heir to a majority of the Company's stock and representative to the Board, smiled self-assuredly at Antonio and the crowd.

"Why so contentious, everyone?" he began, projecting his voice and flashing a winning smile. "We're all in the same business. After all, we have a reciprocal relationship. Without your coffee cherries, we'll miss our revenue projections."

Shouts from several men indicated they were perfectly aware how the relationship worked, but that it needed changing. Antonio appealed for calm and Marco helped him by waving his hands at the crowd and appealing for quiet.

"Unfortunately," continued Phillip, looking suddenly forlorn, "the Company is unable to absorb such a massive increase in certificate cash-outs. Larger market forces are at work, after all. Forces that are well beyond this little corner of the world."

Antonio noticed for the first time that Phillip wore a narrow headset buried in his thick blonde hair. It looked strikingly similar to those worn by the Federals. He half-listened to Phillip as he recalled the incident in the cashier's office.

"So I'm appealing to you right now," continued Phillip, "exchange your coffee and avoid any ugly confrontation. Next year, if the harvest is better and if global prices are more in line with your expectations, perhaps then we can sit down and discuss things."

"No deal, you Penkava rat," shouted a man standing just a few yards away. "You listen to Mr. Richards. He knows all about your profits. You can't hide those anymore."

The rugged farmer pointed up to Antonio as the other men joined in a belligerent response to Phillip's appeal. Phillip's face turned very serious and he looked to Antonio as if questioning his leadership ability.

"No deal, Phillip," echoed Antonio as the noise softened. "This year's prices are high enough to justify immediate compensation. Next year is another year too late, another year of debt and another year of sickness and lack of education for many of our families. We're not asking for a fortune, certainly not by your standards. All we're asking for is fair compensation for our work."

Phillip sighed and placed his hands on his hips. The Public Relations department might be better suited for this nonsense, he thought. It aggravated him that Antonio, someone he confidently took for a simple farmer, could become such an annoyance in so little time. The Board would undoubtedly flip out if he agreed to a penny more for the cash-outs, especially when they faced dropping global coffee prices. These farmers didn't really need more money anyway, he convinced himself. He looked at several standing close by and saw simple, greedy eyes staring back at him.

"I'm sorry to hear that, Antonio," Phillip said in a normal voice. "But we cannot afford that exchange." He shrugged and began to turn back to the mill then stopped suddenly. "Many of you need a cash-out today, I am sure," Phillip yelled out to the crowd while ignoring Antonio. "The mill needs your coffee cherries. Indeed, we *want* to pay you. I'm appealing to you one last time to take the current cash-out.

Following the advice of Mr. Richards will only make you poorer, and all that coffee will go to waste."

A minute of silence convinced him there were still no takers for his offer. He shrugged, and shaking his head in disbelief turned back to the mill while calculating how much bean stock he could tap in order to make up for the losses. A few days without coffee would make little difference, considering the thousands of processed bags stored in Saint Matthew's dockside warehouses. Several days of losses would begin to bite, however, and the last thing Phillip wanted was the Celeste returning to New York City with no coffee on board.

Phillip fingered his headset and whispered a few words into the microphone. Today's coffee cherries were still recoverable even if the farmers did not want to sell them at the current price. They would come around in just a few minutes, Phillip thought, just as soon as their leader was publicly humiliated. Soon, when Mr. Richards ceased being an annoyance, the coffee exchange would continue as it had for generations.

Antonio watched Phillip disappear into the mill while adjusting his headset. Partly surprised, partly annoyed, he looked across the crowd and quickly reviewed his planned speech. Anticipating Phillip's response was like chess, he thought, and planning a counter-strategy where his men could stay motivated was part of the game. He opened his mouth to begin a few inspirational comments when two boys suddenly bolted from a side street and sprinted towards the men. Antonio looked quickly at José, but his friend was already pushing his way to the nearest runner. Then a distant rumble echoed through the streets of Amadica and Antonio suddenly felt sick with fear. Large diesel engines roared, all heading towards the mill.

A large truck carrying well-armed Federals shot out from a side street and skidded to a stop only a few yards from the crowd. Another appeared from an opposite street, and one more from behind the mill. Large dust clouds billowed up from each of their wheels and began drifting over the surprised farmers. The astonished men tripped and stumbled into each other until they stood in a tightly packed circle. Shouts of confusion were immediately followed by angry and frightened cries as soldiers abruptly lifted their rifles and with grim professionalism took aim at Antonio.

A khaki-clad officer leaned out a window and spoke into a bullhorn. "Antonio Richards," boomed his voice from the crackling plastic speaker, "you are under arrest for disturbing the peace." A tremendous roar of protest suddenly exploded from the farmers.

In the confusion of being surrounded by the Federals, Craig became separated from Felix and now stood at the crowd's perimeter directly in front of the bullhorn. Already on a short fuse, he now grew incensed hearing that Antonio was to be arrested. He felt at once hopeless and desperate, but most of all angry that Phillip Penkava could work so closely with President Vasquez to use Salavandra's own soldiers against the island's coffee farmers. Gritting his teeth, he turned to see Antonio standing in defiance on the coffee and almost daring the Federals to force their way through the crowd to fulfill their arrest orders.

"You can go straight to hell," shouted Craig as he turned to face the soldier with the bullhorn. "Antonio isn't going anywhere with you fucks."

The soldier looked at him in surprise but after a moment turned to the driver and made a quick comment. Through the dust-covered windshield Craig watched as the driver broke into a grin that was shared by the man with the bullhorn. They were laughing at him. A confusion of shouted words washed over him from behind, the crowd surged and pushed as everyone packed into each other more tightly. In a blind rage Craig leaned down and pried a rock from the dusty ground. He gripped it until the heavy mass bit into his palm. Its sharp edges cut through his thickly calloused fingers but he held it tightly because it felt like the only legitimate thing left on Salavandra. It felt like justice. He hurled it directly into the cab where it hit the officer squarely in the temple.

The bullhorn began falling from the soldier's hand and Craig watched as the officer leaned into the driver and then disappeared beneath the dashboard. Rifles that were trained on Antonio shifted positions and Craig suddenly stared down the barrels of two assault rifles. The bullhorn finally hit the ground where it released an unpleasant squawk. From the corner of his eye Craig saw another rock suddenly fly through the air.

Despite the packed crowd Leonard still had some space surrounding him. The small group of farmers that huddled nearby when Phillip spoke now gave him plenty of room even as dozens of men pushed and shoved in a desperate attempt to get out from under the aim of the Federals' guns. Leonard looked and acted like a caged animal. His great frame was slightly crouched as if ready to spring upon an unwitting prey. His bent arms and splayed hands looked ready to engulf and crush anything that got too close. While others joined in the chaos of shouting, Leonard remained silent and observant with his jaw tightly clenched.

He looked to Antonio and saw a man swallowing a sickly concern as over a dozen rifles aimed at his head and chest. Leonard saw him watching the farmers mostly, not the Federals, and swore that Antonio yelled something to the crowd that was immediately swallowed by the roaring protest. Behind Antonio, beyond the crowd, Leonard saw the mill's massive doors slide across the opening and block off the dark interior. He turned and saw two rocks fly over José's head and smash into the windshield of the nearest truck.

José never reached the runners. He was blocked by one of the speeding trucks and nearly run over as it slid to a stop in front of the crowd. Frantically waving his arm as the Federal's trap closed, José pointed up the mountain towards home hoping his young sentries would understand and leave the area. He breathed a sigh of relief as the boys bolted away and disappeared behind a nearby building. Even if they did not return home, José assured himself, at least they would avoid any immediate danger.

When José felt confident that both lookouts were out of danger, he turned his attention to the heaving crowd and noticed for the first time how the Federals had their weapons raised. He watched Antonio listen with a drawn face to his arrest statement bellowing through a bullhorn. The novice leader of Amadica's coffee movement looked exhausted but kept his chin high and looked sternly from truck to truck.

Felix stood trapped amongst the pile of other farmers. He watched in horror as Craig yelled at the Federal wielding a bullhorn. His lifelong friend never heard a sound when Felix screamed at him to keep his mouth shut. Felix realized with growing horror that Craig probably needed a firm shake to release him from his tunnel-vision of rage. His entire life he had checked Craig's more violent outbursts, usually accompanying them with a good dose of humor to cool his friend's explosive temper. Now, when facing the most dangerous event of his life, Felix could not reach him no matter how hard he struggled against the pitching crowd.

He cried out in fear as Craig wound up and hurled a tremendous rock at the soldier in the truck. How so much velocity got behind that heavy rock Felix could only wonder. In the split second as it left Craig's hand, Felix's mind flashed to a time long ago when he tactfully suggested that Craig visit Amadica's doctor about his temper. Craig never did, and now it appeared that his temper just got the better of him. A deadly aim, Felix thought, and watched the rock sail into the cab. The crowd roared, it surged, but Felix shut his eyes and tried only to breathe. Antonio would fix this, he hoped, and wondered how the Federals planned to pull Antonio from the crowd.

"It was his headset, Boss," Marco yelled up to Antonio above the growing confusion. Marco wanted to spit in disgust but was suddenly crushed up against the burlap sacks upon which Antonio stood.

Marco saw Antonio look down at him and nod. The face of his boss and friend carried a confused blend of emotions. Fused with overwhelming worry, Marco saw anger and a touch of desperation wrinkling Antonio's brow. He realized for a second that a lesser man might crack at such a moment. He watched Antonio bend, his body seemed to yield under the strain of responsibility, and he momentarily looked less solid than the coffee sacks beneath his feet. Marco reached out and slapped Antonio's calf as hard as he could.

"Don't let them…" he began to scream, knowing Antonio needed a jolt of encouragement. The loud squawk of the bullhorn interrupted him, and he watched Antonio turn towards the sound.

Marco never took his eyes from Antonio even as the arrest statement echoed off the coffee mill's metallic exterior. As a father might look upon a son, Marco now gazed up at Antonio. Older by a generation and having more experiences in more places, Marco still felt tightly allied with Antonio if for nothing more than Antonio's refusal to accept his meager lot on Salavandra. Antonio lived an inspirational life, Marco thought as his own life flashed through his mind. He was landless, drifting from island to island and profoundly discouraged about ever crawling out from under coffee's endless toil.

Somewhere in the crowd a clear voice full of rage rang out above all others. Marco turned towards a sea of men, most backing away from the three trucks and crushing everyone in the process. One man, perhaps Craig, but Marco strained to see through the confusion, stood a little apart from the others. It looked to Marco as if he taunted the Federals. Marco's voice caught in his throat as he saw the lone figure cock back his arm and launch a rock through the air. It seemed to hang in time, the space of a heartbeat or of a generation of coffee growers. The world exploded after the rock found its mark.

Little puffs of smoke erupted from the two rifles aimed at his chest. Thinking they misfired, Craig smiled and bent to grasp another rock as dozens rained over his head. Feet surged around him suddenly, but he remembered that he was standing alone only a moment earlier. He wondered how so many people could congregate around him so quickly. He found another rock, but it stubbornly clung to the earth and refused to budge no matter how hard he pulled and pushed. He grew tired and vaguely noticed the crowd's shouts somehow growing dimmer and yet more desperate. Circular dark spots appeared in the dirt beneath him. Rain did not usually fall in February. Picking coffee in the rain was never any fun. It was always too muddy, and when the molds bloomed the harvest grew more tenuous. At least some of the coffee was already picked.

Antonio choked back a cry when Craig's rock crushed the officer's skull. He watched in shock as two soldiers lowered their rifles and immediately shot one round each into his friend's chest. He wanted to vomit, to cry out and pound the coffee cherries into Salvandra's soil and crush the entire island into the sea. He carried a death on his hands, and though he did not pull the triggers that sent the bullets flying, Antonio still felt responsible. As Craig slumped down and tried prying another rock from the ground, the crowd surged around him. Antonio remembered Craig's son Eric.

More rocks flew, pelting the soldiers and bouncing off the truck's bullet-proof windshield. A sudden and harsh order from an officer stayed any additional firing. Emboldened, the crowd surged around the truck and began rocking it while demanding that the soldiers who shot Craig step down. One farmer jumped up and grabbed the barrel of a rifle. He yanked it down into the crowd and disappeared into the melee. Antonio finally found his voice and screamed out in a futile attempt to stop the brawl. He felt Marco slap him on the calf again and looked down for a moment. Marco pointed desperately at the other two trucks full of soldiers.

"They're moving," screamed Marco. "They're coming to get you."

With the farmers so occupied, nobody noticed the other two trucks. In the confusion they crept closer to Antonio and Marco, who now stood at the back of the crowd. Antonio swallowed his responsibility and stepped down off the burlap sacks to sternly face the oncoming Federals.

"You have to leave," cried Marco, pulling at Antonio's arms and looking at him wildly. "They'll take you away, you'll disappear! You have to leave now."

Antonio shook his head and pried Marco's hand loose. He understood now. The death, the danger, all would cease once his arrest was carried out. Nobody else would die for a lousy certificate.

"I'm going with them," he said loudly to Marco. "It's the only way to end this chaos." He swept an arm across the crowd, still boiling with rage and intent on tipping over the furthest truck. "They don't deserve this," said Antonio sadly, and turned back to face the soldiers.

Four Federals immediately jumped off a truck. Marco backed away as they approached, stunned that Antonio refused to resist arrest. A young soldier with a clenched jaw lowered his rifle butt and rammed it into Antonio's stomach. Antonio sank to his knees but refused to cry out while another soldier cracked him over the head and opened a bloody gash above his patched eye. He dropped closer to the ground and swayed sickeningly over the Federals' shiny black boots. In seconds his hands were bound and the Federals tossed him up onto a truck where he lay in a daze staring at the crowd. With a sudden lurch and a grinding of gears the trucks roared away from the mill.

A window high above the mill's giant door opened and Phillip's head suddenly poked out above everyone. He smiled as the Federals carried away Antonio's limp body. Later, when the coffee was processed and the certificates exchanged, Phillip planned to pay Antonio a visit. Amadica's jail, he was told by a local captain, was an especially unpleasant place.

As the last truck backed away from the crowd Phillip raised his own bullhorn. "The mill is still buying coffee, gentlemen," he announced. His voice boomed across the crowd and everyone turned to look at the mill. He swallowed hard to bite back a smile while thinking about addressing the farmers as gentlemen. "Mr. Richards has been arrested as a public nuisance. One of you is dead. Was this all worth it?"

Phillip let the silence fall heavily. The small cluster of men around Craig's lifeless body gathered together more tightly. Phillip had watched the entire episode unfold, and while not wanting anyone to get killed, considered that one man's death would probably end this certificate nonsense. Anything is worth stopping this headache, he thought wearily. The stunned crowd looked around for Antonio and cried out when they realized the Federals had truly snatched him from their midst.

"You've been deceived by Mr. Richards," continued Phillip through the bullhorn. "You all have coffee cherries to exchange and the mill still wants to help you even after all that's happened. Think of all the things that you need, that your family needs, and how you can get those things by exchanging that coffee. Let's put this unpleasantness behind us. It's Sunday, after all, and not a day for fighting."

More silence followed and several men moved towards their respective sacks. He was winning them over, Phillip thought happily, and in a matter of minutes the mill's giant door would open and the certificate exchange would begin again. Dad would be proud, he thought happily, and watched as a tall man suddenly stepped forward.

"You can't have my coffee, Penkava." The man's voice rose strongly above the crowd and forced the other farmers to pay attention. Phillip watched with sickened fascination as the man sliced into a burlap sack and spilled thousands of coffee cherries out on the ground. He did it again, and once more, while loudly cursing the Penkava corporation and President Vasquez. The giant farmer finally threw the empty burlap sacks atop the pile and again raised his fist into the air, shaking it angrily.

"And just to make sure you know that I mean it…" he cried out as the other farmers looked on. From his pocket Leonard drew a crushed matchbook and bent to light the burlap. The sacks caught fire in seconds and soon a well-defined trail of white smoke rose from the ground. Phillip groaned as another farmer dragged one of his own sacks over and gently laid it on the fire. Others followed and soon dozens of sacks rested atop the fire and voices rose in newfound enthusiasm as flames were lit at various locations. Someone dragged over a bag of trash from an alley and threw it on the heap. Old scrap lumber suddenly appeared and was also thrown onto the pile. In just a few minutes a strong blaze began taking shape.

"Try to take this coffee, Penkava, you bastard," yelled Leonard.

Phillip watched in silent amazement as the flames rose higher and consumed the precious coffee. More farmers dragged their sacks over to the growing blaze. They don't care, Phillip thought. They don't care about the cash-out. Their families would suffer the loss of money. Their lives would be harder by burning the coffee, and yet farmer after farmer dragged his product to the pile and then raised a fist to the mill. Flames appeared in the center of the pile and several men backed away from the growing heat. Shaking his head, Phillip slammed the window and refused to watch as he lost the day.

Eight

"Son, we've got rumors up here that are starting to pressure the stock. Something about the coffee farmers demanding more money. Is anything going on down there that I need to know about?"

The Link's small screen outlined Tom Penkava's worried face. He called just as Phillip finished calculating worst-case scenario loss projections. The Celeste would sail without any coffee by the end of March unless he convinced Antonio to accept the current exchange rate.

"Nothing I can't handle, Dad," replied Phillip, rubbing his temples and wondering when his headache began. The acrid smell of burning coffee and trash still clung to the mill's walls despite two fans blowing fresh air through the meeting room. A manager slid a package of aspirin across the broad table and pointed at a pitcher of water.

"So there is something going on?" Tom looked suddenly more concerned, and his face furrowed. It was the same expression Phillip remembered from his childhood, just before Tom meted out a punishment for some childish prank. Phillip unintentionally winced, recalling his father's belt snapping loudly across his shirtless back.

"We had a little event this morning," Phillip began explaining. "The farmers want more for the certificates."

"You know that can't happen, Phillip," said Tom quickly, interrupting his son.

Phillip sighed, "Yes, Dad, that's what I told them." He hated explaining things to anyone, especially to his father when he knew Tom was in no mood to listen.

"Don't get smart with me, boy. You've always done a good job down there, and I expect you'll find a way to smooth this out, too. Do they have someone you can reason with?"

After years of industry experience, Tom always looked for a representative voice whenever any business dealings stirred up local controversy. He reasoned that Salavandra's problem might be easily erased by somehow bringing the farmers' leader on board with the Company. A similar strategy worked in Indonesia seven years earlier.

Phillip considered his last sight of Antonio, bleeding and curled up like a fetus with his hands roughly cuffed behind his back. Perhaps he would come around now, Phillip thought, especially after spending time with the guards in Amadica's jail.

"They have a leader, of sorts," replied Phillip after a moment's consideration. "His name is Antonio Richards. He's really nothing more than a dumb farmer." Phillip's last comment died in his mouth and he silently admonished himself for underestimating Antonio.

He recovered quickly however, and refused to show his father any sign of indecision. "I'll tell you one thing," he continued. "We owe President Vasquez a huge thank you. His Federals arrested Richards this morning for disturbing the peace. If the traders get hot up there in New York, you can always assure them that this Richards guy is a criminal, and that he's rotting in jail."

"Arrested him?" Tom asked. "That couldn't have gone over well. Was it quick?"

Phillip shook his head and suddenly had mixed emotions about the manner of Antonio's arrest. Humiliating him in public did nothing to calm the farmers' anger. It actually created the opposite of Phillip's intended effect. He could still see them shaking their fists after dumping their coffee on the growing blaze.

"Not exactly, Dad," Phillip said quietly, knowing Tom would keep probing until he learned the entire story. Somehow his father always managed to expose flaws in all his plans.

"There was sort of a..." he struggled to find the words. "There was a, disturbance of sorts, with lots of stones being thrown. An officer is in a coma, and two Federals were forced to defend themselves against a man throwing a huge rock."

Tom fell silent for a moment as he processed Phillip's comment. He shook his head seriously. "Don't let this get out of hand, son," he said quietly. "Do you think Vasquez has enough resources to keep this thing from spilling over?"

Phillip shrugged and said, "Even before this morning, there were Federals all over the place looking for my mugger. I've never seen so many soldiers patrolling the island. I just want to get back to Retribution Point and enjoy the cabin. Since when did coming down here turn into such a headache?"

He watched as his father nodded to someone off screen, and suddenly the Link's view swung to a new face. Senator Bill Wilson looked at Phillip with his most concerned gaze. He really did like Phillip, despite the youthful exuberance and occasional ill-considered remarks.

"Sorry to eavesdrop, Phillip. Sounds like you've got your hands full down there."

Phillip nodded and quickly waved a finger of greeting at the Senator. "You might say that, Bill. February in New York isn't looking so bad anymore. I think I need a real vacation."

"Don't we all," chuckled Bill. "Tell you what, Phillip. I'm going to give President Vasquez a ring and see if there's anything we can do to help him out. A few extra resources for his Federals might make your life a little easier."

"Thanks Bill. I know he'll appreciate anything you guys send him, as usual."

"It's the least we can do, Phillip. Vasquez has always been a solid friend, and I'm sure he's a bit stretched right now."

"In the mean time," said Tom's firm voice from off-screen. Senator Wilson politely moved the Link back to face Phillip's father. "You find out if Mr. Richards has any soft spots. Figure out how to use them, and then try to get him working with the company. When his people see he's come around, they'll drop this certificate nonsense."

Phillip thought of Mary and smiled. "I'm already working on that, Dad. I expect to wrap this mess up shortly."

Phillip shut down the Link and leaned back in his chair with a sigh of relief. He felt in control again for the first time since the morning's blaze. Both his headache and the smoke's bitter odor were finally receding. Antonio clearly had a soft spot. She begged him to keep secret their affair every time he forced himself on her.

"You must go to him," he commanded Mary later that day after once again pulling her from the greenhouses. Mercedes gave him an accusing look when he showed up and tried to talk to Mary. Mary ignored her old friend, however, and immediately ran to Phillip when he called.

She now sat at a small table across from Phillip in his private quarters deep within Amadica's mill. She refused to look at the bed where he thrust himself into her mouth the previous night. Antonio never treated her so poorly, she considered sadly. Antonio never promised, either, to take her away from the greenhouses. He would also never show her Manhattan, or take her to Broadway shows in shoes she could only dream about wearing. Phillip promised all this and more. "Just as soon as the Valentine's Day shipment is secure," he told her repeatedly, "we'll be off to New York."

"What would you have me say to him?" she asked.

Mercedes had commented on her attitude this morning while they tended roses. "You've lost your energy," she said, "and it all started when Phillip Penkava showed up to interview us." As Mary now looked across the table at Phillip, she felt a draining anxiety overwhelming her. Only three more days to the Valentine's shipment, she thought, and many flowers would already leave Salavandra tomorrow. The blood red roses stood ready to bloom.

"You have to convince him to retract this demand for a higher certificate exchange rate," Phillip replied sharply. "The Company will never pay a cent more. Tell him he should give up, because nothing is going to change."

Mary remembered standing on the porch with Rene, José and Antonio. For a few moments last night, she actually forgot about her betrayal and felt at peace and once again tightly bound to her neighbors and the life she knew so well. The comfort she felt during those few moments now grated painfully against Phillip's order.

"I can't see him agreeing," she quietly replied, keeping her eyes focused on the table. "He can be a stubborn man, especially when he's right."

"Right or wrong doesn't matter, Mary," said Phillip roughly and smacked the table with his palm. "The Company, *my* Company, can't have some idiot dirt-bag farmer from this stinking little island screwing up our balance sheets and reputation."

Mary lifted her head uncontrollably. Anger burned in her dark eyes. "My father is a coffee farmer," she said slowly with a hot glare, "and Salavandra does not stink."

Phillip paused in surprise, then smiled, and gestured widely with his arms. "Then why do you keep asking me to take you away? Of course Salavandra stinks. In fact it reeks."

Phillip could see that with each word Mary grew more irritated, but he pushed forward anyway, confident that he could turn her emotions upside down in a moment. Malleable, he told himself.

"Salavandra has nothing for you, Mary. Think of New York. Think of the nice homes, the entertainment and the parties. Then, of course, there's the entire country to explore. You're going to have a great time there."

Mary's expression quickly changed. Every time Phillip talked about New York, she forgot about her troubles and imagined herself amongst tall buildings, wearing wonderful clothing and never having to prune flowers again. "I want to be there, Phillip," she said honestly.

"Of course, of course you do, Mary. Beautiful Mary. How many times do I have to tell you? After all this is over, we're going to fly away from this island and have the time of our lives." He flashed Mary his most perfect smile while reaching across the table and grasping her hand. Confident that he once again had her in tow, he continued with the instructions.

"Now when you see Antonio, don't tell him you talked to me. I want him to think it's just you coming to him. Appeal to his common sense. Remind him that whatever money he and his fellow farmers have will go fast if they continue refusing to sell.

"I told the guards at the jail to expect you this afternoon. They'll let you see him without any questions. If he keeps refusing to listen, suggest to him that he talk to me, privately. Suggest that he could profit, from coming to me and striking a deal."

"What kind of deal?" asked Mary, seeing the intricacies of Phillip's plan and beginning to understand his strategy.

Phillip shook his head. "That doesn't concern you, Mary. Suggest that a deal might be workable, and that he should consider talking to me, one on one."

Mary nodded obediently, but she felt a familiar pain flare-up in her stomach. It happened whenever she planned to see Antonio. Years of being together, of trusting each other, were being turned upside-down so quickly. She hated herself, but continued nodding.

"To review," said Phillip quickly, standing and showing her to the door. "First, try to get him to abandon this idea of a bigger cash-out. If that doesn't work, suggest that there might be an alternative if he talks to me."

Mary stood at the open door and nodded. She swallowed hard and forced back tears that threatened to spill. She wondered how she ever became so wretched. The night on the beach started it all, she thought, and shamefully pushed the muddled images from her mind. It was better than I remember, she told herself. She remembered the starlight and the cool water of the vast Caribbean stretching north. Now she felt trapped no matter how she tried convincing herself otherwise. Phillip bent and kissed her forehead lightly as she turned to leave.

Oh, and Mary," he called to her as she walked down the narrow hallway, "If you have to fuck him to get him to agree, do it."

"You probably don't remember me, Mr. Richards," said the broad-shouldered Federal looming above him. He filled the narrow cell with his bulky mass and exhaled a thick stream of cigar smoke. Only a few inches separated the toes of his shined boots with Antonio's face. "I too have coffee in my blood. I was your neighbor many years ago."

Antonio lifted his head from the cement floor and gazed up at the uniformed soldier. He looked like any other Federal, wearing khaki clothing and carrying a palpable, repugnant arrogance. He remembered Craig shaking his fist at the Federals. Eric would be crushed when he got the news of his father's death.

"I don't know you," whispered Antonio, too weak from the repeated beatings to say anything louder. The soldiers who brought him to jail seemed to enjoy kicking him repeatedly.

"My name is Munoz. Our fathers had adjacent fields when we were children."

Antonio looked more carefully at the soldier's face and dimly recognized his childhood acquaintance. "Ignacio? Ignacio Munoz?" he asked, and weakly laid his head back onto the floor. The man above him grunted, and Antonio recalled a tall kid, a few years older than himself, being called out of school to work the fields.

"It's Lieutenant-Colonel Munoz, now. You remember even in your current state. Impressive." He directed a guard to throw some water on Antonio. The shock stung his wounds and killed his growing lethargy. "No sleep, not yet, Antonio," said Munoz gruffly.

Antonio sputtered the water from his lips. "Your father was a good man."

"Yes, he was a good man. And my mother, a good woman. Both are dead now, and my brothers and sisters, scattered, and off Salavandra, thank God. I sold the land to pay my family's debts."

"I'm sorry."

LTC Munoz grunted, and motioned the guard to leave. The steel doors clanged shut and locked them both inside the tiny cell. Though a beam of sunlight shined through a single small window, the interior remained oppressively damp and carried a stale, moldy odor. Munoz squatted down and politely held his chewed cigar stub away from Antonio's face.

"Why are you here in this stinking cell, neighbor?" he asked softly. Antonio thought he heard a hint of sadness in the LTC's voice.

"Your men arrested…"

"I know they arrested you. I gave them the order," Munoz interrupted loudly. "Why are you being a nuisance? Why are you in my jail, bleeding on my floor, during the middle of Harvest?"

Antonio looked at the LTC and tried to discern his intentions. Something more than a simple interrogation, Antonio surmised; this seemed almost personal.

"Penkava and Vasquez are cheating us. We live like slaves while they get rich."

"Ha! And when did you finally realize this, my friend?" asked Munoz, taking a puff on his cigar. "It's about time you come around."

"What do you mean?"

Munoz shrugged. "That's life, Mr. Richards. That's reality on Salavandra. Vasquez keeps Salavandra quiet, while Penkava gets our coffee, lumber and whatever else. Before Vasquez there was Hugo, and before him, Lopez. I don't remember anyone earlier, but it's always the same, no matter who lives in the President's mansion. As long as there's a body, the actual person matters very little."

"It's not fair, and we can't keep living like this," said Antonio, resting his head on the filthy cement. Darkness flooded in, sleep beckoned, even through his aching limbs.

"Yes," agreed Munoz. "It's not fair, not by a mile. It is Salavandra, however. And I think, my neighbor, you should learn to accept the rules."

Antonio gently rolled his head against the floor in protest. He felt the cement scrape his forehead but did not care. "Rules can change. How can you be a part of this, especially when you came from coffee?"

Munoz straightened slowly and let out a sigh. After a long moment of silence the LTC cleared his throat and carefully selected his words. "We all make choices about how to live, Antonio. I broke free of coffee's shackles years ago. I made something of myself, and now have security, a home, and my two sons can go to school. I'm no longer bound to the land, suffering through each harvest and wondering if I'll make it to the next."

"I make choices too, Ignacio," replied Antonio, looking up at his distant acquaintance and suddenly finding strength he did not know he possessed. "You may have freed yourself from coffee, but in doing so you chained yourself to Penkava and Vasquez. I'm not ashamed that the land is my master. Can you say the same?"

LTC Munoz grunted again. He looked carefully at Antonio lying at his feet and took another substantial puff from his cigar.

"Fuck you," he said, and loudly called the guard to open the cell door.

Antonio drifted down towards sleep as the cell door banged shut. He felt a vague sense of guilt after forcing Ignacio to consider life from a different perspective. It was not his intention to hurt people, but as Antonio thought about the preceding days, it seemed that grief followed wherever he went. He saw Craig's lifeless body slumped in the dirt. He saw his neighbors going hungry because they refused to sell their coffee under his direction. When sleep finally washed over him, it was a fitful series of naps, full of nightmares where Craig, with bloodied lips and blank eyes, threw rocks at truckloads of heavily-armed Federals.

When he awoke, he found Mary staring down at him from the other side of the cell door. Her eyes glistened and she gripped the steel bars tightly but did not say anything. From his curled position on the floor that now smelled of his own urine, Antonio sensed her anguish and wished she would simply go away. It was too painful to see her standing there, watching him with so much pity in her eyes.

"How long have you been there?" he asked with a cracked and dry voice.

Mary barely shrugged. "Twenty minutes, maybe thirty," she whispered. She turned her head and sniffed loudly while blinking away the tears. One rolled down her cheek and she quickly wiped it away.

"You should leave. I don't want you seeing me like this." He pushed himself up against the far wall, gingerly straining against the pain blooming in his ribs.

Mary turned to him suddenly, forgetting Phillip's orders and thinking only of Antonio as her lover, her friend, and how he did not deserve such cruelty. "It doesn't have to be this way, Antonio. You could just be quiet and promise to go home and stop making trouble." She spoke from her aching heart and wished only for Antonio to return to his quite life of farming. This simple act would heal some of the holes the past several days had torn into her soul.

Antonio shook his head slowly. "It's too late, Mary," he replied sadly. "Already there are many farmers behind the movement. Nearly one hundred gathered at the mill this morning. They're sick of this life and want change. I can't leave them now."

A long moment of silence ensued where Antonio shut his eye and listened to Mary's gentle breathing. He remembered that same delicate sound next to his chest and in his ear after an hour of lovemaking. Peace. So much had changed. Those days seemed lifetimes away.

"They'll never let you out," Mary said softly, choking on her own words. "They'll ..."

"Disappear me. I know," he finished her sentence knowing she could not say the dreaded words. Salavandra's infamous disappearances predictably occurred whenever anyone became too difficult for the Federals to easily handle. The thought occupied Antonio's mind since the soldiers threw him to the floor.

"I don't want this, Mary," he tried to explain while waving an arm weakly through the air. "All I want is to go back to how things were, with me farming and us planning to be married and raising children." Images of the Celeste suddenly flashed through his mind. He adjusted the eye patch and thought briefly of the Link stashed at home. "We nearly got there," he whispered. "Forty dollars was enough."

Mary turned from the cell and faced the wall. She could not suffer another moment looking at Antonio while listening to the plans of a former life. She would confess to him, she thought wildly, and tell him everything that happened and how she fell into Phillip's trap. Wallowing in such miserable depths was now partly her doing, of course. She lusted after Phillip's wealth, and especially his promise to take her to America. Antonio might understand, she thought, he might even forgive.

"Can you tell my mother I'm alright, and look after her?"

Mary hung her head and nodded to the wall. More tears dropped from her swollen eyes as she realized she had no courage to confess to anyone, much less to Antonio. Another example of my worthlessness, she thought, and balled her hands into tight fists. She turned suddenly to see Antonio and considered the irony of him behind bars but righteously free, while she walked freely while imprisoned in her own lies.

A guard called down the hall telling her that she had to leave.

"I will tell her."

"Thank you, Mary. Fate seems stacked against us. I wish there was some other way. I love you."

She felt crushed into the cement but stood firmly against the desire to sink to the floor weeping. She suddenly realized that this was the last time she would see him. Her resolve nearly cracked. He needs strength now, Mary told herself furiously, and I can at least give him one last ray of light to ease the end.

"I love you, my sweet Antonio."

She turned and walked quickly down the hallway with her eyes to the floor. She felt the embodiment of misery. Phillip disgusted her, she now freely admitted to herself, and Antonio did not deserve her vileness. She even spurned Mercedes. Losing on all fronts Mary suddenly wondered how she became such a person.

She swiftly passed through the jail's front office without looking at anyone. Phillip lounged comfortably in a corner chair patiently waiting his turn for a go at Antonio. As the door banged shut behind Mary he turned to LTC Munoz who was sitting behind a desk quietly considering his cold cigar stub.

"She looked upset," Phillip said lightly.

Ignacio turned to him with a questioning look. He nodded and sighed heavily. The cigar remains crumbled in his fingers and he carefully brushed the moist tobacco into the trash can.

"Yes, Sir," he replied politely, knowing Phillip had direct communication with President Vasquez. "Mr. Richards is a noble man and she knows he's lost."

Antonio swallowed a groan as Mary's footsteps echoed down the hallway. He listened closely as the door shut and steeled himself against never seeing her again. For what, he asked? Was more certificate exchange money worth such decrepitude? The urine stink from his soaked pants wafted upwards and drove out hot, desperate tears. Truly, thought Antonio, I am at life's bottom.

Half an hour later another click from the hall door jolted his self-deprecating misery. Firm and slow, the footsteps spoke of a confident man. Perhaps a guard, Antonio thought, with some new grief to inflict upon my already battered body. He refused to look up as the footsteps stopped. After a moment the fresh smells of soap and cologne floated into his cell.

"Phillip Penkava," Antonio snarled, recognizing the expensive scents from his stay in Saint Matthew's clinic. He suddenly found himself full of venom, and Phillip was the single person he most desired to spit it upon.

"Save your breath," Antonio hissed, "The farmers are still behind me."

"Oh?" Phillip responded quickly. "Then you must have told them to spend their exchange money in Amadica's shops. Food, clothing, supplies, they're all flowing out of town in record amounts after this morning's massive exchange."

Antonio looked up at Phillip and wanted to crush him. Even in his weakened state he imagined throwing himself upon Phillip and strangling the life from his body. Mary's quick exit still simmered in his mind.

"Nobody told you?" Phillip asked. He shrugged as if to announce that the morning's events were just a minor nuisance, hardly worth his attention. "After you left, everyone came to their senses and exchanged at the going rate. It's a shame you didn't do the same."

"You lie."

Another shrug, accompanied by a wry smile suggesting Antonio would never know either way. Phillip looked around the cell and studied Antonio's ruined clothing while shaking his head.

"You're pathetic and broken. Nobody's following you anymore. Did you honestly believe the Company would agree to a fifty percent increase?"

"You can afford it."

"Of course we can afford it," snarled Phillip, suddenly gripping the bars. "That's not the point, you ignorant farmer."

"Point or not, it's not fair that we continue working while you and Vasquez get rich."

"Vasquez is a good man, Antonio. He's helps make this tiny country safe by keeping it connected to the global marketplace."

"He manipulates the people. Salavandra's elections are a joke and he lines his pockets with your assistance. All this is done on my neighbors' backs."

Phillip sighed and shook his head as he realized how little Antonio understood of geopolitical relationships. "Salavandra is all you know," he began, mildly trying to check his condescending tone. "It's just one little speck of innumerable other insignificant specks all over the world. The U.S. and companies like mine keep you under our umbrella. And how do you repay us? By sowing dissent amongst people that were perfectly happy before you came along. Where's your gratitude?"

"Where's my gratitude?" Antonio yelled, unable to control himself. He stood up, straining heavily against his tender bruises while steadily approaching the cell door. The pungent smell of urine followed him like a cloud, but he disregarded it and ignored Phillip's calculated step away from the bars.

"My father died from your fungicide. Our women's eyes burn with tears from working in your greenhouses. I live in my father's tiny home and sleep on the floor so my mother can have the single bedroom. My neighbors can't send their children to school because they have to work the fields. The list goes on, Phillip, sickness, hunger, endless debt, it's all part of our *happy* lives. And you have the guts to ask me about gratitude?"

"They have eye drops," Phillip replied promptly.

"What?"

"The greenhouse workers. I got them eye drops. It makes their eyes feel better."

Antonio dropped his head heavily against the steel bars. He realized that Phillip would never understand the extent of suffering on Salavandra.

"I talk of profound problems at the core of our lives," Antonio said weakly, "and you offer eye drops. Thank you, Mr. Penkava. You are truly benevolent."

"It's more complicated than that, Antonio," said Phillip. "Everything costs money and stockholders don't like expenses. Competition is always snapping at our heels. I don't expect you to understand, but there are larger market forces at play."

"Again with the market forces, Phillip? That's too vague an excuse now. There are expense issues on your end, yes, I understand this point. However, you are unwilling to negotiate even an inch. You can keep your eye drops. I hope my neighbors kick you and Vasquez off Salavandra." He turned and shuffled to the back wall and slumped heavily to the floor.

"The Federals will make sure that never happens, Antonio. Besides, if Penkava leaves, some other company will replace us." Phillip's voice abruptly dropped to a whisper. "And you know very well Vasquez is nothing more than a puppet and easily replaced."

"True, true, Phillip," replied Antonio nodding. He felt the cement's coldness seeping into his body and wanted to stand again. "Vasquez's goons are too well armed and well trained. They'll arrest whoever replaces me, either tomorrow or next year. But it cannot last forever, Phillip. Not when the rest of the world finds out about what's going on down here."

"Oh that?" replied Phillip, regaining his bravado. "The annoying Link message you dropped onto the stock's bulletin board was erased. We found out early and solved the problem."

Antonio remained silent while feeling his world slipping away. He wondered how the end might feel. A quick end, he thought, a single bullet in the back of the head. He hoped the Federals felt that they had kicked him enough.

Phillip watched Antonio roll his head against the wall. With one eye shut and the other patched Antonio looked bottomed out and desperate enough to grasp anything. "It doesn't have to be this way, Antonio."

"What do you mean?"

"We can solve your problem. Privately, of course. Your neighbors and the other growers can't know anything."

"What are you talking about?"

"Just hear me out. The Company can get you released but you have to accept our offer. We'll give you a settlement of one year's coffee income if you stop your demonstrations and all activity related to certificate pricing. You can go back to your farm and start rebuilding you life. What do you say?"

Antonio nearly stopped breathing. One year's income on top of his current harvest would put him well into the black. Rene could see Amadica's doctor and even travel to Saint Matthew's clinic if necessary. He could buy more land and more robust seedlings that would significantly increase his yield in later years. Mary could have a beautiful wedding. His debt would instantly vanish.

"Antonio?" asked Phillip after an extended silence.

Antonio opened his eyes. "It's a generous offer, Phillip."

Phillip shrugged and thought he saw a familiar glimmer in Antonio's eyes. "We can be magnanimous when necessary."

"My neighbors would appreciate such an offer too."

Phillip shook his head and held up his hands. "Just you," he whispered, and cast a quick glance down the empty hallway.

Antonio shut his eyes again. He struggled with thoughts of his mother needing him as she grew older. Mary too, he considered, deserved a man that would love her. If he disappeared, their suffering would persist long after Leonard, Felix and José began to forget him, and his family name sank into oblivion. Marco would move on to another field on another island and forget about the eleventh of February.

"My father had dreams of getting out of coffee, Phillip. He actually wanted me to leave Salavandra. I hardly understood him at the time, but I see clearly now."

"With a year's income you could easily get out of coffee. Passage to another place is cheap."

Antonio suddenly opened his eyes. Fatigue disappeared and was replaced with anger.

"My father was wrong, Phillip," Antonio said firmly. His voice echoed off the cinderblocks. "There is no escape from Salavandra, no matter where I choose to live. One place is much the same as any other, I am sure. If not coffee it's sugar cane, if not cane it's fruits or vegetables or sewing pants in a factory somewhere. I can as much leave Salavandra as you can understand the depths of hardship in the lives of my neighbors."

"I see," said Phillip. "I also see you've made better use of the Link than I imagined."

"I'll just carry Salavandra with me if I leave. No deal, Phillip. I am here, my neighbors are here, and it is this Salavandra we're going to change."

"Not if you're dead," said Phillip, and stomped down the hallway.

Marco gazed down upon Amadica from the wooded slope overlooking the little town. A few lights shined up through the darkness and feebly pierced the nighttime sky. Overhead, a nearly full moon emerged from behind running cloud cover that skirted across the sky as if on some urgent western mission. Wind blew through the forest and rustled leaves with whistling speed as it flowed across Mt. Tabor in giant, undulating waves.

Shaking off his weariness, Marco concentrated on watching the jailhouse for any sign of movement. Salavandra's earliest hours buried the town in a deep slumber despite the day's protests. He sniffed the air for any sign of the fire, but the late night winds had long ago pushed the burned stench down slope and out to sea. Then the door to the jailhouse opened with a flood of light. A man stepped out and began smoking.

"Only a single man in one hour," whispered Knox. "Antonio doesn't seem heavily guarded."

Marco nodded but pointed to the building next to the jail. The single-story cinder block structure stood low to the ground and stretched into the darkness behind the jail. Two large trucks were parked outside its front door.

"Barracks," he whispered back. "Nobody's awake there either, as far as I can tell."

"José's runners better be right," muttered Knox.

"They're right," replied Marco. "I know both of them. They're good kids and do as they're told. That's why José picked them to watch the jail this afternoon."

Knox abruptly waved an arm into the darkness behind him. The forest seemed to come alive as dozens of shadows materialized from the undergrowth. Feet stirred loose sticks and branches as farmers carefully made their way to the slope's ridge overlooking Amadica. Leonard moved up next to Marco while staying close to the ground. Jonathan eased up to Knox's side and carefully peered over the town and strategically assessed its layout.

When Marco returned to the fields earlier that day he told Knox and his men the entire story about Craig's death and Antonio's arrest. They listened closely but cursed Phillip Penkava and the Federals so many times that Knox was forced to tell everyone to shut up. Diego, of course, remained quiet, and to a lesser extent, so did Hank. In their silence Marco noticed a simmering anger, similar to that of the farmers who gathered on Antonio's front porch the previous evening.

"So what happens now," Will Finkle had asked, kicking a half-full sack of coffee after Marco finished telling them what happened. "Are we still getting paid for any of this work?"

"Shut up, Will," replied Knox firmly. "I have to think. How many farmers were at the mill?" he asked Marco.

"Nearly a hundred."

"And how many are in the hollow?"

Marco estimated that around twenty-five farmers, most looking to Leonard for leadership, were now congregated around Antonio's porch. He remembered comforting Rene before leaving her with Felix. José set lookouts and runners just in case the Federals decided to break up their meeting.

"And what's their mood?" asked Knox curiously.

"They're rightfully pissed-off and worried. You name it, they're feeling it."

"Are they desperate?" asked Knox, looking at Marco with a seizing gaze.

Marco swallowed hard and paused. Something about Knox warned him that prudence might serve best. He held Knox's eyes and nodded.

"They're desperate."

"Boys," called out Knox, and waited for his men to gather around. "We've been picking coffee for a couple days and it's decent work, but it's not a life for us. We'd all like to go back to Hutch, back to our homes and families." Knox paused to look at Stephen and the Warwick brothers.

"Well, as far as I can tell," Knox continued after taking a deep breath. "There's no going back." He waited for the comment to register with the men. "At least not like it was before our little encounter with the Jola crew."

"No shit, Knox?" asked Hank. "What do you really want to say?"

Knox looked sharply at Hank. He was a trusted and reliable friend, but Knox knew Hank liked to be his own man. Following anyone was a bit of a struggle.

"What I'm really saying, Hank," continued Knox, "is that we owe Antonio for not ratting us out to the Federals. We owe him for letting us work his fields when he could have turned us away for being wanted men. We have a common problem, him and us. Sure, we arrived from different paths, but it's now us against the Federals."

"You want to break him out, don't you?" asked Will suddenly. He looked both worried and excited at the same moment.

Knox paused, looked at each of his men. "The least we can do is try to break him out," he replied. "Besides, the jail has more guns and ammunition, and I for one don't want to be running from the Federals without any bullets."

"What about the guards and the soldiers? What do we do about them?" Will's voice seemed a bit high for a grown man. He was always a nervous guy, thought Knox.

"If we have to, we can take care of them just like we took care of the others when they came looking in the Reserve. What else are we going to do? We're dead if they ever catch us. Adding Antonio's break-out to our file isn't going to make our sentences any worse."

"What are you getting us into, Knox?" asked Stephen. "We don't have that much connection with Antonio. I mean, I like him, he's a nice guy and I'm thankful for what he's done for us, but breaking him out of jail? How do we even do that?"

Knox shrugged but remained optimistic. "I'm trying to help out a friend," he said, "just like he would help us if the tables were turned. I'm sure we can free Antonio with a little help."

Knox's men looked at each other and shrugged in mild agreement. Only Will seemed especially anxious, but even he settled down as the others dropped their coffee sacks and began asking Marco questions about Amadica and its jail.

Overlooking the jail with their sixteen carefully chosen volunteers, both Knox and Marco thought their chances fairly good. "Remember to stay in the shadows," Knox whispered to the faceless men. Quick nods from the farmers and loggers signaled an almost impatient understanding, and in just seconds all the men silently flowed down the slope.

Machete blades reflected the moonlight whenever enough broke through the cloud cover. Several men carried rifles stolen from the Federals, and Hank carried his shotgun strapped across his back. Only Knox appeared unarmed, but everyone knew he carried the handgun beneath the thick folds of his jacket. Though well armed, the small party planned a silent operation where bullets would be exchanged only as a last resort. Vasquez's soldiers were simply too numerous for an open confrontation. Before asking for volunteers, Knox and Marco made it clear that machete work might be necessary. Several men declined the invitation to join after that remark.

The jail stood two blocks into Amadica's southeastern section. The men made their way quickly and silently past ramshackle homes with their sleeping occupants. They ignored the sudden whine of a disturbed dog and barely looked as a rooster suddenly squawked in agitation at the unexpected movement on the street. Knox looked back at the trailing men once and was impressed that they stayed under cover and moved silently across Amadica's thinly paved streets. In just a few minutes they reached the last building before the jail.

"That was the easy part," said Knox as he peered around the corner. The smoking guard exhaled one last great puff that shone briefly under the light of a battered lamp. He stretched and then stepped back inside the building. The door banged shut behind him.

"No lock!" observed Marco as he watched the guard enter. It had occurred to him that entering the building might pose a serious challenge, especially when silence was crucial.

"That's good," whispered Knox. He motioned to Leonard, Jonathan and Hank to prepare for the sprint across the open street. Hank quickly handed his shotgun to Felix, who then followed the other men as they took positions in adjoining streets to cover the rescue crew. Initially many more men wanted to enter the jail, but Marco and Knox insisted on a small party that could move quickly and keep silent. Leonard was chosen for his threatening mass, Jonathan because he seemed least hesitant about potential machete work, and Hank came simply because he insisted.

"One more set of hands to carry out the guns," Hank said with a smile. Knox finally gave in and accepted his demand to accompany them into the jail.

"Ok, here we go," said Knox, and gave Marco a little shove out into the street.

Marco took off running and never looked back. He heard boots pounding around him, and in what seemed only a second his hand fell upon the doorknob. In one quick motion he yanked open the door and burst inside the jailhouse. The others followed quickly, with Jonathan lightly pulling the door shut to avoid it banging against the jamb.

Two soldiers sat behind their respective desks facing each other. As soon as Marco entered, the younger one reached for his sidearm. Leonard immediately pounced on him. Papers and pens scattered and the desk groaned under Leonard's great weight. He wrapped a massive hand around the soldier's throat and squeezed firmly while pinning him back against the wall.

"I wouldn't, if I were you," he said quietly.

The soldier's eyes grew wide as Leonard gave the man's neck a suggestive squeeze. He let out a choked grunt and then moved his hand away from his holster.

"Better," said Leonard, and disarmed the soldier with his free hand.

LTC Ignacio Munoz sat on the other side of the room. So lost in thought about burying his father and mother, he barely reacted when the door burst open. He now sat up straight with sharpened machete edges pressed against his neck. Marco and Hank steadied their blades while Knox motioned for Munoz to keep quiet. Silence fell while Jonathan listened at the door for any commotion outside. Knox cleared his throat and addressed Munoz, who clearly outranked the other soldier.

"You will release Mr. Antonio Richards," he said quickly.

LTC Munoz cast his eyes quickly around the room and clenched his teeth. Expecting the blades to bite into his neck, he uttered a few words through tightened lips.

"Can't. I'll get court-martialed."

"No jokes," replied Knox, whispering fiercely. He looked quickly to Jonathan who listened intently at the door. "Court-martialed or not, you're going to open that cell. We've got no time for nonsense. Marco, hold his jaw shut."

Marco obediently holstered his machete and slipped behind the chair. He reached around Munoz's neck just above Hank's thick blade and locked his hands beneath Ignacio's chin. Knox grabbed Munoz's right hand and forced his index finger onto the desk.

"Now, Mr. Munoz," said Knox, reading Ignacio's name off his breast pocket. Knox was breathing hard from the excitement and was nearly panicked thinking about the time already spent in the jail. His mind screamed at him to hurry. "Jonathan over there is pretty good with a machete. I'm sure you would rather keep this finger than make him chop it off."

LTC Munoz made no sound. He looked defiantly at Knox.

"Jonathan, over here." He motioned to Jonathan to leave the door. "Chop off this man's finger. Is everything still ok over there, Leonard?"

Leonard grunted an affirmative as Jonathan stepped to the desk and drew his gleaming machete from his belt. He quickly raised it above his head.

"Last chance," said Knox. He motioned for Jonathan to wait a moment. Looking into Ignacio's eyes, wondering how far the man might go before breaking.

"No?" Knox said, surprised. "Hold tight, Marco."

Marco pulled hard on Munoz's head and locked his jaw tightly. He shut his eyes against the coming horror, having no doubt Jonathan would follow Knox's order. With a quick gesture from Knox, Jonathan's massive blade swept down and chunked heavily into the desk. Munoz jolted back and screamed through his teeth while Marco struggled to control him. In the commotion Hank's blade drew a neat line of blood across Munoz's neck. The LTC's eyes rolled wildly in his head and tears leaked from his eyes. Knox slapped his face twice, hard.

"You see now that we're not joking, Munoz. Next will be your hand. Release Antonio Richards."

"Keys," Ignacio squeezed from his locked jaw. Sweat poured from his forehead into his eyes and he squinted against its salty sting. "Pocket." He looked down at his finger lying on the desk in a bloody puddle. Again his eyes rolled and the color drained from his face.

Knox slapped him again and held up the LTC's mangled hand. Blood poured freely from the wound. "This could have been avoided," said Knox harshly.

Pawing roughly through Ignacio's pockets, Knox finally withdrew a set of keys and motioned to Marco to help the man from his chair. Hank kept his blade poised as the four walked across the room to the hallway leading to the cells.

"Jonathan, start gathering the guns," Knox ordered. "Leonard, bring that youngster with us. We've got to lock 'em both up."

Jonathan threw open a closet door. Twelve rifles stood neatly stacked adjacent to several ammunition boxes. While Jonathan moved into the closet, Leonard walked the young soldier backwards across the room.

"You'd think they'd lock this closet," said Jonathan nonchalantly. He began removing rifles and ammunition and stacking them near the door.

"They don't believe anyone's crazy enough to steal them," replied Leonard while roughly shoving the soldier.

Knox unlocked the hall door and threw the light switch. Long fluorescents snapped on with a buzz and everyone moved quickly down the hall in a tight mass. They stopped at the only occupied cell and looked in at Antonio lying curled on the floor.

"Want to leave?" Knox asked a stunned and groggy-eyed Antonio.

"Knox?" Antonio muttered in disbelief.

"The one and only," Knox said as he thrust a key into the lock and slammed back the bolt. Everyone moved into the cell while Knox helped Antonio stand.

"Gag them," Knox ordered, "and bind their hands to the bars so they can't make any mischief. Make sure Munoz can still reach his hand. No need for some dumb guard to bleed out." He passed the keys to Hank with instructions to lock the cell as they left.

While Hank, Leonard and Marco feverishly occupied themselves with preparing the Federals, Knox walked Antonio down the hallway and into the guardroom. Jonathan just finished stacking everything by the door as they appeared.

"Hey, Antonio!" Jonathan greeted him as warmly as an old friend. "It seems a lot of people want to see you freed."

Antonio quickly thanked them both. He turned to the desk where Ignacio's finger still lay in a pool of blood.

"At least you didn't kill them," said Antonio.

Knox nodded while strapping two rifles across his back. "That'll come later, Mr. Richards," he said formally. "You've got some kind of revolution on your hands now. There'll be lots of killing soon, I'm sure."

Leonard, Marco and Hank hurried into the room and quickly began strapping on weapons. Antonio insisted on helping carry a box of ammunition even while gritting his teeth against the pain still lingering in his gut. With a quick peek outside, Hank motioned for everyone to leave and held the door as they all filed out. Antonio followed Knox and Marco, who took the lead and sprinted down a side street. Armed, shadowy figures closed in on both sides of the running men and escorted them through Amadica and up into Mt. Tabor's densely forested slopes.

Nine

Antonio watched with grim certainty as a thick cloud of gray smoke materialized from beneath the forest canopy. It billowed into the late-afternoon sky, contrasting sharply with Mt. Tabor's luxuriant slopes. Marco and Knox stood at his side quietly watching the spectacle. It came from one place, one home. Though heavily shrouded in green vegetation, they knew the fire burned in the hollow in which Antonio lived, once lived, with many other farmers.

"They won't burn the other homes, will they?" asked Marco, and cast a quick look at the men scattered behind them at the mouth of a cave. All of Knox's men, in addition to Leonard, Felix, José and about a dozen coffee farmers now rested in the little-known caverns on the slopes near Mt. Tabor's peak. Antonio remembered coming to these caves as a child and being dared to enter their dark openings.

Antonio shook his head doubtfully. "Just mine," he sighed, wistfully considering how quickly his few possessions disappeared. He patted the Link, comfortably nestled in a pouch on his belt. "The Federals will assume that's a sufficient deterrent."

"It's enough to make a person think twice about joining us, that's for sure," said Knox. He coughed hard and spat down the steep slope.

"You're sure your mother will be fine?" asked Marco with a worried tone. He considered Rene almost as a second mother.

Antonio recalled the rush up the mountain in the dead of night. The clouds had thankfully disappeared and allowed late moonlight to filter through the forest and illuminate their circuitous route. Pre-dawn's lifeless melancholy cloaked the hollow by the time they reached Antonio's home. In the weak light of the day in which he expected death, Antonio bid his neighbors and rescuers thanks, and told them to return to their families and to expect word. Rene, already awake and dressed, stepped out onto the porch as the men filtered away.

"Mother," Antonio began, abruptly realizing how close he came to never seeing her again. He wanted to tell her about his fear, his anger, but time pushed, and Knox shuffled anxiously. "Mother, the Federals will be here looking for me sometime today. You need to go to Mary's home. They'll look after you."

Rene held her son with a long and pained look. She saw him return home with Victor's cold body wrapped in a muddy blue tarp. She witnessed his innocence drain away that afternoon as he emerged naked from the massive black truck. Not a drop of innocence remains, she thought sadly.

"You've done something to upset the Federals?" she asked.

Antonio nodded. "It's something big, Mother. It's mostly about certificates, but also about Papa's sickness in a way."

Rene placed her aging hands upon her hips and carefully gazed at the passing men. Many of those planning to follow Antonio up into the wild had two rifles strapped across their backs. She tapped a box of stolen ammunition with her foot.

"This is a big fight?" she asked.

Antonio tried considering how large a movement he ignited. In a matter of only weeks he had somehow moved from anonymous farmer to Salavandra's most wanted man, next to Christopher Knox. Now they worked together for some yet undetermined end, but certainly something greater than a simple certificate exchange rate increase.

"Yes, Mother. I'm afraid it is a big fight," Antonio said softly. "This will shatter lives."

He watched as Rene turned to face the only home she knew since being married. It stood plain but in good repair and looked much like the other dwellings in the hollow.

"They burn homes, you know."

"Yes, Mother. They have ever since I can remember."

Antonio watched the back of his mother's head hold steady. She considered the lifetime spent coddled inside its thin walls and recalled the first few nights with Victor under their new roof so many years ago. She thought of Antonio's birth, assisted with a midwife who hiked up from Amadica two days before the delivery. She considered the innumerable coffee workers eating and drinking the food she prepared.

"Such memories in this place," she muttered while shaking her head. "It'll be gone today." She turned on Antonio with a determined and hard look in her glistening eyes.

"This fight, is it just?"

Antonio did not hesitate. "Yes, Mother."

"Then Papa would approve. Have your men bring my clothing, blankets and my pots over to Mary's. Take whatever else you need." Without looking back she stepped off the porch and marched down the road towards the Gonzalez's home. She refused to look at Antonio as she passed.

Mary appeared from the other direction just as Rene marched off. Still sleepy-eyed and with disheveled hair, she stopped several feet from Antonio and stood staring in disbelief. Antonio rushed over to her as the men entered his home and began picking through its contents. He nearly crushed her in a hug.

"There's no time, Mary. I thought I'd never see you again. I have to leave. The Federals are coming for me." His words rushed out in a panic as Knox motioned for him to hurry. He pulled away and looked deeply into her eyes.

"They're still red and irritated. Are you using the eye drops?"

Mary could not speak. She could hardly believe Antonio stood in front of her and it broke her heart all over again that he had to leave immediately. Sadder yet was him mistaking the swelling in her eyes being caused by the greenhouse pesticides. She blinked away her tears and pressed her head sadly against his chest. A sleepless and sobbing night, endless work hours and Phillip's raking abuse strained her resolve to breaking.

"Mary, Mary," Antonio whispered as the footsteps of men began pounding up the road in a desperate hurry to leave the hollow. "This will all be over some day. I'm afraid I'll miss Valentine's Day, but know that I love you. I'll see you when it's safe, whenever I can."

He released her at Knox's prodding and without looking back ran up the road. Fatigue and fear blended mercilessly and his heart pleaded for more time with her. Antonio choked back his emotions and concentrated only on escaping the coming pursuit.

"I'm sure she'll be fine," Antonio said to Marco, swallowing hard against his painful memories. "Mary's father is gruff, but he understands. I've sent word to my uncle in Jola. He'll help if he can."

A distant series of explosions suddenly echoed up the mountain as the gray cloud boiling up from his home turned a shade darker. Antonio looked at Knox who smiled, despite watching Antonio's home transform into a smoking ruin.

"One of your surprises, Knox?" asked Antonio curiously. The logger nodded, quite pleased with himself. Several men lounging against the hillside stepped to the ridge and looked expectantly towards the blasts.

"It seems some of those pesticides don't like heat too much." He chuckled at his own cleverness. "I just hope the shrapnel got a few Federals."

Later, while inside the largest cave, Antonio took stock of the donated supplies gleaned from various neighbors' homes. Not much, he considered strategically, but certainly enough for a few weeks of hard living. Bags of flour, beans and rice comprised the bulk of food along with a precious few pounds of bacon wrapped tightly in salted and wax-smeared burlap. Several large containers of water, lugged up the mountain mostly by Leonard, stood neatly alongside the food supplies. Ammunition and weapons lined a side wall with Hank's shotgun looking quite feeble next to the larger and more powerful assault rifles. Exhausted men slept heavily amongst the gear in a snoring bedlam while scattered lamps cast weak yellow light across the walls.

"What have I begun here," muttered Antonio. He gazed down the length of the gently sloping cavern. It stretched nearly forty feet straight back into the mountain and eventually narrowed with the ceiling dropping to the floor. The cave's size and dry interior made an ideal hideout from which he could observe vast portions of Mt. Tabor. The mountain peak, of course, situated one hundred feet above him, made the best lookout. José now stood somewhere up there, carefully watching the mountain road for any sign of movement.

He sat heavily on a rocky protrusion curiously shaped like a stool and leaned against the wall. Exhaustion swept over him. The sprint up Mt. Tabor had stretched through the day as everyone hustled supplies and weapons into the caves. The men dropped quickly into sleep after storing everything, and now that the sun began sinking Antonio also felt fatigue dragging him to the ground. He rested his head against the wall and quickly blinked away his doubling vision in an effort to stay awake. There was too much to worry about, too much to consider. He squinted and noticed a curious scratching marring the surface of the far wall.

Phillip was here.

Antonio dismissed the markings as his mind moved towards more pressing matters. Thoughts of a broad plan of action, of a focused direction to his movement and how to organize the men into a disciplined force raced through his mind. Too many variables and too many possible outcomes, he thought, and desperately wished for some epiphany that might clarify his role and the role of his men. After an hour of considering this whirlwind of issues, he finally dropped into a heavy slumber while still sitting on his rocky stool. Just then Marco stepped into the cave after conferring with Knox.

"Daniel's probably not asleep anyway," Knox had grumbled, "and José must be as tired as the rest of us." He stomped off to another, smaller cavern to find Daniel Warwick and send him up the mountain to relieve José.

Marco found a blanket and laid it carefully across Antonio's lap. He hoped Antonio would sleep well into the night and regain the strength lost while in jail. The men need you, Marco thought anxiously, reflecting on the entwined events leading him to this moment. It hardly seemed possible that instead of picking coffee, he stood atop Mt. Tabor hiding from Salavandra's Federals while fussing over his boss. He found his own blankets and spread them out on the dusty floor next to Antonio. He drifted off while daring to think about owning his own plot of land and harvesting his own coffee.

"I'm telling you, we need to lay out what we're doing up here," said Hank with considerable animation. He stood in the morning sunshine just outside the main cave where Antonio and most other men had slept. Daniel Warwick, true to his insomnia, kept watch through the entire night and let everyone sleep. He snoozed lightly now in one of the smaller fissures away from the crowd of talking men.

"Staying alive," replied Will quickly. "I'm keeping a bullet out of my skull, if you ask me." A few nervous chuckles rippled through the small gathering.

"It's more than that," replied Leonard. Antonio noticed his towering neighbor becoming more vocal as his role expanded within the group. Men now looked to Leonard for direction, after himself and Knox.

"I didn't leave the rest of this year's harvest to rot on the trees for nothing," Leonard continued. "I want some change on Salavandra, beginning with how we get paid."

"But Penkava's got a lock on our coffee," said Felix soberly. His dark mood hung over him like a cloud since Craig's death and hasty burial. Antonio lamented that virtually no grieving time had passed. He knew Felix suffered sharply for his friend.

"Your coffee and our lumber," said Stephen. He stood next to Logan and passed him a water canteen. The two men were almost as tight as the Warwick brothers. Jonathan Warwick sat quietly off to the side of the cave with Diego.

"Those of us who didn't actually enter the jail can go back home," said Felix. "That is, if we want to go home. Leonard and Marco, along with Knox and all your men, of course, have to stay out of sight. The two guards probably identified you all by now."

"Should have killed them," called Jonathan from behind the crowd. A few affirmative grunts rippled through the men. "Just one word, Knox. It would have been real quiet."

Knox shrugged. "I just wanted to release Antonio. Who can tell if they deserved to die?"

"They're Federals," replied Jonathan. "Isn't that enough?"

"Knox is right," called out Antonio loudly. He did not want the men, *his* men as he now thought of the lot, thinking they carried licenses to kill. He knew that the assault rifles stacked in the cave probably suggested something different, and also realized that convincing Knox's men to follow orders might be especially challenging.

"There'll be no random killings or mayhem, no matter who you are," Antonio continued. He looked at Jonathan firmly and held his eyes for a moment. Off to the side he caught sight of Knox's head nodding and breathed a sigh of relief. The last thing Antonio wanted was a power struggle in a group not yet fully cohesive, and holding objectives no greater than staying away from the Federals.

"Hank's right, too," said Antonio. "Today we'll formalize what we're doing. After all, Vasquez and his Federals are no doubt painting us as criminals. We need to counter that so we have the support of the people. Nobody's going to give food and supplies to a band of murderers and crooks.

"Penkava's lock on our coffee and lumber is our main grievance. Let's not forget about the flowers, too. Many of you, including myself, know women who work in the greenhouses." Antonio thought of Mary's swollen and irritated eyes and how she always seemed ready to cry when returning from work.

"So we should kick Penkava off Salavandra," said Felix.

Antonio shook his head. "Without Penkava we have no way to trade our goods. What we need is some competition. The problem is, the Company has a lock on the entire island. Salavandra is controlled by just one firm."

"So if other firms bought our lumber and your coffee," said Hank cautiously, feeling his way through Antonio's argument, "then we'd play one off the other and get better prices."

Antonio nodded. "Provided the buyers never decided to work together to keep certificate rates low. Or, in the case of logging, the hourly rates you're paid."

"Vasquez will never allow that," spat Will. "He's too close with Penkava."

Antonio nodded again. He struggled for hours with this very problem while hiking up the mountain. Penkava would never agree to more competition, and Vasquez would make sure none arrived on Salavandra. Penetrating and reforming that relationship seemed an insurmountable task.

"That's why we have to get rid of Vasquez," said Knox suddenly. He gripped his belt tightly and cast hard looks at the men, daring them to suggest something different. "He's terrorized Salavandra too long."

"His Federals are nothing but murderers," cried Felix. "Craig died from their bullets and nobody's ever going to pay if we don't do something."

Loud voices of approval rippled through the crowd. Craig's popularity, even after his death, resonated with the farmers. They all suffered his absence.

"The disappearances, the beatings, the house burnings, I'm sick of it all," continued Felix. His passionate rant boiled over with the pain of Craig's death. "It's like Salavandra's not even our island. I think Vasquez is the biggest problem."

Many men loudly agreed with Felix and suddenly everyone seemed to speak at once. Every man had at least one personal anecdote about

Vasquez terrorizing Salavandra in some manner, mostly with his Federals running the island like their own personal property. After nearly an hour of arguing about necessary changes and vilifying Penkava and Vasquez, Antonio finally held up his hands for quiet.

"We are going in circles here, my friends," he called out while standing atop a boulder. Above their heads a clear view down Mt. Tabor's lush slopes revealed an island rich in resources and ripe for change. He could just make out the sparkling Caribbean to the northeast. An inspirational view, Antonio thought, and good for a beginning.

"As far as I can tell, Salavandra needs three major changes. First, we need truly free elections. Everyone knows Vasquez rigs the ballots so there is no way anyone else can ever win. Second, we need some guarantees of our rights. No more beatings, no more disappearances. Last, Penkava Incorporated must release its exclusive control over Salavandra."

His voice carried loudly through to the last syllable and then he paused to take a deep breath and watch his words take hold. Leonard was the first to nod in agreement, then Hank and several of Antonio's neighbors. Soon another wave of discussion erupted, this one centered on Antonio's three objectives.

"To accomplish these changes," Antonio yelled, still standing on the boulder overlooking the men, "there will have to be sacrifices. You've all shown your willingness to work for a cause. I worry about the rest of Salavandra's people, though. I wonder if they're ready for such a challenge."

"The coffee farmers are behind you," said Leonard. "Don't forget about the mill standoff and the fire."

"The loggers too," said Stephen firmly. "We need some big changes, not just with the Jola Reserve but also with getting work on the slopes of Mt. Lucinda." He thought of his sons Carlos and Vicente and how they could inherit a free island rather than the oppressed one they now endured. Knox's men all agreed and even Diego voiced his approval.

"Farmers and loggers," said Antonio thoughtfully. "That leaves one last major group of workers, the flower growers." After a moment of thought and a wish that Mary stood at his side, he lifted his chin and announced, "I'll speak for them. They need change too, even if nobody's here to say so. They have no voice yet, but I know they sorely need one."

"So we'll form a united front against Vasquez and Penkava," said Will excitedly.

"A united front for change," agreed another man, one of Antonio's more distant neighbors.

"More than just change, it's a united front for our liberation," cried out Leonard. "For too long we've been under the yoke of Vasquez and Penkava." Antonio looked in surprise as the towering and normally reserved man forgot his characteristic detachment and joined the crowd's growing enthusiasm.

"Then we'll call ourselves the United Front for the Liberation of Salavandra," yelled Antonio. He threw open his arms as if embracing the island and men. "Vasquez, Penkava and the world will know us as the UFLS."

The men began chanting UFLS. Antonio felt at once pleased and apprehensive. Finally, after a lifetime of hardship capped by a few turbulent weeks there existed some hope for change on Salavandra. He privately wondered if he measured up to the task ahead.

"We must organize a chain of command," Antonio yelled above the excited men. They settled and listened attentively. "I need you, Christopher Knox, and you, Leonard Sherman, in charge of organizing the men. You two will be my field commanders. What do you say?"

Quick acceptance nods followed and Antonio breathed a little easier seeing the men rally around Knox and Leonard. They seemed the most natural choices, Antonio thought, and recalled making the decision last night before falling asleep. Knox already directed the loggers and a small portion of coffee farmers, and Leonard had quickly grown into a powerful leadership role. Together, the two would command the respect and activities of the men, while Antonio concentrated on steering the UFLS towards accomplishing its three main objectives.

Felix hurried down the mountain with the late afternoon sun high above Mt. Tabor. Deliberately rushing, he stumbled several times on the steeply sloped road and cursed as an ankle twisted on a protruding stone. In addition to a head full of instructions, he gripped a formal letter signed by Antonio, as well as a thick stack of paper torn from a notebook that once held Rene's correspondence. The papers numbered nearly one hundred sheets and carried an identical, simple message neatly scrawled across the yellow pages.

As he picked his way quickly down the curving road Felix recalled Antonio, Knox and Leonard calling him into the cave following the morning's gathering. After a brief explanation, the three men appointed him the task of spreading the word about the UFLS and delivering a letter for President Vasquez.

Craig haunted him with each step down the mountain. He kept envisioning smoke lightly puffing from the two rifles, followed by his best friend slumping lifelessly to the ground covered in dust and blood. Telling Eric had forced Felix to relive the nightmare, and now Eric's anguished face appeared often in the reflected sunlight as it scattered off rocks cast alongside the road.

Several hours later when a cheerless dusk settled over the island Felix finally made out his home's familiar shape nestled within a smartly trimmed grove. A picturesque sight, he admitted, a cozy place even in these uncertain times. Intending to rest before continuing his trek to Amadica, he picked up the pace and soon pushed open his front door. His wife Paulina threw herself into his arms the moment he stepped inside.

"Oh Felix," she said breathlessly while squeezing him tightly. "I'm so glad you're safe. The Federals were here, were everywhere, questioning and pushing us around. I thought they might find you."

Felix comforted and soothed his wife. "As far as they know, I'm innocent. They have nothing on me."

Paulina pulled away but still clung to his shoulders. She looked into his eyes with firm resolve, yet Felix saw fear. "Innocent or not," she said carefully, "they do not care. They assume everyone knows something." With a quick nod she directed him to the bedroom where low voices conversed in the dim light.

"Eric was here when the Federals arrived," she said in a low voice. "I was just leaving to fetch his mother. I don't know if she can take any more."

Felix gently detached himself and stepped to the room's threshold. Eric lay on the bed clutching a damp rag across his forehead. A dark red smear stained the cloth and one of his eyes looked angry and swollen. Rosemary knelt at the bed and hung her head as Felix stepped into the room.

"Anything broken?" asked Felix as he tenderly grasped Rosemary's shoulder and gave it a supportive squeeze.

Eric shook his head. "Just a little roughing-up. No worse than a bar brawl. The cut on my forehead will be ugly for the next week."

Felix nudged Eric's hand and carefully lifted the rag. A deeply bruised gash sutured with familiar black thread marked the left side of his forehead. A honeycombed pattern imprinted one side of the wound, and Felix pictured the laced pattern of a rifle butt.

"No more bleeding. Neat stitches. Must be your work." He turned and smiled supportively at Paulina who stood behind him.

"Well, I've stitched you up enough to know how to do it right," Paulina replied. She shook her head though, unable to make light of the situation. "They'll have no mercy when they catch him, Felix," she said nervously. "They'll kill Antonio immediately. I've never seen the Federals so aggressive."

Felix imagined the humiliation they experienced when discovering that their sole prisoner escaped along with a large collection of weapons and ammunition. "I'm afraid that things are going to get harder before they get easier." From the inside of his jacket he pulled out the stack of papers and passed one around. "I'm posting these in Amadica tonight," he said heavily. "Tomorrow I'll deliver a formal letter from Antonio to President Vasquez. We've formed a group to liberate the island."

"The UFLS?" said Rosemary as the paper crinkled lightly in her hands. She read aloud the three demands listed below the title.

Felix nodded. "The United Front for the Liberation of Salavandra. We're now organized and demanding three main areas of change. We're hopeful, but we don't really believe the Federals will take us seriously. Still, we must try to negotiate first."

"First?" asked Eric, sitting up on the bed and gripping the paper tightly.

"Plans are being formulated as we speak for additional and more convincing means of persuasion," replied Felix. "That's all I've been told. If Vasquez counters with the Federals, there'll be some real fighting."

Eric handed the paper back to Felix and stood quickly. "I'm helping you," he announced while gripping the bedpost. With his free hand he lifted Rosemary from her position next to the bed.

Felix nodded once and patted Eric on the shoulder. "Your father would be proud," he said firmly. "Now let's all eat something while I rest a little. Are you able to make it to Amadica tonight, Eric?"

Eric nodded firmly and stepped away from the bed. He placed a comforting arm around Rosemary as she stifled a sob and whispered something in his ear. Everyone moved into the kitchen for a fast meal and to listen to Felix's account of the day's events atop Mt. Tabor.

Later that night, bundled against the evening's chill, Felix and Eric bid the women goodbye and set off down the mountain towards town. Felix told Paulina to tell the neighbors about the movement and handed her ten yellow papers before kissing her goodbye. Word would spread quickly and in a day most farmers would know about the UFLS. In a week, he hoped, all of Salavandra would rally behind the movement.

The full moon cast a cold, hard light on the broken road as they walked quickly towards Amadica. Felix could not recall a time when he felt so uncomfortable being outside after dark. Though familiar sounds echoed throughout the forest and the brisk smells of clean air and leafy vegetation permeated each breath, he still felt an uncomfortable and oppressive sensation. When he commented, Eric seemed not to notice.

"They didn't listen, even when I tried to answer them," Eric said after a short period of silence. Felix thought the steady crunching of their boots across the rock-strewn ground was too loud. "As soon as they realized I didn't know anything, pow, they cracked me in the face with their rifles."

"They're not interested in listening," replied Felix. "They just follow orders."

"So I can say that Vasquez ordered them to do this to me?" asked Eric. He pointed to the stitches running across his forehead.

Felix replied, "Federals may have actually committed the act, but President Vasquez is ultimately responsible. Don't get me wrong, most of the Federals should be jailed, but President Vasquez should get the worst punishment."

"Then I hope the UFLS makes some changes."

The sound of a grinding engine suddenly reverberated throughout the forest, followed by the low whine of a diesel truck struggling uphill. Pushed ever higher by the driver's loud curses, a military flatbed rounded the last bend in the road before Amadica. On the back, a tight cluster of soldiers leaned against the railing and peered out into the night.

"Down the hill, quick," Felix whispered and dove into the forest. Eric followed and found himself nearly tumbling down a steep incline following Felix's fleeting shadow. They came to rest a few feet from each other, clutching a tree's outspread braches in a flailing attempt to stop their descent.

"I thought you had nothing to worry about," whispered Eric once they caught their breath. On the road far above them they heard the large truck struggling to gain traction on the steep incline.

"It's true, they've got nothing on me so I shouldn't have to hide. But I'm in no mood for Paulina to stitch me up just in case they don't feel like listening."

They both watched in silence as headlights pierced the darkness and the big truck slowly moved up the mountain. Neither ducked, confident that the heavy foliage adequately shrouded them in darkness.

"I think a few are smokers," said Eric as the truck passed. "I saw cigarette embers glowing in the darkness."

"Craig always said you had the sharpest eyes," said Felix. He instantly regretted mentioning Craig in front of his son. The young man cast his eyes somberly toward the ground.

"Hey," said Felix, and took hold of Eric's shoulder with his free hand. "You know your dad and I were best friends. I consider you the son I never had, Eric. Those bastards up there, they're the reason we're down here right now. They're the reason why the UFLS even exists. They need to answer for their crimes and for your father's death. I know Craig wouldn't want you doing anything other than what you're doing right now."

"I miss him," whispered Eric, stifling a sob. "He could get so mad, but he was all bark and never laid a hand on us. What the hell got into him that he threw a rock?" He looked at Felix with wet, shimmering eyes that glistened in the moon's white light. Felix suddenly remembered seeing Eric as a toddler and then as a teenager courting Rosemary. He recalled Craig's happy, boisterous laugh when realizing that some day he and Felix would be related.

"He got fed up, Son," Felix whispered coarsely and swallowed his own choking pain. "Come on, we've got work to do." He struggled back up to the road well ahead of Eric.

Amadica's quiet streets appeared foreign and threatening as midnight approached. Deep shadows cast about the little homes and the occasional light burned dimly behind curtained windows as the occupants prepared for bed. A disconcerting and opaque silence encapsulated Amadica's deserted main road as it flowed towards Saint Matthew and Jola. Frozen in time, thought Felix, and motioned Eric to follow him towards the far northeastern part of town.

"We'll start at the edge of town away from the jail and barracks," he whispered, and handed Eric half of the yellow papers. "Slip them onto people's doorsteps and windows, so they'll get noticed. Stay out of sight." Eric vanished into the shadows across the street, intent on working fast and staying quiet.

A minute later Felix gripped his stack of paper and made for the first house. As he stepped up to the small concrete home Felix thought it looked more like a square cement block than a house. He delicately curled a single yellow sheet between the doorknob and jamb. Lightly stepping away and casting a quick glance back, he briefly considered the irony of a single sheet of cheap yellow paper creating the biggest event witnessed on Salavandra since the British left.

"Say hello to the UFLS, neighbors," Felix whispered and quickly ducked over to the next home.

They made steady progress towards Amadica's southeastern section as the small hours passed. Each home presented new challenges, from avoiding anything that might make noise to situating the paper in an appropriately visible area. As they neared the jail and barracks, Felix motioned Eric to keep out of sight and pointed to the single guard posted outside.

"I'd rather not have him see us until morning," he whispered.

Eric nodded and scampered off across a side street staying within the cover of darkness. Felix remembered Antonio's rescue when he too ducked carefully beneath the heavy shadows of the narrower lanes. He's fitting right in, Felix thought with a hint of sadness. Craig would indeed be proud.

The rising sun and growing noise of morning found them nestled in a wooded depression just outside town. After finishing their deliveries the two had ducked off into the woods for a much needed nap before completing their final task. Felix fretted about delivering Antonio's letter and picked nervously at the stale bread that Paulina packed for him the night before. What if they shoot me, he privately worried while watching Eric. What will the bullet feel like crashing into my skull?

"You're only a messenger to them," assured Antonio before Felix left Mt. Tabor's caves the previous day. "In this game both sides need communication. The Federals will let you return, I am certain."

Recalling Antonio's confident tone did little to settle Felix's stomach. He felt the crinkled letter, pressed lightly against his chest, for what seemed the hundredth time. He listened when Antonio had read it aloud and asked for comments before signing his name. This message for President Vasquez would fall like a hammer, Felix thought, and suddenly the thin and insubstantial paper felt quite heavy.

"It's Valentine's Day," said Eric, rubbing his sleep-filled eyes. "I'm supposed to do something special for Rosemary."

His tone indicated that he forgot Valentine's Day was even coming. Felix considered the tumultuous time Eric just lived through and assured him that Rosemary would understand. "Besides," he continued, "you coming home after what we've accomplished here should be special enough."

They walked back through town and blended into Amadica's early-morning hustle. A few vehicles roared by on the road to Saint Matthew. Many people opened their doors to let the fresh air inside and Felix saw several holding their yellow paper and carefully looking around as they struggled with the writing. Many will not be able to read this, Antonio said yesterday as he handed over the stack of papers, but those who can, will spread the word.

Leaving Eric sitting on a curb within clear sight of the jail, Felix stiffened his back and walked quickly across the street. The guard at the door watched him with an air of detached wariness that made Felix's palms sweat. Unsuccessfully willing his heart to stop pounding, he approached the guard and asked for his commander. Without speaking, the guard looked him over as if weighing a potential threat. Finally he thrust his head towards the door.

"Colonel Munoz, inside," growled the guard, and turned back toward the street.

The door banged shut as Felix stepped into the room. He swallowed his nervousness and recalled his excitement while watching Marco lead the rescue party into this very building only a few nights ago.

"What do you want?" asked a big man sitting behind a desk. He shuffled some papers and tossed a bound stack across the room to a second, unoccupied desk.

Felix approached the large man and cleared his throat. He read Munoz's name clearly off his shirt and suddenly remembered the subtle talk of machete work and a missing finger. A thick, fresh notch marred the desk's edge.

"Well, speak up, I don't have all day."

"I have a letter," began Felix, slowly at first but feeling his strength building. "It's for President Vasquez from Antonio Richards."

Colonel Munoz froze. His mind's eye saw the machete drop again. He felt the searing pain of a lost digit and the humiliation of being discovered bound, gagged and locked in a cell sitting in a pool of his own blood. He expected dismissal following his release. Instead, a promotion message appeared on the barrack's Link the following day. President Vasquez personally thanked him for his gallant effort not to release Antonio, even at the cost of sacrificing a finger. Now, on this first full day on the job, Antonio again haunted him. Sighing, he slowly reached out his heavily bandaged hand and carefully grasped the letter from Felix's outstretched palm.

"Sit, please," he motioned Felix to a chair and opened the neatly folded paper.

Felix watched Colonel Munoz mull over the letter. The brief message explained the UFLS objectives and invited President Vasquez to open discussions regarding Salavandra's future political and economic organization. Felix thought he could read the entire letter in less than a minute, but sat watching Munoz re-read it while taking time to pause thoughtfully and gaze up at the ceiling. He dared not interrupt him, so continued sitting while quietly hoping Eric did not get too worried about the passage of time. Finally Colonel Munoz looked at him.

"This letter is serious?" he asked Felix.

Felix nodded. "Yes, Sir."

"This is unfortunate, Mr…?"

"Ramirez."

"Mr. Ramirez, I will pass this letter along but I must tell you that I've been instructed by the president himself to find and kill Mr. Richards. President Vasquez is in no mood to discuss anything."

"Kill him?" asked Felix softly.

Colonel Munoz nodded and sighed again. He leaned back in his chair. "I remember being in school with him for a short time," said the Colonel. "This is such a strange turn of events." He drifted briefly to his childhood and the school where he learned some math and science while sitting in a multi-grade room. Antonio, a few years younger, sat and squirmed like any other little kid.

"I was once a coffee man like Richards," said Munoz.

"Should I take a message back?" asked Felix hopefully. He worried that Munoz's apparent stalling was some trick to keep him in the jail.

Munoz looked at him quickly as if he forgot he even existed and abruptly sat up in his chair. It creaked loudly under his muscular frame. He shrugged once.

"You may tell Mr. Richards and his United...," he paused and checked the letter to make certain he read it correctly. "Tell him and his UFLS that there is no deal, no discussions, and that he's a wanted criminal. I'll be coming for him. Remind him that Salavandra is a small island."

Felix stood immediately. He left the jail feeling at once elated at still being free and alive, but incredibly anxious about the Colonel's message. Fatigue washed over him as he left the building and neared Eric who still sat on the curb trying to look bored and unobservant.

"What happened?" Eric asked as he stood and began walking out of town with Felix.

Felix shook his head. "It doesn't look good."

As Felix and Eric made their way back up the mountain, Antonio turned on his Link and surfed to the various sites where he posted messages the previous evening. Writing about Salavandra's struggle was easier now that he led an organized movement. Though lacking a formal title, he made it clear that he piloted the infant UFLS as it demanded recognition from President Vasquez and Penkava Incorporated. He grew more excited as he scrolled through the message boards. Many people read his postings and typed responses ranging from complete dismissal to offers for arms shipments. One touch away from the Penkava Incorporated stock page, he paused to consider the impact of his Link activity.

"The world is learning about us," he said, leaning against a rock while the cool wind whipped through his hair. Marco crouched next to him sipping coffee and waiting his turn to replace José as lookout. Antonio held up the Link for him to see.

"That, my friend, means over a thousand people read my posting about the UFLS. It's one of nearly a dozen sites where our message is posted."

"That's good," replied Marco dryly. "I hope it makes a difference."

"Cheer up, Marco," said Antonio, seeing his older companion's worried face. "Let's see what's going on with Penkava's stock."

In addition to an already negative opening for the New York markets, Penkava Incorporated's stock weakened significantly under the pressure of Antonio's message. Its ticker was listed in bright red letters on the Link's screen. Losses already topped over five percent and the markets just recently opened. Antonio smiled at the Link and held it up for Marco to see.

"What'd I tell you?" he declared enthusiastically. "Nobody wants to buy stock in a company that acts like a tyrant. Phillip himself will climb this mountain with an offer. Then we'll get Vasquez to the table and real changes will begin."

He scrolled down the screen to access other data and saw listings for various news releases. The first one, posted less than an hour ago from Penkava's Public Relations department, denied any validity to the myriad of rumors circulating on the message boards. The UFLS did not even exist, according to Penkava Incorporated. The news release also confirmed an announcement from Salavandra's government that Antonio Richards was a common criminal wanted for escaping custody and mutilating an officer of the law. Ignacio Munoz's bloody hand flashed through Antonio's mind. He tapped over to the Company's public message board and began composing a response.

In twenty minutes, after re-reading the message a couple of times, he turned to Marco who now stood a few feet away gazing down the mountain towards Amadica. "Marco," Antonio called, feeling the wind pull the words from his mouth, "stand over there with this." He handed Marco the Link. "Face the screen towards me and when I say so, push this button." He pointed to the button that could take snapshots.

Marco carefully propped his coffee cup between two stones and hefted the Link. He did as Antonio asked, a little awkwardly at first, and took several pictures.

Moments later Antonio deleted all but one image. "I look best in the one with the rifle," he said with a wry grin. "It says I'm serious, but my eyes are compassionate and dedicated to our cause. It says all that and more. This is the one I'll post with my message."

He tapped out a few commands so quickly that Marco, who watched curiously over his shoulder, immediately lost track of the movements. Antonio noticed and deliberately slowed his tapping and carefully illustrated the various steps. "You get fast after a little practice," he explained, and designated eleven separate Link sites as message recipients.

"The Company can wipe out any message posted beneath their own stock listing," he explained to Marco, "but it can't erase postings on other sites. I figured that out yesterday evening." With a single tap from the stylus he beamed the message and his picture up to the orbiting satellites.

"Now we'll see what happens," he mumbled, and scrolled back up to the Company's stock listing.

Penkava Incorporated's five percent loss held steady for just over one feverish minute. Antonio imagined the tens of thousands of people opening his message, seeing the photo and immediately placing sell orders. A half point drop suddenly showed on the screen followed immediately by another half point drop. Now down a total of six percent, the losses triggered additional selling until free-fall values flashed across the Link. In five minutes a twelve percent loss registered before the stock finally stabilized. Even Marco cheered up at the sight.

"I guess the Link really does have an impact," he said, wide-eyed and shaking his head.

"It's an information struggle too," replied Antonio. "In some ways it's more powerful than the bullets in this rifle."

Panic surged through Penkava's Public Relations department. All the senior executives recalled numerous information battles fought over the years, but none with weight enough to trounce the stock's price so soundly. A loud roar erupted across the department as Antonio's message and photo appeared on monitors all over the office.

Contrary to the messages posted by Penkava Incorporated and confirmed by my own country's corrupt government, the United Front for the Liberation of Salavandra does indeed exist and is positioning itself to change the island. I, Antonio Richards, wrongly arrested by President Vasquez for speaking out against the unfair labor practices of Penkava Incorporated, am now free and struggling to reform my small country. Posted below are the three agenda items the UFLS wants to discuss with the President or those who represent his office.

Free and fair elections
Guarantees for our basic human rights
Penkava Inc. releasing its monopolistic control on Salavandra

"How am I?" yelled Tom Penkava into his desktop monitor. "The Company's hemorrhaging value by the second, Bill." He sat at his desk with a forgotten cup of coffee and a half-eaten croissant sitting on trim blue china. The Link's stock alert monitor interrupted his otherwise pleasant morning. His heart jumped painfully when he saw the flashing red numbers.

Senator Bill Wilson appeared on the screen looking concerned. He glanced at his own monitor and saw the stock value while quickly reading over Antonio's message.

"I've never heard of Antonio Richards or the UFLS, Tom. Where did this come from?"

"He's the farmer that's been giving Phillip a headache about coffee prices. He gave us a scare the other day but we took care of the problem. It seems he's learning how to scoot around our efforts to shut him up. And now there's this UFLS crap. Vasquez must have his hands full."

"Is Phillip on this?"

"I've been trying to get him on the line but he isn't responding."

"What about Vasquez? Have you talked to him?"

Tom shook his head. "Not since yesterday. I just discovered the stock losses a minute ago. I'm still recovering from the shock."

"Well maybe this will cheer you up," Bill replied. "Supplies for Vasquez are being flown out of New Orleans as we speak. They should arrive in less than two hours."

"Flown? That's good."

"Like I said to Phillip, it's the least I can do. Besides, a boat would take too long, and from the look of this message, the faster this stuff gets there, the better. President Vasquez was most appreciative when I told him what we're sending."

"What is it?"

"The standard heavy trucks and field equipment. There's also new satellite communications to coordinate ground forces. I even managed to include two choppers under the Anti-Terrorism Act. They're already in the air."

Tom nodded and felt his anger subsiding. "You're a good friend, Bill."

"If things keep heating up, especially with this UFLS, I may be able to send a few advisors down there too. We'll have to wait and watch for developments."

Tom nodded and sipped the now tepid brew. He grimaced at the flavor and set the cup aside in disgust. "Damn coffee never stays fresh long enough. Let's hope it doesn't come to that, Bill," he said to the monitor while chewing on the croissant. "I'm calling Vasquez myself and asking about this Richards guy. A coordinated publicity effort against Richards would help dampen his credibility."

"My office can help with that, too."

Senator Wilson passed Tom the names and numbers of his office staffers. He hesitated before signing off, carefully weighing what he wanted to say while considering national security laws.

"Something else, Bill?" asked Tom, reading his old friend's face.

"There is one more thing, but it's got to be kept under wraps." He paused and looked carefully at Tom. Their friendship stretched back many years and he felt comfortable trusting him with sensitive information.

"This end's secure," replied Tom, double checking the monitor's privacy icon.

"There's a way we can identify the exact location of any message uploaded to the Link's satellites." Bill kept his voice low while checking his own security icons. "Under the Anti-Terrorism Act, Link Incorporated forwards all latitude and longitude records of sent messages in any designated hot zone. My Senate committee can designate Salavandra a hot zone."

Tom lifted his eyebrows in surprise. The ripped piece of croissant never made it to his mouth. "How?" he asked, genuinely curious about the technology.

"Simple triangulation. When three or more satellites receive a message, the sender's location can be pinpointed. It's old Global Positioning Systems technology with a backwards sort of twist."

"How accurate is it? After all, we know Richards is on the island."

Bill smiled, impressed at the precise quality of the data. Throughout his career he witnessed several people being captured after assuming they had sent anonymous messages.

"Is less than a foot close enough?"

"How soon?" Tom's excitement drove him to speak in rapid-fire questions.

"A few hours to get started then maybe the rest of the day to confer. By tomorrow afternoon we can start waiting for another message."

"So Mr. Richards will be soured from our publicity campaign and then arrested for disrupting the peace and mutilating a soldier. I can already see it coming together, Bill. Thanks."

"Anything to keep the peace, Tom."

Ten

Over the next week helicopters chopped loudly across Salavandra's blue skies as pilots patrolled the island searching for clusters of men that might be UFLS members. They hovered low over homes and flew slowly across roads making certain that the spinning blades' reverberating echoes asserted Vasquez's dominance over the island. The noise began as distant, low thumping that grew in intensity until the blades seemed to crack through the air like spinning whips that sent children and adults alike running for shelter while covering their ears. No part of Salavandra escaped their deafening booms.

An impossibly loud bullhorn fitted to the helicopters' cabins carried a gruff and demanding voice to the fleeing people. The same message blared every time, recorded by none other than President Vasquez. "All UFLS members will be fully prosecuted as traitors to Salavandra," the announcement blasted. "Spare yourself and your families this unnecessary and useless suffering." Emphasizing the seriousness of the declaration, pilots usually let fly a blast of machine-gun fire after the announcement. So far only leafy vegetation and coffee trees suffered gunfire damage, but that was sufficient to convince many people to take the President's statement seriously. Still, no UFLS members gave themselves or Antonio up to the Federals.

Uniformed and well-armed ground troops also searched for UFLS members. With heavy boots they stomped through the extensive gardens and coffee fields around Amadica. On trucks they scoured Salavandra's roads looking for suspicious movements and large numbers of men. Brutalizing the population around Amadica seemed part of their orders, and many young men received much harsher treatment than Eric Palmer's forehead gash. Mothers across the coffee region began welcoming only stitches instead of broken arms and fingers. Women, especially those intercepted in the darkness as they returned from the greenhouses, received much worse treatment. Humiliating searches and rapes went unreported as Salavandra's population hunkered down against Vasquez's heavy hand.

On Mt. Tabor's peak the remaining core of UFLS leadership watched as helicopters buzzed the island and listened to the reports brought up by José's runners. Most men returned to their homes shortly after pledging UFLS membership and promising to await orders. These men, Antonio knew, now held his future in their hands. Though their orchards hung heavy with ripe coffee, each man promised not to pick. Though food supplies grew increasingly low, each man promised not to trade a single sack of coffee. With most certificates already exchanged in a desperate need for cash, families now supported each other as neighbors banded together to weather the growing crisis.

Several times Antonio fled Mt. Tabor's caves as José rushed down from the peak with news of troop movements on the road below. Only once did the Federals clamber all the way to the peak. They stayed only long enough for an uncomfortable rest at its windswept, chilly heights before descending. Having never bothered to carefully search around the peak, the caves holding the diminishing supplies of the UFLS remained untouched.

"This can't go on much longer," said Antonio to Knox and Leonard one morning while watching a helicopter buzz the hollow where his home once stood. Only a pile of ashes now, a runner reported to Antonio three days hence, and nothing there to see. "People can't hold out being treated like this, and the men need something to keep them inspired and aggressive."

Knox and Leonard agreed quickly. Though all three men formulated the contingency attack plans, Antonio alone decided the precise moment to act. He sighed while considering the danger into which he was about to throw his men.

"Well," he said, so softly that the strong breeze gusting across the slope drowned his words, "I never really expected Vasquez to accept my invitation to talk. It's obviously time for something else."

Antonio turned quickly to Knox and Leonard. His eyes carried a hard glint that spoke of final decision. "Tell José to send down his runners with the instructions."

Ten minutes later four young and wiry boys sprinted down the twisting road. They stepped lightly across the strewn gravel and jostled each other attempting to take the lead. Later, as they tired, their enthusiasm carried them even further. Antonio watched them disappear. By late afternoon, he guessed by the height of the sun, UFLS members across the region would know that tonight would find them far from their homes' simple comforts.

When early evening's broad swath finally blanketed Salavandra, dozens of men began moving through the forest and gathering in discrete, silent bunches at specified meeting places. Dressed in their work clothing, most carried neither gun nor machete but only hope for change and willingness to exact punishment upon Salavandra's notorious leadership. Two separate groups materialized in the darkness. One gathered on the ridge overlooking Amadica's southeastern section, the same place that launched Antonio's rescue party. Another gathered on Amadica's northeastern edge where the coffee mill's hulking mass rose from the ground like a threatening and unassailable shadow.

Leonard materialized from the forest at his designated location with two rifles strapped across his back and carrying an entire case of ammunition. Over a dozen of his neighbors quietly greeted him and several men stashed the bullets next to another case, awkwardly carried down the mountain by Marco and Will. Water and day-old tortillas exchanged hands and Leonard gratefully accepted a few bites while resting from his laborious trek down Mt. Tabor.

"Many are here already and it's not yet ten," said Felix excitedly. He stood next to Eric who insisted on joining him when the older man set out into the night.

Leonard nodded and looked along the wooded ridge. Here and there, spread out amongst the trees and lying low in numerous depressions, the non-descript forms of men rustled quietly in the leafy undergrowth. He identified José only after a short and lean shadow sprinted away into the forest. No doubt one of his lookouts, Leonard thought.

"More will come," whispered Leonard. "We'll start moving at midnight. Until then, everyone rest. If José taps you, you're on lookout duty. Pass that along."

The night deepened and another dozen men appeared along the ridge. Amadica grew quieter as fewer trucks passed though town and people shut their doors and windows against the cooling nighttime air. Leonard quietly greeted the men as they arrived and instructed each of them to wait until midnight for his orders. The sky above grew thickly blanketed with stars and Leonard, who harbored no doubts about his own UFLS commitments, grew increasingly concerned about how far these men were willing to go for the UFLS cause.

"Diego," Leonard whispered as midnight approached and the men began rustling in anticipation. Diego turned to him but Leonard could not see his eyes through the heavy shadows. "When we finally get there remember, the men will need to see some real aggressiveness. I can't have them backing out at the last second."

Diego's head nodded quickly. "I'll run out ahead of you."

Leonard stood and stretched at the stroke of midnight while hoping Antonio and the others successfully moved ahead with the second part of the night's attack plans. If luck served, two in the morning would find Antonio well positioned in Saint Matthew. It heartened him that Amadica remained quiet and undisturbed. "They must have left by now," he muttered and began waving the men over to him.

In a few minutes Leonard's loose cluster of volunteers flowed through the shadowy forest. They headed southeast and walked quickly while keeping the dark ribbon of blacktop to their left. Undergrowth rustled, branches and twigs snapped loudly, but each man walked with confidence knowing José and his lookouts watched all sides as they passed. Though Leonard did not say where he led, word soon leaked through the men that Penkava's greenhouses seemed the only logical destination.

Suddenly a harshly whispered call to stop passed from man to man and the entire column, numbering over two dozen, ground to a halt. Heavy breathing and light wind stirred through the dense leaves as everyone spread out and crouched beneath thickets and amongst the roots of large trees.

"What's happening?" whispered Eric to Felix as the two hunched within the shadow of a fallen and decaying tree. Moldy dust rose up around them as they stirred the ground.

Felix cupped his hand to Eric's ear and told him to be quiet. "Federals," he said fiercely, "one of José's scouts must have seen them."

A minute later a truck grumbled around a curve in the road. It moved very slowly, crawling along so the cluster of soldiers walking beside it easily kept pace. Many other troops walked casually through the woods in a long column stretching up the slope. With each second they drew closer to the hiding men.

Thick voices and the sound of heavy boots grew closer and more threatening. Eric suddenly wished he never left Rosemary's side. He remembered her distraught face wrinkling in an effort not to beg him to stay. Footsteps seemed to fall upon him as two soldiers stopped just a few feet away. With his heart pounding so hard Eric thought it might reveal his location, he tightly shut his eyes and wished the Federals would simply disappear.

"What's Munoz thinking?" asked a strong voice somewhere above him. "Nobody's out here, as usual. The UFLS probably doesn't even exist. Richards too. It's just some bullshit to keep us busy."

Eric heard a lighter snap open and a Federal exhale loudly after taking a puff on a cigarette. As the smoke drifted by on the light breeze Eric squeezed himself into a tighter knot and wished he could shrink down into the decaying loam and disappear amongst Salavandra's worms and beetles.

"Oh, they're real all right," replied the second soldier from somewhere up the slope. "Don't forget about that bonfire in front of the mill. Those dumb farmers are organized now." He paused and drew another long puff from his cigarette. "But it doesn't matter," he continued. "They've got no training, no guns and no gear. They're doomed. Just fill in your time and get paid, that's all it's about. Besides, this is personal for Munoz. Did you see his hand?"

"Just the bandage. We're getting hazard pay too, right?"

The other soldier laughed lightly. "Hazard plus nighttime patrol, plus our regular pay. Not bad for a stroll through the woods, even if it is at night."

"All the same, I can't wait to get back to St. Matthew. I hate it up here. Amadica's a dump. Can't find beer. Can't find women. Can't do shit except play cards with your sorry ass."

"That's why I have all your money. You keep thinking about booze and women, not your cards."

The smoker exhaled loudly and heedlessly flicked his spent cigarette through the air. The glowing butt arced recklessly through the foliage. Eric's eyes popped open in alarm as the glowing stub landed just inches from his feet.

"I swear you'll start a fire with those cigarettes."

The smoker grunted and dismissed his partner's concerns. "Not tonight, at least," he replied and shifted his gear noisily. "Come on, Munoz will want his report, and I don't want to keep everyone waiting."

Eric finally relaxed as the truck's low growl disappeared up the road and the patrols' footsteps faded into the night. Rosemary's anxious face appeared in his mind's eye even as he uselessly tried pushing away her image. He vowed not to tell her about this close call with the Federals. Anything to make her less worried was worth the effort, even if it meant a lie of omission.

"Is it true? Are we doomed?" he whispered to Felix a half hour later as they again moved through the woods.

Felix shook his head and kept picking his way carefully past broken tree limbs and prickly bushes. In places where the forest thinned the blazing starlight above helped ease their passage. "We'll succeed where they fail," he began thoughtfully. "We actually believe in what we're doing. Those Federals back there, they're just working."

Leonard and Diego led the men in a smooth arc back towards the road. But for the wind lightly brushing the leaves, silence enveloped the empty strip of pockmarked road as it twisted down slope towards a flat, rock-strewn plain. Standing alone, clustered with organized and industrial neatness against the emptiness of the rugged expanse, twenty-six greenhouses glowed weakly in the reflecting starlight. A single yellow lamp shone dimly above the door to the small office. Leonard motioned the men over to him and began counting.

"That, gentlemen, is tonight's objective." He jerked a thumb toward the greenhouses. "We're hitting Penkava tonight, and even though the Valentine's Day shipment is gone, it will still hurt operations."

He looked carefully from man to man, trying to measure their resolve. None of them ever took part in anything approaching tonight's planned destruction.

"Each of you take one greenhouse," he instructed. "Inside, you'll have twenty minutes. Tip over as many tables as possible, spread out the fertilizer, cut any watering tubes and create as much damage as possible."

"They're big," replied one of Leonard's neighbors. He sounded willing but anxious about being able to complete his task.

Leonard nodded in agreement. "Concentrate on the most vulnerable areas. If there are only soil tables, tip them over and break their legs. If you come across supplies, open them and throw them around. Each house is probably different. After twenty minutes come back and meet up here."

"What happens after twenty minutes?" asked another man.

"Some of us will begin using these," said Leonard, patting the two rifles strapped across his shoulders. Felix and Diego stepped forward with a box of ammunition. Each carried a rifle tightly strapped across his back. They looked ready and even anxious to begin.

"The shooting will be loud," said Leonard. "It will probably attract the Federals, but it'll take them some time to get here. In the meantime, everyone else head for home. Go by different routes and spread out. Don't stay to watch the fire."

"Fire?" someone asked from the darkness.

Leonard pointed to Diego. "Diego will concentrate on the office. Expect to see flames when you meet back here."

Without hesitating he turned to Diego and nodded once. Diego sprinted out from the forest and ran hard across the road toward the greenhouses. Leonard took off, followed closely by Marco and Felix who struggled a bit carrying a box of ammunition. To Leonard's relief he heard all the men running in step behind him. They crossed the road in a matter of seconds and flowed amongst the fat, vulnerable greenhouses. A waning gibbous moon began rising and cast Salavandra in an ashen hue while the UFLS launched its first attack.

A few minutes before midnight found Antonio clambering up onto the back of a large coffee truck. He looked with dismay at the gagged and bound guard lying in the shadows with his hands tied tightly behind his back. It was necessary, Antonio thought, nestling himself within the hastily stacked pallets, fertilizer drums and empty burlap sacks.

He crouched next to Logan, Hank and Stephen who had some difficulty adequately concealing each other amongst the array of equipment thrown onto the truck. The mill's guard, unwilling to give up the keys until forced, had watched in wonder as men emerged from the darkness surrounding the mill and began tossing all manner of gear up onto the flatbeds. In ten minutes, two trucks quickly pulled out onto the road, bound for St. Matthew. They left him wriggling fiercely in the dust trying to loosen his bonds.

Antonio's mind drifted to his fateful day aboard the Celeste as the trucks descended the winding road and plummeted through the cool air towards the coast. He imagined a descent into Hell as they drew close to sea level with its oppressive heat and humidity. He doubted Knox and the Warwicks felt the same in the truck ahead. Knox's last trip to Salavandra's capital netted him a pile of cash and a handgun. The Warwick brothers probably looked forward to seeing the town, though their tasks tonight would be anything but recreational.

From within his hiding place Knox suddenly felt his truck slow and gently swerve. Fear spiked followed by a flood of relief as he watched another truck pass while climbing the road to Amadica. Federals, he thought grimly, and wondered at the progress of Leonard's team. A dual and coordinated attack, he recalled Antonio saying, would give Vasquez and Penkava the impression of broad-based popular support for the UFLS.

As his truck regained speed Knox coldly measured his own almost accidental role in Antonio's movement. If not for the UFLS opportunity, a life of being on the run as a wanted murderer lay in his future. He wondered if Hank and the others realized so much when presented with the choice of freeing Antonio. Knox knew he convinced his friends to select the only option that might bury their past. He also realized that the infant UFLS might fail, but in the meantime the movement would also protect him and his men from answering for the Jola murders.

"This feels all wrong without a rifle," Daniel yelled to him as he leaned out from behind three large plastic barrels. His voice nearly drowned in the sound of the humming motor and whipping wind.

Knox felt the handgun at his side and wished everyone could have one. Besides Hank's shotgun, it was the only other firearm the group carried. "We won't need them," he assured Daniel loudly, poking his head around a pallet to see him better. "Besides, they'd probably get in the way. We have to be fast and get out before anyone notices."

Daniel shrugged and acknowledged Knox. "I just feel vulnerable," he yelled and tucked himself back into his hiding place.

The motor's high, constant whine suddenly dropped and Knox felt the vehicle coasting while the driver braked to slow their descent. He watched as the second truck rolled close and then backed off as that driver applied his own brakes. Through the windshield and in the dim lights of the dashboard Knox saw the driver's expression suddenly harden. Knox risked a peak at the road ahead and felt a sudden and unpleasant burst of adrenaline.

"What's going on?" asked Jonathan from beneath a pile of empty burlap sacks.

"Roadblock," growled Knox as the vehicles slowed to a crawl approaching the fork that led to Hutch. "Stay quiet and pray those drivers don't panic."

"Nerves of steel, they live close to Amadica and have no record with the Federals," Antonio had explained when Knox asked about the drivers. Antonio expected a roadblock, Knox recalled, and had told him that farmers often pick up odd jobs at the mill to make ends meet. Driving supplies to Saint Matthew, even at night, was not uncommon.

Amongst flashing yellow lights both trucks squeaked to a halt. Footsteps clicked on the pavement near the cab and muffled voices drifted over the hiding men. More footsteps, these stepping quickly, passed Knox heading toward the second truck. He carefully drew his pistol and held it firmly in a sweating palm. If the Federals discovered them, Knox swore the gun's clip would empty and several would die immediately.

More voices sounded, this time from the second cab. He pictured several troops surrounding the flatbeds and peering across the jumbled mass of gear deliberately made to look haphazardly loaded. An unlikely-looking place for hiding a few UFLS fighters, Knox hoped. He stayed frozen in place and imagined himself and the others as more barrels, more empty sacks, and yet another spent office supplies container.

Silence fell upon them. It grew and matured until Knox wondered at his ability to withstand another second of waiting. Are the troops still looking at the gear, he wondered? Are they playing with us and simply waiting, with pointed guns, to shoot at the slightest motion on the flatbeds? A suddenly barked order nearly made him squeeze the pistol's trigger. To his great relief the trucks began moving again, slowly at first and then gaining speed.

"No more of that, thank you very much," cried out Daniel with the roadblock well in the distance. Jonathan poked his head out from under the burlap and looked at his brother and Knox. He smiled with relief while shaking his head.

"I guess you don't have to be too smart to be a Federal," he said quickly. "They could have had us in a second. We should be dead."

"The fun's just beginning, my friends," laughed Knox above the wind. It blew warmly now and the sharp smell of sea salt hung in the air. He tucked the pistol back into his pocket next to a matchbook.

Back in Amadica the bound guard struggled hard against his bindings. Dust rose up around his body and stuck to the gathering perspiration beading on his face. His anger bubbled, mostly from being surprised by Antonio's men, but also from being so ignobly treated. More than anger, however, fear overran his emotions and drove him to twist even harder against the thin rope securing his arms and legs. He shuddered to consider what punishment the mill's management might levy upon him after discovering tonight's theft. Thankfully, the guard thought as he rested a moment before gathering his strength, the big boss vacated the mill's guest room earlier that day.

With the rope shearing painfully against his wrists the knot finally loosened enough to free a hand. Feverishly he pulled his other hand free and strained against his aching arms before untying his legs. They sure know how to make knots, he thought bitterly and wondered at the time that had passed during his struggle. Finally freed, he stood and gingerly stretched before making his way across town to the Federal's barracks and Colonel Munoz.

"They look deserted," said Hank as the trucks pulled up next to the warehouses lining Saint Matthew's docks. The drive along the coast went smoothly following the roadblock, and after a meandering passage through Saint Matthew's streets, they finally reached their destination.

"There might be a guard or two," responded Antonio as he descended from the truck, "but not much more than that." He quickly scanned the area with the other men but nobody emerged from the darkness to challenge their presence. The notable absence of the

Celeste's towering steel mass, Antonio realized, explained the lack of dockside activity.

An unnatural, murky silence oozed over the docks. The air smelled of tarred wood and machine oil and reminded Antonio of the day he lost his eye. He tried shaking a growing feeling of dread and cast a hopeful glance at the sky above Saint Matthew's normally cheerful bay. Starlight glittered fiercely against empty space. The water, however inviting during the daytime, now seemed cold and unfriendly. Across the bay a single bright light shone high on the cliff above Retribution Point. Phillip's cabin, thought Antonio bitterly and recalled waking in Saint Matthew's clinic without an eye while Phillip stood nearby conversing over his Link.

Forcing himself to shift his attention, Antonio looked down the line of seven warehouses lining the docks and considered the shiny padlocks on each of the massive, sliding doors. While securing the coffee inside from the remote possibility of theft, the hardened steel did nothing to prevent the doors from swinging open a foot or two when lifted from the ground. The enormous rolling mechanism over each door simply slid back and forth with the slightest pressure. Antonio showed the men how to slip inside after they gathered around him in the shadows of the first warehouse.

"Just lift and squirm beneath," he explained. "You three, you're the lookouts," he pointed to Daniel and the drivers. "If you see anyone coming, run down the line and knock hard on the warehouse doors." They nodded and sprinted off into the darkness to watch for trouble. Antonio turned his attention to the remaining six men, nearly all Knox's men. Knox himself stood at some distance ready to run to the furthest warehouse on Antonio's command.

"Everyone have their knives and matches?" Antonio asked. A cold sense of authority fell over him. His nagging sliver of doubt disappeared as each man nodded quickly.

"Remember to empty at least three bags, and tuck the loose burlap near the bottom of a stack. It'll catch with a little encouragement. Meet back at the trucks when your blaze is fully caught."

With a quick wave of his hand he sent each of them off to their respective warehouses and watched until they disappeared beneath the doors. Tonight, thought Antonio, Penkava and Vasquez will feel the bite of the UFLS.

Blinded by the interior's opaque darkness, Knox carefully moved through the warehouse with extended arms hoping to find something to lean against. After a frustrating minute he finally lit a single match and held it high above his head. The feeble light barely penetrated the gloom but afforded him a quick look at the thousands of bulging coffee bags stacked to the ceiling.

"This will be pretty," he said aloud, and drew close to a pallet holding a few bags. His voice fell flat and soft, dampened against the coffee stock, and he thought that even a scream would barely carry beyond the warehouse door.

Wasting no time and working in the dark he quickly sliced open three sacks and dumped thousands of hard, green coffee beans upon the floor. They rattled and scattered smoothly, reminding Knox of flowing water. With a match he oriented himself and in seconds was lighting the emptied burlap after tucking it securely near the bottom of a huge stack of coffee.

The fire struggled at first. Knox excitedly lit another match and held the flame's tip to the loose material. Sputtering with dust and crackling in protest, the little flame gathered strength and bit deeper into the burlap. An orange glow radiated around his face and the smell of smoke seeped into the air. Knox gave the little flame a gentle blow. It licked one of the sacks above it and then bit deeply into the material. Knox gave the flame another slightly harder blow and again it spread, gathering strength and depth. The pleasant smell of roasting beans mingled with acrid smoke. As Knox took a step back to assess his work, the fire finally caught fully and a long column of narrow flames raced to the ceiling. Seven feet, twelve feet, fifteen feet high the fire climbed, merrily biting into and consuming the hard won efforts of so many farmers and so much processing. Twenty feet above the floor the flames finally licked the warehouse's dusty rafters and Knox let out a victorious bellow at his destructive creation.

Suddenly a heavy and desperate knocking thumped against the warehouse door. Cold panic exploded through him and forgetting the crackling tower of flame he spun to face the door while gripping his gun. The muffled but indistinguishable sound of gunfire pulsed deeply into the warehouse while pounding boots and yelling voices sounded outside. The blaze behind Knox suddenly brightened and a wall of heat and choking smoke pushed him towards the door. Caught, he thought bitterly. Another second of indecision brought more gunfire and a distant scream.

The door swung up from the ground with a slight push and Knox skittered beneath it on his back while holding his gun ready to fire. His head emerged into chaos. Down the line of warehouses flames leapt through several roofs in a crazy dance of bright yellow and deep orange waste. Smoke poured from the cracks outlining the warehouse doors. A melee of Federals, looking more like faceless, rifle-toting shadows than men, peppered the dock and fanatically dashed about chasing, clubbing and shooting. Shapeless blobs lay at many Federals' feet, immobilized by a bullet or a club or simple fear. Knox squirmed again, desperate to slip away. A confusing series of bright white flashes illuminated the frenzied scene just before a rifle butt smashed down upon his face.

The truck climbing the road to Amadica that passed Antonio and the others carried a desperately needed patrol rotation for Jola. Since the UFLS declared itself, troops had scoured the island uselessly searching for members and their hideouts. With manpower thinly stretched, soldiers endured long stretches of tiresome duty without any sleep. Plummeting morale was a problem, and the platoon in Jola cheerfully looked forward to a day off. Their replacements, however, were considerably less enthusiastic. They stopped at Amadica's barracks for an extended break to rest and refuel.

Colonel Munoz was awake after a forced nap that nearly turned into a deep and heartily needed eight-hour sleep. He greeted the soldiers when they arrived and now sent them on their way while waving a bandaged hand and thinking about his missing finger. As the truck grumbled down the road towards Jola, Munoz spotted a man running towards him from down the street with his hands waving above his head. Probably a drunken fight, Munoz thought with considerable aggravation. He glared at the oncoming figure.

"Thieves," cried the man excitedly. Munoz's attitude quickly changed when the man's bloodied wrists and soiled clothing came into view.

"Thieves," the man repeated, panting and rushing up to the jailhouse. "They took two trucks from the mill and tied me up."

"Come inside, quickly," said Ignacio and held open the door for the mill's guard.

While Colonel Munoz listened attentively to the guard and began making calls, the Jola rotation sped down the steep highway towards Amadica's greenhouses. Diego was just backing away from the blazing office, quite happy with his thoroughly destructive arson when he heard the truck's engine whining. He turned and the large green flatbed suddenly burst into view from around a corner. The startled look on the driver's face turned into fearful determination as the truck veered off the road and rolled directly towards the flaming office.

"Federals!" cried Diego. He screamed it so loudly that his voice cracked. He sprinted off towards the road and the relative safety of Mt. Tabor's forested slopes.

Men still ransacked the greenhouses, he thought with a jolt of fear. Gunfire erupted in short, sharp bursts that echoed against the mountain slope. He turned to look and saw bursts of orange light flaring out from the shadows around the greenhouses. At least they're staying in the dark, Diego thought hopefully, desperately wishing that he too carried a rifle.

Bullets rained across the truck's windshield. Glass cracked, metal popped and dented loudly as the novice UFLS shooters found their marks. Diego kept running toward the road, towards the slopes and away from the chaos. The truck finally skidded to a stop in front of the ruined, blazing office and the Jola rotation suddenly poured from the truck's back with their guns blasting in controlled, professional bursts as each soldier spread out and took cover.

One Federal, the passenger in the cab who stayed behind the windshield's bulletproof glass, opened his door and saw Diego running towards the forest. He lifted his rifle and patiently estimated the seconds remaining before his target disappeared. Five seconds, four, three, he counted. Diego crossed the pavement and his right foot stepped onto the rocky median. Two, one. A single, confidently shot bullet sped through the air. Diego heard nothing. Nor did he see his chest explode out onto the leaves in front of him. He finally made it into the forest.

Men rushed from the greenhouses as soon as bullets began flying. They mistakenly thought that they lingered too long tipping soil tables and dumping fertilizer, and that Leonard was already beginning to shoot out the glass. They stepped into pandemonium. Screaming voices mixed with flying lead and fire flashes. Many ran towards the blazing office, directly into the midst of gunfire. They were slaughtered by rounds from both sides. Glass shattered everywhere as the soldiers let loose round after round, aiming towards the UFLS light flashes and hoping to hit something in the dark.

Leonard shot, panicky at first with a rush of adrenaline, then more controlled as he gained cover behind a mound of topsoil and assessed the situation. With two rounds left he somehow detached himself from the fray. Between fifteen and twenty soldiers had sprung upon them and were now steadily making their way around the greenhouses, gradually trapping the UFLS forces. He stopped noticing the dying men. The distinctive gunfire cracks disappeared into an ocean of noise. Preserving the few remaining UFLS men overtook his thinking.

"Felix," Leonard shouted, waving an arm towards a shadowy figure, heedless of the danger. "There's too many. We have to back up and escape out onto the plain behind the greenhouses. Pass the word."

Felix nodded and sprinted away from a stack of pallets. Several men already realized the danger near the office and were running towards the empty darkness of the expansive rocky plain. Felix rushed up to Eric and fiercely pushed him towards safety.

"Go back there," Felix screamed, and pointed towards the end of the greenhouses where they stretched into the gloom. Eric crouched tightly against a concrete base, frozen with fear. He held his hands across his ears and rocked back and forth with a nervous, jerking motion.

Felix screamed at him again, "Eric," he yelled into his ear. Several bullets popped into the concrete and a nearby glass pane shattered. Felix turned and fired in desperation. He needed to get Eric to safety; Rosemary waited at home. Her worried face watched him from afar, saw the danger that he knowingly drew Eric into, and suddenly hated him. Felix fired again and again until he gradually discerned the terrifying clicking of a spent clip. Throwing the rifle down in disgust, he turned back to Eric, but the boy was gone.

Startled, Felix looked up and saw Eric's thin figure racing away past the greenhouses and deep into the distant plain. He felt a sudden crack ring through his head and Rosemary's face suddenly grew softer, pleasant, and then smiled with joy. Paulina stood behind their daughter, clasping her hands and beaming, happy that Eric had at last made it to safety so that Rosemary could someday wed. Then, like a heavy veil, shadow draped through Felix's mind. He dropped to the ground and died.

Marco's rifle emptied just a few seconds after he began shooting. The Federals startled him so much that he forgot all he learned about firing the gun and simply held down the trigger, praying that the rounds would somehow stop the oncoming soldiers. The ammunition at his feet, an entire box that he and Felix lugged for miles up and down Mt. Tabor's slopes, lay opened but unused. There was simply no time to reload.

Will's voice called out his name through the rifles' repeated popping. He looked sick with worry, but in the cold moonlight Marco saw the intensity with which he controlled the rifle.

"Move back, Marco. Run," Will cried out and let a controlled burst fly off towards the Federals. "I'll keep them back a bit longer."

Will stepped out from the shadow of a fertilizer barrel and waved an arm down between the greenhouses towards safety. Marco followed his arm and saw a man, a shadow really, sprinting towards the rocky plain to safety. He turned back to Will for a split second and saw the horribly exposed position of his new friend.

"Get down, Will," cried Marco, and looked towards the burning office where the Federals crouched. A quick series of orange bursts flashed near the truck's shot-out headlights and Marco heard the sickening thuds of bullets finding their mark just a few feet away. When he dared look, Will's body lay partially in the shadows, quiet. With an anguished cry Marco stood and sprinted off into the darkness.

Pinned behind his pile of earth, Leonard saved his two remaining rounds while hoping Felix successfully passed on the retreat order. He imagined Antonio's expression when learning of tonight's casualties. From his crouched position he saw two lifeless UFLS bodies lying on the ground.

Their families will suffer, he thought sadly, but immediately turned back to the fight as a sudden quiet bloomed. The smell of smoke drifted heavily through the greenhouse complex. The office burned with gusting roars and glass cracked and fell everywhere from its steel framing even as the silence grew. A minute crawled by before a Federal officer finally barked an order to his soldiers. Leonard looked behind him and breathed a little easier. It seemed that Felix had succeeded.

"Around...check them...contact..." Leonard strained to hear a crackling radio. One pitched hiss sounded off to his left and another much weaker one far to the right. The soldiers were surrounding the complex, he remembered, and he carefully peered out from behind his hiding place.

Two Federals with ready guns stepped towards his loose mound of topsoil. They swept their weapons in careful arcs and were ready to fire at the slightest provocation. Leonard noticed how their smoothly professional gestures contrasted with the rag-tag movements of the UFLS. Those farmers were his neighbors though, Leonard thought angrily, not suited for fighting but for working hard and raising families. The sole purpose of these Federals was to crush their dream of a better life. Leonard suddenly realized how much he missed his day-to-day work and seeing his fellow coffee men. He wished he had been a friendlier neighbor.

From the darkness he held his breath and carefully took aim. A single shot at each Federal, one immediately following the other, dropped both soldiers just fifteen feet from his hiding place. He ducked back behind the soil and listened to spitting radios suddenly discharge everywhere in the darkness around him. The radio strapped to one of the downed Federals repeatedly called out for a response as other soldiers tried discerning the location of the gunfire.

"This way," shouted a voice nearby. Booted feet pounded through the aisles between the greenhouses. Three shadows passed in front of him running for cover. He turned around to make a dash for the distant plain when he saw a single figure crouched protectively at the corner of a greenhouse near the end of his aisle. Another figure appeared and suddenly two narrow beams of red laser light shot through the smoky haze.

Leonard tried wiping the two spots off his shirt. They slipped over him effortlessly and though he squirmed away, the beams followed and steadily climbed his chest.

"He's pinned, Sir," cracked the radio from a dead Federal. "Do you want him alive?"

Time stretched in the brief pause before the officer answered. Leonard gripped the loose earth; Salavandra's rich soil trucked up from the fertile coastal plains to coddle Penkava's roses. It smelled healthy, like moist new life. It gave way as his fingers dug deeply, clawing, thirsting to root into the island.

"No."

Two empty cabernet bottles reflected the television's glowing light as a satellite feed streamed down into Phillip's cabin on Retribution Point. News, movies, sports, every conceivable form of entertainment flashed across the wide screen as Mary sat transfixed, clicking from channel to channel, unable to absorb enough of the flashing images. Phillip found this endearing at first, but soon grew tired of her innocent fixation.

"Enough, Mary," he said, firmly taking the remote from her hand and clicking off the television. An image of a news anchor faded away as the screen darkened. "It's late. I'm exhausted and we should go to bed."

Mary's eyes glittered in the cabin's low light. She seemed excited to be spending her first night in the cabin, and yet more distant and reserved than Phillip remembered. She reached for her glass where the last few drops of wine pooled. She drank more tonight than Phillip thought possible.

"What else does this place have?" she slurred, clearly drunk from the wine and not at all ready to sleep. Phillip sighed and wished he had brought her out to the Point earlier in the day.

"It's all just normal stuff, Mary." Phillip heard his voice getting short. He spent the last week communicating with Colonel Munoz regarding the search for Antonio while strategically scheduling coffee shipments and assuring New York that Salavandra's farmers would soon get back to work. The thought of now feeding Mary's bubbling enthusiasm tipped his patience.

"What about this?" she asked, reaching to a nearby shelf for another remote control. Rows of black and gray buttons lined the plastic in orderly columns. Mary pressed the big red button and Phillip groaned. Music suddenly flowed through the cabin, spilling from speakers embedded in nearly every wall and ceiling. Mary's face looked around in wonder at the sound.

"This cabin plays music, too?" she asked, and reached for a wine bottle. Finding it empty, she tried the other and then shook her glass suggestively at Phillip. He ignored her and stood up from the sofa.

"I'm going to bed. Stay up as late as you want."

Mary looked around the room at all the splendid accommodations. Thick rugs lined the polished wooden flooring, a huge refrigerator stood at one end of a well-stocked kitchen and there were so many electrical appliances it would take a week to figure out all their functions. The bathroom alone, Mary thought in wonder, had a tremendous spa-tub and wonderfully smelling soaps and lotions. She recalled her own home's thin, unadorned walls where crickets and other insects often sneaked inside.

"Aren't you afraid this stuff will get stolen?"

With a foot on the steps leading upstairs Phillip paused and looked back while shaking his head.

"President Vasquez lends us a soldier to watch the peninsula road. You didn't see it, but there's a little guard station in the woods." He stepped up on the first stair thinking about the smooth softness of his bed sheets.

"Is New York this nice?" asked Mary hopefully.

"Nicer. Lots nicer."

"How soon are we leaving?"

Phillip stopped climbing the stairs and wrestled with a sudden shot of anxiety. He wanted to save this until tomorrow, or another day when he had more energy.

"About that, Mary," he began. He saw the corner of the bed inviting him upstairs. "With the UFLS interrupting the coffee shipments, I'm afraid we'll have to postpone that for a little bit."

Her silent pause seemed to shout up the stairs. He took another step.

"How long?" she asked, her voice suddenly serious and carrying none of the energy of just a few moments ago.

"As soon as things settle down," replied Phillip testily. "Antonio's costing the Company a lot of money and now I have to coordinate the warehouse bean discharge."

Mary's normal reserve around Phillip vanished. "It's probably cheaper to simply pay us more for the certificates." She recalled her father grumbling that very morning about the poor exchange rate and swearing to help the UFLS. She left the house feeling like a thief, stealing away from one life to meet Phillip in another. New York called, but she felt like a traitor to her island and her people.

"Besides," she continued, "I don't think Salavandra's going to settle down anytime soon."

Phillip turned and faced Mary from the steps. Fatigue melted away and anger warmed his chest. "It'll settle," he announced loudly. Images of the Board and his father raced through his mind. He was not about to allow the woman he dominated in bed begin pressuring him about his work. "The dirty rat will get caught and Salavandra will return to normal. The UFLS is a hopeless band of ignorant, filthy fucks and..."

He ducked as Mary's wine glass flew through the air and crashed on the steps below him.

"Don't you dare talk about my people like that," Mary screamed. "They are not ignorant or filthy. They simply do not have all this," she cried out and gestured wildly around the room. Her long black hair tossed around her shoulders and a stern glint shined in her dark eyes. Phillip stepped heavily down the steps. Broken glass crunched loudly beneath his shoes

"First," he said, drawing closer and thrusting a finger under her nose. "They're not *your* people anymore, Sweetheart. You cut yourself loose the day you climbed back into my truck. Second, they *are* ignorant, especially that fuck Antonio. He has no idea what economic forces are in play around his simple, stupid beans."

Mary tipped back onto the couch under Phillip's heavy presence. He stood over her and glared down into her glazed, drunken eyes. "You don't fit in here anymore, Mary," he said a little more quietly. The shirt she borrowed from his wardrobe hung open and exposed a heavy breast. A stirring quiver tickled Phillip's crotch. "I'm you're only salvation off this wretched rock. Without me, you've got nothing."

Still seething, Mary tried to squirm out from under Phillip but he caught her hair and violently yanked her head back. She gasped as pain exploded across her scalp.

"Nothing without me, you island whore," whispered Phillip fiercely, and tore open Mary's shirt. She slapped at him and violently twisted while trying to free herself from his grip. Phillip pinned her to the sofa with a knee pressed heavily into her chest. A free hand rose high above his head. Mary screamed once before it landed.

"Now hold still, bitch. And when I'm done, we're going to sleep and you are never going question me about my work again. Got it?" He raised his hand threateningly.

Tears streamed from Mary's eyes and she nodded weakly. Phillip tore at the rest of her clothing and threatened to hit her again if she resisted. The TV, Mary thought, think about the television programs. Images blurred into one another in a dizzying array of skits, commercials and canned laughter. Scenes from around the world filled her mind and she bit her cheek against a wave of shame. Where was her strength, she wondered? How had this one man leached it away so quickly? She closed her eyes and wished herself free of this treachery.

To Mary's great relief Phillip finished quickly. He immediately left her on the couch and disappeared into the bathroom.

"Here," he called out roughly a moment later. "Take two of these." He tossed her a small pill container that rattled loudly when she caught the vial.

"What are these?" Mary asked, wiping away the last of her tears and hoping Phillip failed to notice her crying.

"They'll make you feel better. Trust me, they're nice. I've been taking them for years."

"Two?"

"You're a wreck. Better take three. Tomorrow morning take three more, and then every day after that. I'll make sure we have enough."

Mary stepped into the kitchen and with trembling hands filled a glass of water. A distant pump kicked in and drew water from deep below the cabin. She swallowed three little pink pills and drew another glass. The cool water tasted like nothing, so different than the metallic stuff she was accustomed to drinking. Her eyes drifted out the window as she swallowed.

"What's that across the bay?" she asked suddenly, setting the empty glass on the counter.

Phillip stepped up behind her and kissed her neck. Mary stiffened against his touch and checked an involuntary shiver.

"Just Saint Matthew's lights…"

A red glow drew Phillip's eyes towards the docks and warehouses on the western side of town. His knees grew weak and he suddenly gripped Mary for support.

"Not that," he whispered. "Anything but that."

"What is it?" Mary asked, seeing panic wash over him.

Phillip ignored her. He spun from the sink and raced to the door where binoculars hung on a peg. The door banged violently against the cabin as Phillip ran to the cliff's edge and peered out across the bay.

His distressed cry reached Mary, still standing at the sink. She suddenly understood, and a secretive grin crept to her lips. Her heart let out a cheer for the UFLS and for all the people on Salavandra wishing the movement success. Tonight, she thought wickedly, Phillip would finally receive some of the pain he deserved.

Eleven

In the ensuing week Salavandra's people bowed under the Federals' domineering presence. Dozens were arrested, and soldiers stared with suspicion at even the most benign exchanges between neighbors. Residents of Amadica especially suffocated under the stifling and constant presence of patrolling Federals. The names Antonio Richards and the UFLS fell from tongues in hushed whispers. They escaped off the island, some said. Others thought that Antonio and his men awaited counterattack on Three Sisters, the remote, northeastern peninsula of the island. Some even said the UFLS was destroyed and that Vasquez was simply reasserting his authority. Whatever the truth, few doubted that the UFLS struck a heavy blow to Penkava Incorporated and President Vasquez.

Government compiled UFLS casualty lists appeared posted on buildings in Amadica and Hutch. Wives and mothers claimed bodies under the eyes of wary soldiers. They returned home to find flames consuming their possessions while soldiers guarded their acts of vengeance with ready guns and bitter silence. Destitute mourners wept on ashes of homes that once provided shelter and a modicum of comfort.

The dawns of many mornings found hastily painted slogans scrawled across Amadica's mill, the jail and even the Federals' barracks; Penkava out, Vasquez is a pig, UFLS. Upon discovery, soldiers immediately set to work obliterating the dissenting cries of a population too frightened to speak aloud.

John Doddard and the mill's other pick-up drivers began moving along the coffee region's back roads hoping to score a few sacks for processing. With incomes stretched to breaking, a few desperate farmers clandestinely picked the rotting beans and looked ahead to the end of March and the harvest's close. The few certificates Doddard exchanged were cashed out at the going rate, many that same day.

José's runners still moved through the region and reported everything back to Antonio and the few remaining active UFLS fighters. Some boys however, did not return from their scouting missions. José assumed they simply went back to their homes, depressed by the heavy losses and lonely for their parents. He assured the remaining boys of their work's essential character and told them that things would soon improve.

"The peoples' will is crumbling," said Marco after talking quietly with José. He crouched with Antonio near Mt. Tabor's peak, sipping the last of the morning's coffee. A few men near the caves mumbled softly to each other over the blowing wind whipping across the mountain.

Antonio sighed. "I expected as much," he replied. "I'm surprised they're not all back in the fields by now."

"Some are, but most aren't. Lots of people still look to you for leadership."

Antonio turned suddenly to face Marco. His week-long bottled anger and doubts about his own leadership abilities welled up within him. He snapped, "What kind of leadership have I provided, Marco? Leading dozens of men to their deaths? Stirring up the Federals' anger so much that people are scared to even walk about? You just told me that some farmers are picking again. What kind of leadership is that?"

Marco leaned away from Antonio's sudden volley, but his experienced eyes belied a patient understanding. "Your leadership, Antonio, is all the people have right now. You forced them to examine their lives, to question their circumstances. They realize now how different things could be were it not for Penkava and Vasquez."

A big gust of chilling wind suddenly raced across the peak and bent the hardy grass tufts to the ground. Antonio looked to the sky. Far off in the distant northeast heavy clouds lined the horizon. Behind him came the gentle sound of plates clinking as the men near the caves took care of the breakfast dishes. He shrugged and thought of the prosaic necessities of life; eating, sleeping, doing dishes, all taking precedent over his ideals.

"I wish we could support them," he replied weakly. No matter how much he rested he could not shake his overwhelming fatigue. His narrow escape from Saint Matthew's docks and subsequent week-long excursion back to Mt. Tabor's peak sapped all his energy. "I just wish people didn't have to pick."

"They're holding out as long as they can. I'm sure they have no other choice."

"Well that's just the point, isn't it?" Antonio asked heatedly. He stood and gestured out across Salavandra. His arms sailed over rich green forest, distant fields and tidy coffee orchards far below. "We picked before the UFLS existed because we had no choice. Now at the cusp of change, we again have no other choice and again must pick to stay alive."

Marco shook his head and looked back at the men clustered near the caves. He cringed seeing how they watched Antonio. "There is still hope," he began. "So long as we believe, we can inspire change in others." He motioned Antonio to sit down. After a moment his leader and friend grudgingly returned to his place in the grass.

"You can't let them see you like this, Antonio," Marco lectured beneath his breath while gazing out across the island. "If you think our numbers are thin now, wait until these few remaining men see you lose faith."

Antonio gritted his teeth and nodded. He knew Marco spoke the truth and dared not look back. He kept his voice deliberately low. "I'm afraid it will take something much larger than the UFLS to change Salavandra. We simply do not have the means."

A minute of silence ensued as Marco recalled the single, empty rifle that lay propped against a cave wall. All the other guns and ammunition fell into the Federals' hands after the greenhouse massacre. All we have left are machetes, Marco thought bitterly as he imagined the futility of leading attacks against Salavandra's well-armed soldiers.

"What about the Link?" Marco asked suddenly. "You once said that this was a war of information, too. Maybe there's help out there and we just don't know it yet."

Antonio shrugged despondently. "I haven't looked at it for days."

His lackluster reaction surprised Marco. He remembered Antonio's enthusiasm about the Link's information network leading them to victory.

"I'll go get it. It's time we take a look."

It felt heavy and foreign in Antonio's hands as he pushed the Link's power button and poised the stylus above the small screen. So much hope in such a little device, Antonio thought, and yet it netted no men, no guns and no supplies. He surfed over to Penkava Incorporated's stock listing and stared at the solid green numbers for several seconds before showing the Link to Marco.

"It's recovered everything it lost and more since my first upload."

"What about the news releases, and the messages boards?"

Antonio clicked across the screen, poking here and there trying to catch up on the Company's news. One deeply embedded listing caught his eye: *Salavandra Returns to Normal Operations.*

> *Operations on Salavandra returned to normal today as authorities swept up the few remaining criminal elements sowing dissent throughout the island's population. The newly-formed UFLS, that earlier this month caused so much stir, "has essentially disappeared," said Phillip Penkava, Executive Director of Operations currently stationed on the island. When asked the whereabouts of Antonio Richards, the supposed leader of the island's roaming band of lawbreakers and murderers, Penkava stated the following: "Antonio Richards is still out there but largely impotent against Salavandra's legal establishment. He won't be destroying people's lives anymore with his inflammatory rhetoric and warmongering. Be assured that he's on the run and the Company's interests on this island paradise are picking up."*

Antonio threw down the Link in disgust. "Hopeless," he whispered as Marco picked up the Link and read the posting.

"You have to reply, Antonio. You have to let them know the UFLS is still a viable force on Salavandra."

"What force? We've got no guns, no ammunition and hardly any supplies."

"Damn you, Antonio," growled Marco. "Enough of this self-pity. I didn't join the UFLS because I thought it would be easy. Neither did the men behind you or those who died last week. We expected it to be hard, and it was, and is, breathtakingly hard. You owe it to us to stand tall and be strong. Lots of men died believing in you, so you'd better make it worthwhile as long as possible." He angrily shoved the Link into Antonio's chest and glared at him.

Antonio clutched the Link, surprised at Marco's reprimand. He looked back at the men going about the morning's business and ready to follow any orders he issued. He remembered the bullets flying across the docks, the raging fire and the screams of pain as men succumbed beneath heavy rifle blows. He envisioned the carnage at the greenhouses that José and the few who escaped recounted when he finally returned to caves.

"You're right, Marco," Antonio said firmly. "They deserve better. All of them deserve better. I'll compose a quick response now, and a longer one later."

Antonio's brief message assured people of the continued UFLS presence on Salavandra. He capped it with a snapshot of Saint Matthew's burning warehouses.

"I took it as I sprinted away into the darkness," he explained when Marco asked him about the picture. It showed three warehouses clearly engulfed in flames with smoke pouring out against the bright spotlight of a military truck.

"This will convince a few people that we're still around," said Antonio. He raised the stylus to the send button and tapped lightly.

The message shot out from the Link and sped towards the satellite network orbiting high above. In seconds it passed from one, to another and then to several other satellites and in under a minute his message circled the globe. Recipients began reading the posting immediately. At that moment a discreet alarm began sounding on a single computer terminal deep within the Pentagon. The stationed officer forwarded the information to the posted listings and immediately called Senator Bill Wilson's private line.

"Phillip," said Tom excitedly to his son. "We just got an upload from Mr. Richards and sent his exact coordinates to Colonel Munoz. I expect he'll be mobilizing immediately."

Even on the Link's small screen Tom Penkava's face looked red. A shine of perspiration glistened across his forehead. Phillip recognized his father's expression and read an array of emotions from agitation to worry and anger. He is still trying to clean up my mess, thought Phillip, and flipped to the stock's bulletin board to view Antonio's message. The image of the burning warehouses made his stomach tighten. He recalled that night's chaos, its destruction, and especially the screams of captured UFLS troops.

"Not to worry, Dad. We already know where he's located. We've been watching him for a few days and last night troops began closing in around him."

Tom looked genuinely surprised. "How did you find out?" he asked. "Bill said there was only one upload and that it was sent within the last half-hour."

Phillip shook his head and smiled. "None of that high tech anti-terrorism stuff down here, Dad. All we needed were a few convincing minutes with some of Antonio's troops." Phillip cast a smile around the table at the Federals sitting quietly and listening to the exchange. They nodded one after the other and consulted their own communication laptops, generously provided by Senator Wilson.

"If I could explain?" interjected Colonel Munoz. He eased himself up from his chair and moved behind Phillip. Tom Penkava peered behind his son at Munoz.

"I received the coordinates just a few minutes ago, Sir," Colonel Munoz began. He leaned closer to the Link to see Tom Penkava more clearly. "They match what we already knew about the position of the UFLS. We've got a coordinated movement on the roll as we speak. The pressure won't let up until Richards and his men are captured."

"And you're coordinating operations from the mill?" Tom asked.

"On my invitation, Dad," Phillip responded quickly. "The Federals didn't have anywhere to host a sizeable operations center, and Amadica's mill has lots of room and resources.

Tom nodded, pleased at the appropriateness of his son's invitation. "Nice going, Phillip," he said quickly. "Anything we can do to help nab Richards is fine by me. How's the cleanup coming along?"

Colonel Munoz returned to his seat and sat heavily on the thick upholstery. He listened with one ear as Phillip gave his father an update on the insurance estimates and rebuilding schedules.

"What's ironic," Phillip said with a little laugh, "is that after all the structural improvements, we'll actually come out ahead. Those idiot farmers actually made our presence here grow stronger!"

Munoz looked up from his laptop as Phillip signed off with a promise to keep the Company informed of any major developments. He watched as Phillip waved over a young, shapely woman with flowing black hair and a vacant expression in her dark eyes. Phillip fondled her in front of everyone.

"The best ever, boys," Phillip announced as he grasped Mary provocatively around her waist and gave her a strong pinch. She appeared not to notice, and most of the officers averted their eyes in embarrassment. "In a few minutes we'll start scrubbing Salavandra clean, and in a few days everything will return to normal."

Colonel Munoz turned his attention back to the laptop and flipped to a screen illustrating Salavandra's topographical relief. He zoomed in on Mt. Tabor's peak where a single red dot located Antonio's last known position. On the slopes, moving in groups of twenty men, Federal soldiers encircled the mountain and steadily made their way towards the peak. Munoz pushed a key and the Federals' exact positions, illustrated as little yellow squares that moved every thirty seconds, popped up onto the screen.

"I can't tell you how much this technology is helping," said an officer from across the table. "Without this equipment it would take months to find and apprehend the UFLS."

Phillip nodded appreciatively. "My government has invested a lot in counter-terrorism technology. What better place to use it than Salavandra, where the UFLS is terrorizing your country?"

With a slap on her backside Phillip sent Mary from the room with instructions to get the Lexus packed up and ready to go. "We'll stay one more night at the cabin, baby," he called after her. "Then we're off to New York and civilization."

She turned from the door and smiled weakly. Colonel Munoz thought she might fall were it not for her suddenly gripping the doorknob.

"Is she alright?" he asked Phillip, and discreetly gestured towards Mary.

Phillip dismissed Ignacio's concern. "Just too many feel-good pills, that's all," he replied. "It keeps her calm and keeps me happy, if you know what I mean."

A few chuckles rippled around the table as the men glanced after Mary's retreating figure.

"Local girl?" asked Munoz.

"More local than you can imagine. Hey, when do we send in the choppers?"

Colonel Munoz turned his attention to the laptop and estimated the time before the helicopters' scheduled buzz of Mt. Tabor's peak. He would issue the order himself, and as he thought about the operation he imagined the hard conditions atop the mountain's wind-swept peak. Munoz knew that the few UFLS fighters still loyal to Antonio would be difficult to uproot. Young or old, their hardened attitudes might pose a real challenge for the troops now moving up the mountain. He remembered his father's strength before sickness took him. Backed into a corner, Juan Munoz could unleash a terrible fury belied by his thin and wiry limbs.

"Soon," he replied to Phillip. "I'd estimate no more than fifteen minutes. They'll be on the run before long."

"Not much change this time," mused Marco as he watched the Link's screen waiting for the stock's price to plummet. It dipped a fraction of a percent then rose again, exhibiting nothing of the roller-coaster ride following Antonio's first posting.

"Maybe people don't read the news on Fridays," he said, and showed Antonio the Link.

"Maybe people don't believe we're for real," replied Antonio, "even after our offensive. Check those headlines, Marco. See if there's anything about the UFLS that I missed."

Marco scanned the listed headlines but found nothing. He was about to give the Link back to Antonio when the Company posted another press release. He opened the posting and gasped.

"What is it?" asked Antonio in alarm.

"We have to get off the peak," shouted Marco, standing suddenly and looking down the mountain. "They know we're here. Somehow they figured it out."

Antonio grabbed the Link and read the succinct the message.

> *Salavandra's security forces today surrounded the remaining UFLS criminal elements as they gathered atop Mt. Tabor hoping to avoid legal prosecution for crimes against the State and against Salavandra's people. Government troops expect to incarcerate the entire gang of outlaws by late this afternoon.*

Antonio looked up towards Mt. Tabor's peak wondering if José spotted anyone coming up the mountain. Only wind moved across the stubbly grass. He looked down the slopes towards the coffee fields and further on towards Amadica. Not a movement disturbed Salavandra's apparent tranquility. He heard Marco harshly ordering the men to prepare to leave.

"Marco," called Antonio sharply. Marco ran over clutching a sack containing a pan and a few handfuls of beans and rice. "Maybe it's a trick," said Antonio. "Maybe they had this response ready so when I posted they would have some reply prepared for the public."

Marco's eyes darted from Antonio to the slopes and back up to the peak. He recalled the bodies at the greenhouses and knew the Federals showed no mercy.

"I'd prefer not to guess," he said quickly. "I think we need to get under the cover of the forest. Mt. Lucinda would make a good hiding place for awhile. It's more remote and a lot harder for troops to move around."

Marco's departure orders had the UFLS fighters moving about in a hurry. Most carried very little and stood ready to leave in under a minute. Others gathered the few supplies needed for living in the wild; a machete, blankets and extra clothing. Antonio sighed as he watched the men, but pride swelled in his heart seeing their determination.

"Seventeen men, plus you, José and myself. Not much of a force against the Federals." He stood and nodded. "I agree, Marco. Let's make for Mt. Lucinda. We can regroup there and start rebuilding our forces."

He stepped towards the caves to collect supplies when a distant chopping clacked through the wind. The noise evolved, grew louder and changed into the clear chop-chop of helicopter blades. Suddenly José appeared, wide-eyed and sprinting down from Mt. Tabor's peak.

"They're coming," he cried out, nearly tripping downhill towards the caves. "They're moving up from the south, east and west. I didn't see them because I was watching the road to Amadica."

"How many?" asked Antonio, forgetting his supplies and racing up to meet José. He grabbed the breathless lookout just before he tripped. Helicopter blades chopped the air and grew more threatening each second.

"Hundreds," said José with an ashen look. "We have to leave now."

"Down the road," cried Antonio to the men and swung an arm quickly towards Amadica. "Make for Mt. Lucinda, leave everything and..."

Suddenly two helicopters popped up over Mt. Tabor's peak. Their pounding blades obliterated Antonio's orders and struck fear into the men. They needed no additional orders and sprinted down the road trying to outrun the horrible noise. Antonio and Marco followed the fleeing men.

Upon orders from Colonel Munoz, the helicopter pilots followed the fleeing UFLS. They hovered a few hundred yards behind while radioing back to Amadica's mill and reporting the absence of any firearms amongst the fighters. When Antonio glanced back towards the peak he spotted dozens of camouflaged figures moving quickly amongst the caves and gathering in groups to catch their breath before continuing the pursuit.

The ground dropped quickly beneath Antonio's feet. With each step he felt ready to tumble into the rocky gravel lining the road. The thought of falling headfirst steadied him somewhat, and he forced himself to slow down and check his panic.

"We'll lose them in the forest," Antonio yelled to Marco as the two ran side by side.

Marco nodded while breathing heavily. His face carried a determined but pained expression. "Are you alright?" Antonio yelled while looking ahead to the other men. Several already disappeared into the woods.

"Just too old for this," cried Marco, dismissing Antonio's concerns. After a few more seconds he called out loudly. "Too easy," he yelled above the steady chopping. "Why aren't there any Federals on the road?"

Antonio shook his head and kept running. He felt his throat and lungs burn with effort. He no longer looked back at the helicopters or the Federals. The forest's edge loomed larger with each step and he saw with relief that most of the men already vanished off the road and into the thick vegetation. Antonio wondered briefly if he would ever see them again.

Suddenly leaves and braches whipped past his face as he ran headlong into the brush. Marco stayed at his side and they kept each other in sight while the remaining UFLS forces scattered and disappeared. The sound of the choppers faded, and then to Antonio's relief, disappeared altogether. He finally motioned Marco to stop and rest.

"Drink?" Marco asked, offering his canteen while they both panted heavily. Antonio accepted the water and swallowed gratefully.

"Have to keep moving," Antonio said raggedly. "Let's walk a little until we catch our breath."

Marco led the way through the forest, steadily making headway down through the thick vegetation. The going was slow, but neither man wanted to risk traveling on the road.

"We can stop at our neighbors and get supplies," said Antonio. Half an hour had passed and he was beginning to plan for the trek up Mt. Lucinda. Marco nodded and kept moving.

They picked up their downhill pace as the morning wore on and thick clouds gradually blanketed Salavandra's normally blue skies. Leery of the road, they constantly watched for soldiers and strained their ears for the sounds of troops moving through the woods. They often crouched and listened fearfully as harsh voices and gunfire resonated through the trees. Several times they carefully peered out from the forest at a farmer's home where they hoped to rest and get supplies. Each time they turned away when Federals appeared, ostensibly guarding the home.

"It's like they're pushing us," observed Marco after several hours of moving downhill and numerous, futile attempts to stop at homes for food and rest. "Every house has Federals hanging around. They're behind us, their on our left, our right, yelling and shooting all the time. The only way open is down, always leading to Amadica."

"I noticed it too. They're picking us off one by one, and constantly herding us."

"It's not like we have a choice either," cursed Marco, suddenly turning to his left as a rifle fired and a distant scream echoed across the hills. "God I wish I had a gun."

Updates flowed constantly from the soldiers in the field to the Federals' command center inside Amadica's mill. Phillip sat transfixed to his laptop watching the progress unfold with calculated predictability. He watched with boyish glee as the small yellow squares moved across his screen and continually pushed the few remaining UFLS fighters towards the final trap. The entire operation was a massive undertaking and stretched Vasquez's budget, but Phillip had assured him that the tremendous expense was worthwhile. His assurances materialized as several distinct groups of soldiers drew near Amadica.

"Not much longer now, gentlemen," he said happily and cast a quick look around the table. The officers acknowledged him briefly and returned to their screens to issue supplementary orders to their respective field units.

By mid-afternoon Phillip's communicator illustrated a collection of little yellow squares finally reaching Amadica's outlined border and spreading out through the streets. Phillip raised his head as each officer confirmed the return of his soldiers.

"Let's flip the view now," said Colonel Munoz. With a touch of a button everyone's laptop screens suddenly exploded with small yellow squares. "Obviously there is no way out of Amadica. Whoever we pushed down off the mountain is now trapped."

Phillip let out a little shout and jumped up from his chair. Running from the room he grabbed Mary and tugged her out onto the mill's catwalks toward the small window overlooking the mill's expansive yard. The charred patch of ground from Leonard's fire still bothered him, but he ignored the black reminder and excitedly looked down into the narrow streets radiating out from the mill.

Silence enveloped the town and no movements disturbed Amadica's deceptive tranquility. The entire population had vanished into their homes. The hundreds of soldiers displayed on the officers' communication laptops stayed out of sight.

"What is it?" asked Mary slowly. She leaned heavily into Phillip and gazed outside. Heavy, moist clouds blanketed the sky and partially blocked the sun. Amadica felt charged by an eerie luminance radiating from above.

"Just wait," he replied, and looked at her quickly. "Those are nice pills, aren't they?"

Mary let out a little laugh and nodded dizzily. "They make me feel all light," she replied.

"Did you at least get the truck packed?" asked Phillip. He thought he told her to do it sometime in the morning.

"Just finished," said Mary and leaned against the wall where she promptly slid into a sitting position. Phillip shrugged and looked back out the window.

Three men suddenly ran towards the yard from a side street. They paused before venturing out into the expansive area but then risked it and sprinted into the open. Two others immediately followed. Suddenly the entire yard exploded with pounding feet and blaring bullhorns. Soldiers poured from the mill, the side streets and from nearby homes.

Five unarmed, ragged men, sweating, filthy and exhausted stood surrounded by hundreds of soldiers, all with rifles held ready to shoot. The five men, shocked by the trap and the sheer number of Federals, slowly raised their arms high above their heads and backed up against each other in a tight circle.

Phillip let out a shout, grabbed Mary off the floor and pushed her back across the catwalks where they caught up with the officers quickly making their way downstairs. As they walked towards the huge, open bay door, Phillip heard the arrest orders being issued. When he stepped outside beneath the overcast sky, the five men stood with their eyes cast earthward and their hands tightly cuffed behind their backs. Phillip's face split into a wicked grin as he recognized Antonio amongst the beaten and miserable group.

"The others?" he heard an officer ask a sergeant.

"All dead, Sir."

"And these five are all that's left of the mighty UFLS?" asked Phillip loudly. He hefted the Link from Antonio's belt and stepped back a few paces. None of the five men acknowledged his presence or even looked up when he relieved Antonio of the Link.

"Smile, UFLS. This one's going around the world." Phillip snapped a few pictures and then directed a nearby soldier to lift the chin of each man for a full face snapshot. He saved Antonio for last.

"And finally him," Phillip said, and motioned the soldier to force Antonio's head up. Phillip involuntarily stepped back when Antonio met his eyes and he nervously checked to make sure Antonio's hands were bound. With a forced smile he lifted the Link for the final picture of the day.

"On second thought," he paused, lowering the Link, "I think this one might be better taken by my assistant." Phillip turned to the officers clustered a few steps away and motioned to Mary. She shook her head and refused to move until one of the officers gave her a shove. She tripped and stumbled out in front of Antonio.

"Thank you, Lieutenant," said Phillip cheerfully and shoved the Link into Mary's hands. Antonio looked quickly from Mary to the officers. Shocked, he turned to stare in disbelief at Mary. He clamped his jaw shut and watched her coldly.

"As you can see, Mr. Richards," said Phillip lightly. "Your movement is dead, your men are dead or captured, and your most precious possession is now mine." He lifted Mary's chin and forced her to look at Antonio.

"Take his picture, Mary," Phillip ordered and thrust her in front of Antonio.

With a sob Mary lifted the Link. Tears flowed freely down her cheeks. Depression and a great wave of sadness pushed up through the medication slowing her mind. She felt sick, strangely agitated, but was still able to think without emotions overwhelming her actions. She vaguely recalled Phillip watching her take the three little pills earlier that day.

The Link flashed. Mary immediately dropped it to the ground and ran off towards the mill. She knelt by the giant door and vomited repeatedly while the soldiers watched her with morbid fascination. She felt her life spilling out like so much thick, yellow bile now staining Salavandra's soil. Exhausted, she curled up in the dirt with her head throbbing and lay still.

"Enough," shouted Colonel Munoz. Mary's spectacle made his stomach flare up and Phillip's snobbish and patronizing attitude disgusted him. "Mr. Penkava, your woman is sick. Tend to her. You men," he gestured at the nearest cluster of soldiers, "escort the prisoners to the jail. The rest of you, return to the barracks. Today's activities are over."

Antonio and the others then stumbled through Amadica's streets surrounded by troops. Marco walked next to him and gritted his teeth against each painful step. The three UFLS men that were also captured, Antonio's distant neighbors but determined and loyal followers, stepped ahead of them. Antonio's breath ran short and ragged as images of Mary raced through his mind. How quickly things change, he thought, and looked to Marco at his side. His older friend acknowledged him with a resolute nod.

"I'm sorry about Mary," said Marco under his breath. One of the soldiers slapped him across the face and told him to shut up.

Antonio cast his eyes downward. Tears would not flow even as he repeatedly envisioned Mary lifting the Link and snapping his picture. He swam in a sea of confusion and disbelief and forgot all about the UFLS, his loyal men and those that died for the movement. Forty dollars, Antonio recalled, tracing the events of the last several weeks back to one ill-fated afternoon. His wrists suddenly strained savagely against the steel handcuffs and he wished they would bite into his skin and bleed him to death. Anger boiled, and the destitute march toward the jail compounded his humiliation. No eye, no woman, no land, no friends and no future he thought bitterly. He suddenly looked forward to the end.

"Bring out Antonio Richards," ordered Colonel Munoz as evening fell and the sky grew heavy with billowing storm clouds. He stood outside the jail peering upwards as daylight faded.

"Sir?" asked a soldier. Several casually guarded the jail and warded off any unlikely rescue attempt.

"Bring Mr. Richards to the truck. I have orders directly from President Vasquez to transport him to Saint Matthew immediately. Two of you must come along to guard him. Any volunteers?"

Most of the soldiers caste their eyes to the ground and shuffled nervously while avoiding Munoz's steady gaze. Their shift ended in a few minutes and with clouds gathering overhead they felt no desire to stand in the rain on the back of a speeding truck while guarding a prisoner.

"Private Crespo, Sir," announced a particularly heavy-set soldier as he stepped forward from the bunch. "Will there be any stops before reaching Saint Matthew, Sir?" Munoz looked at him silently. "My friend was killed at the greenhouses, Sir," explained Private Crespo. "That, and of course, your hand, Sir."

Munoz rocked back on his heels for a moment considering the request. "A stop can be arranged, Private."

"Thank you, Sir."

"Anyone else?"

Rain fell from the sky and peppered the dusty ground with random, symmetrical dots. The barrack's metal roof rang lightly as drops by the thousands plummeted from the clouds. The remaining soldiers looked even less likely to volunteer now, so Munoz made a quick decision.

"Then one will suffice. You others, report to the Sergeant and volunteer for the rest of the night's guard shift without pay. Crespo, go get Antonio. I'll wait in the truck."

Munoz stepped into a truck's cab amidst groans and curses erupting from the soldiers. He smiled, remembering the same treatment he received many years ago after refusing to volunteer for a similarly unpleasant duty. That was shortly after making the decision to join Vasquez's Federals, a decision he now looked back upon with a critical eye. Still, he thought with some distress, the military income provided a life unlike anything a coffee farmer could ever afford. He lit his last cigar and with a sad and listless breath puffed thoughtfully.

A thump from the flatbed announced Antonio's presence. Munoz peered back through the rearview mirror and watched as Private Crespo administered a hearty kick to Antonio's curled frame. The prisoner looked rightfully humble, Munoz thought, just right for the trip down to the coast. He shook his head sadly while starting the truck and fiercely gunning the engine. Rain scattered across the windshield and the wipers smeared a muddy sheen across the glass. With a gentle lurch the truck rolled away from the jail and headed down the road toward Saint Matthew. Its headlights sliced through the growing twilight and cut sharply across the steady rain.

Antonio steeled himself against Crespo's repeated kicking but soon lost his strength and simply absorbed each blow while trying to maneuver a few inches away from the private's boot. Rain soaked his thin clothing and as the truck gained speed the wind pulled wracking chills from his body. Once he peered up at Crespo and met the man's empty stare. He never looked up again. Crespo's eyes carried nothing but a brutish intention to hurt, and Antonio shivered harder while staring at the pavement rolling beneath the truck.

After darkness fell the road leveled and a sharp, salty smell of ocean water finally pushed through the steady rain. Crespo grew bored of kicking him some time ago so Antonio breathed fully and was beginning to grow more cognizant of his surroundings. He gradually realized his position and expected to reach Saint Matthew in the next few minutes. The truck began slowing, however, and then it veered off the roadside and eventually squealed stop.

"Just a little break, Mr. Richards," said Crespo politely. He smiled down through the darkness. Antonio shrank from the Private's reaching grasp but the heavy man grabbed his cuffed wrists and roughly dragged him from the truck and out into the headlights.

Heavy waves crashed on a nearby beach but Antonio dared not look for fear that Crespo might hit him. The truck's door slammed shut but the engine still pulsed through the falling rain and pounding ocean.

"How long?" Crespo called back to Colonel Munoz, standing off to the side.

"Ten minutes, so make it good."

Crespo clutched Antonio's throat and squeezed. Antonio choked against the crushing pressure and his breath rasped painfully. He clamped his jaw shut and squinted against the rain and the coming blow. Crespo raised his free fist and held it above Antonio.

"This will hurt, Mr. Richards," he growled. Rain poured over his surly face and dripped from his nose. Antonio absurdly wondered if the rain bothered Crespo at all, or if the man even noticed.

A huge crack suddenly erupted and Antonio winced against the blast and involuntarily shut his eye. He felt Crespo's grip weaken and then grow dim until the soldier's hand slipped away completely. He heard a weighty thump land at his feet. Only then did Antonio dare to look. Private Crespo lay on the ground, a huge bulge of a man, facedown and quite dead. A bloody hole opened one side of his skull and falling rain diluted the river of blood pouring out onto the sand.

Stunned, Antonio felt his hands lifted up into the truck's headlights and heard a set of keys rattling against the steel handcuffs. With an easy click his bindings snapped open. Colonel Munoz threw them to the ground and gently turned Antonio.

"I loved my father, my mother and my family, Antonio," Colonel Munoz said to him firmly. The stump of his missing finger still pained him but he ignored the throbbing ache. The bandages began peeling away in the rain. They hardly mattered now, he thought, and kept hold of Antonio's shoulders.

"We suffered like you cannot imagine. Sickness all the time. No medicine and hardly any money to go see the clinic's doctor. Death took them, slowly, and what death left me I had to sell to repay our debts."

"I'm sorry," whispered Antonio, still processing what just happened. Munoz shook his head angrily and squeezed Antonio's shoulders.

"I do not want your pity," he yelled through the wind. "I want you to leave Salavandra. It's impossible to change this place. I have seen the forces and all the equipment and resources. It's hopeless here. Take the truck, find a boat and leave. Only death waits here."

From his pocket Colonel Munoz withdrew a pistol and forced it into Antonio's hand.

"Take it," he demanded. "You're not safe yet."

He gave Antonio a mighty shove towards the truck and walked off into the darkness towards the crashing waves. His vague form disappeared into the showering gloom.

"But where will I go," whispered Antonio as water droplets ran down his face.

A single shot suddenly cut through the darkness.

Antonio dropped to the sand and wept. Rain fell in pounding torrents but he hardly noticed. So much death, he lamented, so much wrong with Salavandra and no way to fix this wretched place. He considered the gun clutched in his wet fingers and knew a bullet would hurt less than the pain he now felt. Salavandra offered him nothing, yet it was all he had in the entire world. He saw Mary again, her image shimmered in the spattering rain as it fell through the truck's burning headlights. He missed her terribly, but also felt a profound, simmering anger.

Chilled and shivering uncontrollably, Antonio eventually stood and walked slowly back to the truck where the heater struggled to warm his body. As he pulled away from the beach the headlights swept over

Private Crespo. The wheels bit deeply into the wet sand and the truck roared out onto the empty road and sped towards Saint Matthew.

Boats rocked and bobbed against the docks as turbulent waves curled around Retribution Point and rolled into Saint Matthew's waterfront. The wet, dark misery pouring over the harbor inspired no confidence, and Antonio sat like a dead man in the truck's cab staring listlessly out across the array of booms and wheelhouses. A few fishermen sprinted along the soaked planks headed for one of the many nearby bars to drown the night in cheap beer and cheaper rum. Even if there was somewhere to go, Antonio thought despondently, who would take him?

An insignificant little machine, Antonio realized, packed with information and spilling truths and lies alike, changed his life. He jealously wondered at the relative peace and certain ignorance of not stumbling across the Link. He supposed that matrimony and a life of comparative tranquility would have followed. Peace and poverty, he reminded himself bitterly, along with a simmering sense of being trapped. He remembered swallowing the Link's data, suckling the information and thirsting for more. Hank's addiction was insignificant compared to this insatiable desire for information.

As the truck's blasting heater finally warmed him Antonio realized that even with his life a shattered ruin, given a second chance he would reach for another Link all over again. What started as a hopeful effort to improve the lives of his fellow coffee farmers evolved into a righteous struggle for something greater than he fully comprehended. Phillip was right, Antonio reflected, forces larger than him, the UFLS, Penkava Incorporated or even the Federals ultimately determined Salavandra's end. Still, Phillip made a convenient target, Antonio thought, and bore much responsibility for this current misery.

Exhausted, he leaned back against the seat trying to determine his next move. A faint light struggled to shine through the night's rain from far across the bay. Phillip's cabin, Antonio remembered angrily, where Phillip this very moment probably toasted the destruction of the UFLS. Mary too, he reminded himself, at least partially chose to be there with him. With cold certainty Antonio knew his next move. He checked the pistol Colonel Munoz forced him to accept and carefully pulled away from the docks.

The single guard remained under his shelter and waved Antonio's truck up through the sodden forest without bothering to identify the driver. Phillip occasionally played host to higher ranking Federals and the soldier was in no mood to interrupt their plans. Antonio drove with deliberate caution up the muddy, winding road through the rain. A low crack of rolling thunder echoed above as the storm matured.

"It's really coming down now," said Mary, standing at the expansive window overlooking the Point. She swallowed another large gulp of wine and stared out into the darkness at the lightning now flashing above the bay. She had learned to check her movements and control the dizzying combination of alcohol and tranquilizers. "We usually don't have such heavy rain in March. Is it supposed to let up by tomorrow?"

Phillip looked up from the kitchen table, mumbled a quick affirmative and turned his attention back to the Link. Tom and the Board wanted his final report posted as soon as possible so he worked quickly to place the finishing touches on the electronic document. Everyday more coffee cherries flowed into Amadica's mill. The foundation outlines for the new warehouses in Saint Matthew were already laid and greenhouse replacement parts would arrive on the Celeste in three days. The afternoon's ruin of the remaining UFLS put an end to any further business disruptions.

"What time are we leaving tomorrow?" asked Mary, turning from the window. Phillip seemed less threatening sitting at the table, almost nice, Mary thought as she approached him. He could even be charming, she convinced herself, as long as she did not make him angry.

"Early. Maybe around ten."

She lost her balance a little and steadied herself against the table. Despite the dizziness and the traumatic afternoon she felt almost cheerful now. Phillip gave her another kind of medicine when they arrived at the cabin and the effects were quite pleasant.

"I can't wait," she replied and let out an excited laugh.

Phillip wrapped an arm around her waist and squeezed. "Tomorrow," he began, reaching for the wine bottle and refilling Mary's glass. "You'll see all the sights I've been telling you about. You'll totally forget this wretched little island and all its accompanying filth."

"And the clothing?" Mary asked. "When will you take me to get some nice clothes? I can't go in my old rags."

Phillip laughed and swallowed some of Mary's wine. "We'll get you some right at the airport when we land, that way you'll look somewhat presentable. After that, we'll get settled and find something the next day."

Mary's watery eyes sparkled as she imagined all the wonderful new things waiting for her in New York. Her head swam with possibilities and she asked Phillip to once again show her pictures of the city with the Link.

"In a second," Phillip replied, "I have to send…"

The cabin's door suddenly crashed open and Antonio stepped in from the downpour with hair plastered to his head and dark wisps curled around his eye patch. His wet clothing hung off his lean frame in damp, wrinkled folds and the heavy patter of falling rain echoed loudly behind him. He raised the pistol and aimed it at Phillip's heart. Mary let out a scream and leapt away from the table.

"You!" exclaimed Phillip, wide-eyed. "How…"

"Quiet," Antonio yelled. "Get up off the chair." Antonio gestured with the gun. Mary let out an anguished moan and slipped to the floor in a wave of dizziness and nausea. Phillip stood slowly, trying to judge if Antonio really intended to shoot him.

"Outside," Antonio ordered.

Phillip looked at the Link lying on the table and briefly noted the irony of his report. Nearly ready to send and in the next minute a bullet might be lodged in his chest. Strange, he thought, that his stay on Salavandra would end this way after all the help from the Federals and Senator Wilson. He moved past Antonio and stepped outside into the heavy rain.

"To your left," Antonio ordered loudly. The pistol's barrel jammed savagely into Phillip's back and he stumbled forward. With a horrible jolt of fear Phillip looked ahead toward the cliff's sharply defined edge. A gaping emptiness loomed before him as he neared the rim. Far below, the sound of waves smashing into sharp rocks pushed upwards through the rainfall. He turned to face Antonio.

"This won't solve anything," Phillip screamed through the rain. Lightning flashed above and briefly illuminated the cabin behind

Antonio. Mary stood at the doorway coldly watching them and gripping the doorknob for support.

"I'm not trying to solve anything anymore, Phillip," Antonio replied. "I'm only putting an end to your presence on Salavandra."

Phillip shook his head. Cold, shivering fear gripped him. He could not shake the image of those sharp rocks waiting for him far below. A well-aimed bullet would be better, he thought.

"My end, Antonio?" Phillip screamed hoarsely. He felt barely strong enough to stand. "Don't you get it, even now? Me, my father, President Vasquez, we don't actually matter. Not much, anyway. If it wasn't us it would be another group of men. It would be the same miserable story on this miserable little island, only with different names."

"Yes, Phillip, I do get it," Antonio replied loudly, shouting above the pounding raindrops. More thunder rolled overhead and Antonio waited a moment for the noise to fade. "I understand better than you realize," he continued. "I even agree with you. That's why I'm here now, because I've got just one fight left in me and see no reason why I shouldn't kill you."

For once in his life Phillip struggled to find an appropriate response. No argument, no snappy comeback popped into his mind. From behind Antonio he saw Mary emerge out into the rain and carefully step in their direction.

"What about Mary?" Phillip asked.

Antonio dismissed him. "My beloved is dead to me," he lied. "As I am dead to her." He raised the pistol and aimed between Phillip's eyes.

Mary closed in behind Antonio and raised the Link high above her head. She wavered, caught her balanced and suddenly crashed the unit down onto Antonio's skull. The sturdy unit cracked loudly and Antonio staggered forward against the blow. Mary sank to the ground sobbing.

Phillip abruptly stepped away from the cliff and seized the gun. He wrestled it loose from Antonio and shoved hard. Antonio wavered and tried to catch his balance as the cliff's sheer drop loomed beneath his feet. He turned and saw Mary, sitting in mud, weeping where pools of water danced beneath the falling rain. The Link lay next to her, its luminescent screen glowing vibrantly green against Salavandra's soaked earth. She looked up at Antonio and revealed an absolute misery.

Antonio stopped trying to steady himself and tipped into the brink.

As he rushed towards the rocks he saw his father's deep and concerned eyes staring at him sadly. Finally, Antonio thought, I am leaving Salavandra.